# WASHINGTON, D.C.

## SEWER SYSTEM

LOGAN
CIRCLE

AVENUE

N STREET

M STREET

MASSACHUSETTS

L STREET

NEW YORK AVENUE

K STREET

YORK AVENUE

AVENUE

I STREET

H STREET

UNION
STATION

G STREET

RY
MENT

F STREET

4TH STREET

XECUTIVE
E

E STREET

PENNSYLVANIA AVENUE

ONSTITUTION AVENUE

CONSTITUTION AVENUE

ADISON DRIVE

U.S.
CAPITOL

H E    M A L L

JEFFERSON DRIVE

INDEPENDENCE AVENUE

INDEPENDENCE AVENUE

AVENUE

# HARD TARGET

ALSO BY CHRISTOPHER HYDE:

*Jericho Falls*

*Crestwood Heights*

# HARD TARGET

## CHRISTOPHER HYDE

William Morrow and Company, Inc.
New York

*Fiction*
*Hyd*

Recognizing the importance of preserving what has been written, it is the policy of William Morrow and Company, Inc., and its imprints and affiliates to have the books it publishes printed on acid-free paper, and we exert our best efforts to that end.

Library of Congress Cataloging-in-Publication Data

Hyde, Christopher.
    Hard target / Christopher Hyde.
        p.    cm.
    ISBN 0-688-09053-2
    I. Title.
PS3558.Y36W48 1991
813'.54—dc20

90-44460
CIP

Printed in the United States of America

First Edition

1  2  3  4  5  6  7  8  9  10

BOOK DESIGN BY PATRICE FODERO

In loving memory of
Little M.,
too short a life,
but lived with utmost joy

# AUTHOR'S NOTE

The research in *Hard Target* is accurate, as is all the information relating to the history, structure, and day-to-day routines within the White House. In the interests of public safety a small number of technical details have been altered slightly.

# PROLOGUE

Hotel Washington
Washington, D.C.
April 10, 1945
7:05 P.M., eastern time

The two men occupying the opulently decorated sitting room of the suite in the Hotel Washington were dressed in civilian clothes, but it was clear from the way he stood and moved that the older man, dark-haired and heavyset, was uncomfortable out of uniform.

While the younger man read, his companion stood by the window, teeth clamped around the end of his long, fuming cigar. It had been dull and overcast all day, and the fading of light into darkness was a barely perceptible exchange of one shade of gray for another, shadows for night. Below him he could still see the classic roofline of the Treasury Building and, beyond it, surrounded by trees, the White House itself.

Roosevelt wasn't there, of course; he'd been absent since the last days of March, traveling to the Little White House in Warm Springs, Georgia, for three weeks of recuperation after Yalta. The First Lady was there, as were dozens of other people, but without the Boss in residence, the grace and power of the famous building were somehow diminished.

The younger man, thin-faced, balding, and wearing rimless eyeglasses, tossed the report onto the coffee table in front of him. He lit a Murad cigarette from the package in his suit jacket, then leaned back against the flowered cushions of the chesterfield.

9

"Is it true?" the young man asked.

"Yes," the older man answered, turning away from the window and speaking around the end of his cigar. "He's reversed his position entirely."

"It's unbelievable, General."

"He wants to show them films after we test."

"It won't be enough," said the younger man, shaking his head. He took off his glasses and began polishing them with a handkerchief from the breast pocket of his suit jacket. "The entire committee was in agreement about that. Stimson, Vannevar Bush, Fermi . . . my God, even Oppenheimer said the only thing that would do it would be a full-scale military operation."

"Does he really think Hirohito is going to give up just because we show him some pictures?" The general bit down hard on his cigar.

"It goes beyond that," said the younger man, replacing his glasses, using pinched fingers to seat them neatly on the bridge of his long, patrician nose. "There's Stalin to consider, for one thing. He'll swallow Europe whole if we let him; this atom bomb might be just the thing to make the son of a bitch stop and think for a minute or two."

"What about Truman?" the general asked. "Would he use it?"

"He's not even supposed to know about it," the younger man replied. "But yes, we have his word on that."

There was a long, thoughtful pause. The general went back to the window and stared out into the gathering darkness.

"We'll have to act quickly," the general said finally, his back to the younger man. "A month or two ago it wasn't as important. The test wasn't going to be until August. We thought perhaps—"

"You thought that Roosevelt would be dead by then," the younger man said bluntly. "According to the reports we're getting from Warm Springs, it looks as if he's getting better."

"What does the admiral say?" the general asked.

"He's guarded; so is Dr. Bruenn." The younger man shrugged. "But he's gaining weight, eating more, swimming in the pool. On the other hand, he could die tomorrow."

"We knew that when we convinced him to run for a fourth term. That's why Harry Truman, not Henry Wallace, is Vice President," the general growled, turning. His cigar had gone out long ago, but he appeared not to notice.

The younger man lit another Murad. With a faint smile on his face he reached into the inside pocket of his elegantly cut jacket and took out a plain leather cigarette case and a pack of Camels. He laid them on the coffee table, then sat back.

"What the hell is that?" the general asked, frowning.

The younger man sighed. "You and I have known each other for some time, General. You know who my family is, and you know what we believe in. That's why you brought me into this in the first place. I assumed you were serious."

"I am," the general snapped. "We all are."

"Good," the younger man said, nodding. "I'm glad to hear it." He took a long draw on his cigarette and slowly let the smoke out through his nostrils in twin plumes. "The cigarette case is an exact duplicate of the one used by Mr. Roosevelt. The cigarettes are exactly what they appear to be—Camels, the President's brand, if you recall."

"I've never noticed," the general said.

"Believe me, he smokes Camels," the younger man said. "Exactly six a day, according to Dr. Bruenn's new regimen. Our information is that he actually smokes almost twice that number, although this is down considerably from his previous two and three packs."

"All right, so you and your friends on E Street created a replica of the President's cigarette case. I appreciate dramatics as much as the next man, but perhaps you could get to the point."

"Certainly. The cigarettes in this pack have been doctored, if you'll pardon the pun."

"Go on," the general said.

"The material in the cigarettes is a by-product of work being done for us by the people at Du Pont. A fiber. I'm not entirely sure of the chemical makeup, but when you ignite the substance, it gives off a poison gas. The effect is much the same as a cerebral hemorrhage."

"Sounds like something out of a dime novel." The general grunted.

"Perhaps," said the younger man. "It does work, however, and it leaves no trace behind."

"What are you suggesting?" the general said finally.

"That we substitute our cigarette case, along with one of our cigarettes, in among some perfectly normal ones."

"And who performs the dastardly deed?" The general scoffed. "One of Donovan's daredevils?"

"No. Someone from outside. Someone with a reason to be in Warm Springs."

"Who."

"A friend of mine. His name is Hollis Macintyre."

11

"Any relation to the admiral?" the general asked, stiffening.

"No. None at all. He was assistant to Roosevelt's senior military adviser."

"General Watson?"

"That's right, the one who died on the way to the Yalta Conference in February. Hollis was so useful at the conference they kept him on. They've got him working as a courier for the time being, bringing the White House bag back and forth."

"He says he'll do it?"

"Yes." The younger man nodded.

"Why?" the general asked coolly.

"Because he's a patriot for one thing. Roosevelt is dying; it's simply a matter of time. Hollis is as aware as you or I that the President is in no condition to negotiate a peace in Europe with Stalin, and if we don't use the atom bomb in Japan, we'll be committing a million men to an invasion. If blood is going to be spilled, Hollis would rather it was Jap blood than American."

"I don't suppose your Mr. Macintyre sees any personal benefit for himself," the general said wryly.

"Our grateful thanks will suffice," the younger man replied, looking directly into the general's eyes.

"When does he leave for Warm Springs?" the general said, looking down at the familiar pack of cigarettes on the table.

"Tomorrow afternoon," the younger man answered quickly. "He flies to Fort Benning, and then a Secret Service detail drives him to Warm Springs."

"Call him," said the general after a moment. "Call your patriot. Tell him to come to the hotel."

"Of course." The younger man nodded.

The general went back to the window and looked down. The Treasury Building was dark, and there were only a few lights on at the White House. "He's dying anyway," the general said softly, speaking to his own reflection in the dark glass of the window. "It's not as though it's murder."

"Excuse me?" said the younger man. He was standing at the desk on the far side of the room, the telephone receiver in his hand. "Did you say something, General?"

"No," answered the older man, shaking his head slowly. "I didn't say anything at all."

12

The Little White House
Warm Springs, Georgia
April 12, 1945
1:15 P.M., central time

The compound at Warm Springs, Georgia, was made up of more than a dozen buildings, most of them for the use of polio victims who came to enjoy the benefits of the hot springs pool close to Georgia Hall. Franklin Delano Roosevelt, in addition to being President of the United States, was one of the founders of the Warm Springs Foundation and regularly traveled to the health spa to recuperate from the rigors of Washington life.

His own estate at Hyde Park, New York, was much larger and more comfortable; but for Roosevelt it would always be his mother's house, and he much preferred the simple pleasures of the six-room clapboard cottage on the hill above Georgia Hall. It had the added advantage of being located near the residence of his longtime love, Lucy Mercer Rutherfurd.

Arriving at the compound almost two weeks before, the President had been exhausted and depressed, but after twelve days of rest, light exercise, and Dr. Bruenn's closely supervised medical treatment he was feeling considerably better. His blood pressure had improved, there was color in his cheeks, and he was even beginning to enjoy his food again. He'd even agreed to sit for a watercolor portrait by his cousin Polly Delano's friend, the imposing Madame Shoumatoff.

Sitting at his desk in the main room of the house, Roosevelt began opening mail and going through the contents of the recently delivered pouch from Washington. The room was bustling with lively activity as Polly and another cousin, Daisy Suckley, moved about, arranging flowers, while Madame Shoumatoff worked behind her easel. Bill Hassett, his appointments secretary, was also in and of the room while his darling Lucy supervised the lunch preparations with his messboy, Joe Esperancilla, and Daisy Bonner, the cook.

Blinking, the President came out of his reverie, realizing that Madame Shoumatoff was talking to him. The heavy Russian accent made her speech difficult to understand.

"I beg your pardon?" he said politely. To the woman's right, by the door leading to the hall, he could see Lucy, hands demurely in her lap, satisfied simply to be in the same room with the man she'd loved so deeply for almost thirty years.

"I was saying, Mr. President, I saw a new Florida centennial stamp. Did you have anything to do with that one?"

"I certainly did," Roosevelt answered, distracted. Behind the artist he could see Joe bringing in the place settings for lunch. "Now, Madame." He smiled, relieved that he wouldn't have to hold his pose for much longer. "We have about fifteen minutes—"

"Yes, yes," Madame Shoumatoff said, her head bobbing. She stepped forward and adjusted the folds of the dark blue navy cape around the frail man's shoulders. She nodded, pleased. The cape went well with the President's dark suit and the red-and-blue-striped tie she had chosen for him. Returning to the easel, she began filling in the tie. Polly Delano came out of one of the bedrooms, talking to Daisy Suckley about getting another vase for one of the arrangements.

Surreptitiously Roosevelt reached out and opened his cigarette case. Bruenn had insisted he smoke no more than six a day, but he usually kept the case full. He reached out and removed one of the cigarettes, then twisted it into one of his favorite ivory holders. Lighting it, he saw Lucy out of the corner of his eye. He winked, and she replied with a mock frown.

Roosevelt dragged deeply on the cigarette, enjoying the familiar nut-bitter taste. Suddenly he smelled lemons, as though someone had sliced one directly in front of him. He felt a sudden, blinding pain behind his eyes and lifted one hand. He gripped his forehead and squeezed it.

"I have a terrific headache," he whispered. He fell back in his chair, the cigarette and holder falling to the floor.

"Did you drop something?" asked Daisy Suckley, smiling. At that moment Roosevelt's eyes half closed, and he slumped to his left.

"Franklin, are you all right?" asked Polly Delano, putting her vase of flowers down on the mantelpiece.

There was no response. Roosevelt was motionless, eyes half closed. His jaw fell open slowly in a macabre imitation of a yawn. Madame Shoumatoff, only a few feet from the desk, began to scream. Joe Esperancilla came out of the kitchen as the Russian artist ran to the front door. She spotted James Beary, a Secret Service agent, leaning against the President's Packard.

"Call a doctor!" yelled Madame Shoumatoff. "Something terrible has happened to the President!"

14

On April 12, 1945, at 3:35 P.M., central time, Dr. Howard G. Bruenn pronounced Franklin Delano Roosevelt dead. According to Dr. Bruenn, the cause of death was a massive cerebral hemorrhage. No autopsy was done, however, and therefore, the diagnosis was never proved to be accurate. Furthermore, within twenty-four hours of the President's death, all medical records relating to Mr. Roosevelt had vanished from the Bethesda Naval Hospital. There is also no trace of any records for the more than twenty-nine pseudonyms Roosevelt used over the course of his years at the White House. Neither the Navy Medical Center nor the federal Office of Personnel Management has any explanation for this occurrence.

On July 16, in Potsdam, Germany, President Harry Truman was informed of the successful test of the atomic bomb in Alamogordo, New Mexico. On August 6, while journeying home from the Potsdam Conference on board the heavy cruiser USS *Augusta,* President Truman was notified that an atomic bomb had been dropped on Hiroshima, Japan, the previous day at 7:15 P.M., Washington time.

On August 9, 1945, Hollis Macintyre, now working as a special adviser to the War Department, completed a twenty-two-page report describing his role in the events leading up to the death of Franklin D. Roosevelt, including the code name for the operation: Romulus. It also listed the names of all other people involved in the conspiracy, including their functions. When the report was completed, he placed it in a small sealed document case, which was then consigned to the fireproof safe hidden under the floor of his bedroom at Stoneacres Farm, Virginia.

# PART ONE

*WE WERE SURE THAT OURS WAS A NATION OF THE BALLOT, NOT THE BULLET, UNTIL THE MURDERS OF JOHN KENNEDY, ROBERT KENNEDY AND MARTIN LUTHER KING.*

—JIMMY CARTER,
*speech at the White House*

# CHAPTER 1

The torrid sun glowed like a hot coal on the Maryland horizon, its shape hazed by the stunning waves of heat rising from the city, its color stained a bruised orange-green by a thousand different airborne pollutants. Sinking slowly, it cast a long, rippling trace across the Potomac, briefly slicing through the hull of a sleek rowing shell making its way downriver like a graceful, multilegged insect.

Except for the shifting blade of light across the water Washington had given itself up to the night; Theodore Roosevelt Island was a dark mass of shadow on the river, and the ghost blue landing beacons at Washington National Airport were already shimmering in the distance.

Hudson Haines Cooper, dressed in an ornate blue and yellow dressing gown and with a lead crystal glass of scotch in his hand, stared out through the living-room window of his Watergate apartment. He was alone, the ten-room luxury suite was dark behind him, and the only sound was the low hum of the central air conditioning. Cooper swirled the ice cubes in his glass and shook his large bald head. The view was perfect, but like most things in Washington, the surface served only to shroud the lie beneath. The Potomac was a sewer, Roosevelt Island at this time of night was a rapist's haven, and National was a pilot's nightmare.

"When you defile the pleasant streams, /And the wild bird's abiding place,/ You massacre a million dreams /And cast your spittle in God's face." The verse from the John Drinkwater poem had come unbidden into his mind, but it was apt enough. He shook his head again and turned

19

away from the window. Apt perhaps, but ironic coming from his lips. He sipped his scotch and stared into the shadows of the apartment. Shadows and lies, his stock-in-trade.

He was sixty, tall and gaunt, the skin on his skull and across his cheeks taut and seamed like parchment, his neck above the fine silk of the robe a twist of ropy tendons. Sixty years and every one showing. Forty of them spent with Central Intelligence, twenty as deputy director of operations, ten here at the Watergate, without Miriam, alone, a widower, childless. "Shadows and Lies." The perfect title for his auto-biography but wasted, of course, because DD/Operations didn't write their autobiographies; it was against the law.

The doorbell chimed, and Cooper crossed the long, broad living room and went down the short hall to the entrance. He put his eye to the peephole. Barron, in civilian clothes, looking very nervous. Cooper threw the locks and opened the door. Barron stepped inside. He was wearing a winter suit, and his pudgy face was sheened with perspiration. He looked as if he'd been drinking.

"The living room," Cooper said, pointing the way. He locked the door and followed Barron into the large room. Cooper sat down behind the gate-legged table he used as a desk and switched on the green-shaded lamp. He indicated a chair, and Barron sat down. The chair and table, like everything else in the apartment, were early American or Victorian, Miriam's choice, not his, but something Cooper had never bothered to change.

Barron squirmed on the hard pine seat, a thin leather case in his lap. The lamplight made him look sickly. Behind him Cooper could see the last slice of sunlight vanish. Full night.

"I was surprised when you called," said Cooper. He flipped open a small wooden box on the table and took out a cigarette. He lit it with a dull gray Cartier lighter that had been Miriam's and sat back in his chair, waiting.

"I thought it was important," Barron answered. "I thought you'd want to know as soon as possible."

"Presumably this has something to do with President Tucker's phys-ical."

"Yes." Barron nodded. "I'm afraid it does." He opened the case in his lap, fumbling with the zipper. He was still sweating, even in the air-conditioned apartment. Cooper could see beads of it on the man's pink forehead and cheeks. Barron pulled a file folder out of the case and handed it across the desk, but Cooper waved it away.

"I'm not a doctor," he said quietly. "You are. You're the President's doctor. Tell me in your own words." Dr. John Barron was senior resident medical officer at Walter Reed Hospital, a full colonel in the Army, and the man in charge of the President's semiannual medical checkups. He was also one knot on the string of Washington "contacts" personally run by Cooper as DDO.

"The President checked in with us three days ago," said Barron hesitantly. "I ordered up all the regular tests, but Mrs. Tucker had previously told me, in confidence, that the President had been having headaches and the odd memory lapse. Nothing extreme, but enough to worry her. President Tucker made no mention of it himself." Barron paused, blinking. He used his index finger to wipe away the sweat on his upper lip, then cleared his throat.

"Go on," said Cooper.

"I added several other tests to the series. CAT scan, PET scan, full blood and endocrine workup."

"Yes."

"The PET scan showed some atrophic shrinking. There were anomalies in the blood serum and the endocrine. I still wasn't entirely sure, so I asked the President if he'd help me with one of my research projects while he was waiting for the test results. I told him I was doing a paper on stress. He agreed, and I put him through the Wechsler Adult Intelligence Scale. There are eleven subtests, each one scored separately. The Wechsler is given to gauge memory function primarily and also simple logic. Why are dark clothes warmer than light clothes? In what way are an egg and a seed alike? Repeating a series of digits in order, that kind of thing."

"And?"

"He has definite aphasia—the inability to find the correct word, ataxia, short-term memory loss . . . a number of other symptoms."

"Symptoms of what exactly?" asked Cooper gently. Barron tried to see beyond the light, blinking again.

"I think the President has Creutzfeldt-Jakob disease. There was no sign of anything like this in the tests I ran just after the inauguration. The differential in the PET scan is marked. There's no other dementia with an onset that rapid."

"Dementia?"

"CJD is a primary undifferentiated dementia. Very much like Alzheimer's," Barron answered, taking refuge in the language of his profession. "If I had a sample of his brain tissue, it would almost certainly show

21

the classic plaques and tangles associated with the disease. I'm not an expert; but I pulled everything I could out of the research library, and it matches up with all the information I have on the President."

"The prognosis?" asked Cooper.

"Poor. The Alzheimer-type symptoms will become more pronounced. There is a possibility of violent behavior, hypersexuality, even incontinence."

"Over what period of time?"

"Six months. Certainly less than a year."

"Until the dementia is fully formed?"

"Until he's dead," said Barron bluntly.

Cooper stubbed out his cigarette in a bronze shell ashtray on the desk. There was an economic summit in four months and a trip to China in five.

"How long can the symptoms be disguised? Surely there must be drugs. . . ."

"According to what I read, there's only one. Nalaxone. It's experimental. At best it dampens the symptoms only briefly." The young man paused, fingers twisting in his lap like fat little worms.

Cooper looked beyond the glare of the light, trying to read Barron's expression. The doctor was in his early thirties, playing out a family tradition of military service before opening up his own practice in Boston, and that itself would be no more than a jumping-off point for a political career. If he played the game and drank scotch in the right parlors, he'd be surgeon general in ten or fifteen years. A flabby, pale, and frightened fool suddenly charged with the responsibility for a deadly secret.

"How many people know about this?" Cooper asked quietly.

"No one," said Barron, trying to make his voice firm and failing. "Everything is in this file." He handed the folder across to Cooper, visibly relaxing as it left his hands. Cooper took it but left the file unopened in front of him.

"What about Mrs. Tucker? What has she been told?"

"Nothing."

"No explanations for her husband's headaches, the memory losses?"

"Normal stress reactions for a man in his position. I suggested she have him take more vitamins with breakfast." Cooper could see a vein twitching on Barron's temple. The burden was too much; he wouldn't last long. A born confessor. "My God! Mr. Cooper, what are we going to do?"

"Nothing," the DDO replied. "At least for now." He paused. "Do you have any leave due?"

"Yes. Two weeks. I was going to take my boat to Cape Cod and visit my parents." The doctor frowned. "Why?"

"Take the leave. Starting tomorrow. Call in sick if you have to. I want you at home, close to the telephone for the next few days." The tone was firm and paternal, but they were orders, not suggestions.

"All right."

"Tell no one about this, do you understand? No one." Cooper leaned forward slightly, letting the puddle of light on his desk etch his cheekbones and eye sockets with shadow. "For your own sake," he added, after an almost imperceptible pause.

"Pardon?" Barron blinked and wiped his upper lip again.

"You're a cardiologist, Dr. Barron, not a neurologist. What if your diagnosis is incorrect? We need time to get another opinion on this." Cooper tapped the file on the desk in front of him with a long, bony finger.

"The diagnosis is accurate," answered Barron.

"Are you willing to stake your reputation on that?" asked Cooper. "Willing to stake your career on it perhaps?"

"I—"

"Go home," said Cooper, standing up. He tightened the knot on his robe and stepped out from behind the desk. "Try not to think about any of this. If you have a problem, call me and no one else, all right, Doctor?"

"Yes." The voice was still frightened, but it was meek now; Cooper had him under control for the time being. Barron stood, and Cooper led him to the door. They shook hands briefly, and then the doctor left.

Cooper went back to the desk, picked up the file, and carried it to one of a group of high-backed upholstered chairs arranged close to the big picture window. He put the file down on a small table between two of the chairs, then went into the kitchen. He made himself a small plate of sliced raw vegetables and carried it back to the living room.

Eating slowly, pausing occasionally to sprinkle a few grains of salt on a slice of cucumber, he read through the file twice, then set it aside. He took his empty plate back to the kitchen, poured himself a cup of decaffeinated coffee from the Braun percolator, and returned to the desk. He lit a cigarette, then switched off the desk lamp, darkening the room completely. Since Miriam's death he'd rarely had more than one or two lights on at a time in the entire apartment, using them only as needed, turning them off as he departed each room.

Through the picture window Maryland was nothing more than a tan-

23

gle of suburban light, breached in the center by the huge caldron of black marking Arlington National Cemetery. Over there a hundred thousand men were sleeping, some of them his friends, all of them past the time for secrets. Frowning at the thought, Cooper sipped his coffee and smoked, his mind playing over the problem Barron had given him like a pianist's fingers on a keyboard, trying to coax an answer out of dissonance.

He *would* get a second opinion, of course, that was easy enough, but he knew intuitively that Barron's diagnosis was correct. Geoffrey James Tucker, the youngest President of the United States since Jack Kennedy, was going to become clinically insane by Christmas. The corrolary to that appalling fact was the consequent ascension of Vice President Vincent Teresi to the chief executive office.

He reached out in the darkness, picked up the telephone receiver, and punched out a number in Burning Tree, Maryland. It was answered on the third ring.

"Macintyre?"

"Yes?" A voice like ragged thunder. Power in a single word.

"Cooper."

"Yes."

"Do you recall our conversation sometime ago concerning crossword puzzles?"

"I do."

"I have a clue."

"Go on."

"Seven letters. Raised by a wolf on seven hills, wanders until he finds eternity."

There was a long silence on the other end of the line. Finally Macintyre responded. "Romulus."

And so it began.

# CHAPTER 2

Stephen Padgett Stone woke at 7:00 A.M. to the tinny sounds of the Beach Boys on his clock radio. They were singing "California Girls," and instead of making him feel eighteen again, it made him feel exactly what he was, a forty-year-old sentimental fool who could still quote from "Desiderata." He snorted angrily at himself and sat up in bed, peeling the sweaty sheets away from his body. He'd come a long way in twenty-odd years: closet hippie at USC to FBI counterintelligence specialist. On the way there'd been a tour in Vietnam, Quantico, endless postings to field offices in places like Sioux City, Iowa, and a failed marriage without children.

He made a small groaning sound, trying to ignore the taste in his mouth and the humid air in the apartment. Scratching at the thick trail of salt-and-pepper hair that curled up his still-flat belly, Stone yawned and eased his legs out over the edge of the bed. He yawned again, blinking, and stood up, heading for the bathroom, wondering when the condominium committee in his building would get around to fixing the central air-conditioning system.

Reaching the bathroom, he flipped on the light, squinting in the sudden glare. He washed and shaved quickly, avoiding the face that stared back at him from the medicine chest mirror. He was already on intimate terms with every crack, crevice, and cranny, thank you very much, and while women had once commented that he looked like a dark-haired Robert Redford, the best he got now were comparisons with a weathered Alan Bates.

Bathroom rituals over, Stone went back to the bedroom, threw on his dressing gown, and went to the kitchen for phase two of the morning routine. He fired up the coffee machine, put a couple of eggs on to boil, and wandered around the apartment, picking up after himself. He ended up back in the bedroom, where he dressed, putting on a fresh shirt, underwear, and socks, followed by lightweight trousers and suspenders.

Breakfast ready, he carried eggs, coffee, and cigarettes out onto the balcony. The view was one of the best things about the apartment. The building was located on Foxhall Road between Georgetown University and the reservoir, and from where he sat Stone could look out over the Potomac to Theodore Roosevelt Island, and beyond, obscured now by the heat haze of another blistering day, to the Lincoln Memorial.

Humming an off-key medley of Beach Boys tunes, he worked his way through the eggs quickly, then sat back with his coffee, lit a Camel Light, and allowed himself twenty minutes of peace before he pole-vaulted himself back into the arcane realities of being a modern day G-man. He shook his head and took a long drag on his cigarette. Debbie, his ex-wife and still-occasional lover, liked to tease him with the G-man label.

He hardly fitted the mold of the classic Hoover FBI agent. His degree was in engineering, not law, he wasn't much with a gun, and worst of all, he couldn't bear wearing a hat. The truth was he'd never even thought about the FBI until coming back from Vietnam.

In country he'd been assigned to an intelligence unit, and he'd spent most of his time working the back streets of Saigon, following hookers and hotel busboys suspected of being VC agents. After a year he finally realized that virtually everyone in the country was potentially a Victor Charlie; but by then he'd been bitten by the intelligence bug, and the bureau seemed the logical place to go. Slightly less than fifteen years later that decision had taken him to the deputy director's slot in a bureau counterintelligence program called Rednet.

Rednet's job was to track, monitor, and, it hoped, snare any and all Soviet Military Intelligence, or GRU, agents working out of the D.C. area. It was a tall order, considering that the GRU operated twenty-five active, registered agents out of the Soviet Military Office on Belmont Road as well as an unknown number of "illegals" and paid contacts. On top of that the GRU also "owned" Aeroflot, the Soviet state airline, and Stone and his people had to keep an eye on that operation as well. It was an exhausting job, and most of it consisted of boring routine; but Stone loved every minute of it.

It was that very love for his work that had cost him his marriage.

Debbie, his ex, was a go-getter with half a dozen degrees to her credit, most of them to do with European and specifically Russian history. She worked as an analyst for ESI, the European Studies Institute, which they both knew was a discreet arm of the Central Intelligence Agency.

Right from the beginning of their relationship Debbie recognized that Stone was in a dead end as far as promotions were concerned. His boss, William Ruppelt, was in for the duration, and Stephen's only hope was a lateral transfer to a different division with more chance of advancement. Debbie had argued for the transfer, but Stone had been adamant; he liked the work he did and wouldn't trade it for a promotion to work he enjoyed less. His apparent lack of ambition had been a wedge between them, and as Debbie Stone rose through the ranks at ESI while Stephen languished, their relationship began to fall apart. Last year, after almost a decade of marriage, they ended it formally. Oddly, or perhaps inevitably, their sex life together flourished after severing the legal bonds, and they now "dated" regularly. Neither of them really had time for a full commitment and their arm's-length "friendship" seemed to suit them both.

Stone refilled his coffee cup and lit another cigarette. Ten more minutes, and he'd start the day. He grimaced, remembering some of the arguments he'd had with Debbie; right up until the end he'd taken most of the blame on himself, but it finally occurred to him that although his lack of ambition may have been part of the problem, her jealousy about his job was an equally important factor. He didn't just like his work, he loved it, and that was something Debbie simply couldn't understand.

Travkin had been the straw that broke the camel's back.

Eighteen months ago Dmitri Aleksandrovich Travkin had been no more than a name on a file folder. Up until then the GRU major had been working out of the Soviet legation in New York and came to Washington rarely. Then the deputy resident at Belmont Road had died of a heart attack, and Travkin had taken on the job, thinly disguised as a member of the Soviet Trade Mission.

Almost immediately Stone and his Rednet operatives saw that Travkin wasn't the lackadaisical deputy resident his predecessor had been. Within a few weeks he'd reestablished connections with the previous man's agents and informers as well as cultivated his own. Unlike his KGB colleagues, Travkin rarely trolled the bars and bistros looking for disaffected civil servants whose information barely justified the expense of gathering it. Instead, the young, good-looking Russian dressed himself in clothes right out of *Gentlemen's Quarterly* and searched out his quarry at gallery openings, diplomatic receptions of every stripe, and as many blue-ribbon social events as he could crowd into his overloaded datebook.

Early on Stone had manufactured a meeting with Travkin at a Corcoran Art Gallery cocktail party. Stone introduced himself as a patron of the arts, and Travkin countered by calling himself a director of Soveca S.A., a computer corporation based in Paris. Soveca was a real company, with real offices and a real interest in computer technology; but the name stood for the Soviet Economic Agency, and the technology it traded in was of questionable origin.

Both men were entirely aware of each other's identities, but enough tidbits of positive and negative information passed between them to make continuing their relationship worthwhile. From that point on both Stone and Travkin made a point of going to the same parties and events, and once or twice the two men had actually played racquetball together, using Travkin's membership at the Westin Fitness Center.

Stone had devoted enormous amounts of time to Travkin, with the eventual hope of turning him, or co-opting him as an agent in place. Debbie had called it an exercise in futility. Whatever the case, Stone became fascinated with his Soviet alter ego, and that fascination and the mental energy it required had been too much for his wife.

Now, after a year and a half, it was obvious that either Stone or Travkin would have to make a real move toward recruitment or co-option. Ruppelt was beginning to make noises in that direction, and Stone assumed that Major General Gennadi Mikhailovich Koslov, Ruppelt's opposite number at the GRU, was becoming equally impatient.

If Travkin moved first and made some kind of overture to Stone, Rednet would have just cause to request an expulsion order from State, and Travkin's whole network would collapse. On the other hand, if Stone made the first move and Travkin didn't bite, their covers would be blown irretrievably and the operation would collapse.

Stone wasn't looking forward to either eventuality. He'd grown to like and respect Travkin over the past months, and he also knew that it was unlikely that he'd ever find himself pitted against such an intelligent and resourceful opponent again. The FBI man stubbed out his cigarette, stood up, and slipped on his sports jacket. By definition two intelligence operatives on opposite sides could not be friends; on that score both GRU and FBI agreed. Friendships, even strange and distant ones like his relationship with Travkin, were essentially dangerous, if for no other reason than the fact that they weakened judgment.

"To hell with it." Stone grunted. He swilled down the last few sips of cold coffee and left the apartment.

By eight-thirty he was parking his overworked Rabbit convertible in a slot behind the CI-Q Rednet offices overlooking Folger Park. The building had once been a mansion belonging to a U.S. senator, and as far as Stone was concerned, it was one of the major blessings of his job at Rednet.

Because the program was not quite "official" by bureau standards, it had been exiled from the J. Edgar Hoover Building on Pennsylvania Avenue, and Stone couldn't have been happier. The old mansion had none of the crisp, bureaucratic efficiency of FBI headquarters, but by the same token, it also didn't have any of the bureau's well-known empire building and political infighting. Counterintelligence had always attracted oddballs, and Rednet seemed to attract the weirdest of the lot, with the exception of William Ruppelt. As the Rednet senior administrator Ruppelt had to attend regular weekly meetings at the J. Edgar, but Stone rarely set foot in the place at all anymore. For the most part CI-Q was allowed to do its job in peace.

Stone locked up his car, crossed the small lot, and ducked under the awning that shrouded the rear entrance to the building. He showed his photo ID to the security guard at his station behind a scarred old wooden desk, then rode the creaking old cage elevator up to the third-floor Operations Center, a rabbit warren of cubicle offices, narrow wood-floored corridors, and a single monstrous blower beside the stairway that was supposed to provide air conditioning in the summer and heat in the winter. In reality all it did was make an incredible amount of noise.

At that hour of the morning Operations was almost empty except for a couple of bleary-eyed night watch special agents in communications. He poked his head in, picked up the log from one of the yawning men, and continued on to his own office, which stood across from Ruppelt's at the end of the corridor. He glanced out the tall, recessed window and caught a glimpse of the Capitol dome rising over the trees around the park, then stripped off his jacket. He sat down behind his desk, buzzed the basement cafeteria for coffee, and began going over the night log, checking on the movements of visitors, guests, and clients. In CI-Q terminology a "visitor" was a registered agent of a foreign nation. A "guest" was a Soviet intelligence operative, and a "client" was one of that operative's known clandestine agents.

Every visitor, guest, and client had a file and code name, and each of the special agents attached to Rednet had his own "patch," or group of files to maintain. Operations was divided into thirteen subsections, one for each Red Zone, or area of concern, each subsection with a special agent in charge, usually an inspector, who reported to Stone. Stone, as deputy director, then reported to Ruppelt, who in turn reported to headquarters.

To an outsider it might have seemed like an overly complex system, but in fact, it was necessary. There are eight Soviet establishments within Washington: the main Soviet Embassy on Sixteenth Street NW, the huge top secret Mount Alto complex on Wisconsin Avenue, an Information Office on Eighteenth Street, the Soviet Military Office on Belmont Road, the Soviet Fisheries Office on Decatur Street, the Soviet Trade Office on Connecticut Avenue, the Soviet Consulate on Phelps Place, and the Maritime Attaché's Office on L Street.

In addition, there is the Tass news agency in the National Press Building; *Pravda* in Chevy Chase, Maryland; *Izvestia* on Willard Avenue, also in Chevy Chase; and the Soviet dacha, or country place, a forty-five-acre estate at Pioneer Point just outside Centreville, Maryland. In all, there are slightly more than a thousand East bloc employees in the D.C. area, and approximately one third of these are visitors and guests.

And that didn't include the clients.

Thankfully, it had been a good night, at least according to the log. No major activity at any of the main Soviet installations, nothing special at any of the half dozen ongoing special surveillance projects, and, best of all, no car rentals. By federal law no Soviet diplomat or agent was allowed to travel more than twenty-five miles out of the capital area without a special permit, and none of them was allowed to drive any vehicle other than one with the special red, white, and blue DFC license plates: *D* for "diplomatic corps" and *FC* for "fucking Communists" according to local mythology. When a Soviet agent wanted to make a drop or contact in and out of Washington, he regularly rented a vehicle, usually from the Avis booth at the Visitor Information Center. Just as regularly he was watched, followed, and photographed.

By the time Ramona, the woman in the cafeteria, had brought him his coffee it was almost nine o'clock and his perusal of the night log was almost complete. The Russians might be atheists, but it seemed that they took Sundays off just like everyone else.

"You really are going to have to get this place decorated." At the sound of the voice Stone looked up. Mort Kessler was standing in the doorway, glancing around his office with a mock frown on his face. Kes-

30

sler was on the short side for bureau material, muscular with a shock of red hair and eyebrows so pale they were almost nonexistent. Quirky, given to fits of temper when frustrated, he was also a natural blood-hound, and he had a photographic memory for faces.

He was also right about the office. Except for a map of Washington pinned up on one wall, the room was bare. The only furniture was a desk, an office chair, a wooden armchair for visitors, and a wood-ve-neered credenza behind the desk loaded with old engineering text-books Stone hadn't opened in years.

Kessler dropped down into the armchair, reached out and snagged Stone's coffee cup, and sat back with it cradled in his hands as though for warmth. He lifted the cup, took a sip, and frowned.

"Jesus, Stef, how can you drink this shit?" Kessler put the cup back on Stone's desk.

"It's espresso." Stone grinned, lighting a cigarette. "Ramona makes it specially for me every morning."

"Ramona has a crush on you."

"She's a woman of taste," countered Stone blithely.

"She's at least sixty, she barely speaks English, she has a mustache, and she probably works for DGI," replied Kessler. (DGI was the Dirección Generale de Inteligencia, Cuban intelligence.)

"Tell me what's going on out at the airport," said Stone, changing the subject. Kessler, with his phenomenal memory, was a floater within CI-Q, attached to no particular patch, going where he was needed, but paying special attention to Washington National and the Baltimore-Wash-ington International Airport. The red-haired man could watch two or three hundred people get off an international flight and pick out the one face he'd glanced at in a file folder six months before.

"Nada." Kessler shrugged. "But I followed up on that advisory we had yesterday on your friend Travkin."

"And?" said Stone.

"He landed at Gander, went on to Ottawa, and spent the night at the embassy there. He's booked in on an American Airlines flight that gets in at ten this morning. You want a team on him?"

"No. He's holding the bag; that means he'll go straight to the SMO. We can pick him up there."

"Okay." Kessler glanced at his watch and then bounced up out of the chair. "Nine-o-five. God's on his way up." God was Bill Ruppelt, the most punctual man in the world. Using a stopwatch, Kessler had once timed the CI-Q boss through his daily routine over a weeklong period,

31

and Ruppelt hadn't deviated by more than a minute throughout the five-day test. Arrival at 9:05, park car, enter building, into elevator at 9:07, arrival in office 9:08. Meeting with Stone, 9:15 to 9:35, bathroom 9:40 (morning edition *USA Today* indicates bowel movement), return to office 9:55.

Laughing, Stone waved Kessler out of his office and picked up the night log again. In three minutes Ruppelt would pass the open doorway, and it wouldn't do to be seen gazing out the window. Trying to look as studious as possible, he stared down at the pages of the log, waiting for God to reach the third floor.

As deputy director of Central Intelligence Hudson Cooper was allowed office space in all of the CIA's buildings, including the headquarters building behind the wire in the Langley compound and the laboratories at Curry Hall. The offices he liked best, however, were in the original OSS building at Twenty-fifth and E Streets, both because of the historical significance of occupying the same suite of rooms once used by Wild Bill Donovan, and because 2430 E Street was a lot closer to downtown Washington than the brooding pile of marble and steel squatting in the middle of a forest on the other side of the Potomac. Few of his predecessors had liked the Langley compound, insisting that it had been obsolete before it was finished in 1963, and Cooper showed his disdain for the campus-styled complex by rarely going there.

Like most of the senior executive offices within the CIA, the DDO's suite was expansive, oak-paneled, and furnished with a men's club combination of dark wood and old leather. His offices consisted of an antechamber, a main office, a full four-piece bathroom, a private dining room, and a kitchen. All this took up almost a third of the building's second floor on the southeast corner, with five high windows looking out over the landscaped grounds and screening trees down to the head-high chain-link fence surrounding the property.

The antechamber, high-ceilinged and oak-floored, was reserved for his assistant. It was decorated in deep blue and white, the wall behind his assistant's desk filled by a huge circular CIA seal, complete with eagle and "The Truth Shall Make You Free" motto.

The main office was large, carpeted with a deep blue shag, and almost empty of furniture. At the center of the room, its back to the three high windows looking out onto the E Street side, was a massive late-eighteenth-century partner's desk, polished to a deep cherry shine and invariably empty except for Cooper's multiline phone and scrambler unit. The chair behind the desk was ultramodern, black leather and high-backed. To his right was an enormous Gouchard globe, while to the left, on its own stand, was a terminal connecting him to the various mainframe computers utilized by the agency. In front of the desk there were three leather-covered armchairs for visitors to the office.

Cooper, dressed in a dark three-piece suit, sat behind the desk and went over Barron's file yet again. He'd slept poorly the night before, plagued by the information the file contained and furious that he could see no realistic solution to the problem. Even so, there were steps to be taken, and he'd arrived at the office before seven, to get as much work done as possible before the official day began.

Finishing Barron's report, he slipped the file into the center drawer of his desk, which he locked with the key he kept on his watch chain. He turned to the computer terminal, cleared the screen, then pressed the intercom button on the telephone, calling for his assistant. A few moments later the door to the main office opened, and a tall middle-aged man with glasses and thinning sandy hair stepped into the room, a thick buff-colored file envelope in one hand. The diagonal blue stripe across the envelope marked it as a CIA soft file, which meant that it had no circulation beyond the DDO's office and did not even exist in any official sense. Paul Mallory crossed the room and sat down in one of the visitors' chairs, the file in his lap.

"You've found something, I see," said Cooper, lighting a cigarette and nodding at the file.

"Yes, sir."

"Quick work," the DDO murmured; there was a note of disapproval in his voice.

"I came across the subject while I was in Threat Analysis several years ago," Mallory explained. "He seemed to be what you were looking for, so I went and found the jacket on him." The bookish man seated across from Cooper had been a project threat analyst before coming to the deputy director's office. His work had involved taking project plans from Operations and running them through a variety of computer-generated "threat evaluations" to see if the plans were feasible.

"Your opinion?" Cooper asked.

"The subject is completely nonjudgmental. Emotionless, practical, straightforward. Follows orders to the letter. On the surface you'd probably say he was sociopathic, but there's nothing to indicate that in his psych profile."

"Let me see his summary," said Cooper.

33

Mallory opened the file, slid out the top sheet, and handed it across to the deputy director. Cooper found himself staring at a four-by-five color photograph clipped to the top of the page. The face was tanned and intelligent, square-jawed, lean, with deep-set dark-gray eyes and a thick mass of black hair, tinged with gray at the temples. He appeared to be in his late thirties or early forties.

"His agency acronym is QJ/RAIL," said Mallory, pulling the file out of its envelope. "He operates under the name of Eric Rhinelander."

"His real name is Phelps?" asked Cooper, reading from the summary sheet.

"Hard to say," answered Mallory, poking his glasses up onto the bridge of his nose. He hunched over the main file, peeling back the pages. "He was an orphan, picked up in Germany in 1945. He appeared to be no more than a month or two old. He'd been given to a local priest just prior to the Allied advance."

"Who adopted him?"

"A British signals officer. He married a German girl during the occupation. Couldn't have children because of measles, so they adopted and settled down on the wife's family farm outside Frankfurt."

"How did he get here?"

"Parents died when he was ten," said Mallory, consulting the file. "Phelps had a brother who'd emigrated here before the war. They took the kid in. New York. He went to school there, dropped out of Columbia and enlisted in the Air Force. They sent him back to Germany because he spoke the language, and he wound up flying special operations with the Ravens into Laos and Cambodia. That's how we found him."

"Did we train him?"

"Yes, sir. The full curriculum. The Farm, Quantico, and Lake Mead. He was good when we picked him up and just about the best when we finished with him. That was in '73. He's worked on contract from then on."

Cooper nodded. QJ/RAIL had been trained as an assassin, a job description denied by every President since Ford signed an executive order stating that no employee of the federal government would have any involvement in any political assassination. By signing annual contracts, QJ/RAIL skirted the ruling in its strictly legal sense.

"Where is he now?" Cooper asked.

"Jamaica," answered Mallory. "At least he has a house there. He hasn't worked for us in five years now."

"Who does he work for?"

"Anyone who'll hire him. People who know him by reputation. Most of them appear to be Southeast Asians involved in the drug trade. He made a lot of connections in the Triangle during the late sixties and early seventies. So far he's avoided anything red, white, and blue. According to our records, he hasn't set foot in the States in years, let alone worked here."

"Then he has no record?"

"No, sir," said Mallory, shaking his head. "Nothing except this file. When he was with the Ravens, they wiped all his military notations, and since he was contract for us, the agency has no hard file. He's clean, just as you requested."

"Do we have anything on his recent movements?"

"No, sir." Mallory smiled; he'd anticipated the question. "I did run a check on drug-related killings over the past few months." He let it dangle.

"And?"

"Three days ago five Cambodians were assassinated in an Amsterdam loft. All of them were big in the Khmer Rouge, Pol Pot's inner circle, including his sister-in-law. There was a sixth corpse as well, a man named Charles Yang. Heavyweight in the opium business."

"You think it was this man Rhinelander?"

"It's a good bet sir. The killing was done with a Carl Gustav rocket launcher from across the street; no fooling around with sniper rifles or anything like that. The description of the man in the rented room across from the loft fits QJ/RAIL well enough."

"Where does that lead us, if anywhere?" asked Cooper.

"Yang's main competition in Europe is a French-German named Philippe Groman," Mallory replied. "According to our information, Groman has been handling all the opium and heroin base the Khmer use to finance their weapons purchasing on the Continent. If Yang was cutting him off, Groman might have hired our man to snuff the opposition."

"Where is Groman?"

"Paris."

"You think Rhinelander might be there as well?"

"It's possible," Mallory answered, shrugging his narrow shoulders. "If he was going back to Groman for the payoff."

"I see." Cooper swung around in his chair, turning to the giant globe on his right. He spun it slowly. It was old and showed a world that had vanished long ago. Belgian Congo, Siam, French Equatorial Africa, Dutch Guiana, British Honduras. Back then the greatest instrument of foreign policy had been a gunboat; now it was surveillance satellites and "Star Wars." He found Paris, covering it with the tip of his index finger. He smiled wanly. If only it were that easy. He turned back in his chair and faced Mallory.

"Find him," he ordered. "Go to Paris. Today. Tell him I wish to speak to him on a matter of urgent business, and give him the number for my white telephone. If he is not in Paris, go to Jamaica and wait for him to return. I want to speak to him as soon as possible. I want you to get back to me on this within twelve hours."

"Yes, sir." Mallory waited for a moment, but Cooper was obviously finished with him. He stood up finally and left the office.

The DDO turned in his chair and stared out the window. Another blistering day. He glanced at the old-fashioned Hamilton on his wrist, an anniversary present from Miriam. It was almost noon, and by now the Barron operation he'd initiated last night would be under way; there were no answers yet, but at least the tracks were being covered.

In his personal and professional life fear was something that Colonel John Barron had rarely encountered. Too young and far too well connected for Vietnam, he had spent his adolescence and early adulthood following a comfortable pattern of proper schools, proper friends, and proper women. His success as a doctor was assured, and his position as senior resident medical officer at Walter Reed had been decided over lunch at the Jockey Club. The fact that he was a reasonably good doctor with a definite talent as a diagnostician was irrelevant. If he'd been Sweeney Todd, the course of his life would have been unchanged.

A year before, when Hudson Cooper had quietly taken him aside and asked him to be his eyes and ears at Walter Reed, Barron had been flattered. For someone used to a life of utter predictability, the thought of working for the CIA had been seductively appealing. It never occurred to him that Cooper had wanted nothing more than a monitor on the new President's general health or that he had half a dozen other informers at Walter Reed and Bethesda, each one paid to keep him up-to-date on the medical status of the Joint Chiefs and anyone else of note at the Pentagon. Not that it would have mattered; Barron enjoyed his secret cloak-and-dagger life, occasionally meeting with Mallory, the DDO's assistant, and passing on some tidbit he thought might be of interest.

But that had changed in an instant. It wasn't a game anymore, and after his meeting with Cooper the night before, the full implications of what he'd done had struck him like a hammerblow. Not only had he

36

violated his oath as a doctor by divulging patient information, but he'd prejudiced his future and put his reputation and that of his entire family into the hands of a total stranger.

By dawn, bleary-eyed from lack of sleep, hands shaking from a dozen cups of coffee, he'd come to the only decision possible. Morally he had no choice: He was going to have to blow the whistle on the whole affair, no matter what the consequences. But first he'd have to clear it with his family.

By nine he'd managed to clean himself up a little, and he'd put on a clean uniform, more for the sake of his own morale than for any official reason. He booked himself onto a Boston flight, called in sick at the hospital, and left his McPherson Square apartment. He took the elevator down to the parking garage beneath the building. He reached the basement, took out his keys, and walked along the echoing concrete, heading for his reserved space at the rear of the first level.

Barron reached his car, a late-model black Thunderbird, and unlocked the door. As he did so, he heard a crashing sound. He turned in time to see two men slam open the sliding door of the dark blue van in the spot beside him. Before he could utter a sound, the two men had dragged him into the interior of the van while a third dropped down to the ground, slid the panel closed, and took the keys out of the Thunderbird's lock. He then climbed into Barron's vehicle and drove off slowly, heading out of the garage. A few moments later a fourth man, behind the wheel of the van, followed the Thunderbird.

Inside the van Barron struggled desperately, but it was no use. The larger of the two men holding him had one hand clamped over his mouth while the other arm snaked around his neck. Using a roll of nylon-reinforced fabric tape, the smaller man bound Barron's legs together and then his arms. Together, rocking jerkily with the movement of the van, they dragged Barron over to a fifty-gallon plastic drum. The drum had been lashed to a pair of cleats welded to the side wall, and each time the van turned or changed lanes water sloshed out onto the bare metal floor.

Staggering, the two men upended Barron's bound body. The big man took his hand away from the doctor's mouth just before it was forced underwater. They held him there, grunting with effort as the body whiplashed back and forth, dousing them both. When the movement stopped, the smaller man went to the front of the van and opened a large vinyl overnight bag. He began removing a selection of casual clothing they'd taken from Barron's boat earlier that morning.

The larger man stayed beside the drum, supporting the doctor's lax, overturned form. Barron was probably already dead, but it was absolutely necessary for the lungs to be filled. The water in the barrel had been taken from the Potomac, and when the autopsy was performed on Barron, the findings would be consistent with accidental death by drowning. Sometime within the next twenty-four hours the doctor's body would be found close to the *Tarantella*, dressed in appropriate clothing, right down to the Top-siders on his feet. His car would be found in the Buzzard Point Marina parking lot.

The van, complete with the fifty-gallon drum, would be taken to a wrecking yard in Alexandria, Virginia, and burned down to the axles. When the vehicle had been completely "sanitized," it would then be put through a crusher and turned into a four-foot square cube of scrap metal.

The four men, hired out of Miami through a series of cutouts, would return to Florida that evening and rendezvous to receive their fee at a house south of the Calle Ocho in Little Havana. When it was certain that all four men were in the house, a second, independently hired two-man team would radio detonate the seven charges of C-4 explosive strategically placed under the floorboards of the house, instantly vaporizing the structure and its occupants.

By midnight any connection between Colonel John Barron, Hudson Cooper, and the mental health of the President of the United States would have vanished.

# CHAPTER 3

After twenty years as a professional soldier, twelve of them spent in Soviet Military Intelligence, Dmitri Travkin was positive that he had discovered the essential flaw in the philosophy of Marxist-Leninism.

Humor or, more precisely, the lack of it was the key. The Russian people were funny enough, but after two weeks of leave in Moscow the GRU major was convinced that to become a card-carrying member of the Communist party involved compulsory surgery to remove the part of the brain responsible for laughter.

Jokes gained you nothing but blank stares, a funny anecdote was enough to have you brought up on charges, and a Politburo pun was probably good for a one-way ticket to the gulag of your choice. It was too bad; a couple of dirty stories told at a summit conference would do more for world peace than dismantling a few dozen obsolete missiles.

Comedy was what he liked most about Americans; even Reagan had managed a few good lines during his presidency, and Ford had an act worthy of the Marx Brothers. It was also rumored that Richard Nixon had a personal collection of utterly obscene jokes that made Richard Pryor look like an amateur. Of course, the essence of the best American humor was satire, a word which simply didn't exist within the Kremlin walls. The rules of the game had changed since the East bloc upheavals of 1989; but for the most part, at least in the intelligence field, the players had remained the same, and if anything, their dour, humorless outlook on the world had only intensified with the looming specter of democracy

39

on the horizon. For the twentieth-century spy or counterspy, peace was a nightmare.

Travkin was reasonably sure that his enjoyment of American comedy had been noted on some file deep within the bowels of the Mount Alto complex on Wisconsin Avenue, and there was probably some grimy little KGB shithead who kept track of his record purchases, right down to his latest Howie Mandel album. It didn't bother him; after two years as GRU deputy resident he'd established his reputation more than adequately, with a score of well-placed informants and illegals sprinkled all over the District of Columbia and beyond. At thirty-eight he was the youngest deputy resident in the Second Directorate, and on rotation in a year or two he was virtually guaranteed a full residency or a posting back to Moscow Center and the "Aquarium" on the perimeter of the old Khodinka Airfield.

Travkin glanced at his watch and frowned. Three o'clock. He wouldn't be posted anywhere if he were late for his meeting with Koslov. The deputy resident yawned, sat up in the lumpy, overstuffed armchair, and adjusted his tie. He stood up and made his way to the bathroom of the small apartment. The living quarters were located on the fourth floor of the Soviet Military Office on Belmont Road. Travkin had his own apartment closer to downtown, but he'd arrived on a late flight the night before, doubling as a courier and carrying the military pouch from Moscow Center. He'd come directly to the SMO on Koslov's orders and had slept off his jet lag before the afternoon briefing.

He stared at the reflection of his narrow, almost feline face in the mirror, pushing back an unruly strand of the cornsilk blond hair he'd inherited from his mother's side of the family. The deep-set hazel eyes and the patrician nose came from his father, God rest his soul. Now *there* was a man who knew how to laugh! Travkin grinned, remembering his father's great, booming laugh, knee slapped, head thrown back as he roared at some joke.

"Faith and begorrah, but you're a handsome boyo!" he crooned, the accent a mind-boggling blend of Russian and Irish. He brushed a spot of lint from the shoulder of his Joseph Wilner silk made-to-measure and left the apartment. He took the rear stairs down to Koslov's second-floor office.

From the outside the SMO is a handsome red-brick Georgian building surrounded by a discreet wrought-iron fence. Inside, it is a maze of small offices, narrow hallways, and low-watt lighting that gives the place and its occupants a pale, sickly look. The furniture is utilitarian, the floors are

CHRISTOPHER HYDE

40

bare wood, and there is not a single piece of artwork in the entire building. During the summer months the central air conditioning is permanently set on "cold," and in winter the furnace keeps the building boiling hot. The windows are allowed to accumulate soot, making surveillance photography difficult. To Dmitri Travkin's delicate nose, the place always seemed to smell faintly of damp wool socks.

Koslov's office was a suite of three cubicles, each one slightly larger than the next. The first was for the resident's male secretary, the second was for Koslov himself, and the third was for meetings of senior staff.

The major general was reading at his desk when Travkin entered the middle room. The desk was metal, the swivel chair behind it was wooden, and with the exception of one wooden office chair directly in front of the desk and half a dozen dark brown filing cabinets against the far wall, the room was bare of furniture.

Travkin seated himself on the wooden chair and waited patiently. He could see Koslov's scalp beneath a thin covering of nicotine-colored hair. The scalp was pink and smooth, like a baby's. Then Koslov lifted his head, and the image vanished. The heavy, dark-jowled face was anything but babyish: thin, colorless lips, permanently crimped around the soggy end of a foul-smelling Opal cigarette; large coal black eyes set deeply above the sagging cheeks and topped by shaggy yellow-white brows; a nose that made Travkin's look tiny by comparison, nostrils flared, thick with curling hair. The voice, when he spoke, was the rasping product of fifty years of smoking and a quart of vodka every day for almost as long.

"Dmitri Aleksandrovich. You are looking well after your leave."

"Thank you, General."

"Your family is well?"

"Yes, thank you, General. My mother sends her best wishes and greatly appreciated the box of chocolates you sent."

"One should not forget old friends," said Koslov. He and Travkin's father had fought together in the Great Patriotic War. According to his mother, Koslov and his father had competed for her favors and his father had been the successful suitor.

Travkin blinked, trying to erase the absurd image of Koslov on bended knee in front of his mother with a bunch of flowers in his hand. Fits of laughter in front of one's superior officer were not wise, especially when the officer was Major General Gennadi Mikhailovich Koslov of the GRU.

"Thankfully things were quiet during your absence." The old man grunted. He pushed a sheaf of papers across the desk, transcriptions of

41

coded messages from his source agents. Travkin left them where they were for the moment. "Little of interest," said Koslov, tapping the sheets with a nicotine-stained index finger. "Borovsky handled the drops."

"Yes, sir." Borovsky was an idiot who could barely tie his shoelaces, but even he was capable of emptying a few "letter boxes."

"Your relationship with this man Stone," said Koslov, after a moment's pause while he relit his Opal. "It concerns me."

"Sir?"

"We know he is an agent of CI-Q, the FBI's Rednet program. By the same token he is certainly aware that you are not a member of our trade mission."

"Yes, sir."

"I see no productivity from the relationship. His intent is clear; he has hopes of turning you."

"I am aware of that, General."

"Then why continue the charade?" Koslov asked, the wide brow furrowing into a dozen bulldog creases.

"Better an enemy one knows than one who is hidden." Travkin shrugged. "I am the passive partner. I expend no energy or manpower maintaining a casual friendship. On the other hand, I've counted as many as six of his men keeping me under surveillance. When I wish to avoid them, I do so and go about my business. The product is their wasted expenditure of time and personnel."

"I see." Koslov nodded.

Travkin knew that he didn't see at all. Koslov was old guard, capable of little in the way of subtlety. As far as he was concerned, the general population of the United States was a bubbling pool of corruption, and any individual was capable of co-option for a price. If you couldn't appeal to a potential source's greed, you trapped him with sex or drugs or a combination of all three. It was true up to a point; but people like Stephen Stone were the hounds in this particular fox hunt, and Travkin wanted them in plain sight at all times.

If his friendship with Stone and their once-a-week racquetball game deflected Rednet's attention away from Travkin's real work, then it was worthwhile. There were other, more complex reasons for continuing the friendship, but Travkin knew enough about the politics of the Soviet military not to reveal all his sources, to his boss or anyone else.

"All right, Dmitri, continue the liaison for the time being, but be advised that Older Brother has been sniffing at your tail." "Older

Brother" was the GRU term for the KGB. "Perhaps it is your expensive clothing, Dmitri Aleksandrovich."

"Of course," Travkin replied, his expression serious. "I will be the first Soviet intelligence officer to defect to the West over a question of wardrobe." He snorted. "My God, sir, don't they have anything better to do?"

"Perhaps not, Dmitri, but I beg you to take their interest seriously. Gurenko would like nothing better than to see me with egg on my face." Vladimir Gurenko was the KGB station chief in Washington and Koslov's opposite number.

"I'll try to be careful," Travkin said. He stood up and gathered the pile of messages from Koslov's desk.

"Do that," said the old man. He waved a hand; it was a dismissal. Walking softly over the creaking floorboards, Dmitri Travkin left the office. Forty minutes later he was back in his apartment, soaking in a hot tub and listening to Bill Cosby moan and groan about his childhood while he went through the stack of messages Koslov had given him. He was halfway through an old Weird Harold skit when he reached the brief note from his source in the file room at Walter Reed Hospital.

In Paris night had fallen, bringing darkness to the city but no relief from the oppressive heat that had left its occupants stunned for the last three days. The August *fermeture annuelle* was in full swing, and any Parisian who could afford it had fled to cooler climes, leaving the sweltering city to the tourists.

Unlike most major cities, Paris, arrogant to the point of martyrdom, refused to believe that pollution existed. Factories belched smoke, automobiles went without emission controls, and the city still used diesel fuel in large parts of the metro system. Because of this, the effect of the heat wave was multiplied a thousandfold and the city choked under a colossal bell jar of umber-colored air, its particulate count high enough to obscure the top of the Eiffel Tower and its stink reminiscent of an animal-rendering plant.

Eric Rhinelander, naked, lay on his narrow bed in the Pension Lipp and tried not to breathe too deeply. He was hot, tired, and angry. If it hadn't been for Groman's stupid attempt to double-cross him, he would have been back at Goldeneye on Jamaica's north coast, enjoying the evening breeze as it swept across the cliffs of Oracabessa.

He had completed the assignment in Amsterdam exactly as Groman had requested, extracting Yang and the others with the precision of a dentist pulling half a dozen rotting teeth. He'd taken the train to Paris that same night, expecting the final portion of Groman's promised payment. It had not been forthcoming, and the pig-eyed whoremaster refused to answer any of his calls.

The money was of less concern to Rhinelander than his reputation. Groman was too well connected to be ignored. If Rhinelander allowed himself to be cheated by the man, others would make the same attempt. It was an irritating waste of time, but Groman had to be taught a lesson that would be heeded by anyone who came along after him.

The assassin sat up and swung his legs off the bed, skimming the film of sweat from his broad chest with the palm of one hand. He picked up the old stainless steel Rolex from the bedside table and glanced at the time. Nine-fifteen. Groman wasn't expected at the Cardinal's Cap for another three quarters of an hour, and the flight to Montreal didn't leave until midnight. There was plenty of time.

He padded across to the small porcelain sink on the other side of the room and sponged himself down. He had the body of a much younger man, shoulders, back, and chest knotted with muscle, thighs hard, the hair over his groin thick, curly, and dark. The only real clues to his age were the faint wings of gray hair at his temples and the fanning web of tiny lines at the corner of each eye.

Opening the freestanding armoire beside the sink, he took out his clothes and dressed: white, open-necked shirt, dark, slightly pleated trousers, cream-colored linen jacket, and a pair of soft, well-used English loafers. He wore no jewelry except for the watch. The rest of his clothing was already at Charles de Gaulle and would be put onto his flight automatically.

Dressed, he reached up to the upper shelf of the cupboard to bring down the rest of his equipment. Going to the side of the bed, he lifted one foot up onto the mattress and strapped the small eight-shot Sauer automatic pistol to his ankle, using two thick rubber bands. He dropped his foot to the floor, shaking down the cuff, then walked across the room and back, adjusting to the weight and feeling for slippage. He added a third rubber band for insurance, then gathered up his wallet, airline ticket, keys, and small change. His passport, a Canadian one in the name of John Duncan, would be retrieved at the front desk of the pension. The last item, a chrome-plated ball-point pen, he clipped to the breast pocket of his shirt.

Rhinelander left the room and went down the narrow stairs to the main floor of the pension. He paid his bill and was given his passport in return. Business completed, he stepped out into the narrow confines of the Rue des Anglais. The street was dark and empty and smelled of cats. He turned left, made his way quickly to the Boulevard St.-Germain, and picked up a taxi from the rank beside the Place Maubert metro station. The driver was reading a paperback book and barely looked up as Rhinelander climbed into the back of his vehicle.

"Impasse Souris."

"*Pardon?*" asked the driver, glancing into his mirror.

"Impasse Souris," Rhinelander repeated. "Montmartre."

"*Ah, oui.*" The driver laid his book down on the seat beside him and threw the old Mercedes into gear. He took another look in the mirror and frowned. His passenger wasn't a local, but he was no tourist either. The clothes looked Italian, but he was too tall, at least six feet. A journalist perhaps. The driver shrugged off his curiosity. Anyone traveling to that part of Montmartre at this time of night was looking for trouble, and he didn't want any part of it.

Rhinelander sat back against the dry, cracked leather of the seat and let his mind go blank. He barely noticed as they crossed the Pont au Double and passed beneath the looming towers of Notre-Dame. After a ten-minute chase through the almost-empty streets they began to climb the hill toward Sacré-Coeur, following the twisting maze of one-way streets and alleys until they reached their destination.

His passenger delivered, the driver took his fare and drove off quickly, heading south toward the more civilized environment of the Left Bank. Rhinelander watched him go, then turned and entered the deeply shadowed recesses of the narrow dead-end alleyway.

The end of the street was blocked by a tottering four-story building, its walls grime-encrusted, the main-floor windows bricked up, and the entrance secured by a heavy wooden door, strapped and studded with iron. Once upon a time the building had probably been the home of a well-to-do merchant, but now it looked like exactly what it was: a whorehouse.

He stepped up to the door and knocked once, his hand balled into a fist. After a moment a small peephole opened at shoulder height.

"*Was?*" asked a tired voice, speaking in German. The eye peering dimly out at Rhinelander was small, wary, and ringed with graying skin.

"*Ich suche Fraülein Harriet,*" Rhinelander answered, slipping easily into his mother tongue. "*Beeilen Sie sich, bitte. Es ist dringend.*"

"*Ja, ja,*" muttered the voice wearily. "Of course, it is urgent. For you

45

men it is *always* urgent. You think only with your balls." The peephole slammed shut, and Rhinelander heard the sound of a bolt being drawn back. The door opened, and he stepped inside quickly. The gray-haired drudge who'd answered his knock locked the door again and shuffled away without a backward glance. Rhinelander kept his jacket on, ignoring the empty row of metal coat hooks in the foyer. From the looks of it, business at the Cardinal's Cap was slow.

He went down the short passage to the main hall and looked around in the dim light. There was a faintly stylish aura about the broad vestibule with its high, ornately worked plaster ceiling and the big wrought-iron spiral staircase that led to the upper levels. But time had passed, taking the grandeur of the house with it. There were holes in the plaster and stains of mildew and rot. The ancient Oriental carpet on the marble floor was threadbare, and there was the dull odor of sour cabbage in the air, mixed with the reek of linen left too long between changes.

Ranged around the oval room were several tables and half a dozen mismatched chairs. A few velvet-shaded lamps threw pale smudges of light across the faces of the women in the room, most of whom were playing cards or simply staring into space, their features blank.

One of the women, older than the rest, was nude, an empty bottle of Stella Artois beer on the floor beside her chair. Her legs were spread wide as she dozed, head lolling against the gray wall at her back. Her breasts hung like empty bags of sugar, the nipples purple and extruded from the white flesh like gigantic moles. Rolls of fat slithered down into her lap, melding with the creped skin of her thighs, her belly running like still-warm lava above the spreading forest of black between her legs and the gaping raw-meat slash of her pudenda.

Rhinelander looked away, trying not to breathe too deeply; the room was like something out of Breughel and far too reminiscent of his dreams. A moment later a middle-aged woman appeared on the stairs. She was dressed in a long blue and orange kimono, her dark hair knotted casually at her neck. At first glance she seemed as blase and desolate as the others; but there was a hint of intelligence in her gray-green eyes, and the lines around her painted cupid's lips were from laughter, not despair. Reaching the bottom of the stairs, she held out a thin, long-boned hand. Rhinelander took it briefly, nodding.

"Herr Duncan," she said softly, her voice a practiced croon. "How nice to see you at the Kardinalen Kap again. What can we do for you tonight?" The woman's German was stiff and formal, the accent forced. She was French; but Groman wanted authenticity, and the Cardinal's

Cap was supposedly a re-creation of a prewar brothel of the same name in Berlin. The woman had a good memory; he'd been at the whorehouse only once before, for his original meeting with Groman.

"I need your help," said Rhinelander, holding the woman's eyes. "Can we go upstairs?"

"You want me?" asked Fraülein Harriet archly, cocking one hip, the bone standing out like a blade beneath the thin synthetic silk of her robe. "You realize that it will cost you more, Herr Duncan?"

"Money is not a consideration," he answered, still speaking German. "I want your time, not your body, *meine Dame*."

"Ah, so I'm a lady now!" She laughed. "Hear that, girls?" she said, speaking French. "A slut no more!"

The other women paid no attention.

"I can go elsewhere," Rhinelander said quietly.

"*Nein, nein, teuer Knabe*! If it is Harriet you want, then Harriet you shall have. Come along."

She led him up the staircase to the narrow corridor that ran the length of the second floor, each cell-like room blocked by a plain, anonymous door.

"How does a woman know which room is hers?" Rhinelander inquired.

"If the room is not locked, it belongs to her." Harriet laughed. "Only the special rooms are marked, and my own room, of course." She winked at Rhinelander and grinned. "Rank hath its privileges, even here, Herr Duncan."

She stopped in front of a blue-painted door and drew a key ring out of the pocket of her robe. She opened the door and led Rhinelander inside. She closed the door and then went to the center of the room, where she stood on a small square of Oriental carpeting, its design almost completely worn away. There was a metal bed and a small bedside table on one side of the room and a fabric-covered folding screen on the other, presumably hiding the chamber pot and other toilet facilities.

The woman kept her smile fixed and her eyes on Rhinelander as she undid the belt of her kimono and let it fall to the floor with a shrug. She was fit enough for a woman her age, the breasts full and sagging only slightly, the belly a single curve, the pale patch of her sex unobtrusive.

"So, what shall it be, Herr Duncan?" she asked, her eyes flickering to the narrow iron bed and the thin mattress.

"I want you to get down on your knees," he instructed.

47

She nodded, at ease with the familiar request and did as he asked, then stared up at him, arms outstretched, hands beckoning.

"Come on then," she murmured.

He moved closer until he was standing directly above her. "Close your eyes," he said.

"Shy?" she asked, laughing.

"Just do it."

"*Jawohl, mein Herr!*" She grinned, obeying. Her lips parted expectantly, waiting for him to begin.

Rhinelander bent slightly, reached down, and pulled the pistol away from its rubber band holster. He placed his left hand on the top of Harriet's head, then slipped the barrel of the gun between her lips and teeth. Her eyes flew open at the cold metallic touch, and she blinked up at him, terrified. He pushed the barrel more deeply into her mouth.

"Don't move, not even an inch," he said quietly. He took his hand away from her head and pushed back the slide, cocking the weapon. "The slightest pressure, and your teeth will be blown out the back of your head along with your brains," he whispered. "I will ask you questions; you will answer. Lie, and you are dead. If you understand, blink your eyes." She did so, rapidly. He slid the barrel out of her mouth, the metal wet with saliva. He backed away, keeping the pistol trained on her. "When Groman comes here, who does he fuck?"

"Me. Usually."

"This room?"

"No," she answered, her voice quavering. "The special room. The furniture there is nicer."

"That is the room with the peephole, yes?"

"Yes."

"What about Max, the bodyguard?"

"Herr Groman doesn't let him come in. He stays with the car."

"Where does he park?"

"Rue Poulbot."

"Good." Rhinelander nodded. "You're doing well. Now then, when Groman visits, how long does he stay?"

"An hour, sometimes two or three if he takes cocaine."

"Does he take it often?"

"Often enough."

"Is there a rear exit from here?" Rhinelander already knew there was, but he wanted to know if she'd tell him the truth.

"Yes." She nodded. "There is an alley. Follow it, and you come to the stairs at Rue Drevet."

"Good. Stand up and put on your robe." The woman did so, her eyes never leaving the pistol in Rhinelander's hand. "Take me to the room. Not the bedroom, the one with the peephole."

He followed her out of the room and along the corridor. They made several turns until she reached a door close to a narrow flight of stairs."

"The stairs lead to the back kitchen," she said, following his glance.

"Fine. Show me the room." She nodded and took out the key ring again. She opened the door and stepped aside, gesturing into a tiny, closet-size space. In the weak light from the corridor he could see that it contained nothing but a high stool and a single coat hook. Rhinelander eased into the room and sat down on the stool. By crouching slightly, he brought his eye to a hole in the wall about the size of an American dime.

The room on the other side of the wall was clean, with freshly painted white walls and a bland selection of modern furniture. There were a few landscape prints on the walls, and the floor was covered in subdued green wall-to-wall carpeting. It looked like something out of a Holiday Inn.

"The hole is covered by the shadow of a wall sconce," explained Harriet nervously, standing in the corridor. "You can see everything that goes on." She paused. "Some people like that."

"So I've heard." Rhinelander nodded, climbing down from the stool. He stepped out into the hallway and stared at the woman silently. Finally he spoke. "It is almost ten o'clock. Groman will be here any moment."

"Yes," Harriet said.

"Bring him here. Do whatever is necessary to distract him. I want him between your legs and thinking of nothing else, understand?"

"Yes . . . yes."

"Tell him anything, warn him, and I will know. And I will kill you."

"You will be watching?"

"Yes." Rhinelander pushed her gently. "Go. Be downstairs to greet him."

The woman gave him a brief, frightened look and then retreated down the hallway. Rhinelander returned to the cubbyhole and closed the door, leaving it slightly ajar. Without hurry he slipped off his shoes and socks and hung up his jacket on the hook behind him. Then he settled down on the stool to wait.

Less than five minutes later he heard the muffled sound of voices coming from the corridor. He leaned over and put his eye to the peephole again. The door to the bedroom opened, and Harriet appeared, followed by Groman's heavyset figure. Once the drug dealer had taken pride in his longshoreman's body, but too many years of indulgence had taken their toll. Even in his expensive suit and handmade shirt the man's belly bulged far over his belt, and the big peasant's face was stained on cheek and nose with blossoms of broken blood vessels.

Without a word Harriet began working at Groman's zipper, then dropped down in front of him. She slipped the brown worm of his limp organ into her mouth and began to suck noisily. Within a few moments the worm had become a hooded snake, thick and long, standing out absurdly from his trousers, the head a slick-wet glistening purple in the bright light from the ceiling fixture.

"The bed," Groman ordered, his voice hoarse. By the time he'd stripped off his clothes, Harriet was already on the mattress, one leg raised, waiting for him. He climbed into bed with her, pushing her legs apart, and she spit into her hand, wetting herself. Without any preliminaries he lowered his large body over hers, plunging himself deeply inside. She grunted, wincing with pain, and then gripped his pale, furry shoulders as he began a jerking, angry rhythm, buttocks clenching with effort, toes digging into the bedding.

Rhinelander stepped gingerly off the stool and out into the corridor. It was empty. From somewhere below he could hear the faint sounds of a stereo playing Charles Aznavour. There were no voices, just the music and the sound of cards being dealt. He stepped along to the door of the peephole room and paused, standing on the balls of his feet, his ear an inch from the thin wooden partition. Groman was grunting loudly with each stroke now, counterpoint to the squeaking of the bedsprings.

Silently Rhinelander reached into his pocket and removed the "ballpoint." It was actually a metal telescopic pointer of the kind used by university lecturers, and Rhinelander had altered it by removing the plastic tip and replacing it with the last half inch of a tungsten steel leatherworker's awl. He clicked the knurled button on the top of the pointer, unlocking it, then pulled it out to its full eighteen-inch length and twisted the end in a half turn, locking it in place again.

He opened the door carefully, the steel tube of his weapon held lightly between the thumb and forefinger of his right hand, while the left hand turned the doorknob. He slipped noiselessly into the room on bare feet, crossing the carpeted floor in three quick steps. Groman had his face buried in Harriet's right shoulder, powerful hands clutching her upraised buttocks as he pounded into her, his large, sagging testicles slapping at the puckered bud of her anus with each stroke.

Almost without pause, Rhinelander found his point and moved, thrusting forward with the pointer, driving the awl tip into the vulnerable four-inch target of Groman's perineum. The foot-and-a-half-long weapon sliced neatly up into the big man's bladder, intestine, stomach, liver, and heart, the tip finally poking out at the base of his throat. With a grimace, Rhinelander pressed his thumb against the end of the device, pushing the last inch into Groman's writhing steel-skewered body. The drug dealer made a choked, mewling sound as every organ in his body ceased functioning simultaneously, and then his head dropped down onto Harriet's chest, a smothering dead weight.

Rhinelander grabbed the hair at the back of the corpse's head and pulled it back. White-faced and paralyzed with fear, Harriet stared up at him, Groman's dead penis slithering out from between her legs.

"Remember this," Rhinelander snarled, bringing his face down to within an inch of the woman. "Remember how he died, and tell anyone who wants to know." He pulled harder on Groman's hair, dragging him off Harriet and rolling him over onto the mattress beside her. Mouth working soundlessly, she crabbed off the bed, staring at the corpse. There was a damp stain on the sheet, and Rhinelander smelled urine. The woman had wet herself with fear.

"Who are you?" she managed to say, her voice stuttering.

"A ghost," he answered. "Someone who never existed."

"Are you going to kill me as well?"

"Of course not," Rhinelander answered. "You didn't cheat me; he did." He smiled at her, his expression almost gentle. "Stay here for at least thirty minutes," he commanded, his voice quiet. "That way there will be no trouble."

"Yes . . . yes, of course," she said. He turned and left the room, returning to the cubbyhole for his jacket, socks, and shoes. He put them on quickly, then took the rear stairs down to the back kitchen. Fifteen minutes later he took a taxi to the Aerogare station at Porte Maillot, and from there he boarded the shuttle bus for Charles de Gaulle. At midnight exactly his Air Canada 747 took off en route to Mirabel Airport, Montreal.

# CHAPTER 4

T he fat man sat in the conference room of the Georgetown safe house, the nib of his heavy Mont Blanc fountain pen gliding easily over the surface of the yellow legal-length pad on the table in front of him. The hand holding the expensive pen was small and very pink, the skin smooth and hairless, the nails perfectly manicured.

At the other end of the long table Hudson Cooper watched the hand and the pen, mesmerized by the smooth movement of the glittering solid-gold nib and the soft, almost feminine fingers wrapped around the thick black-lacquered barrel. The delicate hand was completely at odds with the rest of the fat man's body and had a life of its own, giving no hint of the immense power it could wield with a single stroke of that same black pen.

The fat man was Hollis C. Macintyre, and with the exception of the President he was probably the most important man in Washington, if not the entire United States. Physically he was either dramatically imposing or repulsive, depending on one's point of view. At eighty he still had all his hair, a crowning glory of thick pure white atop a massive, leonine head. Cheeks and jaws were draped in Churchillian jowls, the eyes were large, dark, and hawk-hooded, and the short tree-trunk neck was wedged between massive shoulders and arms. He dressed impeccably, custom-cut three-piece white silk suits from Hong Kong in the summer, dark pinstripes in the fall and winter, and always with his trademark red, white, and blue polka-dot bow tie.

Macintyre's formal occupation was the chairmanship of the President's political party, but that was really nothing more than a flag for him to fly under. After almost half a century in the shifting sands of federal politics he had innumerable allies in both houses of Congress, sat on the boards of a score of institutions and multinational corporations, and was owed favors by virtually every important figure in Washington from bureaucrats in the Budget Office to the Joint Chiefs. In addition, he was chairman pro tem of the Romulus Committee, a position not noted in any biography, official or otherwise.

"I believe I have the salient points," he said, capping the pen. Macintyre's voice was rich and deep with the rolling timbre of a natural orator. The large, hooded eyes stared blandly down the table at Cooper. "I presume Colonel Barron's diagnosis has been verified?"

"Certainly." Cooper nodded. "By one of the best neurologists in the country. He had no idea who the patient was, of course."

"What about this Barron fellow? How far can he be trusted?" asked Macintyre.

"The question is moot," Cooper answered, smiling briefly. "Colonel Barron had a boating accident today. A fatal one."

"I see," Macintyre answered. "This was necessary?"

"By my estimation there was no alternative. To have taken him any further would have involved Romulus. I felt it was better to forestall any possible complications."

"Yes. You're probably right." The fat man leaned back in his chair, the small hands clasped together over his enormous belly. He glanced briefly at the trays of hors d'oeuvres and wine on the sideboard to his left. The refreshments had been brought in by stewards from Cooper's own staff, who had long since left the building. They would return in the morning to clean up the remains. Macintyre turned his attention back to the DDO. "How much have you told the others?" he asked finally.

"Nothing," Cooper answered, shaking his head. "I wanted the chance to confer with you first." He paused. "Romulus has never dealt with anything of this magnitude before."

"True," said Macintyre. "And like your Colonel Barron, some of them are not altogether trustworthy, at least in this instance." The "others" included the head chairman of the Joint Chiefs of Staff, the secretary of state, the assistant secretary of the treasury, and the attorney general. In fine, Romulus was made up of people who covered most major elements of the federal government and the armed forces.

"So what do we tell them?" Cooper asked. He checked his watch. "They'll start coming within the next half hour or so."

"We tell them the truth," said Macintyre, shrugging his massive shoulders. "Or at least a part of it. The President is ill, but at this point we're not certain how ill. We do know that the illness could well become disabling in a short period of time. That should cover things for the moment."

"Fair enough, but what about Teresi?" Cooper asked, referring to the Vice President, Vincent Teresi.

"Our Italian friend bullied his way into the vice presidency," Macintyre responded, a note of anger in his voice. "If I hadn't outmaneuvered him at the convention and offered him the position on the ticket, he would have split the party in half."

"Or become President," said Cooper dryly.

"Indeed," said Macintyre, "in which case we all would be out of work, believe me."

"Romulus wasn't created to deal with questions of partisan politics," said Cooper, an edge to his voice. "It was devised to deal with a potentially disastrous oversight within the Constitution. Our employment or lack of it is hardly a consideration."

"Don't be naive, Hudson. The Romulus Committee was created because Franklin Delano Roosevelt was dying of heart disease and had a fellow traveler as Vice President. If he, or Eleanor, or any of his close friends had known how sick he was, he would never have run for a third term, and Wallace would have become President. We needed the third term, and we needed Harry Truman. Or would you rather have had Dewey negotiating with Stalin?"

"This is hardly the same situation," said Cooper.

"I disagree," replied Macintyre, shaking his large head slowly. "I think the situation is almost identical. In less than six months we're going to be hosting a major summit. In terms of world politics that summit is even more important than Potsdam. There they were cutting up Europe; this time the entire world is at stake. Beyond that you know as well as I do that with the democratization of the East bloc we've got billions of dollars in the military appropriations riding on this, not to mention the fate of NATO, Star Wars, and our relationship with the third world countries when Central and South America get on the bandwagon. Those bastards in the Kremlin have taken away all our enemies, Hudson. All we have left is that idiot Qaddafi. That summit is the single most important political event of the past seventy-five years. It will set the standard of international relations well into the twenty-first century. Do you want Vincent Teresi representing our interests? He'd give the Soviets Central

America on a platter if they allowed mass to be said in Moscow. Among other shortcomings, the man is a sentimental fool. Simply in terms of national security I think the question of his assumption of executive power certainly falls within the mandate of this committee."

Macintyre paused and sat forward, hands splayed on the surface of the conference table. "Consider this, Hudson. The Romulus Committee has been convened only seven times since the death of FDR." He lifted his hands and began counting off each instance on his fingers. "Eisenhower's heart attack, the Marilyn Monroe affair, Oswald, Ruby, twice during Watergate, and once following the Hinckley attempt on Reagan. Of the seven meetings, only two resulted in direct action, but partisan politics was a part of every one."

"What exactly are you suggesting?" asked Cooper. He knew the answer, since there was only one, but it would come from Macintyre's lips, not his.

"I'm not entirely sure at this point," the fat man said thoughtfully. He stroked the underside of his fleshy chin with the thumb of one hand. "I do know one thing though: Under no circumstances can Vincent Teresi be allowed to assume the presidency of the United States."

There was a soft buzz from the foyer behind Cooper. The first of the other committee members had arrived. Macintyre rose ponderously to his feet. As chairman he would act as host and greet his guests. "I think we should delay discussion of the details until after the meeting," he warned quietly. "I'm afraid some members of the committee might be a trifle squeamish about that sort of thing."

"As you wish," Cooper said. He remained seated while Macintyre walked heavily past him and left the room. He stared at the empty chair at the other end of the table, remembering the pink, soft hands. "'Who will rid me of this turbulent priest?'" he quoted, whispering softly. But he was alone in the room, and there was no one close at hand to hear the tortured question or to answer.

# CHAPTER 5

After the standard forty-five-minute ritual of meandering metro rides, double backs on foot, and switched cabs, Dmitri Travkin arrived at the main entrance to the Smithsonian. He was well aware that the paranoid arabesque he'd just gone through was normal operating procedure, but he found it all more than just physically tiring. He lived in a world of nagging fears and doubts, where everything and everyone were suspect. A picnic in the park was cover for a dead drop, a friend might well be an enemy, or a visit to the museum might be a clandestine meeting between agents.

Sighing, Travkin jammed his hands into the pocket of his sports jacket, jogged up the steps, and went into the Great Hall. How did you keep your sanity in a business where nothing was as it seemed? No wonder so many of his colleagues were alcoholics. He skirted the crowd of tourists around the Washington planning exhibit and headed for the Mall exit. Give it another couple of years, and he'd be ready for that job at the Soviet Military Academy Koslov had been hinting about. A normal life, or something close to it. Perhaps even a wife, children?

Travkin snorted at his fantasy and pushed out through the doors and into the sunlight. He slipped on his sunglasses, then followed the main footpath through the neatly planted elms to the Mall proper. A good place to meet. The greensward was more than four hundred feet across, stretching from Madison Drive to Jefferson, and two miles long, going from the Washington Monument to Capitol Hill. If anyone were following either him or his contact, he'd be clearly visible from a long way off.

He walked east along Jefferson, taking his time, pausing at the sunken sculpture garden behind the drum-shaped Hirshhorn Museum.

He lit a cigarette and glanced around. No sign of any Rednet people and no sign of Scanlon either. Travkin dragged deeply on the cigarette and exhaled, frowning. He'd give the man two minutes, no more; it was very bad manners to keep a deputy resident waiting, especially when you expected to get money from him.

Scanlon, a clerk in the library at Walter Reed, had been one of Travkin's first enlistments, and still rated as the easiest. The man was a racist white-supremacist pig, and representing himself as an anti-gun-control lobbyist, Travkin had explained that he wanted access to health information at Walter Reed to keep track of their enemies in Congress. Scanlon had taken the bait and the money that went with it, something Travkin could prove with photographic evidence if the man ever became a problem.

Travkin dropped the butt of his cigarette onto the gravel path and ground it out with the toe of his shoe. In any other circumstances he would have ignored Scanlon's request for a meeting, but coming so soon after the death of Barron, the President's doctor, Travkin had been intrigued. President goes into Walter Reed for a physical, President's physician has a fatal accident on his boat, then the summons from Scanlon.

"Mr. Smith?" Travkin turned at the sound of the low-pitched voice. It was Scanlon, white shirt billowing over a fat gut, dark wet patches under the arms, a wrinkled seersucker jacket hooked on one finger and draped over his shoulder. Sweat was beaded in the short man's curly hair, and he was breathing in short, hard gasps. Scanlon was feeling the heat.

"Let's walk," said Travkin. Without waiting for an answer, he struck out across the Mall, heading for the Museum of Natural History. He could hear Scanlon, panting behind him, trotting to keep up. On the far side of the open space Travkin found an empty park bench and seated himself. Scanlon dropped down beside him with a grateful sigh. Travkin lit another cigarette and waited for the man to catch his breath.

"Jesus, it's hot," the clerk muttered, his breath still coming in harsh little gasps.

"Why did you ask for the meeting?" Travkin asked bluntly. It *was* hot, and intrigued or not, he didn't like the idea of spending any more time with Scanlon than he had to.

"Barron."

"The President's doctor. The one who died."

57

"Right." Scanlon nodded. He pulled a crumpled handkerchief out of his pants pocket and wiped his face.

"What about him?"

"I'm not sure if it means anything, but I switched to the morning shift the same day Dr. Barron drowned."

"Yes?"

"Well," Scanlon said, wiping his face again, "one of the things you do first thing in the library is go over the request log."

"Explain," Travkin interrupted.

"The request log. It's all on computer. It's got all the requests for material on it from the previous shift. It shows what material was sent up to which doctor so the guys on the next shift can make sure it gets back to the library."

"What does this have to do with Dr. Barron?"

"I'm getting to that," said Scanlon. "I mean, I didn't know Barron was dead, so I didn't think too much of it at the time, but it clicked later on."

"What clicked?" Travkin asked, annoyance creeping into his voice.

"The night before Dr. Barron called in a request for anything the library had on something called—shit." The fat man dragged his jacket into his lap and fumbled in one of the inside pockets. He brought out a folded sheet of paper and opened it. "Here it is. He wanted information on Creutzfeldt-Jakob disease."

"Spell it," Travkin instructed. Scanlon did so. Travkin stubbed out his cigarette and looked up and down the Mall. He checked his watch. Another fifteen minutes, and the lunchtime crowds would begin to appear. "What is this illness?" he asked.

"Beats me." Scanlon shrugged. "He asked for some stuff on Alzheimer's at the same time if that means anything. Anyway, that's not what I thought was so interesting."

"Oh?"

"Yeah." Scanlon nodded. "What got me was that when I put in a call to Barron's office the next day to ask for the material back, I got told he'd never asked for the stuff in the first place. They said it must be a computer glitch. So I checked." Scanlon paused and wiped his face a third time.

"And?"

"I went back through the log, and by Christ, if there wasn't any sign of a request from Dr. Barron. I even went back into the stacks and checked out the material he was supposed to have asked for. It was all there, filed just the way it's supposed to be. Damnedest thing."

"What do you think it means?" Travkin asked, already forming his own opinion.

"Obvious." Scanlon grunted. "Barron died. He was asking about something somebody didn't want anyone else to know about. So they cleaned the slate and put everything back nice and tidy."

"*They* cleaned the slate?" Travkin asked. "Who do you think 'they' might be?"

"Dunno." Scanlon shrugged. "Have to be somebody pretty high up to start fiddling with the computers that way."

"You have access to personnel files, don't you?" Travkin asked suddenly.

"Sure." Scanlon nodded, frowning. "Why?"

"I want Barron's."

"All of it?"

"Yes," Travkin answered, biting his lip thoughtfully. "Right back to his medical school days. You can call me at the usual number when you're ready to hand it over."

"I'll see what I can do."

"One more thing," Travkin said slowly. "How do they keep track of telephone calls at Walter Reed?"

"Computer," Scanlon answered. "They've got a call-accounting system tied into the central control unit."

"Can you get into it?"

"Sure." Scanlon nodded.

"I want to know if Barron made any outside calls around the time he called down to the library."

"Okay," Scanlon said, "but it's going to cost extra." He dabbed at his upper lip with the handkerchief.

"I'm aware of that," Travkin answered, nodding curtly. "There will be another five hundred in the envelope this month."

"Fine." Scanlon beamed.

"I want the information quickly," said Travkin, standing. He turned and headed back down the Mall toward the Washington Monument. Scanlon watched him go and then stood up himself and walked away in the opposite direction.

*   *   *

Stephen Stone sat in the dark basement screening room and stared at the grainy telephoto image on the large-screen television. He worked the remote control in his hand, moving the picture back and forth. Mort Kessler sat on his left, while the lip-reader sat on his right. The lip-reader was Norman Traynor, a bullet-headed bureau man of the old school who'd gone deaf ten years before. He'd avoided being put out to pasture by learning how to lip-read for long-range surveillance operations like this one.

". . . 'I want the information' . . . something," Traynor said as Stone ran the last few seconds of the tape again. "I can't make out the last little bit. Your target turned away at the end."

"Sorry about that," said Kessler. "Your boy is pretty cautious. We couldn't risk getting much closer. We were up in the tower at the Smithsonian for this. That's maybe four, five hundred yards."

"That's all right." Stone shrugged. He turned to Traynor. "You get all of it?" he asked. The heavyset gray-haired man nodded, snapping the cassette out of the small tape machine in his lap. With the videotape running he'd transcribed directly onto the cassette.

"I'll take it up to technical and match audio to the picture. You should be able to see the mix in a couple of hours. I'll let you know."

"Great." Stone nodded. "Thanks, Norm."

"My pleasure." The lip-reader stood up and left the screening room.

"Well?" asked Stone as the older man left the room. Kessler clambered to his feet, found the light switch on the far wall, and turned it on. Stone lit a cigarette and leaned back in the theater seat. Kessler began to pace back and forth in front of him and described the surveillance.

"From the Mall he went up to the Library of Congress, on foot, mind you, and went through the card indexes for about half an hour. After that he took a cab to an antiquarian bookstore on M Street. McCann's. They specialize in medical and technical reference books. He bought two books on dementia and a general text on brain diseases. From there he went to three more bookstores. Same thing. Books on Alzheimer's, dementia, mental illness, and brain diseases. Then he went back to his apartment. Paid cash at the antiquarian store and at the other three as well."

"Smart." Stone grunted. "You have to give your name and provide ID to get stuff out of the stacks at the Library of Congress. He probably used the card index to get an idea of some titles to go after, then hit the stores working off that list."

"I wonder what he's up to," said Kessler.

"Dunno," Stone muttered, watching the thin line of smoke from his cigarette trail up to the low ceiling of the screening room. "But we're one step ahead of him." He pulled himself up in the seat. "Let's see if we can come up with some material on Barron's practice outside the President. Find out who he's been treating lately and if we can find some connection between a patient and this Creutzfeldt-Jakob thing."

"Do we pull in Scanlon?"

"No, not yet. Let him run a little longer."

"Anything else?" Kessler asked.

Stone tapped his fingers on the arm of the chair. "The pathologist," he said finally, staring at the blank television screen a few feet in front of him.

"Who?" asked Kessler.

"The pathologist. Whoever it was at the coroner's office who did the autopsy on Barron. See if you can get me his name, would you?"

"You sound like you're on to something."

"Not really," Stone said thoughtfully. "But if Dmitri is interested in the dead Dr. Barron, then so am I."

Rhinelander moved easily through the pale green water, fins pumping in strong rhythmic strokes as he cruised above the reef. He swam in a long-established pattern, pausing at each float on the grid to take another set of photographs. The bright yellow plastic spheres bobbed at the end of ten-foot-long nylon cords anchored to the reef, providing him with a standard position from which to shoot so that the same portion of the reef's surface could be documented each time he made a run.

He paused at the outermost marker and lifted the Data Scan console dangling from his waist to check the readout. This was his second dive of the day, and he'd been down seventy minutes. According to the display on the console, he had eleven minutes of bottom time left. Not enough time to make another pass, and with the sun almost directly overhead the usual shoals of brilliantly colored reef fish were absent. Another time. Turning away, he let his arms dangle at his side and followed his bubbles toward the surface and the bobbing spearhead shadow marking his thirty-foot Boston Whaler, *Whisperland*.

Reaching the stern of the high-sided sport cruiser, he spit out his mouthpiece and stripped off his mask. He slipped off his flippers, tossed them into the boat, and boosted himself up onto the metal dive step bolted to the transom. He flipped inboard and began to strip down, beginning with the Nikonos camera and ending with the dark green wet suit

61

CHRISTOPHER HYDE

he'd been using for the past six years. Dressed only in his Speedo bikini, he ducked into the lower cabin, pulled a bottle of Red Stripe out of the little bar refrigerator in the galley, and took it back on deck. He climbed into the cockpit seat and settled back against the sun-hot tan leather. Squinting through the lightly tinted windshield, he could make out the steep green hills above Discovery Bay, almost four miles away.

He sipped the cold beer, savoring the crisp bite as it struck his tongue. The sun felt good on his bare skin, and he was already beginning to feel the tensions of the last few days begin to recede. If there was any security to his life, any sense of belonging in a real world, it was here, on the reef, feeling the gentle swell lapping at the *Whisperland*'s hull. Before Jamaica, the boat, and the house at Oracabessa his life had been little more than reactions to events. Born with no real identity of his own, he adopted them to suit his needs and the requirements of his work; trained to kill, he killed, perfecting the assassin's trade to the level of art.

Rhinelander smiled, reached out, and took a cigarette from the pack of Senior Service on the cockpit shelf. Setting his beer down, he lit the cigarette, then plucked a few shreds of tobacco from the tip of his tongue. On the pages of some secret file deep in the vaults at Langley he was probably listed as a psychopath, but he knew the psychiatrists on staff at the agency used the word only to comfort themselves and rationalize the insanity of their own positions.

Not that it mattered. Some years before, he had finally come to see the truth of his life: Unlike most people, he lived on two planes of existence, call them Overworld and Underworld. Overworld was his life here, the life that the general population would see as "normal." Underworld was an existence populated with the Breughel nightmares of people like Philippe Groman and the snake pit politics of Pol Pot's grisly henchmen. Both worlds had their own natural laws and constants, both had their own loyalties and lies, both had their separate sets of rules that had to be obeyed, and with care, both worlds could be lived in, feeding on each other in an endless, delicately balanced cycle. Rhinelander took a long swallow of the warming beer. If that was madness, then so be it. He closed his eyes and let his head fall back against the seat. An hour in the sun, another cigarette or two, and another beer. After that he'd weigh anchor, head for the dock at Ocho Rios, then home to Breakers.

Paul Mallory, special assistant to CIA Deputy Director of Operations Hudson Cooper, reached Jamaica aboard the noon American Airlines flight, landing at Montego Bay's Sir Donald Sangster Airport. Already

62

wilting in the wet heat, he endured the tooth-rattling electrified steel band on the main concourse and threaded his way through the scattered off-season crowds to the Budget booth. Half an hour later, after confirming his reservation at the Ocho Rios Americana, he piloted the bruised Toyota he'd rented out onto the Queens Drive, took the A-3 west, and began the fifty-mile drive to Oracabessa.

The switchback narrow road along the coast was an odd combination of bright white modern resort hotels and tumbledown shacks, mangrove swamps and blue and silver beaches; gigantic ferns choking flaking billboards advertising Red Stripe Brewery Fresh Beer and Tropigaz; cane fields and coconut palms; stone-hut villages, long abandoned, broken windows like dark, staring eyes. Mallory ignored all of it, concentrating on the road. For him, Jamaica was no island paradise; it was a trap waiting to be sprung.

Mallory had been recruited into the CIA during his last year at MIT and joined the agency six months after Richard Nixon became President and Richard Helms took over as director of central intelligence. Already comfortable with the fledgling field of computers, he was assigned to the Threat Analysis and Plans division of Operations, spending most of his time gathering information about countries in Central and South America. During his tenure with the TAP group he went on occasional fact-finding missions to the countries in question, but those trips bore no resemblance to his recent journey to Paris and now to Jamaica.

In the past Mallory had never found his work difficult to justify, and he'd certainly never felt himself to be in any personal danger. He thought of himself as a statistician who happened to work in the field of intelligence, nothing more, as a demiscientist in a secure job, with all the best computer toys in the world at his disposal.

This was different. As DDO Hudson Cooper had a broad mandate within the CIA, but it was clear that this operation had been conceived and put into effect well outside the normal protocols. Cooper's interest in the QJ/RAIL-Rhinelander file was more than casual, and Rhinelander was much more than your average ex-Company man. He was an assassin who'd never even come close to being caught or even implicated in a political killing. If Cooper was fishing around for a man like Rhinelander, it could mean only one thing: The DDO wanted someone dead. Mallory also knew that you didn't hire someone of QJ/RAIL's "quality" for a bit of minor housecleaning. The target of Cooper's interest had to be big-league.

Mallory frowned and pushed his glasses back onto the bridge of his

63

nose with a practiced finger. Big-league, but who? Ever since Cooper had shown interest in the QJ/RAIL file, Mallory had been going through his mental Rolodex, trying to figure it out. The most likely target was someone high in a foreign intelligence operation, but there had been nothing in the wind recently except for yet another mole turning up in the UK.

One thing was certain, if Rhinelander was being used, the prospective victim had to be a so-called hard target, a person, or persons, surrounded by a lot of protective security or situated in a difficult location—the Kremlin, for instance. Mallory sucked air through his clenched teeth and tapped his fingers on the sticky plastic of the steering wheel. Being involved in some clandestine and possibly unsanctioned operation of Cooper's made him very nervous, especially when it involved assassination, which, in Mallory's expert estimation, was an outmoded and statistically ineffectual instrument of foreign policy.

Passing through the tiny village of Salt Gut, Mallory eased off on the gas and began paying attention to the directions he'd been given at the airport in Montego Bay. A few miles down the narrow highway he spotted the abandoned remains of a Shell station blasted by the '88 hurricane and turned off onto an even narrower dirt road leading toward the coast. As promised, he came to a pair of overgrown gateposts, each one topped with a large carved black-painted falcon.

There was no gate blocking the entrance, so Mallory turned the small sedan down the jungle-choked trail. After a hundred yards the canopied track ended in a small clearing facing the ocean. There was a modest cement-walled bungalow in the center of the open space, angled slightly away from the gleaming water and the low cliffs above the beach: Breakers, built next door to the summer house once owned by Ian Fleming, creator of James Bond, and now occupied by Eric Rhinelander, a man who possessed the real-life version of that fictional character's license to kill.

Mallory parked the Toyota and stepped out into the bright sunshine. Squinting, he adjusted his glasses again and took a deep breath. An odd combination of smells: the rich blossom and rot scent of the screening foliage, mixed with the salt-bitter breath of the onshore breeze. He turned, and shading his eyes with one uplifted hand, he examined the house: single-storied, deep-set window openings blocked by fat-slat venetian blinds. Jalousies; that's what he remembered his Deep South grandmother calling them; like something you'd expect to see on the windows of a plantation house in Georgia.

The roof was covered in worn shingles, whole sections looking much newer than others. The hurricane? Mallory did a full circuit, his shoes crunching on the crumbling perimeter of patio stones around the house. All the windows were shuttered against the early-afternoon heat. The building was constructed in a thick L shape with two entrances—one through a set of shuttered French doors that faced the overgrown sunken garden on the ocean side, the other through a narrow wooden door on the short side of the house to the right of where Mallory had parked the Toyota. The French doors were locked. Completing his circuit, he knocked hesitantly on the narrow door and waited. He looked around, but there were no other vehicles other than his own. Mallory knocked again, harder this time, then tried the old-fashioned thumb latch handle. The door swung open, revealing a cool dark vestibule. Wishing the door had been locked, he stepped inside, carefully closing the door behind him.

The bare walls were roughly plastered; the floor was concrete, painted a dark blue and partially covered by a scattering of thin plaited fiber mats. Directly in front of Mallory a narrow hall ran down the length of the house, while to his left a doorway led into a small galley kitchen. Beside it an archway opened onto the large, low-ceilinged living room. Ignoring the kitchen, Mallory stepped into the living room, peering into the gloom. The only light came from the cracks between the shutter slats creating knife-blade beams alive with eddying motes of dust.

Again the walls were bare, rough plaster. The furniture was sparse and nondescript: two club chairs upholstered in a fabric to match the dark blue floor, a small two-seater couch done in a lighter blue, and a rectangular coffee table made of some buttery, thickly varnished wood. Set close to the French doors at the far end of the room was a small dark wood dining-room table with two plain chairs. The room said nothing about Rhinelander at all.

Mallory returned to the vestibule and paused for a moment, listening hard. Slight rattle of the shutters, distant surf, birds, the hard, echoing beating of his heart: Get out, get out, get out. Rational thought told him that invading the privacy of a professional assassin was not a good idea, but his own curiosity and Hudson Cooper's insistence on contacting Rhinelander led him down the short hall to the other rooms. If Rhinelander came back to the house, he'd hear the car pull up in plenty of time.

The first door led into a cramped bathroom with toilet, basin, and shower stall, no tub. Mallory checked the long shelf over the basin. Pear's soap, a Harrod's shaving brush with an ivory handle, and a Wilkinson's straight razor, neatly folded. A two-thirds-full bottle of Lagerfeld and a nail clipper. He took the top off the Lagerfeld and sniffed, wondering if the deep, rich scent was the last thing Rhinelander's victims knew before they died. He shivered, spun the silver top back on the bottle, and backed out of the room quickly.

The second room was no more than a Spartan sleeping cell: single bed on a metal frame, freestanding closet, lamp on a bedside table. There was a book on the table, *Caribbean Reef Fishes* by John Randall. Mallory picked it up and flipped to the title page. Rhinelander had purchased the book in Hong Kong. He put the book back down on the table and glanced around the room. Rhinelander was still a cipher; so far the house was about as interesting as a Holiday Inn. He turned toward the door. Cooper wanted an edge, but it didn't look as though he were going to get it. Mallory went into the last room at the end of the hall. Dark as a tomb. Fumbling, he found a light switch beside the door and flipped it on.

"Jesus Christ."

All four walls of the twelve-by-fifteen room were covered in bookshelves from floor to ceiling. A long counter-style work station was ranged along one of the book walls, fitted with a Compaq 386/25 computer, Hewlett-Packard laser printer, scanner, plotter, the works. All of it was right up Mallory's alley, and he knew he was looking at a good fifty Ks worth of hardware. Resisting the temptation to sit down at the keyboard and boot up Rhinelander's hard drive, he turned his attention toward the books.

The wall behind the work station was given over to a wide-reaching array of books on oceanography, marine biology, marine technology, and naval history. The wall opposite was a library of travel books: Fodor's, Fielding's, and Baedeker's guides, both modern and old, shelves full of neatly filed map folders, one whole shelf devoted to European rail guides and a score of Kodak Carousel boxes, each one marked with the name of a different country or city. The bulk of the travel books concentrated on Southeast Asia and Europe, but there were also a number of them covering the Caribbean, Central America, South America, and the Orient.

The bookcases facing the door were the most telling. The upper shelves contained rows of *Jane's Weapon System* yearbooks going back to the middle sixties, books on Soviet and American weaponry, various U.S. Army handbooks on unconventional warfare and ring-bound catologs from every major arms manufacturer in the world. Below the ordnance books were dozens of titles relating to intelligence, both domestic and foreign: *CIA in Central America, Agency, Rise and Decline of the*

*CIA, The Puzzle Palace, Soviet Military Intelligence, Deep Black, The President's Secret Wars, Society and the Assassin, The Assassin's Art, Low-Intensity Warfare.* The list went on and on. Below that, filling out the lower shelves, were titles dealing with the drug trade: Alvin Moscow's *Merchants of Heroin, Trail of the Triads, Inside the Golden Triangle.*

Except for the books on the sea, the library made sense in a macabre fashion. The average fictional assassin was a bullet-headed sadist like Nash in *From Russia with Love* or a faceless, slightly effete nemesis figure like the killer in *The Day of the Jackal.*

Rhinelander, on the other hand, his psychotic character profile aside, was a professional killer who took his job seriously. The books on ordnance kept him up-to-date on available weaponry, travel guides told him what to expect in various airports and hotels, and books on the intelligence community and the drug underworld gave him some basic research on what to expect from both enemies and possible employers. Neat and tidy, very businesslike. Still . . .

Mallory pursed his lips, eyes blinking behind the lenses of his glasses. He felt a dull twisting in the pit of his stomach, and for a moment he tasted bile in his throat, remembering. In Paris, Henri Faligot of the Directorate for Surveillance of the Territory (DST) had shown him coroner's photographs of Philippe Groman's corpse, *in situ* at the Cardinal's Cap brothel in Montmartre. *That* was Rhinelander's profession, and no well-ordered room like this could change the reality of those stark, obscenely clinical black-and-white images.

He thought of leaving then, simply turning tail and fleeing. He could report back to Cooper that he hadn't been able to locate QJ/RAIL, and that would be the end of it. He'd probably wind up being dumped back down to Threat Analysis or worse for his failure, but at least he'd be in a world he understood.

Mallory eased his glasses back up onto his nose and made a little snorting sound. Melodrama. All he had to do was make contact with the man, arrange a meeting, and that would be that. Part of his mandate from Cooper was to find out as much as he could about Rhinelander before the meeting, and that was precisely what he was doing now.

Ignoring the cramping sensation in his gut, he sat down in front of the computer and began booting it up, enjoying the familiar routines. He pulled up the main menu for the hard drive and stared at the screen. Rhinelander was running a variety of software: word processing, filing, bookkeeping, and telecommunications as well as a computer-assisted design program.

67

According to the screen, about a third of the hard drive's eighty-megabyte memory was given over to a series of files referred to in the main menu as RAC. Poking at the keys, Mallory opened the main file and saw that it was subindexed with dated, smaller files. They were chronological, going back three years in seven-, fourteen-, and twenty-one-day intervals. He tapped open a file from a year before and was instantly rewarded with a three-dimensional grid, the lines in glowing amber on a dark blue ground. It looked like a radar screen. The title in the top left corner gave the date and then the name: Reef Analysis Chart.

It took him a few minutes, but Mallory figured out the codes and deciphered the screen. The grid was a representation of a section of reef, and by keying in different commands, he could include temperature, currents, tide levels, schooling fish . . . anything. Mallory sat back in the chair and poked at his glasses. This explained the books on oceanography. Rhinelander's hobby?

"Enjoying yourself?" The voice came from behind, and Mallory whirled, heart smashing at his ribs, glasses almost flying off his nose. He could smell himself, the acid sweat of fear, and his mouth was cotton-dry, all in a split second. Rhinelander stood in the doorway, wearing a dark blue short-sleeve knit shirt and tight pale gray shorts. His feet were bare, and he held a small flat automatic pistol in his right hand. He held the pistol loosely, barrel aimed at the floor.

"Uh . . ." It was all Mallory could manage.

"Get up," Rhinelander ordered. Mallory did as he was told, legs rubbery, barely able to support him. Rhinelander stepped aside, motioning with the pistol. "The living room."

Mallory nodded weakly and began to walk, the sensation of his shoes on the hard floor numb and distant. Rhinelander followed him down the hall and through the arch. He motioned Mallory to the couch and then sat down himself, easing down onto one of the club chairs, the pistol held in his lap, honey bars of sunlight striping his face and chest.

"What's your name?" asked Rhinelander. The tone was even, the voice unaccented. Not American, not British, not anything. Mallory stared at the gun hand, unwilling and unable to look into the man's dark, dead eyes.

"Mallory, Paul Mallory."

"Washington." It wasn't a question. There was no point in lying.

"Yes."

"CIA?"

"Yes."

"Who?"

"Cooper."

"How can I know that?"

"I have ID," Mallory answered. His eyes flickered to Rhinelander's face for an instant. The expression hadn't changed. Neutral, uninterested, as though Mallory were nothing more than a crawling insect on the floor.

"Anyone can have ID. Do better."

"Your file designation is QJ slash RAIL. Your operating name for the Company was Eric Rhinelander. You were . . ." Mallory hesitated, frightened.

"Yes?"

"You were recently in Paris." Mallory swallowed hard, wondering how much he'd have to say.

"Yes." No change in expression, the gun hand motionless. Mallory saw the eight-by-tens of Groman, sprawled on the whorehouse bed, the seeping perfect puncture, like a blood-oozed second anus. It would take Rhinelander less than a second to lift the automatic, aim and fire. In his mind's eye he could see the spray of blood and brains, caught for an instant in the light slatting through the shutters.

"You—you were responsible for the death of a drug dealer named Philippe Groman."

"He cheated me," Rhinelander replied calmly, explaining a simple fact of life. "He was responsible for his own death. He knew the rules."

"I see," muttered Mallory, wondering what the rules said about entering Rhinelander's home uninvited.

"No, you don't see at all." The automatic shifted slightly in Rhinelander's lap. There was a long pause, and then he spoke again. "Why are you here?"

"Mr. Cooper would like to speak with you."

"Speak with me?"

"See you."

"Why?"

"I have no idea."

"What are you to Cooper?"

"I don't understand."

"What do you do for him?"

"I'm his special assistant."

"Before you worked for him, what department were you in?"

"Threat Analysis and Plans."

"No operational experience? Fieldwork?"

"No."

"Were you given any instructions about setting up a meeting?"

"No. He said you wouldn't trust anything he set up."

"He was right." There was another long silence. Mallory could hear the surf pounding somewhere in the distance. Rhinelander seemed to be looking past him, lost in thought. The wings of gray at his temples looked pure white against the darkness of his tan, and the lines around the eyes and the deep caliper creases around the mouth made his face look too old for the hard athletic body.

"Do you have a number for him?" Rhinelander asked finally.

Startled, Mallory gave a quick nod. "On a card," he answered. "In my wallet."

"Take it out."

"Yes," Mallory answered, head bobbing. His glasses had slipped again, but he made no move to reposition them. He reached into his jacket slowly, took out his wallet, and extracted the printed card with Hudson Cooper's telephone, teletype, and fax numbers printed on it.

"Leave it on the coffee table."

"Yes." Mallory leaned forward and placed the card gently on the table.

"Now get out of my house," Rhinelander ordered. Mallory stood up, sweat running down his jawline. Fright sweat, cool and oily. A terrible spasming cramp in his bowels. Knowing how lucky he was to be alive.

"What do I tell Mr. Cooper?" he asked. "About the meeting?"

"Tell him anything you want," Rhinelander answered. "Anything at all." He made a small, flicking gesture with the pistol in his lap. "Go."

Mallory went.

# CHAPTER 6

**S**toneacres, ancestral home of the Macintyre family, was located on the Virginia bank of the Potomac, thirty miles southeast of Washington, halfway between the town of Woodbridge and the FBI National Academy at Quantico. It was neither stony nor particularly ancestral. The four-hundred-acre estate was a mixture of natural woodlot and rolling meadows, and the twelve-bedroom brick colonial mansion had been built in 1910 by Charles Macintyre, Hollis Macintyre's father. Macintyre, Sr., a naturalized American born in Glasgow, had been trained as a dental technician. In 1901 he invented and patented a process to make cheap amalgam for fillings, and within five years he was a millionaire.

After tripling his money by investing in the fledgling Ford Motor Company, he married the daughter of an influential congressman and retired to the life of a respectable country gentleman, his days spent polishing porcelain dentures discreetly forgotten. Within a very few years, through the good graces of Macintyre's father-in-law and wife, Stoneacres had become an accepted part of genteel Washington society, its lofty halls and oak-beamed chambers playing host to an endless array of princes, politicians, and presidents.

Hollis Crandall Macintyre was born on February 6, 1911, sharing his birthday with the man who eventually became the fortieth President of the United States, Ronald Reagan. Macintyre was the first of five children and the only male, and his early life was a well-ordered series of events designed to groom him for a position among the nation's power-mongers: a private school education at Lockhart Academy, a degree in business from the University of Virginia, and then a commission in the Army.

Returning to civilian life in 1933, Macintyre immediately went to work as assistant to General Edwin M. Watson, President Roosevelt's senior military aide. A number of the Macintyre family's Republican friends were infuriated by what they perceived as a treasonous betrayal of upper-class values; but Hollis Macintyre had been born a realist, and even as a young man he was acutely aware of power and its usefulness.

Franklin Delano Roosevelt had been elected by a landslide, and for all its welfare state overtones Hollis Macintyre saw that the New Deal centralized power in the federal government, particularly in the hands of the President. Working in the White House was the perfect place for a man like Hollis Macintyre to learn the savagery and subtlety of life in the nation's capital, and by the time Pearl Harbor arrived, he was known throughout the bureaucratic offices of Foggy Bottom and the corridors of Congress as the detail man, always willing to give a favor in the present for the promise of two in the future. By the time of Roosevelt's death in 1945 he was one of the least liked and most respected men in Washington.

Macintyre's career from that point on had been given over to consolidating the gains he made in those early years, building a ziggurat of favors and foibles, secrets and lies. His titles and job descriptions within the political and governmental structures of Washington were irrelevant; he took power where he found it and dispensed favors without prejudice.

The only constant through all those years was his membership in Romulus. An accident of fate had made him instrumental in the group's creation, thus making him privy to all its secrets, a cachet he shared with no one else. Through the eleven presidential administrations since Roosevelt it had been Hollis Macintyre who vetted each new member of the committee and Hollis Macintyre who ensured that retiring members maintained their pledges of secrecy. It was a measure of his abilities that in almost fifty years none of the 111 members, past and present, had ever mentioned the Romulus Committee in public, and with the exception of a few vague rumors that surfaced from time to time, virtually nothing was known of its existence.

On the fifth day following the initial meeting of the Romulus Committee regarding the Barron diagnosis, Hollis Macintyre awoke at 6:30 A.M. and worked his way slowly through a breakfast of poached eggs, crisp bacon, and whole wheat toast, followed by several cups of freshly brewed Jamaican coffee. He ate on the balcony of the second-floor master bedroom, already fully dressed in suit and tie as he watched the light mist on the Potomac being shredded by the rising sun. At 7:00, with breakfast over, he took his last cup of coffee into the bedroom, seated himself in an oversize silk-upholstered chair beside the four-poster Sheraton bed and began to work his way through the morning papers. Normally his reading would have taken place in the limousine on his way into the city; but today was Sunday, and his only meeting for the day was to take place here, at Stoneacres.

Flipping open the bulky parcel of the Sunday *New York Times*, he pulled out the magazine section. The cover story was a profile of Vincent Teresi, Vice President of the United States. Macintyre felt his breakfast sour within the confines of his enormous belly, and he frowned, staring at the smiling, cap-toothed face on the cover. A modern version of Frank Sinatra with thick black hair, twinkling dark eyes, and his patented "trust me" grin. At forty-four he was the media's darling and, since the death of his wife in childbirth three years before, Washington's most eligible bachelor.

With a grunting sigh, Macintyre pushed the stack of newspapers off his lap onto the floor. He didn't have to read the article to know what it said; he'd had the "sheet" on Teresi ever since he'd come out of nowhere to claim the vice presidential ticket. The white-haired man glanced around the large, richly decorated room. Herez carpets on the pegged-oak floor, the canopied four-poster bed, a prizewinning collection of American paintings by Thomas Moran, David Kennedy, and Andrew Melrose, the D'Avulo marble fireplace—all of it marked a life given over to the serenity of order, position and wealth, icons of power that appeared to be anathema to the Vice President.

Born in New York and raised in California, Vincenzo Santino Michelangelo Teresi came out of the classic immigrant stewpot of brickworkers, fruit vendors, and dockworkers who made up the Brooklyn of the late forties. Vincenzo's father, Antonio Teresi, was a skilled mechanic and moved to San Diego in the early fifties, taking advantage of the growing aerospace industry. Somewhere between New York and the West Coast, Vincenzo became Vincent, and the middle names were dropped completely. By the time he was graduated from high school, any trace of Brooklyn was gone and Vince Teresi was the quintessential Californian.

He was also smart enough to know that he had neither the academic qualifications nor the money for a university, so he enlisted in the Air Force, qualified for both officer training and flight school, and wound up spending the next two years flying high-altitude reconnaissance missions

73

over North Vietnam. His tour over, he returned Stateside and reupped, accepting a posting to the Air Force Directorate of Operational Intelligence at the Pentagon. The work wasn't particularly demanding, and he put his free time in Washington to good use, managing to obtain a basic law degree from Georgetown University.

After almost six years in the military he left Washington and returned to California, where he worked for a number of law firms as well as dabbled first in local and then in state politics. With hindsight, Hollis Macintyre could see a familiar thread running through the Vice President's political history, reminiscent of his own, studied climb to power. Teresi was willing to do favors for just about anyone and volunteered for everything, one favor leading to another, methodically propelling the young man from the Los Angeles district attorney's office to the state legislature and finally to the governor's office as a low-profile member of the Reagan palace guard.

Instead of following Reagan and his cohorts to the White House in 1980, Teresi decided to follow his own path, remaining in California, where he specialized in environmental law and began building a position within the party's National Committee. By the end of the Reagan administration he'd quietly managed to consolidate the less conservative, younger factions within the party, and the day before the convention to nominate Tucker for President he made his move. A succession of problems, including the last Quayle scandal, had convinced Bush not to run for another term, leaving the field wide open.

During his brief meeting with Macintyre Teresi had been friendly but firm. Either he rode the ticket as Tucker's running mate, or he'd start a fight on the convention floor to split the vote. Teresi didn't have enough delegates to carry the nomination, but a weak win for Tucker at the convention would be the kiss of death for his chances at the presidency.

Macintyre knew that his failure to spot Teresi's end run marked the beginning of the end for his own career, but he had no choice. Teresi got the nod and became Geoffrey Tucker's running mate. Ironically, after the election most of the media credited Teresi's good looks and oratory as being the factors that boosted Tucker over the top, giving him the narrow margin needed to win over his opponent.

The result for Hollis Macintyre had been inevitable. After slightly more than a year in office, the Tucker administration was in good shape, and Teresi's image was getting bigger and better by the minute. In three years Tucker would run again and win, and four years after that Vincent Teresi would take the nomination.

By that time, if he was still alive, Hollis Macintyre would be almost ninety and long since relegated to elder statesman status. The king had his heir, succession was assured, so there was no longer any need for the kingmaker. On inauguration day Hollis Macintyre's invitation was overlooked, and from then on he had been slowly but surely cut out of the loop of protocol and communication giving access to the White House.

Macintyre smiled thinly and turned in his chair, lifting the porcelain cup and saucer from the serving table at his side. He took a small sip of the cooling aromatic coffee and nodded to himself. At eighty he was perfectly willing to give up the reins of power and take his place in the history books, but it would be on his own terms, not those of the upstart son of a Brooklyn tool-and-die maker.

There was a faint knock, and the bedroom door was opened. Benjamin, Macintyre's butler-chauffeur-bodyguard, stepped into the room. The stooped gray-haired black man was the son of Charles Macintyre's houseman and had been in service at Stoneacres his entire life. Like Hollis Macintyre, Benjamin had never married. He lived in his own three-room apartment in the east wing of the house and was in charge of the housekeeper, cook, two maids, and the gardener who made up the staff of the estate.

"Good morning, sir." The dark-suited aging servant spoke in a harsh whisper.

"Good morning, Benjamin." Macintyre nodded. "Have our guests arrived?"

"Mr. Cooper called to say he'd be a few minutes late," said Benjamin. "Mr. Swanbridge is waiting in the sun-room, sir."

"All right, Benjamin." With a groaning sigh, Macintyre levered himself up out of the chair, leaning heavily on the arms for support. "Coffee and orange juice in the library when Mr. Cooper arrives," he ordered. "Tea with lemon for Secretary Swanbridge, and ask Mary if the scones are ready yet."

"Yes, sir," Benjamin answered, nodding again. "Will there be anything else?"

"No, thank you, Benjamin. Just see to it that we aren't disturbed. No telephone calls or other interruptions."

"Of course, Mr. Macintyre." Benjamin withdrew, and after straightening his bow tie in front of the circular Tiffany mirror beside the door, Macintyre followed.

He went down the broad carpeted staircase, crossed the main hall, and went through the open mahogany and lead glass doors leading to the large beam-ceilinged sun-room. Like the floors of all of the halls and "public" rooms at Stoneacres, the floor of the sun-room was done in a dull moss green Greuby tile. The far wall was made up entirely of floor-to-ceiling windows and a double pair of French doors looking out onto the sloping lawn and the river, a hundred yards away. The furniture, a scattering of wicker and enameled white wrought iron, was part of the original decor.

"Joseph," said Macintyre, entering the sun-bright room. "Good of you to come."

Cigar held slackly between thin lips, Geoffrey Tucker's tall, bald, and professorial-looking secretary of state turned away from the French doors and crossed the room to greet Macintyre with an extended hand. At sixty-eight Joseph Saxon Swanbridge was not wearing his age well. The eyes behind his old-fashioned wire-rimmed spectacles were deeply inset and bagged, his skin had an unhealthy pallor, and the man's brown-spotted hands were twisted with the tree-root gnarling of arthritis. He drank too much, smoked too much, and worked too hard, but the brain behind the watery blue eyes was one of the best in the country. Of all the other members of Romulus, Swanbridge was the only one who had been told the extent of the President's illness.

"Hudson's not here yet, I gather," said Swanbridge, his voice wheezing slightly around the cigar.

"Not yet," said Macintyre. He took Swanbridge by the elbow and guided him toward the doors leading back into the hall. "You can have tea in the library while we wait for him."

The library was a twenty-by-twenty room immediately to the left of the main entrance. The high-ceilinged chamber was windowless on three sides, the walls sheathed in books of all descriptions, many of them leather-bound. A delicate Hepplewhite writing desk stood in one corner, a large glass globe beside it, while a black and gold-flecked Egyptian marble fireplace rose against the end wall, its shiny surface glowing in the soft light from the recessed fixtures in the ceiling. Like the floor in Macintyre's bedroom, the floor here was pegged oak, the wood covered by a scattering of Oriental carpets. In the center of the room a collection of small couches and comfortable chairs was arranged around a huge coffee table of striated green Italian marble, its surface inlaid with an insect motif.

Once inside the large, comfortable room, Macintyre sank into one of the upholstered chairs and watched as Swanbridge, an inveterate pacer, moved slowly around the room, examining the spines of books with a close eye and occasionally picking up knickknacks from the small tables set here and there. It took a little while, but eventually, like some gangly, bald-headed insect, Swanbridge settled, choosing a love seat on the far side of the coffee table from Macintyre.

A few minutes later Benjamin appeared, wheeling a serving dolly. He laid out scones, preserves, butter, a frosted tall beaker of orange juice, crystal goblets, coffee and tea, cream, milk, and sugar, a dish of lemon wedges, cups, and saucers. He nodded silently to Macintyre, turned the dolly around, and retired. Before he was out of the room, Swanbridge had poured himself a cup of tea and was busily buttering one of the scones. Macintyre watched without serving himself anything. Like many fat men, he wasn't a particularly enthusiastic eater and took almost as much pleasure from watching other people enjoying their food as he did from the actual act of eating. He smiled briefly as the secretary of state spilled crumbs down the front of his rumpled suit. Except for state occasions, when he was forced into formality, Swanbridge was an archetypical slob.

"You've had several days now to assimilate the information regarding the President's condition," Macintyre said as Swanbridge smoothed butter onto his second scone. "Have you formulated an opinion?"

"An opinion regarding what?" asked Swanbridge. He popped half of the second scone into his mouth and began to chew, staring blandly across the table. He took a swallow of tea, then set the cup down again. "According to your information, the President is suffering from a degenerative brain disease, so what is there to opine? He either has the disease or does not."

"You're being tediously academic, Joseph." Macintyre sighed. "And you're evading the question. Geoffrey Tucker has Creutzfeldt-Jakob disease. He will die from it. Before he dies from it, he is potentially capable of a number of demented acts. It behooves us to do something about the situation."

"Now you're the one being tedious," Swanbridge answered, his voice cold. "You've known about this for a week. Your information came from Hudson Cooper. In the meantime, the President's attending physician at Walter Reed dies in a boating accident. You inform me of the President's condition, and then you call this meeting."

Swanbridge dropped the remains of his scone onto the plate and sat back. He reached into the pocket of his jacket for a fresh cigar, unwrapped it, clipped the end, and lit it with a pocket match, tossing the burned sliver of wood into his tea saucer. He puffed the cigar into life, staring at Macintyre through a billowing haze of smoke. "You don't want my opinion, Hollis," he said finally. "You want my complicity in whatever scheme you and Hudson have cooked up between you."

Macintyre smiled and let out a small, coughing laugh. Swanbridge's Secret Service designation was "Nutcracker," and he'd been given the code name with good reason. The toughest secretary of state since John Foster Dulles, Joseph Swanbridge had made his political bones as deputy director of the Rand Corporation's Hudson Institute, working with the infamous Herman Kahn, followed by three years as American ambassador to the Soviet Union. Until his appointment as Tucker's secretary of state he'd spent his time as dean of the Georgetown Institute for Strategic Studies. He might have crumbs on his lapels and gravy stains on his tie, but he also had the shrewdest political sense Hollis Macintyre had ever known.

"I prefer to think of it as a contingency plan," the fat man replied. "We are facing a serious political crisis of which you, by necessity, are a part."

"If the President is unable to function, Section Four can be invoked," Swanbridge responded, referring to the paragraph in the Twenty-fifth Amendment to the Constitution covering presidential incapacity.

"It would tear the country apart," Macintyre said flatly. "Section Four is a panacea, Joseph, and you know it. The words sound good on paper, but putting them into effect is virtually impossible."

"I'm aware of the problems." Swanbridge nodded, tapping ash into his saucer. "Teresi would have to get a consensus from the Cabinet, then apply to the speaker of the House and the president pro tempore of the Senate. If Tucker took it into his mind to fight, he could ask for a vote in both houses of Congress."

"He has forty-eight hours to call the vote if Congress is in session," said Macintyre. "Twenty-one days if it is not. As you are aware, Congress has recessed for the summer."

"Indeed." Swanbridge nodded. "Even without a vote, invoking Section Four could well be a long, drawn-out affair, and that presumes Mr. Teresi's cooperation."

"Something we're not likely to get," Macintyre grumbled. "And even if we did, we'd wind up with him as President."

"Quite so." Swanbridge nodded, puffing on his cigar. He rubbed a free hand thoughtfully over his bald scalp, as though polishing it. "Regardless of what effect Section Four might have, Mr. Teresi's assuming the presidency would have catastrophic results, I'm afraid."

"The media loves him, but he's made a lot of enemies on Wall Street," said Macintyre. "And he has every military contractor along the Beltway biting his nails."

"If Vincent Teresi became President, we certainly would lose a great many friends," Swanbridge said.

"We'd lose more than friends, Joseph," Macintyre warned. "We'd lose everything."

"Which brings us back to your so-called contingency plan," said Swanbridge. "Presumably you've come up with a number of options."

"Certainly." Macintyre nodded. "Several." He cleared his throat, waving a discreet hand at the smoke generated by Swanbridge's cigar. "The most obvious is the least attractive. We simply do nothing and let nature take its course, in which case the transition of power becomes a simple one: Teresi becomes President and chooses someone to fill his position as Vice President, much the same way as Ford took over from Nixon."

"And I'd be out of a job within twenty-four hours," interrupted Swanbridge, smiling around the stogie.

"Along with the rest of the Tucker Cabinet," said Macintyre. "We'd go from a relatively conservative and evenhanded administration to progressive chaos overnight."

"That's not the point," said Swanbridge, shaking his head. "The real problem is that Vincent Teresi thinks he's Jack Kennedy reborn, and he's not. He's a babe in the woods when it comes to foreign policy, and he doesn't have the strategic smarts of a gnat. Lots of charm and élan, but not much depth. He has too many weaknesses. Fatal flaws you might call them. So we rule out option one. What's next?"

"We dirty Teresi's diaper, find a Chappaquiddick, real or otherwise," said Macintyre. "Hudson has worked up a few scenarios."

"From the tone of your voice I gather the scenarios weren't sufficiently workable," said Swanbridge.

Macintyre shrugged. "The scenarios weren't the problem; it was their net effect. First Tucker dies of a degenerative brain disease; then the Vice President is scandalized into resigning. The Dow-Jones would go through the floor. You wouldn't be able to elect one of our people to the White House for a hundred years after that. It would be political suicide for the party."

"The third option?" asked Swanbridge.

"The final one," said Macintyre. "The simultaneous death of both President Tucker and Vincent Teresi."

"An accident?" queried Swanbridge, no sense of surprise in either his expression or voice.

"We considered it." Macintyre nodded. "The most realistic plan would involve Air Force One. Hudson feels the logistics and possibility of discovery rule it out."

"So?"

"Assassination," Macintyre replied, biting hard on the word.

"An ugly term." Swanbridge's cigar had gone out while they were talking. He tapped off the cold ash directly into his teacup and relit the butt with another match. "An ugly act as well, even when considered hypothetically."

"Agreed," said Macintyre. "Nevertheless, its results can sometimes be justified."

"In a banana republic perhaps," Swanbridge answered, lifting his shoulders in a shrug. "In this country it has done nothing but lead to tragedy and confusion."

"Granted," Macintyre replied. "There have been eleven assassinations and assassination attempts from Andrew Jackson to Ronald Reagan. The man who tried to kill Jackson was a mentally disturbed house painter, and John Hinckley, Jr., got off on an insanity defense. Even the two Puerto Ricans who tried to kill Truman were mentally disturbed."

"Make your point, Hollis." Swanbridge sighed.

"The point is, Joseph, the reasons for a madman to assassinate a President are usually clear only to the madman. The act itself serves no positive function; it only disrupts."

"You're saying that your plan is somehow different?" asked Swanbridge, the skepticism clear in his voice.

"Not my plan so much as Hudson Cooper's," Macintyre answered.

The secretary of state let out a braying laugh. "Good Lord, Hollis! There's no need to cover yourself quite so soon! This mysterious scenario is still in cloud-cuckoo-land as far as I'm concerned."

"I'm afraid it's already gone beyond that," said Macintyre. "And like it or not, you *are* involved. Jack Reynolds is speaker of the House; he's seventy-three, and he has a pacemaker. Charles Whittaker is president pro tempore of the Senate. He's had cancer twice already. They would almost certainly disqualify themselves as presidential material."

"You're saying the office would devolve to me?"

"According to the Succession Act of 1955, you would be next in line."
It was the carrot that would allow Swanbridge to swallow the stick.

"I see." Swanbridge paused, rolling the cigar between his lips. "You said the scenario was already operative. I presume you mean the supposedly accidental death of Dr. Barron?"

"Yes."

"Hudson's work?"

"Yes."

"I have doubts concerning Hudson's judgment," said Swanbridge slowly. He dropped the last half inch of the cigar into the dregs of his tea. "Recently he's shown what I would term an unhealthy obsession with his wife."

"His wife is dead, Joseph," responded Macintyre.

"My point exactly," Swanbridge murmured.

Macintyre shrugged off the comment. "He'll be here in a moment, Joseph. I'll let him tell you the details of his plan, and you can judge for yourself. Personally I find the man's idea rather cunning."

Swanbridge gave a small snort and reached into the pocket of his jacket.

"Too much cunning undoes," he said, pulling out another cigar and stripping off the plastic wrap.

"Good Lord, Joseph!" Macintyre laughed. "A proverb?"

"A warning," Swanbridge answered flatly, then popped the cigar into his mouth.

# CHAPTER 7

Geneneral Vladimir Arkadyevich Gurenko, senior KGB resident in North America, stood at the picture window of his penthouse office in the Mount Alto complex of the Soviet Embassy and stared out at central Washington spread out below him. Directly in front of him and less than half a mile away he could see the rooftop of the Vice President's house on the Naval Observatory grounds, and to his right, in the distance, he could easily make out the White House and the Capitol building a mile beyond it.

Gurenko, a lean dark-haired man in his early fifties, had risen through the ranks in the KGB, forging his career on the basis of productivity rather than the more common route of bribery (*klass*) and the secret lists of the *nomenklatura*. Opting for the most onerous and dangerous assignments and serving in places like Cambodia, Cuba, and Afghanistan, Gurenko had leapfrogged over less ambitious colleagues. He worked his way up through the system and finally captured the plum: chief of the Washington residency. With much of Central Europe in a state of political and economic flux since the "housecleaning" in 1989, the Washington residency was more important than ever before. Like it or not, the Americans were having to make some serious adjustments of their own, especially in terms of military spending. Gorbachev's upheavals had led to massive problems within the USSR; but his foreign policy had left the United States holding the bag, and it was clearly labeled "warmonger." Running the KGB in Washington had become an even more sensitive posting now, and Gurenko knew it required some very careful footwork;

82

the lines between enemy and ally had blurred, making everyone's life more difficult.

Wisely, since taking over the position after the retirement of his predecessor a year and a half before, Gurenko had not practiced the classic KGB pattern of reassigning and firing. Instead, he'd done his best to interact with his people, forging new alliances and relationships, while getting the job done as efficiently as possible. It seemed to have worked, and the reports that Valentin Ivashutin, his deputy, was sending back to Moscow Center were mostly favorable.

Gurenko himself reported to only one man, Sergei Yulevich Kuryokhin, chief of the First Department of the First Chief Directorate. This was the division of the KGB responsible for the residencies in Washington, New York, San Francisco, and Ottawa as well as for coordinating the operations of East European and Cuban intelligence services against the United States. Except for the Yurchenko coup in 1985, the First Department had been on extremely shaky ground politically, and so far it appeared that Kuryokhin appreciated Gurenko's efforts to keep things on a smooth and even keel in Washington. Gurenko intended to keep it that way; that was why he had been so disturbed by the memo he'd received that morning from Yuri Sidorov, director of Technical Support.

"Well?" he asked, turning away from the window. "What do you think?" Seated on a couch at the other end of the sparsely furnished, low-ceilinged room, Valentin Ivashutin went over the memo from Technical. It was almost thirty pages long and included transcripts of several different telephone conversations.

"It would appear that Comrade Travkin is overstepping the bounds of his authority," answered Gurenko's deputy. Ivashutin was as lean as his superior but was taller; his black hair thinned in a widow's peak. In the Mount Alto complex he was known as the Weasel, a nickname that suited him perfectly.

Gurenko crossed the room and sank into a chair across from Ivashutin. A low, highly polished birchwood table sat between them, resting on a brightly colored Afghani "war" rug, Gurenko's most prized possession, purchased during his two years in Kabul. The rug's motif was a repeating series of tanks, antiaircraft guns, helicopters, and soldiers. The red-faced soldiers were Soviets; the yellow ones, Afghani partisans. Inevitably the Afghanis were shown killing the Soviets, complete with lines of bullets flying from the barrels of the Afghani rifles. The design, minus the political implications, was exactly the kind of thing Gurenko and his friends had drawn on the covers of their notebooks as schoolboys.

"Is it worth pursuing?" Gurenko asked, gesturing at the report in Ivashutin's hands.

"As an officer in the GRU Major Travkin should be addressing matters of military intelligence. Instead, he has now met twice with this clerk from Walter Reed Hospital. As you know, we had Comrade Travkin only under light surveillance prior to that, standard procedure for a deputy resident. The second time we were able to get better information."

"The telephone number reference?" said Gurenko, indicating the file again.

Ivashutin nodded. "Yes."

"Which you then traced to Hudson Cooper?"

"Yes. The number was unlisted but not difficult to obtain."

"Presumably Comrade Travkin has done the same thing."

"Certainly," said Ivashutin. "His contacts in the telephone company are probably as good as ours."

"If not better." Gurenko nodded.

Ivashutin smiled at the oblique reference to the GRU's propensity for lavishing money on their informers and hired field agents.

"An interesting puzzle," said Ivashutin, dropping the report onto the table between them. He let the observation dangle, allowing Gurenko to come to the obvious conclusion.

"Does Cooper have his medical checkups done at Walter Reed?" asked the KGB resident.

His deputy nodded. "Yes. His doctor is a man named Weinstein."

"Then we may conclude that Comrade Travkin knows something about Mr. Cooper's medical condition that we do not," mused Gurenko. It opened up a number of intriguing possibilities. With only a few notable exceptions the position of director of central intelligence was political, not based on any real experience with the intelligence community. The last DCI with a long-standing intelligence background had been William Colby. The various deputy directorships, on the other hand, were truly powerful positions, and as DD/Operations Hudson Cooper had the most powerful position of all.

"I wonder . . ." Gurenko murmured.

"*Osin?*" asked Ivashutin, using the Russian word for "autumn."

"It occurred to me, yes." Gurenko nodded. He stood up and went back to the window overlooking the city, hands clasped behind his back. For Gurenko, Ivashutin, and a few other well-chosen KGB officers abroad, "autumn" was more than a word for a season. It was also the code name for the near-mythic KGB "tapeworm," or mole, buried within the Central Intelligence Agency.

The senior resident knew virtually nothing about the agent, other than the presumption that he was highly placed within the agency. Gurenko didn't even know who Autumn's handler was. Twice during his tenure in Washington, Gurenko had played brief host to a courier sent from Moscow by Kuryokhin. On both occasions the courier had arrived at Mount Alto without warning, carrying the bag, or diplomatic pouch, from Moscow. After presenting Kuryokhin's respects, the courier had vanished for twenty-four hours, then reappeared in time to carry the return pouch back to the Soviet Union.

Six months before, when Gurenko had been on a short leave to attend his mother's funeral, suspicions had been borne out when Kuryokhin, in the privacy of his dacha and under the influence of a considerable amount of vodka, had congratulated him on handling the Autumn courier with such discretion. The very fact that his superior had mentioned the tapeworm's code name to him was a compliment and a sign of trust, and now Gurenko had a way to return the favor.

If Autumn was as valuable as he seemed, it was likely that he was highly placed in a sensitive division of the CIA. The most sensitive and certainly most useful division from the KGB's point of view would be the Directorate of Operations, which included covert action, foreign espionage, and counterintelligence and counterespionage, making it the exact equivalent of his own First Chief Directorate.

If Autumn was somewhere in the CIA Directorate of Operations, any information regarding the health of the man in command of that directorate could be vitally important. As he stared out over the heat-hazed city, Gurenko suddenly realized that Autumn could conceivably be in line for Hudson Cooper's job. He turned from the window again, trying to keep his expression as blank as possible. Ivashutin was *osnovnoi*, high in the ranks of the elite, the *nomenklatura*, and God only knew whom the man was reporting to other than Moscow Center. The senior resident knew he had to walk a fine political line as well as cover himself in case things went wrong.

"We should look over the file on Hudson Cooper," Gurenko said finally.

Ivashutin nodded and reached into the breast pocket of his jacket. He took out a small notebook and scribbled a reminder. "What about Travkin?" Ivashutin murmured, ball-point poised over the open notebook.

"Full surveillance. Tap his phone, follow his car. Complete documentation and at least two men on him at all times."

"Will you be reporting to Center?" asked Ivashutin calmly. It was the key question. Autumn was Kuryokhin's asset, and to interfere with him was potentially dangerous. Even the use of his code name in a communication was a risk. On the other hand, Hudson Cooper's medical condition might well have a vital bearing on Autumn's continued safety. Gurenko cursed silently; it was another example of how politics within the KGB interfered with the real work at hand.

"I want you to complete the report," Gurenko said finally, making the best of the situation. "Sign your name under my authority."

"Of course." Ivashutin nodded. "What kind of encryption and transmission?"

"Use your own code," Gurenko replied. "I don't want it going anywhere near the U-three people." U-3 referred to the third level below ground, where signals were coded and then transmitted. Logging a transmission through Sidorov's people was like shouting over a party line. "When you have the report coded, send it by pouch," Gurenko added. Using the diplomatic courier meant that Kuryokhin wouldn't have it for at least thirty-six hours, but there was no other way of keeping Autumn secure.

"Will that be all?" asked Ivashutin. He climbed to his feet, snapped the notebook closed, and returned it to his pocket.

"I'll want to read the report before you send it off, of course," Gurenko said.

"Of course."

"And I want you to destroy every copy of the memo report from Sidorov with the exception of the one you just read," Gurenko went on. "Append that to your own report."

"Very well." Ivashutin left the office silently, leaving Gurenko alone with his thoughts. He turned back to the window, looking out again over the sunbaked city.

In KGB parlance, Washington, D.C., was symbol and center of the "Main Enemy." It sounded silly, of course, as infantile as Reagan's infamous description of the USSR as the "Evil Empire." But the average American *was* fundamentally suspicious of the Soviet Union, assuming its citizenry was made up of mindless, bullet-headed robots, just as the average Muscovite *did* see the United States as a pernicious wasteland of corruption, immorality, and nauseating overindulgence. Neither description was accurate, but both contained grains of truth. Tearing down the

Berlin wall, firing corrupt politicians, and changing governments all over Eastern Europe hadn't done very much to change any of those opinions. It was ironic really, since both Soviets and Americans prided themselves on "patriotism," and both nations had been born out of armed rebellion. At its simplest level the antagonism between the two superpowers was easy enough to understand: It was just an old-fashioned, deeply rooted fear of strangers. Shoot first and ask questions later. Gurenko shook his head. He was no better than the rest. Children playing games with incredibly dangerous toys.

Autumn was a case in point. A tapeworm lodged deep in the belly of the Central Intelligence Agency and a secret symbol of its ineptness and inadequacy, the phantom asset was also capable of pointing out the paranoias and internal politicking of the KGB with embarrassing accuracy. Gurenko sighed; none of it was going to change, at least not in his lifetime. He, like every other intelligence officer, Soviet, French, British, or American, lived in a world of lies that went from purest white to deepest black.

The KGB resident smiled, his memory taking him back to his classes at the Foreign Intelligence School. The school was located a short distance from Moscow just off the Volokolamskoye Highway and consisted of a depressing four-story brick monstrosity hidden behind a yellow masonry wall topped by barbed wire. To Gurenko it had looked more like a prison camp than an institute of higher learning, but if nothing else, the English classes introduced him to the Romantic poets, particularly Byron, a man who well knew the world of lying, in both his personal life and his writings: "And, after all, what is a lie? 'Tis but the truth in masquerade." It could easily have been written to be the motto for either the KGB or the CIA.

"*Shtoi!*" Gurenko moaned ruefully. It was a damn good thing the Weasel couldn't read minds or he'd be on his way to the psycho ward at Lefortovo Prison. Idly the resident picked up the high-powered Meade binoculars and focused them on the roof of the White House, three miles away to the southeast. During the Carter and Reagan administrations, extensive renovations had been done on the third, or attic, floor of the executive mansion, and on warm days, using the binoculars, Gurenko had occasionally seen people sunbathing on the roof of the solarium. Today the roof was empty except for a shirt-sleeved Secret Service agent, sweating away his shift in a lawn chair set up below the limply hanging Stars and Stripes.

Gurenko put the binoculars gently back on the windowsill. Pointless voyeurism, like Byron's poetry, was counterproductive to the cause of Soviet intelligence, and he, for one, had work to do. Turning his back to the view, he went to his desk and sat down. He pulled his ashtray within easy reach and took out a package of Opals and a lighter from the drawer on his left. He buzzed his secretary for coffee and then settled down to examine the pile of weekly expense reports in front of him. Within a few moments he was totally immersed in the columns of figures, and he had completely forgotten about Dmitri Travkin.

While Vladimir Gurenko of the KGB tried to decipher the inevitably inflated expense reports of his junior officers, Dmitri Travkin of the GRU was seated in front of a computer terminal in his cubicle at the Soviet Military Office on Belmont Street trying to unscramble a puzzle of his own.

The terminal he was using, like all the others in the SMO, was an out-of-date Zenith hooked into an equally archaic mainframe in the basement. Both mainframe and terminals were bug-checked regularly and protected from electronic eavesdropping by copper sheathing in the walls, but Travkin still got twitchy when he worked classified information on the screen.

Not that anyone "ghosting" his data would get much for his trouble; with the few facts he was trying to stitch together he might just as well have been trying to spin straw into gold. Grumbling under his breath, he straightened up in his chair, stretched, and then lit a cigarette. He glanced around the room, squinting through the haze of cigarette smoke and frowning. His office was no more than a twelve-by-twelve box, most of it filled with filing cabinets and archive boxes piled to the ceiling. At least it had a small window, almost opaque with dirt and soot, but still admitting enough light to let him know if it was night or day.

"Shit," he muttered, looking back at the screen. For the last three days he'd been devoting almost all his time to the Scanlon material, and Koslov was badgering him to get back to more productive work. As deputy resident Travkin was responsible for management of all the operational officers in both Washington and New York, supervision of the specialist officers and the material they were preparing for transmittal to Moscow, and the monitoring of the various illegals and their controlling operational officers.

Travkin cursed again, scrolling through the meager dossier he had assembled. Perhaps Koslov was right; what he had didn't amount to very much. At first it had seemed as though he were on to something, but it seemed now that the more he looked, the less he saw.

Barron, for instance. After doing some very basic research, Travkin had learned that Barron hadn't been the President's personal physician at all, merely the attending physician who oversaw the chief executive's semiannual checkups. The real presidential doctor was a man with the faintly sinister name of Hacker. Hacker and a support staff of sixteen had a full-scale clinic in the basement of the White House itself. According to Travkin's information, Charlie Moorehead was a high school friend of the President's and was a general practitioner with no specialty.

Travkin's initial reaction had been to connect Barron, the President, and the library request, but now he wasn't so sure of that either. As far as he could tell, Barron really had died in a boating accident, and as it turned out, his uncle had Alzheimer's. Everything could be explained away easily enough except for Scanlon's photocopy of the printout from the Walter Reed telephone log. According to the log, Dr. Barron had placed only one outside call, and that was to Hudson Haines Cooper, deputy director of operations for the CIA. A simple check revealed that Barron was not Cooper's physician at Walter Reed.

Digging a little deeper, Travkin had followed up by meeting with one of his contacts in the telephone company. The contact, a systems engineer named Zaritski, thought that Travkin was an alcoholic West German journalist with more money than brains; the GRU deputy resident had done nothing to change the man's mind, paying him well on the few occasions he'd been used.

At Travkin's request, backed up by five one-hundred-dollar bills in an envelope, Zaritski had spent a few off-duty hours tracing Hudson Cooper's Watergate number through the telephone company's labyrinthine computer billing system, and like Scanlon, he came up with a number, this one in Virginia. Zaritski, reporting back to Travkin, said that the number, although unlisted, was traceable through the billing office. According to the engineer, the number was billed to someone named Hollis Crandall Macintyre of Woodbridge, Virginia. The name obviously meant nothing to Zaritski, probably just as well, but it put another wrinkle of confusion onto Travkin's brow. What was the connection between an Army doctor at Walter Reed, the DDO for the CIA, and a cranky old bulldog politico like Macintyre. None of it made any sense, but there obviously *was* a connection.

Barron had called for the information relating to Creutzfeldt-Jakob disease and associated dementia at 6:15 P.M. At 8:30 P.M. he placed his call to Hudson Cooper. At 10:15 P.M. Cooper in turn called Hollis Macintyre in Woodbridge. The call from Barron to Cooper had lasted for one minute and seventeen seconds; the call from Cooper to Macintyre had lasted twenty-two seconds. Within twenty-four hours of Cooper's call, Dr. John Barron was dead.

Travkin sighed. Every instinct told him there was some sort of elusive relationship among the three men; but coming up with real proof was something else again, and real proof was what Koslov was calling for if he wanted to continue with the project.

Barron's call for information on C-J disease might have been for a paper he was writing. The call to Cooper could have been a social one, as could the call from Cooper to Macintyre. None of it was even mildly suspicious except for Scanlon's assertion that the request logs at the Walter Reed Hospital had been tampered with, and Scanlon's testimony could hardly be called fact.

The telephone beside the computer terminal buzzed, and Travkin picked up the receiver. It was Gregor Savin, the operational officer Travkin had assigned to keep an eye on Hudson Cooper. So far Cooper had done nothing out of the ordinary.

"Yes, Savin?"

"I have a transmission."

"Just a moment," Travkin answered. Like every other intelligence organization operating in Washington, the GRU had a variety of ways to ensure that radio, telephone, and microwave transmissions remained secure. With Koslov's tacit approval Travkin had outfitted his operations people with a Swedish-made encrypting device called a Transfertex SR22. The machine, attached to a normal telephone, had a nine-digit numerical pad, and the random numbers for both transmitter and receiver were changed once a week. Travkin connected his base unit receiver, set the nine numbers, then picked up the telephone again.

"Savin?"

"Yes. Connected."

"Good. Go ahead," Travkin urged.

"Hudson Cooper and his assistant—"

"Mallory?"

"Yes. They arrived at Dulles about half an hour ago. Cooper went to the VIP lounge for international flights, and Mallory went to the American Airlines desk. I sent Lovchikov to join the line behind him. He came back and told me that Mallory picked up two first-class tickets to Barbados. The flight leaves in ten minutes. Lovchikov is watching the gate to make sure they actually get on that flight."

"Are they using their own names?" Travkin queried.

"No," Savin answered crisply. "Cooper is traveling as a Mr. John Barnes. Mallory is using the name Akroyd. Thomas Akroyd."

"All right, Savin. Good work," Travkin said. "Stay there until the flight takes off; then get back here as fast as you can."

"Fine." There was a burst of electronic noise as Lovchikov ended the transmission from his end. Travkin unhooked the Transfertex device and hung up the telephone. He sat back in his chair, scratching his chin thoughtfully. Another anomaly and something to tweak Koslov's imagination at last. It was unlikely that traveling with Mallory and using a false name, Cooper was going to Barbados for pleasure, and it was unheard of for a man at Cooper's level to appear at field level on an operation. Ergo, something very strange was going on, strange like the phone call from Barron to Cooper. Nodding to himself, he picked up the telephone again and dialed a three-digit internal number.

"Documents, Lieutenant Kapalkin speaking."

"This is Colonel Travkin."

"Yes, Colonel, what can I do for you?"

"I need cover." Travkin rubbed a clammy palm against the fabric of his trousers. Pray that Koslov sees this the way I do, he thought.

"Of course, Colonel, anything in mind?"

"Swiss?" Travkin suggested. His English was good but accented enough to mark him as a foreigner. "Visas for the United States and Great Britain. A few credit cards, some pocket litter."

"Do the cards have to work?" asked Kapalkin.

"No," Travkin answered. "I'll be using cash."

"Good," Kapalkin answered pleasantly. "That will speed things up considerably, Colonel."

"I want it all by four," Travkin said, glancing at his watch. It was already one-thirty.

"Fine," the documents officer said breezily. "We have your photos on file. Give me an hour or so." The Documents Section at the SMO was the foreign division of the GRU First Department (Passport) and had instant access to a gigantic data base of information relating to passport regulations, identity cards, driving licenses, passes, military documents, police documents, and air, sea, and rail tickets.

At any time of the day or night, using a secure satellite link, Kapalkin could find out the entry requirements and documentation for any given control or passport point in the world, including the types of questions likely to be asked and what stamps should be on the passports or other travel documents. The First Department also kept Kapalkin's office and others like it supplied with a variety of blank passports, identity cards, and driver's licenses.

After thanking the documents officer, Travkin put down the telephone and then shut off the computer terminal. He had an overnight bag already packed in the courier's apartment on the top floor. If he could convince Koslov of his suspicions, he could be on his way to Barbados while the trail was still warm.

Stephen Stone pulled the nondescript car pool Chevy into a no parking zone on H Street, killed the engine, and pulled down the passenger-side visor to display the regulation FBI "on duty" sticker. Already dressed in a D.C. Public Works coverall, he picked up the hard hat from the seat beside him and put it on, completing the image. Scooping up an official-looking clipboard from the top of the dashboard, he climbed out of the car and locked the door behind him.

He fumbled around in the coverall pockets for his sunglasses and put them on to ward off the bright midafternoon sun. It was another hazy, humid day in the nation's capital, and he could already feel the sweat trickling down his ribs. Feeling a little idiotic in his disguise, he walked quickly down H Street past the Decatur House, then turned right on Jackson Place. Across the street on his left was the parched brown-edged grass of Lafayette Square. Pennsylvania Avenue and the northern perimeter of the White House grounds were less than a hundred yards away to the south.

Still not quite sure how a top Soviet agent like Travkin had managed to swing an apartment within spitting distance of the President of the United States, Stone shook his head. It was especially ironic considering the sinful amount of money he paid in rent for his own high-rise hole in the wall on Sixteenth Street, a mile to the north.

The FBI man glanced down the street. Jackson Place allowed angle-parking on the west side, and as far as Stone could see, every spot was taken. He slowed, spotting the surveillance vehicle, a light green high-sided van with "D.C. Public Works" stencils all over it. Kessler had managed to put it into perfect position, just south of Travkin's building.

The narrow town houses on Jackson Place had been erected in the mid 1800's and been narrowly saved from demolition by John F. Kennedy. Under his sponsorship the houses were restored and renovated, and anachronistic, newer buildings, such as the small apartment building Travkin occupied, were remodeled to conform to the nineteenth-century ambience of the little street.

Most of the town houses were now occupied by lawyers and Capitol Hill lobbyists, but a few, like Travkin's, were still used residentially. On Seventeenth Street, directly behind the block-long row and looming over it slightly, was the modern brick-and-glass rear facade of the new Executive Office Building.

Stone stepped out onto the street, went around to the rear of the truck, and gave the proper coded knock. He waited for a few seconds, then pulled open the rear door and stepped inside. His nose wrinkled as he was hit by a wall of hot soup-thick air tinged with the scent of male perspiration and old socks. Mort Kessler and a Communications Division jock named Dofney were seated at a bank of electronic equipment bolted to the side wall of the truck. Both men were stripped to the waist with headphones clamped over their ears. The van was lit dimly by a single fluorescent fixture in the ceiling.

Seeing Stone, Kessler pulled off the headphones and tossed them onto the console in front of him. Face almost as red as his hair and a nasty look in his eyes, he swiveled around in his chair. Stone took off the hard hat and dropped down onto a bench seat opposite the electronic console. He found himself staring at a quartet of video monitors providing exterior coverage of the van.

"This is a surveillance vehicle, right?" said Kessler, his voice sour.

"Right." Stone nodded, trying to keep a straight face.

"More precisely it's a fucking surveillance vehicle for use in Washington goddamn D.C., am I correct?"

"Right as rain." Stone nodded.

"Got all the best equipment," Kessler snarled, waving a hand at the stacked electronic equipment. "We got Cougarnet here, we got Comsec speech security, Scanlok for radios, Voicelok for phones, fiber-optic video capabilities—shit, we've even got your basic microwave resonating cavity bug—*but* by God, we don't have fucking air conditioning."

"I'll take it up with Director Ruppelt." Stone grinned.

"Sure you will, and Mr. God will tell you all about his budget problems." Kessler snorted. The red-haired man lit a Kool, adding to the already foggy atmosphere within the truck. "Did you get it?" he asked finally. "It" referred to wiretap authorization from the Foreign Intelligence Surveillance Court. The court, undoubtedly the least known division of the American judicial system, was supposed to judge the

93

relevance and legality of submissions by the FBI and other federal agencies for the electronic surveillance of suspected foreign agents. Not once in the court's history had it ever turned down such a submission.

"Of course, I got it," Stone answered. He reached into the bib pocket of the coveralls and pulled out a thick folded cream-colored document.

"Good." Kessler nodded. "Especially since we've already done the work." The FBI man looked expectantly at Stone.

"What do you mean, you've already done the work?"

"Just that," Kessler answered blandly. He hooked a thumb at Dofney. "Chuck planted 'em, and I kept a lookout." He nodded toward the video screens. The tiny fiber-optic lenses were mounted high on the van body, giving a 360-degree view from four cameras, all connected to a VCR and an effects panel in front of Kessler.

Dofney looked like a college football player: overmuscled with an out-of-date crew cut, and no more than twenty-five years old. He turned in his chair and gave Stone a broad collegiate grin.

"Radio bug in each room," he said proudly. "And an RF flooder on the main junction box. Already got it tuned in. This guy Travkin does have air conditioning by the way; his apartment was nice and cool."

"Did you find any telltales?" Stone asked.

"You mean, like hairs on door cracks, talcum powder on briefcase locks?" Dofney asked, surprised. "James Bond shit?"

"Something like that." Stone nodded, sighing. The young agent was looking at him as though he'd just been released from an old folks' home.

"Uh, no," Dofney said finally. "You mean, people still do things like that?" he added.

"Sometimes," Stone replied. He decided it was time to change the subject. "Tell me about his apartment. Describe it."

"Do better than that." Dofney grinned. He tossed Stone a thick packet of Polaroids bound with a rubber band. "Old Mort here said you'd want them."

"Old Mort was right," said Stone. Eager for a more intimate view of his quarry, he flipped through the photographs.

A large one-bedroom apartment with a bay window looking out over the statues in Lafayette Square. White walls, highly polished hardwood floors, and lots of small Oriental rugs. The bedroom was sparse, furnished with a lot of modern plastic.

Kitchen hi tech, complete with Cuisinart and all the bells and whistles: espresso machine; pasta maker; Braun coffeemaker. Living room: fireplace with a pot of dried flowers in the grate, collection of vaguely antique stringed instruments on one wall, Bang and Olufsen stereo, complete with a CD player, television set, and one whole wall filled with books.

Dofney wasn't quite as brainless as he looked; he'd taken more than a dozen close-ups of the book titles: a lot of American military history, biographies of a number of conservative politicians, and a huge collection of books on Hollywood, leaning heavily on comedy and comedians. Taking up a whole shelf above it were at least a hundred jokebooks, some of them apparently quite old. Except for a small section of murder mysteries and thrillers, there didn't seem to be much in the way of fiction.

"Interesting," Stone said, slipping the rubber band around the pictures again.

"I'd say Comrade Travkin was taking full advantage of his tour of duty in the decadent West." Kessler grinned. "According to Chuck here, your boy has got about fifty different kinds of condom in his bedside table."

"All colors and flavors." Dofney snorted. "That guy's no spy; he's a pussy hound."

"Don't underestimate him; he's a spy all right," Stone answered. "Just remember, this man is a GRU deputy resident for D.C., and he's not even forty yet. He's working at least a dozen people we know about and probably a whole lot more besides." Stone paused and wiped sweat off his forehead with the sleeve of his coverall.

"You went through his apartment, Dofney, and I'll bet you didn't find one thing in it with any kind of personal connotation. No address books, no letters, not even a postcard from home. You can bet your ass he empties his pockets every day before he leaves work, just to make sure he doesn't bring back any incriminating pocket litter. Don't kid yourself, Agent Dofney: Dmitri Travkin is a professional, and he's dangerous."

Dofney opened his mouth to reply, but Kessler's voice cut him off.

"Company," the red-haired man said sharply.

"Where?" Stone asked, leaning forward, his eyes scanning the video monitors.

"Camera one, north," Kessler answered crisply. He stabbed the record button with his left index finger and the auto zoom with his right. Stone watched as the image on camera one tightened, showing the street and a few cars. "The dark blue Ford," said Kessler. "Dip plates. DFC six-seven-seven." Kessler squeezed his eyes shut for a fraction of a second, thinking. "She's out of the Mount Alto complex, not the SMO. I'd say she's KGB."

95

"What do we do now?" asked Dofney, his voice nervous.

"Nothing," Stone answered, keeping his eye on the screen.

"They're sniffing," explained Kessler. "They'll make a pass and go around the block."

"I don't get it." Dofney frowned. "If they're KGB, what are they doing here?"

"They don't teach you much in ComDiv, do they?" Kessler asked rhetorically. They all watched as the Ford slid off the camera one screen, then reappeared on camera two, moving away toward Pennsylvania Avenue. "It's Big Brother, Little Brother," the red-haired agent explained. "There's no love lost between the KGB and the GRU, so they watch each other. These guys are probably just making a routine run on the building. The GRU has a lot of its people housed outside the Mount Alto complex and the killer bees are jealous."

"It sounds stupid to me." Dofney shrugged.

"You think it's any different here?" Kessler asked. The Ford turned right onto Pennsylvania Avenue and vanished. "The CIA watches the DIA, and the NSA watches them right back. It's the same thing, except we dress better than they do."

"I think it goes a little deeper than that." Stone laughed.

Kessler lifted a single, expressive eyebrow and turned back to the video monitors. He punched up the zoom on camera one, waiting for the Ford to reappear. Less than a minute later it did.

"Here she comes," Kessler murmured. He hit the time counter, the display running in the lower-right-hand corner of all four screens. The car was definitely going more slowly the second time around. It slid past the van's position, and Kessler went to camera two again.

"They're stopping," Stone whispered, watching the screen and ignoring the puddling sweat under his eyes. The body heat from the three men and the heat of the equipment had turned the truck's interior into a jungle.

The rear door of the Ford opened, and two men appeared, both carrying small black bags. The tall one was dressed in shorts, a Hawaiian shirt, and a straw hat; his shorter companion was wearing a jogging suit. "Two doctors going to a costume party." Kessler grunted. The KGB men reached the sidewalk, and Kessler punched up camera three, giving them a view of the sidewalk and Travkin's front door. On the camera two screen the Ford was pulling away. The two men appeared on screen, walking toward Travkin's building. "Straw hat is a Line KR boy named Stefan Gontar," said Kessler as the two men entered the building and disappeared from view. "I've never seen the other one." "Line KR" stood for the KGB counterintelligence section.

"Technical support?" Stone suggested.

Kessler nodded. "Could be." The agent turned to Dofney. "Give us some sounds, kid."

"Sure," Dofney answered. He hit several switches, and there was a faint hum as the recorders began to turn. Obviously worried, the technician turned to Stone. "You think they're sweeping the place for our bugs?" he asked. Stone shook his head.

"Too much of a coincidence," he said. "I think we just stepped into some interagency shit here."

"You mean, they're bugging his place, too?" said Dofney.

"Probably." Stone nodded. "Are they likely to trip over your stuff?"

Dofney thought for a moment, then lifted his broad shoulders. "They might, but I doubt it. The RF flooder is two blocks away."

"What about the other bugs?"

"C-Comms," Dofney answered. "We get them custom-made to look like Duracells. I took the real batteries out of his smoke alarms." The muscular agent laughed. "Mind you, we're shit out of luck if he has a fire."

Stone heard a faint crackling sound from the PA speaker. Kessler slipped on his headphones, and Dofney boosted the volume. Stone could hear the creaking of a door, then footsteps—metal clips on hardwood.

"They're in," Kessler murmured. Stone joined the two agents at the electronics console, crouching down between them and listening. There were more footsteps, sniffing noises as though one of the intruders had a cold, and then voices.

"*Sveyarlo*—something about a drill," said Stone, straining to hear. He'd spent four months on a Russian-language course after joining Rednet, but he was far from fluent. A few seconds later he heard a high-pitched whining sound.

"Portable drill," Kessler said, "probably taking a chunk out of the baseboard."

"Radio bug?" asked Stone, glancing up at Dofney.

"No, sir," the technician answered. "We can service ours from any building around here; they don't have that kind of access." Dofney paused, thinking. "Probably an MRC at some inaudible frequency . . . . real high, say three thirty megaHertz." An MRC was a microwave resonating cavity bug of the type used by the Soviets to monitor conversations in the U.S. Embassy in Moscow. In that case the bug, less than three

97

inches long, had been secreted inside the carved seal of the United States that hung behind the ambassador's desk.

"It won't interfere with our signals?" asked Stone.

"Nope," Dofney answered, shaking his head. "They'll run a tight beam off the roof at Mount Alto to pick it up."

"One of them is leaving," said Kessler. The men in the van watched the video monitor, but after two long minutes no one appeared. There were more drilling sounds from Travkin's apartment.

"The other guy is probably tracing the phone line," suggested Dofney. "Tapping the junction box."

"All of a sudden your boy is a very hot item," said Kessler, giving Stone a meaningful glance. He returned it silently; there was nothing about the situation they could discuss in front of Dofney.

A strident electronic buzz filled the interior of the van, and Kessler picked up the scrambled radiophone handset from the console in front of him. He listened for a few seconds, nodded once, and then turned to face Stone.

"What?"

"It's Midbrook," Kessler answered. "He's got the service watch at SMO. He says Travkin just got into an airport limo, carrying an overnight bag. He wants to know if he should follow."

"Yes," Stone responded quickly. "But only until he figures out which airport they're going to. Once he's done that, tell him to get one of our people there before the limo if that's possible, but for Christ sake, be discreet!"

"Right." Kessler nodded. He turned back to the radiophone.

Stone stood up and went back to the bench seat on the other side of the van. He sat down heavily and lit a cigarette. If Travkin was acting as a courier again, he would have used a vehicle from the SMO or Mount Alto car pool. The fact that he was carrying an overnight bag and hadn't come back to his own apartment to pack meant that he was in a hurry. But why, and for what? Stone shook his head.

"What the hell is the little bastard up to?" he whispered.

# CHAPTER 8

As the name implies, Garrison Savannah, home track of the Barbados Turf Club, is situated on a field across from the old British garrison. The eighty-year-old facility is a mile or so from the center of Bridgetown, capital of the island nation, and operates two full seasons of regular six- and seven-race cards.

For off-island afficionados, used to modern track facilities, Garrison Savannah is an archaic eyesore. The rickety old grandstand is made of wood, and with the exception of a few private box seats for Turf Club members, hard bench seats are the rule. Smoking is allowed, so there is the constant threat of fire, the overhead canopy leaks when it rains, and during each race the entire grandstand structure shakes as the horses thunder past.

Outside the track, parking is haphazard with no real lots, the stables to the north of the field are a slum, and the inside rail around the paddock is decorated with scores of garish, brightly colored billboard advertisements for everything from Chez Monique's to Willie's Watersports.

Eyesore or not, the track is one of the most popular attractions on the island, and on the regular Saturday race days or for special stake races, the grandstand is filled to capacity with fans from all over Barbados, as well as hordes of tourists from the nearby Hilton and the other hotels along the Highway 7 coastal route to Grantley Adams International Airport.

Seated deep in the shadows on the top bench under the grandstand canopy, Eric Rhinelander watched as the horses assembled for the last

99

race on the card, the Concorde Stakes. The race, underwritten by British Airways, had been sponsored to celebrate the fifth year of Concorde service to Barbados and with a ten-thousand-pound stake it had attracted every Thoroughbred racing enthusiast on the island.

Rhinelander, appropriately dressed in sneakers, jeans, and a "Barbados Wildlife Trust" T-shirt, sipped at his large cup of Banks beer, occasionally lifting his mid-range Tasco binoculars to look down at the track. The bench beside him was filled with a boisterous party of Bajan locals, hooting and yelling to friends below them. Rhinelander ignored them, and each time he lifted the binoculars to scan the track he allowed himself a few seconds to focus on the lowest box in the private Turf Club section at the north end of the grandstand.

There were five people in the booth, two couples and a single man. The two couples were dressed casually, the men in jackets and open-necked shirts, the women in skirts and blouses. The single man was dressed nautically in a blazer, white ducks, and an officer's cap. Once upon a time the man had obviously been quite good-looking, but through the binoculars Rhinelander could see the fine-line strawberry booze marks on his cheeks and nose. He was fiftyish and jowled, thick through the middle, and when he took off his cap to wipe the sweat from his forehead, Rhinelander could see a broad patch of tanned, hairless scalp. What hair remained, once blond, was now a nicotine-colored white. His name was William Harper, and he was the CIA station chief for Barbados.

Deeming that the island was neither economically nor strategically important, the State Department had seen fit to assign a chargé d'Affaires rather than an ambassador to the small Caribbean nation. The tiny diplomatic staff was housed in a suite of offices in the Canadian Imperial Bank Building on Broad Street in Bridgetown. Visiting the offices shortly after his arrival, Rhinelander had made a quick visual reconnaissance, picked up a few pamphlets, and left.

On the basis of what he had seen and the information in the pamphlets, Rhinelander came to some quick conclusions. According to the brochure describing the office of the chargé d'Affaires and its services, there were eight people employed: the chargé d'affaires himself, a man named Howard Sawyer, his assistant, two secretaries, a receptionist, an immigration officer, an information officer, and a public affairs officer.

From past experience with CIA stations abroad, Rhinelander suspected that Harper, the information officer, was the man he was after. His office was almost the same size as the chargé d'Affaires', and it was obvious that he had more money than his boss. He drove a two-year-old Volvo, lived aboard sixty thousand dollars' worth of motor sailer moored on the Waterfront Arcade at the foot of Bay Street, and dressed expensively. By contrast, Sawyer, the chargé d'Affaires, drove a five-year-old Isuzu sedan and lived with his wife and two children in a relatively modest bungalow.

After renting a canvas-roofed open-sided mini-moke, Rhinelander spent two days keeping tabs on Harper, and by the end of the second day he was positive that the man was CIA. He worked no more than an hour or two a day at the office, spending most of his time aboard his boat and doing the rounds of Bridgetown clubs and bars in the evening.

Not that he wasn't working. If Barbados was like other small CIA stations, Harper's mandate from the people at Langley was probably to cultivate, emulate, and infiltrate the upper echelons of Barbadian society. The long-term results of his hobnobbing would be a good selection of dossiers of both locals and their visitors, some of which might be useful to the agency. In CIA parlance, Harper was "trolling," with the car, boat, and Turf Club private box as both bait and cover.

During the Grenada invasion and the CIA destabilization efforts that had preceded it, Barbados had also proved its strategic value as an intelligence and military staging base, and Harper's continued presence also ensured that other nations, especially those in the Caribbean and Central America, recognized that the long arm of the U.S. military was never far away.

Somewhere along the line, however, Harper had developed a private sideline. Focusing on the box again, Rhinelander took another look at the two couples seated with the station chief. They weren't really couples at all, of course; the women were imports, tall and blond, probably from Miami or Nassau, and the two men were both employed by the government of Colombia. The older of the two, a short, bearded man named Torres, was assistant to the Colombian chargé d'affaires, and his younger, taller, and clean-shaven companion was supposedly a chauffeur. If Rhinelander was reading the signs correctly, the Colombians and Harper had some sort of drug scam going, probably involving the "special," a regularly scheduled diplomatic pouch used only by the CIA and utterly taboo.

Rhinelander had noted, since putting Harper under loose surveillance, that the station chief spent a great deal of time with Torres and the chauffeur, most of it on the boat. That morning, prior to leaving for the track, Harper and the two Colombians had spent a couple of hours

101

loading food, liquor, and water onto the boat as well as topped up its fuel tanks. It was two hundred miles from Bridgetown to the Venezuelan coast, half that to a midpoint rendezvous with a drug ship, all in all, at least a twenty-four-hour round trip on a boat the size of Harper's.

Rhinelander couldn't have cared less about Harper's involvement in the drug trade; he wouldn't be the first CIA employee to use his position for personal gain, nor would he be the last. What did matter was that Harper's interests were elsewhere for the moment. If the red-faced station chief were en route to a cocaine rendezvous, he wouldn't be interfering in Rhinelander's affairs.

The grandstand crowd, noisy to begin with, let out an exuberant, blossoming roar of appreciation as the car-mounted starting gate yawned open and the horses broke into the first straightaway. All around Rhinelander spectators had leaped to their feet, waving their arms, screaming for their favorites, betting slips clutched in their hands. Ignoring the race and the frenzied crowd, Rhinelander began to move, pushing his way along the aisle until he reached the main stairs leading to the track.

By the time the horses thundered into the second turn, Rhinelander had made his way down to the base of the grandstand. A commentator was calling the race order incoherently over the public-address system that all he could make out was the name of the favorite, a three-year-old named Charlie Muffin. According to the race program, the horse was owned by a syndicate headed by William Harper.

Ducking into the cool shadows, Rhinelander headed down the broad dark passage that led back under the grandstand, pushed through the turnstile, and stepped out into the sunlight. Behind him he could still hear the roaring crowd, but the parking lot in front of him was silent. Just outside the chain-link fence a group of luridly painted private buses was waiting for the last race to end, hoping to steal away passengers from the public bus line.

He found his rental mini-moke, slipped behind the wheel, and fired up the little vehicle's ignition. A few moments later he pulled out onto the highway, heading north into Bridgetown. Even with the racing program well under way the traffic was still horrendous, and it took Rhinelander almost fifteen minutes to navigate the mile or so of road back to Trafalgar Square and the yacht basin by Chamberlain Bridge.

After guiding the moke over the bridge separating the Careenage from the Inner Basin, he turned left around the statue of Lord Nelson and threaded his way along the wharf until he reached the parking lot at the far end of the harbor. He lifted the binoculars again and panned

102

down the forest of ship masts and tightly clustered buildings along the pier until he picked out Harper's boat, *Sandpiper,* the name clearly visible on the transom. The boat identified, he sat back against the seat and closed his eyes.

Forty minutes later, on his fourth check with the binoculars, Rhinelander spotted movement aboard *Sandpiper.* Harper, Torres, and the driver were making ready for sea. There was no sign of the two women. Rhinelander assumed that they were either below in the cabin or hadn't been invited along on the covert journey. If Harper had any sense, it would be the latter.

At almost exactly 4:00 P.M. *Sandpiper* came puttering along the Careenage, sails partly unfurled and ready to be hoisted once they reached open water. Keeping well back in the shadows of the moke's canopy, Rhinelander watched as the motor sailer went by. Harper, officer's cap firmly down over his forehead, was at the wheel, while the Colombian chauffeur, now stripped to a pair of skimpy shorts, was scrambling around the foredeck, making a show of gathering up tackle for the benefit of the two blondes lounging in their bikinis against the cabin bulkhead. Rhinelander shook his head. Not smart.

He waited until *Sandpiper* cleared the harbor entrance, then started up the moke again. If things went according to schedule, Mallory and Cooper would be arriving at Grantley Adams on the seven-thirty flight from Dulles. That gave him a little more than three hours, and there was still a lot to do.

The Tropicana Court Hotel was located on the beach off Highway 7 just beyond the village of Hastings and about three miles from the center of Bridgetown. The hotel, isolated from its more luxurious neighbors by several hundred yards of rocky cliff on either side, consisted of a main building, a pool, an open-air restaurant, and a modest stretch of pleasant, shallow-water beach.

The main building consisted of eighteen units on three floors with a pair of exterior staircases at the rear of the building leading up to motel-style open-air walkways. The units were identical, each having a kitchen to the left of the entrance and a bathroom to the right. The kitchen was separated from the bedroom-living area by a waist-high counter outfitted with barstools.

Beyond the counter and against the wall were a bureau and desk, which faced two single beds. A small drop leaf table and two chairs stood between the beds and a sliding glass door leading out to the balcony. The

103

balcony of every unit had a view of the pool and restaurant as well as the ocean beyond while the balconies themselves were separated by full-height privacy walls of roughly stuccoed concrete, each one fitted with a bolted connecting door. There was another table on the balcony, this one with a pair of aluminum canvas-seat lawn chairs.

The decor of each unit was also identical: Floors were uniform pale green linoleum tile, walls were blush pink, and the furniture was heavily varnished maple. Linens and towels were the same watery green as the floor, and the heavy hotelware crockery in the cupboards was a reasonable match for the pink walls.

On his arrival in Barbados, Rhinelander had chosen the Tropicana Court for both its isolation and the straightforward access to the units. He'd rented two adjoining units, 13 and 14, located on the third floor at the eastern end of the building. He told the manager that he was expecting friends from the States and was renting the second room on their behalf. He took the units for a week and paid cash in advance. Watching as the manager tapped the requisite information into his computer, Rhinelander could see that rooms fifteen through eighteen were not booked for that time period. He would have the top floor to himself.

Following the departure of Harper and his companions Rhinelander piloted the moke back to Garrison Savannah and beyond it to the hotel. He parked the car in the lot, then climbed the stairs to the third floor. After removing the telltale sliver of cellophane from the lock, he inserted his key and opened the door. Remaining in the open-air walkway, he listened carefully and sniffed the air. Everything seemed in order. He entered the room, closed and locked the door, then checked bathroom, kitchen, living area, and balcony. Empty.

Standing on the balcony, Rhinelander lit a cigarette and glanced down at the pool. A middle-aged man with a sunburn on his fleshy shoulders was doing slow laps, while two women in bikinis lay tanning in a pair of green plastic-webbed lounge chairs. They were paying no attention to the man in the pool. Rhinelander sat down at the balcony table, tipping his ashes into a butt-filled saucer. Through the screening line of trees between the pool and the sea, he noted that the beach was almost empty as well. Things were quiet at the Tropicana Court.

He sat on the balcony for a few minutes longer, smoking his cigarette and listening to the shrill sound of crickets and the muttering of the ocean. When the cigarette was finished, he butted it into the saucer and went back to the living area. Squatting down, he reached under the overhanging coverlet of the bed nearest the balcony and withdrew a well-used

104

pale blue vinyl flight bag emblazoned with the Pan Am symbol. He un-zipped the bag and began removing the contents: hand drill, a package of hacksaw blades, electrical tape, an eyeglass screwdriver, a roll of speaker wire, a tube of liquid solder, insulated wire cutters, and a squeeze pack-age of plumber's putty.

Also in the flight bag was a shoebox containing a Panasonic voice-activated memocorder, one 120-minute BASF micro audiotape, a pack-age of Duracell AAA batteries, and a large fifties-vintage behind-the-ear Beltone hearing aid. Rhinelander had purchased all these, including the flight bag, at a number of stores in Bridgetown over the previous three days. Taking a selection of tools and instruments to the table by the bal-cony door, Rhinelander began to work.

Using the eyeglass screwdriver, he carefully removed the flesh-toned cover of the hearing aid and examined the device closely. As he had expected, the mechanism consisted of a miniature transistorized receiver connected to a microphone and battery. Using the screwdriver as a lever, Rhinelander delicately removed the microphone from the earpiece, then separated it completely from the rest of the unit by snipping the wires leading to the receiver. He clipped a six-foot length of speaker wire and rebuilt the hearing aid circuit with it, bonding the new length of wire with a minuscule amount of the liquid solder.

Leaving the solder to harden, he went back to the bed, picked up the drill and the hacksaw blades, then carried them to the party wall between his room and the one next door. Sitting cross-legged on the floor, he chose a spot directly over a wall socket and quickly drilled two pairs of parallel holes about eight inches apart directly above the outlet. Using one of the hacksaw blades, he joined the four holes, then pried out the square of wallboard. He slid down and peered into the opening; his mea-surements the day before had been accurate: The electrical box and wall socket on the other wall matched the one on his side.

He boosted himself up, went back to the bed, picked up the batteries, memocorder, and the electrical tape, then carried them to the table. The liquid solder had set up nicely, making a solid connection. Rhinelander tore off two six-inch strips of electrical tape, then gently picked up the receiver end of the hearing aid. He butted the receiver end to the con-denser microphone in the memocorder and attached it with the two strips of tape. The end result of his labors was an unsophisticated but perfectly workable bugging device.

After replacing the tape machine's batteries with the new Duracells, Rhinelander loaded the tape, then ran a quick check, setting the tape machine on record and whispering into the microphone end of the hearing aid, his eyes on the voice-level needle on the recorder. It worked perfectly. He rewound the tape, then carried the electronic package to his newly opened hole in the wall.

He picked up the drill again, reached into the hole, and ran his finger under the cast steel box covering the outlet in the other room. Using his finger as a guide, he drilled a small hole through the plasterboard just under the box. That done, he withdrew the drill and set it aside. He took the package of putty out of his jeans, kneaded it for a few seconds, then tore it open. After balling a wad of the gray compound between thumb and forefinger, he made a thick collar around the microphone from the hearing aid. He reached into the hole again, found the tiny hole below the electrical box, then carefully used his other hand to place the microphone, pressing firmly to ensure that it would hold. With the microphone in position he eased the memocorder into the hole, letting it rest on the wooden framing joist between the two panels of plasterboard. He replaced the square he'd removed, secured it with more putty, then cleaned up after himself, using the flight bag as a catchall.

Ten minutes later he was finished, satisfied that any evidence of his modest renovations had been removed. Finally, he pushed the bureau a foot to the left, hiding the scored area of wallboard above the electrical outlet. He looked around the room again, then checked his watch. The whole procedure had taken less than an hour; there was plenty of time left.

Rhinelander went out onto the balcony, pulled back the heavy bolt on the connecting door, and stepped across onto the adjoining balcony. He slid open the glass door and entered the living room. The unit was the mirror image of his own, the furniture and decor duplicated exactly. He crossed the room to the electrical outlet beside the bureau and got down onto his hands and knees. There was a tiny dribble of plaster dust on the baseboard. Rhinelander licked the tip of his finger and dabbed it over the offending area. The plaster dust vanished. Bending even lower, he checked the drill hole. The opening was completely invisible, a pinhole lost in the shadows of the plug plate and the baseboard.

A thorough search by a team of trained debuggers from the agency would be able to spot it eventually, but Rhinelander wasn't giving Hudson Cooper the luxury or the time for that. Returning to the balcony, Rhinelander bolted the adjoining door, then left the unit through the regular door and locked it behind him. He returned to his own room, dropped the key to unit 13 into a Tropicana Court envelope, and sat down at the desk to write a brief set of instructions for Cooper.

Five minutes later he was back outside and climbing into the minimoke. Two minutes after that he was on his way to Grantley Adams International Airport.

According to established CIA tradecraft, Hudson Cooper and Paul Mallory should have traveled separately from Washington, but Cooper had decided to forgo procedure. Since they both were flying on diplomatic passports, with Mallory handcuffed to the Central Intelligence "special" diplomatic bag, it seemed absurd to sit apart during the flight and go through customs and immigration singly.

The flight came in exactly on time, and the sun was only just lowering on the horizon when the two men reached the bottom of the steps and began walking across the tarmac to the terminal with the rest of the passengers.

"What on earth is that noise?" asked Cooper. The air was filled with a continuous creaking whine, like thousands of tiny squeaking wooden wheels in need of grease.

"Crickets," Mallory responded. While Cooper had spent the four-and-a-half-hour flight staring blankly out the window, his assistant had passed the time by reading three hundred pages of the *Insight Guide to Barbados*. "They have a plague of crickets in Barbados. They're everywhere."

"Oh," Cooper answered, not even mildly interested, his thoughts focused on Rhinelander and their meeting.

They ducked under the concrete canopy over the main entrance doors and stepped inside the terminal. Having sidestepped the main line of passengers winding its way through customs and immigration, they flashed their red-covered passports and were given priority treatment. Within ten minutes they had reached the main concourse.

"The message said we should go to the American Express kiosk," Cooper said, obviously uncomfortable. The whirling currents of humanity that eddied through the concourse were dressed in a wild assortment of brightly colored tourist clothes while Cooper wore a dark gray business suit complete with white shirt, striped tie, and black wing tips.

"That way," Mallory said, pointing down the concourse to the familiar blue and white sign. Cooper's assistant was dressed more appropriately in an open-necked shirt and a cream-colored summer-weight sports jacket. The large metal-sided attaché case handcuffed to his left wrist was a dead giveaway, however, and for anyone who cared to notice, the two men were clearly not tourists.

With Mallory in the lead they made their way through the dense traffic on the concourse and eventually reached the small Amex booth. A pleasant, smiling woman greeted them, and Cooper asked if there were any messages for him. The woman checked a bank of pigeonholes on her left and handed the deputy director an envelope. Cooper thanked her, then moved to one side with Mallory.

"A key," he said, tearing open the envelope. He read the message on the Tropicana Court letterhead, then handed it to Mallory.

The instructions were simple and clear. They were to take a taxi from Grantley Adams to the Tropicana Court and use the key to get into unit 13. Rhinelander would meet them there, and after their meeting Mallory and Cooper would return to Grantley Adams for the midnight British West Indies Airline flight to Miami, connecting to an Eastern flight to Washington, D.C. The BWIA tickets would be found on the desk in their room. The note reiterated what they had been told previously: If Rhinelander became aware of any surveillance of himself or the room at the Tropicana Court, he would not appear for the meeting.

"Fair enough." Mallory nodded. It wasn't fair at all, of course, at least not as far as he was concerned. He was becoming more and more deeply involved with Cooper's subrosa escapade, and he liked it less and less with each passing day. Being party to some sort of clandestine operation involving the deputy director of operations was bad enough without the complication of involving a soft file assassin like Rhinelander. He'd seen the photographs in Paris, and he'd seen the cold, dead eyes of the man in Jamaica. Mallory had the sinking feeling that if he made it through this alive, he'd wind up explaining his actions in front of a congressional investigating committee.

Thus far the only positive note was the fact that Cooper had offered no information about the nature of the project, and Mallory, of course, had asked no questions. Still, he wasn't a fool, and all those years in Threat Analysis had jaded him severely when it came to field operations. Back then, of course, it had never occurred to him that he would one day be taking an active part in one.

Leaving the Amex kiosk, they continued on through the concourse until they reached the outer doors. Ignoring the line of strange-looking Japanese minivans waiting to shuttle incoming passengers to their hotels, they found a taxi and gave the driver the address. Like all the cabs in

Barbados, theirs was unmetered; but neither Cooper nor Mallory was interested in bartering the fare, and they agreed to the first price mentioned by the driver. Muttering under his breath about "assified" American tourists, the driver popped the clutch on the little Daihatsu sedan and flung the car into the stream of traffic heading for the highway.

By the time they reached the Tropicana Court night was falling and the sun was no more than a narrow slash of color on the western horizon. The driver, still talking to himself, sped off toward Bridgetown, leaving Cooper and Mallory at the foot of the winding stairs leading up to unit 13. Cooper slipped a hand into the side pocket of his suitcoat and gave Mallory the key. The implication was clear. If Rhinelander were waiting up there to spring some sort of trap, it would be sprung on Mallory. The deputy director's assistant started up, Cooper trailing a few steps behind.

Slightly out of breath and heart beating hard from more than simple exertion, Mallory reached the top of the stairs and walked a few paces to unit 13. Glancing over his shoulder, he saw that Cooper was waiting at the head of the stairs. He gave his boss a brief nod, inserted the key in the lock, and stepped inside. He reappeared a few moments later, poking his head around the doorframe.

"Clear," he called out softly. Cooper joined him at the door, and both men went into the unit, Mallory standing aside and closing the door after Cooper had entered.

"Sweep it," Cooper ordered. The deputy director switched on the lights in the main room and looked around carefully. Inspection complete, he went to the balcony door, slid it back, and stepped outside.

In the meantime, Mallory unlocked the handcuff on his wrist and set the metal case down on the bed. After taking a ring of keys out of his pocket, he opened the case and flipped back the lid. Inside was a second, slightly smaller case, which he also opened.

The second case contained an ISA countermeasures receiver and a separate chart and screen scanner. The receiver scanned all radio frequencies from 20 kiloHertz, which was just beyond the range of human hearing, up to 1 gigaHertz, which was the end of television and the beginning of microwave. The scanner, once connected to the receiver, offered a panoramic display of any and all radio signals in that range, detecting any evidence of snuggling, a common bugging practice in which the surveillance device uses a frequency close to that of a major radio or television station and hides in its shadow. On both chart and screen, a major carrier such as a radio station would show up as a sharp peak, with any bugs showing up as minor, subcarrier peaks close to the major signal.

109

Mallory connected the receiver to the scanner, carried both across the room to the desk, then plugged the receiver into the wall. Because of both the harsh overhead lighting and his own lack of experience, he failed to notice the tiny pinhole just beneath the plastic outlet cover.

Back at the desk he toggled the power switch and checked the display lights. A flat carrier signal appeared on the dark green monitor screen, and there was a sharp buzzing sound as a blank tongue of paper slid out of the slot at the bottom of the control panel. He adjusted the controls, then put the machine into the scan mode.

The curved line on the screen instantly jumped into a series of peaks and valleys, and the chart paper began to stream out of the machine. Mallory carefully examined both, then reached into his jacket for the *Insight Guide* book.

"Anything?" asked Cooper, stepping back into the room and closing the sliding glass door.

"Spikes at seven-ninety and nine hundred. Three FM and one television." He gestured with the guidebook. "It fits in with local radio and TV."

"Any snuggling?"

"No."

"Then the room is clean." Cooper nodded to himself and sat down at the table between the bed and the balcony door. The deputy director relaxed visibly, satisfied that they weren't under any kind of audio surveillance. His assumption was wrong, of course, since the ISA unit was capable of digging out sophisticated radio devices but was blind, deaf, and mute to the basic wire and microphone bug Rhinelander had used.

"Now what?" Mallory asked, packing up the equipment.

"Presumably our man will show up when he's satisfied that we're alone," Cooper answered. "Until then we wait."

Eric Rhinelander sat at one of the umbrella-topped tables between the bar and the pool of the Tropicana Court. He sipped his bottle of Banks beer slowly, his eyes on the square of light that marked unit 13 in the main building. A few minutes previously he'd seen the silhouetted figure of a man on the balcony. Cooper or perhaps his assistant, Mallory.

He lit a cigarette, careful to keep his face turned away from the window, even though he was shielded by the umbrella. He took a drag on the cigarette and exhaled slowly, the smoke dribbling between his parted lips and pluming from his nostrils as he considered his situation. His instincts told him not to meet the two men in unit 13. Mallory's finding him in Jamaica had been a warning; his ex-employers knew where he was and what he was doing. That was bad enough, but the fact that Cooper wanted to meet him personally was worse. The deputy director of operations for the Central Intelligence Agency did not meet with a "wet affairs" operative unless he was putting together something even the CIA didn't want to be involved in.

Rhinelander took another long drag on the cigarette, eyes drifting up to the lit window of unit 13 again. He'd gone over all the I-know-that-you-know-that-he-knows permutations a hundred times, and he still hadn't come up with any clear answer. In the final analysis, though, there were only two real possibilities: Either Cooper wanted to hire him or, for some obscure reason, Cooper wanted to kill him.

Not that it mattered very much. One way or the other his days in Jamaica were over, and one way or another he'd have to confront Cooper, so it might as well be now. He checked his watch, took a final sip of beer, then butted the cigarette into the plastic ashtray on the table. It was time.

He made his way around the pool, the rubber soles of his sneakers making small hissing noises on the water-stained concrete. He kept close to the wall, out of unit 13's line of sight, then went around the side of the building, heading for the stairs at the rear. In the darkness the only sounds came from the crickets, the sea, and the gentle wind that whispered through the leafy branches of the nearby trees.

Rhinelander reached the stairs and climbed them, two steps at a time. He reached the third floor and without hesitation went to the door of unit 13 and knocked. He hadn't risked bringing a firearm into Barbados, and it was equally unlikely that Cooper or Mallory had tried either.

The door opened. It was Mallory. He was dressed in an open-necked shirt and trousers. To the left Rhinelander could see a jacket hanging on a hook. Wise move; by taking off his jacket, the CIA man was showing that he was unarmed. Looking over Mallory's shoulder, Rhinelander could see a slim, balding man seated in a chair by the balcony door. Hudson Cooper, jacket still on and tie neatly knotted. Mallory extended a hand, which Rhinelander ignored. He closed and locked the door, then gestured to Mallory, indicating that he precede him down the short hallway between the kitchen and bathroom of the unit. Mallory did so.

As they came into the main room, Cooper rose from his seat and extended his own hand. This time Rhinelander took it. The grip was warm, firm, and dry. If the DDO was nervous or frightened, he was hiding it well.

111

"Hudson Cooper," he said, letting go of Rhinelander's hand. "We did everything you asked."

"Good." Rhinelander nodded. "We should get down to business; you don't have much time."

"No," Cooper said. "You've put us on quite a tight schedule, I'm afraid."

"It was necessary," Rhinelander replied. "Especially after the violation of my privacy a few days ago." He looked pointedly at Mallory.

"I'm sorry about that," Cooper answered. He cleared his throat and gestured to his assistant. Mallory crossed the room and leaned down as Cooper whispered something. Mallory nodded, then went out onto the balcony of the unit, shutting the sliding glass door firmly.

"You don't trust him?" Rhinelander asked.

"Of course, I trust him," Cooper said. "But this is need to know."

"I see," Rhinelander said. "What he doesn't know won't hurt him."

"Something like that," Cooper answered. He cleared his throat again, nervously. There was a short silence.

Rhinelander frowned, his expression irritated. "The whole process of arranging this meeting has taken up a lot of my time," he said quietly. "Let's not waste any more of it. Why don't you tell me what you want?"

"We want to employ your services."

"Who is 'we'?" Rhinelander asked. "The agency?"

"Not exactly," Cooper replied. "Let us simply say that 'we' is a group of highly placed and influential people."

"I was trained by several organizations, including yours, Mr. Cooper. You know what I am and what I do. Let's get to the point. You want me to kill someone. Who?"

The deputy director hesitated for a moment. After this there would be no turning back; he and the other members of the Romulus Committee would be committed. He gritted his teeth, silently cursing the twists of fate and circumstance that had brought him to this moment. Finally he spoke.

"Geoffrey James Tucker, the President of the United States," Cooper answered coldly. He kept his eyes on Rhinelander, waiting for some clue to his emotions. There was none. He simply nodded, then lit a cigarette.

"Why?" he asked a moment later, blowing out a long tail of smoke.

"He's dying," Cooper explained. "A degenerative brain disease. He'll be dead in less than a year. The disease takes the form of a progressive dementia which might prove to be . . . embarrassing, considering his position as chief executive."

"I see," Rhinelander said, his face still a mask. "Does President Tucker know that he has this disease?"

"No."

"But you do. And several others, I presume?"

"Yes."

"If Tucker dies, Vincent Teresi becomes President. I can't believe you'd want that."

"No," Cooper answered.

There was a brief moment of silence as Rhinelander digested that piece of information. He nodded to himself.

"You want me to kill them both," he said finally. He reached out and stubbed his cigarette into the ashtray on the table between them. He didn't light another.

"Yes."

"You have something in mind," Rhinelander said thoughtfully. "Something else you want to accomplish."

"Yes," Cooper replied. "We thought of having Teresi die 'accidentally,' but that still left us with the problem of Tucker's progressive dementia. A Vice President dying accidentally, a new Vice President chosen by a President whose health is ailing, and then a presidential resignation or death in office—it would be too much." The deputy director hesitated for a moment, then went on. "But we came up with another idea." He hesitated again, almost as though unwilling to say what had to be said.

"Go on," Rhinelander said. He glanced over Cooper's shoulder. Mallory was outside on the balcony, leaning on the railing and studiously presenting his back to the proceedings within the room.

Cooper spoke again. "Two months ago we were advised by our station chief in Beirut that a new terrorist group was being organized by a senior member of the Abu Nidal Group. The man's name is Nezar Assad. The focus of the group was to be the United States. We put Assad under surveillance, and ten days ago we caught him trying to enter the country illegally at the Niagara Falls border crossing. We now have Assad under protective custody. Learning of the President's tragic disability, we knew that drastic measures had to be taken, and it occurred to us that perhaps Mr. Assad could be of some assistance."

"You want to use him as an Oswald," Rhinelander said, following Cooper's line of thought. "I do the work, and he takes the fall. In the end Libya gets the blame."

"Precisely," Cooper answered. "If we had absolute proof that both the President and the Vice President had been assassinated by a Qaddafi-

113

sponsored killer, we could write our own ticket in the Middle East. Everyone would be on our side."

"When?" Rhinelander asked.

"Soon. Six to eight weeks at the most. It has to be done before the President's symptoms become more noticeable."

"Where?"

Cooper hesitated again. He and Macintyre had put the scenario together. A terrorist strike at the heart of America. An act so fundamentally violent and obscene that any form of retaliation would seem justified. It seemed like madness, sitting here with this man, but perhaps that was the object of the exercise.

"The White House," Cooper said bluntly. "For maximum effect, the Oval Office."

Rhinelander thought for a moment and then shook his head. "It may not be possible," he responded finally. "At best it would be a very, very difficult proposition."

"We concede that," Cooper said. "But as a symbolic target it's unquestionably ideal. Second best would be Camp David; third and fourth would be Air Force One or the *Sequoia*."

"I'd need to do some research before I agreed to proceed with it," Rhinelander warned. "Presidential assassins have a poor record of escaping intact."

"I can understand your hesitation."

"I'd also like a question answered," Rhinelander said.

"Certainly."

"Why me? I can think of half a dozen people with my . . . qualifications."

"Anonymity," Cooper answered. "As you say, there are a number of highly qualified people in your field. None of them is as invisible as you, however. As far as we can tell, the soft file held by our office is the only documentation of your existence on this planet. You vanished officially when you joined the Pheonix program. Since then everything about your identity has been manufactured. It's as much an asset to us as it is to you."

"Especially if the project goes wrong and I have to be erased," Rhinelander put in.

"Far more to the point is the fact that if you ran into difficulty and were captured or killed, nothing would lead back to us," Cooper responded. "Anything else?"

"Terms."

"Go on," Cooper said.

"First, understand that I haven't agreed to anything at this point. I'll do some research to see if it's feasible. If it is, I'll let you know."

"How long?" Cooper asked.

"A week, ten days at the most."

"Agreed."

"For that I want two hundred thousand dollars, up front and nonrefundable, plus the nontraceable ID I'll need to make use of it."

"Agreed."

"Any hint of surveillance by any of your people and I disappear. I need the anonymity as much as you do."

"Certainly, that's clear enough."

"Mallory, your assistant."

"What about him?"

"I deal with him only. After this he's the only one I see or have any contact with. He supplies me with anything I want."

"He's not a fool. In fact, he's already nervous," said Cooper. "To tell him any more about this is the same as signing his death warrant. He'll know that."

"He knows you want someone killed, he doesn't know who," Rhinelander answered. "Tell him something he'll believe."

"All right."

"Another thing. The final payment is going to be heavy."

"How much?" Cooper asked.

"As much as you can afford," Rhinelander answered, showing a brief, flashing smile. "I'll want it all in uncut gemstones. No diamonds; they're too hard to sell and too easy to trace. Emeralds only and nothing over a carat."

"That can be arranged," said Cooper. "Anything else?"

"Yes," Rhinelander said, his voice calm. "Cross me, make any attempt to set me up or throw me to the wolves, and I'll kill you . . . all of you."

"I understand. You have no reason for concern."

"Good." Rhinelander nodded. "Then our meeting is finished." He lit a cigarette and leaned back in his chair.

Cooper checked his watch, then went to the balcony door and rapped lightly on the glass with one knuckle. Startled, Paul Mallory turned, a surprised look on his face. Cooper crooked a finger, ordering him inside. Mallory obeyed.

**115**

"The meeting is over," Cooper said. "We should be getting back to the airport."

"Yes." Mallory nodded. He skirted the table where Rhinelander sat smoking and picked up the polished metal case containing the ISA equipment.

"Find anything with that?" Rhinelander asked.

Mallory shook his head. "Nothing," he said.

"I didn't think so." Rhinelander nodded. He turned to Cooper. "Before you leave Barbados, try the seafood platter at the Voyager restaurant in the airport. It's quite good, and there's no meal on the flight to Miami."

"Thanks for the advice. We'll do that," Cooper answered. He extended his hand to Rhinelander. "We'll be in touch," he said lamely.

A few moments later the two men had gone, leaving Rhinelander sitting alone in the room. He waited, smoking quietly, giving them time to call for a taxi from the manager's office on the main floor. After two cigarettes and a quarter of an hour he stood, turned off the lights, and left unit 13, locking the door behind him.

In unit 14 he retrieved the tape machine and pulled off the hearing aid attachment. He rewound the tape and listened for a moment. The improvised bugging device had picked up everything clearly; he had his insurance policy.

Slipping the tape into the pocket of his jeans, he went to the balcony and stepped outside. Three floors below the pool was a shimmering blue rectangle, glowing eerily, empty at this hour of the night. Faint sounds of laughter and conversation wafted up from the restaurant, and in the distance he could hear the faint pummeling echo of the waves as they struck the beach.

The tape had been essential, the covert insurance vitally important, especially now that he knew about the operation Cooper was planning. There was no way in the world a man like that would leave anything to chance. Somewhere out there Cooper had a backup, blind to the operation itself, hired to clean up loose ends when it was done, win or lose.

Rhinelander stared down at the pool, thinking about the reef. That was over now; Cooper had discovered it, destroyed it for him. So he really had no choice now; he'd see if the operation was feasible, and if it was, he'd do it. If he survived, then he'd become someone else again, go somewhere else again, and this time he'd go forever.

116

# CHAPTER 9

Sergei Yulevich Kuryokhin tightened the knot of his tie around his thin, wrinkled throat, idly glancing out the third-floor window of his apartment on Moscow's Zhdanova Street. A bright sun pouring down from a clear sky, and warm too, to judge by the light summer clothes worn by the few pedestrians on the street below. It was after nine, and the early-morning crowds heading for the metro station on Dzerzhinsky Square had long since thinned and vanished. Taking a deep breath, the white-haired, slightly stooped old man smiled happily. The apartment he had occupied for the better part of forty years was located above the Sardine Café, and today, by the succulent odors wafting through the vents, it appeared that the cooks were making *pyelmeni*, spiced, meat-filled dumplings usually served in a vegetable broth. Before going to work, he would place an order to be set aside for his dinner that evening. He shrugged on the jacket of his decades-out-of-date Bond Street-tailored three-piece suit and examined himself in the mirror hanging from his closet door. An old man certainly, there was no escaping that, but a dapper old man, by God!

Kuryokhin twisted a Lucky Strike into his old-fashioned amber holder and lit it with the Strategic Air Command Zippo lighter he'd confiscated from the U-2 pilot Francis Gary Powers in 1960. The elderly man took a long, indulgent drag and smiled. *Pyelmeni.* A good omen for the day.

After leaving his atticlike apartment, Kuryokhin placed his order with the café owner, then crossed the narrow street and went in through the main entrance of the five-story Hotel Berlin. It was another benefit of his

117

apartment's location; the Berlin was a hotel for foreign tourists, and he could buy his Lucky Strikes at the kiosk there, using hard currency.

Cigarettes purchased, Kuryokhin went back out into the sunshine, blinking behind the thick lenses of his spectacles. Humming a tuneless melody, he walked the short block to Dzerzhinsky Square and the metro. Approaching the subway entrance, he glanced at the low pink-stone building on the far side of the square. Once upon a time it really had been the center, focus of all KGB operations, both domestic and foreign, but the building had long since grown too small, even with the black marble blockhouse to the left and the annex building on the right side of the square.

Kuryokhin went down the escalator and caught a southbound train on the Green line. As chief of the KGB First Department of the First Chief Directorate Kuryokhin certainly rated one of the big Chaika sedans with the MOC license plates and a driver to go with it, but he preferred public transportation. Any KGB driver he used would probably be spying for someone else, automobiles could be bugged, and anyway, he enjoyed the quarter-hour ride beneath the Moskva River and Lenin Prospekt.

His train was almost empty except for a few ancient *babushki*, their thick, gnarled fingers gripping the handles of innumerable *sumka*, the inevitable paper and plastic shopping bags carried by the well-prepared Muscovite consumer. As the train headed deeper into the southern suburbs, the train emptied even more, and by the time Kuryokhin reached the Belyaevo station he had the car to himself.

He left the subway at the next stop, Teply Stan, the blandly named "Warm Field," which the First Chief Directorate had adopted as its headquarters. The Teply Stan metro station aboveground was a small modern glass-and-steel edifice just inside the K Ring Road on Trade Union Street. There was no other building within five hundred yards, and except for the trucks on the K Ring, there was almost no traffic at this time of day. As usual, one of the van-size dark green minibuses was waiting just outside the station, its sole purpose to ferry First Chief Directorate personnel to and from the metro station.

Flashing his pass, Kuryokhin boarded the bus, and a moment later they were in motion. The bus drove south briefly, then took an exit off the cloverleaf surrounding the K Ring. A narrow road led west into what appeared to be an isolated pine forest. As they continued west, the road began to climb slightly, the low sun broken into shattered beams by the dark branches of the trees.

Ignoring the No Smoking sign at the front of the bus, Kuryokhin lit

118

another Lucky Strike, enjoying the pastoral scenery, knowing that it would soon vanish. It did, abruptly, as the bus entered a huge clearing in the forest, a quarter mile on a side. In the center of the clearing, rising above the trees like some alien artifact was the real Teply Stan, a nine-story building constructed in three wings to form something approximating the Mercedes-Benz star. There were an additional six stories underground, including the hardened bomb shelter, and the flat roofs of all three wings sprouted a forest of telecommunications antennas. The only bare space was the rooftop helipad located at the apex of the three wings. In all, the building had space for fifteen thousand employees.

The minibus stopped at the bleak, unlandscaped main entrance to the building. Kuryokhin thanked the driver pleasantly, climbed down from the bus, and went through the tall armored-glass doors leading to the lobby. He handed his pass to the armed and uniformed officer standing in front of the metal detector gate. The officer examined the pass briefly, then handed the laminated card back and nodded toward the oval detector gate. Kuryokhin stepped through successfully.

Kuryokhin crossed the lobby, his highly polished British-made shoes tapping across the huge inlaid "Sword and Shield" insignia of the KGB. At a single elevator to the right of the main bank, he took a small key from the vest pocket of his suit, inserted it into the appropriate slot beside the elevator door, and waited. A few seconds later the door swished open, and he stepped inside. Kuryokhin tapped the button for the B-6 level, and the doors shut. Normally he would have gone directly to his ninth-floor office, but Baklinov, his man on the Washington desk, had requested a meeting in the "Egg."

The Egg, like its counterparts in most major embassies and intelligence installations, was a room-size capsule invulnerable to any and all surveillance procedures. As well as being insulated, both physically and electronically, the interior of the chamber was also swept prior to each meeting, as were all those people in attendance. In the case of the Teply Stan capsule, the chamber was located ninety-two feet underground, next to the bomb shelter hardened against nuclear weapons.

The elevator doors opened on the B-6 level, and Kuryokhin stepped out into a small vestibule manned by yet another uniformed warrant officer. The elderly man showed his pass, then turned right. He followed a narrow corridor to the large copper-lined room housing the Egg. Once more there was a guard, this one in civilian clothes. He ushered Kuryokhin through a heavy rubber-edged door, then shut it, confining the First Department chief in a small steel-walled air lock. A few seconds later the door at the other end of the tiny room opened, and he stepped into the Egg.

The chamber was twenty feet long and twelve wide, just big enough to accommodate the blond oak conference table and a dozen chairs. The walls were made of a black plastic substance, the floors were thickly carpeted in dark blue, and the only light came from four recessed panels in the ceiling. In addition to the basic furniture, there was a portable paper shredder and a water cooler. The overall effect was somber and slightly claustrophobic. Each time he entered the secured area Kuryokhin felt as through he were being buried alive.

Baklinov, seated to one side of the armchair at the head of the table, was waiting for him. The man was of medium height and broad-shouldered, his dark hair receding on both sides to form a long widow's peak. At forty-two the jowled, thick-browed man looked more like a wrestler than an intelligence officer with an academic background.

Kuryokhin sat down at the head of the table, pulling a large, cut glass ashtray closer to him. He glanced at his wristwatch. Ten-thirty and he'd had only three cigarettes since awakening; the indomitable Dr. Trepov would be pleased. The intelligence chief rewarded himself by plunging a fourth Lucky Strike into his holder and lighting it.

"Well?" he asked, turning to Baklinov.

"It concerns the report from General Gurenko," replied the Washington desk controller. "There have been developments."

"Go on."

"Travkin, the GRU deputy resident, was seen boarding a flight to Barbados in the Caribbean. He returned some twenty-four hours later."

"A brief vacation," Kuryokhin murmured, puffing on his cigarette.

"When it was discovered that he'd gone, Gurenko had a watch put on the airport. There was a late-night flight from Barbados, and there was a possibility Travkin might be returning on it. As it turned out, he wasn't, but according to Gurenko's surveillance team, Hudson Cooper was on board the flight, along with his executive assistant, a man named Mallory."

"Interesting," Kuryokhin nodded. He slouched down in the chair, eyes half closed, the cigarette in its holder pointing up to the ceiling. "The presumption, I suppose, is that Travkin had a meeting with Cooper in Barbados."

"I can't think of anything else." Baklinov shrugged. "I'd say he was being turned."

"With a man of Cooper's stature as case officer?" Kuryokhin scoffed. "Possible perhaps, but highly unlikely."

"What if Travkin specifically asked for Cooper?" Baklinov suggested.

"Why would he do that?" Kuryokhin asked, sitting forward. "And more important, once asked, why would Cooper respond?" The question hung in the air for a long moment.

Finally, frowning, Baklinov spoke up hesitantly. "Because he had something to offer?" the husky man suggested.

"Indeed." Kuryokhin nodded. One-handed, he pinched the cigarette out of its holder and stubbed out the remains in the ashtray. "I wonder what?" The old man pursed his lips thoughtfully. "We need links. Puzzle pieces."

"In his initial report Comrade General Gurenko brought up the possibility of Osin," Baklinov said delicately.

Kuryokhin shook his head. "Autumn is not a factor in this," he said slowly. "There is no way that Travkin could know anything about him." Without thinking the old man took out another cigarette and placed it in the holder. Bringing up the subject of the tapeworm was undoubtedly the reason behind Baklinov's request for a meeting in the Egg. Only a dozen people within the KGB knew about the deep-cover agent, and fewer than half that number knew the code name.

Autumn had been Kuryokhin's asset from the beginning, going back to the First Department chief's days as KGB resident in Budapest. Since then he had nurtured the agent's rise to prominence within the United States intelligence community. The old man lit his cigarette, clamping down on the worn amber holder with his teeth. Autumn was his insurance policy, the jewel in the crown of his achievements, and any thought that he might have been compromised was deeply disturbing.

"What about Travkin's interest in this man from the military hospital?" Baklinov suggested. "Could there be a connection?"

"Perhaps." Kuryokhin nodded. "But we need to know more. A list of patients treated by this man Barron, for example."

"That should be easy enough," Baklinov responded. He paused, then spoke again. "I assume that the surveillance on Comrade Colonel Travkin should be maintained."

"Certainly," said Kuryokhin. The white-haired man smiled thinly, gray eyes pale behind his eyeglasses. "But suggest to Gurenko that he try his best to keep from stepping on the toes of Gennadi Koslov. We have troubles enough without rousing that old bear."

121

"Of course," Baklinov answered, inclining his head slightly. He stood up, aware that the meeting was over, and exited, leaving Kuryokhin alone in the Egg.

"Interesting," the old man said quietly to himself. "But why Barbados?"

He sat for a few minutes, thinking hard, digging into his recent memory. Something he'd heard or read about in a monthly status report. Finally he had it. He rose from his chair and headed for the air lock door. To confirm his suspicion, he'd have to see Lemesh, his opposite number in the Second Department, handling Central America.

William Arnold Ruppelt, director of the FBI's Rednet program, sat behind his desk and listened attentively as Stephen Stone and Mort Kessler brought him up-to-date on the Travkin surveillance. Ruppelt was the ideal bureau man: Happily married with three children and a ranch–split-level in McLean, Virginia, he'd worked his way methodically up through the FBI bureaucracy, going from one field office to the next, slowly building up brownie points, taking night courses, attending special seminars, and reading all the right books. He even looked like an FBI man: slim, tall, invariably dressed in a navy or dark gray suit, wing tip shoes, conservatively cut hair in salt and pepper and bifocals for the Washington *Post*.

Behind Ruppelt an air conditioner wheezed noisily in the high, narrow window. Outside, the sun streamed mercilessly down out of a hazed blue sky. Stone grimaced; no wonder Congress began winding down as the first cherry blossoms began to fall. The city really was unfit for human habitation between mid-June and late August.

"I'm not sure I see where all of this is going," Ruppelt said as Stone finished his briefing. "Is this man Travkin going over to the Company?"

"Appearances would seem to suggest that." Stone nodded. He shifted uncomfortably in his seat. Ruppelt's wife, Connie, had done the decorating in his office, and it was full of low leather-and-chrome furniture that suited neither the high-ceilinged nineteenth-century architecture of the building nor the 1950's personality of her husband.

"But why Barbados?" Ruppelt asked, frowning.

"We think we've got that figured," Kessler answered. "Central Intelligence has no mandate to operate within the United States; Barbados makes the whole thing kosher."

"But it's still poaching," Stone insisted hotly. "Travkin's no walk-in.

He's GRU deputy resident for Washington and New York. That's our turf, and Cooper knows it. We advise the agency of our activities through the Interagency Committee; that's by presidential directive. He knows Travkin is ours."

"Perhaps Travkin came to him," Ruppelt said placatingly. "We have no control over that. The question we should be addressing is why."

"It has to be the Cabrera thing," said Kessler, glancing over at Stone.

"Cabrera?" Ruppelt asked. "Francisco Cabrera, the president of Costa Rica?"

"That's right." Stone nodded. He hadn't wanted to bring the subject up until he was sure, but Mort was right to mention it now; another five minutes, and Ruppelt would have thrown in the towel and given Travkin up without a fight.

"I'm not sure I understand," Ruppelt said, confused. "What does Costa Rica have to do with this?"

"Costa Rica is just about bankrupt," Stone explained. "Things have been going from bad to worse for years now. For the past year or so Cabrera has been playing footsies with the Soviets. Rumor has it he's offering them a Pacific port in exchange for all sorts of aid. State knows about it, and it's been backing someone named Juan José Morazán. He's chief of the Policia Nacional. Five thousand men, American-trained and -armed. It's what passes for an army in Costa Rica."

"I still don't see," Ruppelt said.

"We found something interesting when we went after Dr. Barron's patient list," Stone continued. "Three days before Dr. Barron died Morazán was at Walter Reed for some fairly serious abdominal surgery. State brought him up from San José as a courtesy; I think Morazán is a West Point graduate or something. It was kept pretty hush-hush; nothing in the papers. Anyway, as senior resident medical officer Barron was given overall control of the case, even though he wasn't doing the surgery or anything else." Stone let it hang, hoping that Ruppelt would make the association on his own. He didn't.

"Go on." The Rednet director prodded him.

"Morazán is seventy-one. From what I've been able to find out that makes him a prime candidate for this Creutzfeldt-Jakob disease Travkin was so interested in. If Morazán is on the verge of going into some sort of Alzheimer's state, that makes it a whole new ball game for State and for any kind of covert action Cooper might have had planned to install him as the new *presidente*."

"It also throws a new light on Barbados," added Kessler, sitting for-

123

ward in his chair. "There's a good chance of a third party being present at the meeting, someone from Costa Rica."

"Do Dr. Barron's records show any sign of the disease being present in Morazán?" Ruppelt asked.

"Impossible to say one way or the other." Stone shrugged. "Walter Reed won't tell us a thing, and we can't get any kind of court order because officially it's a military reservation."

"Maybe we should ask Travkin," Kessler said, his voice sour. The redheaded agent was clearly frustrated by the whole thing. "He seems to have better connections at Walter Reed than we do."

"I think we should back off the whole operation for a while," Ruppelt said calmly. "We don't want to tread on the Company's toes."

"Why not?" Stone shot back. "Cooper's treading on ours."

"That remains to be seen," said Ruppelt. He stood up, planting his palms flat on the desk in front of him, signaling the end of the meeting. "For the time being I'd like you to leave it alone. I'll bring the case up privately with Cooper at the next interagency meeting."

"When is that?" Stone asked.

Ruppelt leaned forward and flipped through the large leather-covered datebook on his desk. "Two weeks today," he said finally, looking up.

"Wonderful." Stone sighed, standing. "So what are we supposed to do for the next fourteen days?"

"At last count there were several hundred Soviet registered aliens in Washington," Ruppelt answered blandly. "Perhaps they might deserve some of your attention?"

"Come on, Stef," Kessler said, knowing when they were beaten and heading for the door. "Let's go catch some Commies."

A few minutes later the two men regrouped in Stephen Stone's office. Mort Kessler had taken a brief side trip down to canteen, returning with a plate of microwaved Danishes and two big mugs of coffee. Ignoring the hot, soggy rounds of jam-smeared pastry, Stone lit a Camel Light and sipped at his coffee.

"So now what do we do?" he asked, glancing at Kessler, seated on the other side of the desk.

The red-haired agent lifted his shoulders wearily. "I hate to say it, but the Roop is right. Dmitri Aleksandrovich isn't the only game in town. We've got at least a dozen of Gurenko's boys and girls trolling for good-ies in every fern bar around the Beltway, and we still haven't finished up with the list of known illegals working for Travkin and Koslov. Just tagging the new fish from the last embassy rollover in January could keep us going all summer."

"Statistical work." Stone grunted. "Glorified filing."

"That's the kind of thing Ruppelt likes," Kessler answered. "He's a slogger. Does things by the book." The agent made a snorting sound and took a bite out of his strawberry Danish, then spoke around the mouthful. "The last thing he wants is some kind of glitz and glamour operation. He'd crap if he ever saw his name in *Time* magazine."

"There are eighty-six people working out of this place," Stone answered. "They follow people, take pictures of people, and listen to people. I'm supposed to coordinate all that and report to Ruppelt. That's what the book says."

"So?" Kessler asked.

"So that's what I do most of the time," Stone said bitterly. "You know as well as I do that we're a watchdog operation, and we do it pretty damn well; but every once in a while we get a Dmitri Aleksandrovich Travkin."

"A player." Mort Kessler nodded.

"Exactly," Stone said, poking the air with his cigarette. "Someone who's playing the game. A challenge. And he's on to something, Mort. I can smell it from a mile off. He's on to something, and we're going to miss it."

"You think the Roop is going to hand off Dmitri to Cooper?" Kessler asked.

"Of course." Stone nodded. "It avoids a confrontation and gives him a few brownie points."

"So what do we do about it?" asked Kessler. "Buck the system?"

Stone sat back in his chair, the mechanism squeaking. Eight agencies and thirteen committees of the National Foreign Intelligence Board handled counterintelligence procedures in the United States and abroad. Like everything else in the nation's capital, the question of counterintelligence was a political and logistical maze that seemed made for professional bureaucrats like William Ruppelt. It had not, however, been created for Stephen Stone.

He knew exactly where he stood within the bureau; his only promotional opportunity was to take over from Ruppelt, a position he neither wanted nor would be given. At forty his career was blocked and he knew it, so when push came to shove, he had very little to lose. The choice was clear: Play Ruppelt's game and back off, or be the cop he wanted to be and go after Travkin. Stone sat forward in his chair again.

"It would be risky," he said at last. "Cooper is deputy director of operations. That's a nice euphemism for covert action. He wouldn't be handling Travkin personally unless the stakes were very high. The whole thing smells really political to me."

"You think it's more than Cabrera?" Kessler said, filching one of Stone's cigarettes.

"I think if we dig much deeper, we're going to find ourselves up to our necks in stuff we might not want to know about," Stone warned. "If we keep going, we're going to have to do it very, very quietly."

"That can be arranged." Kessler grinned. "You're the deputy director. Come up with an operation, give it a code name for the file jacket, and make me special agent in charge. I'll put a group of people together who can keep their mouths shut. The Roop knows I'm a floater, so he won't notice if I'm not around for a while."

"This could get us into trouble," Stone said quietly, "a lot of trouble."

"Is that an out you're offering?" Kessler asked.

"I suppose so." Stone shrugged.

"Screw it," answered the red-haired agent with a broad smile. "Anything beats counting Eastern bloc heads coming off the Aeroflots at Dulles." He butted his cigarette and took another from Stone's package. "So what are we going to call this operation anyway? It should be something nice and bland for the Roop."

"I'll check," Stone said, turning in his chair and booting up his computer terminal. Like every other division of the FBI, Rednet used a book of file code names selected randomly by computer, then arranged in alphabetical order. As a name was used, the file name was removed from the book.

"What is it?" asked Kessler watching as Stone jotted down a name from the screen.

"Couldn't be better," Stone answered, keying off the machine. "The jacket title for the file is Back Door."

On the other side of the city Dmitri Travkin was seated at an umbrella-topped table in the courtyard café of the Georgetown Four Seasons, enjoying a midafternoon glass of frosty tea. The open area was almost empty except for a few late lunchers, most of the hotel's guests preferring the air-conditioned confines of Aux Beaux Champs or high tea in the plushly decorated lobby. Dressed in a lightweight off-white Armani suit and wearing his favorite pair of Serengeti Driver sunglasses, Travkin was the quintessential Four Seasons type, and with proper Washingtonian politesse, no one paid him the slightest attention except the waiter, hoping for a better than average tip.

Sipping his iced tea, the GRU colonel tried to concentrate on the sheet of notes in front of him, making a vain attempt at giving his thoughts some kind of order before he went back to the SMO on Belmont Drive to brief Koslov on the Barbados trip, something he'd managed to avoid for the past twenty-four hours. He sighed, then lit a cigarette. On top of everything else he was being followed, and that was worrying him.

The surveillance itself wasn't the problem, he was used to Stone's Rednet squads tracking him, and he knew that Gurenko's people sometimes had him on watch as well; but Stone's FBI and Gurenko's KGB followed set patterns and routines that were as recognizable as they were easy to shrug off. Neither Stone nor Gurenko made any real attempt to keep his tracking covert. Both knew Travkin was a player in the game and let it go at that, their surveillance nothing more than flag-waving, a method of letting him know that he wasn't the only wolf in Washington walking around in sheep's clothing.

This was different. The team working his movements today had been topflight professionals, and if it hadn't been for a few very minor errors, Travkin never would have noticed he was being tailed. Even so, it was almost noon before he realized he was being tailed, and it took him another hour to identify his watchers. By the time he'd made his way to the Four Seasons he was positive that the men were neither FBI nor KGB. The cars were wrong, the clothes were wrong, and so were the routines and patterns.

So who were they, and why the sudden interest? The average American, when he thought about it at all, might be able to name four or five intelligence organizations but Travkin knew better. At last count there were twenty-four *American* intelligence organizations operating in Washington, from the standards like the CIA, DIA, and NSA to more obscure groups like the Bureau of Intelligence and Research at the State Department. On top of that there were at least fifty-seven foreign intelligence groups operating within the D.C. area, from the United Kingdom's SIS to Japan's Naicho and the Italian's SISMI. The Germans had the BND, the French had the DGSE, and the Israelis had Mossad. Even Morocco had an intelligence service—the DGED. Travkin knew that any one of these groups might be the one on his tail, but why?

Washington was a dead issue during the summer months, it was a time for staff rotations, holidays and make-work projects. Except for the regular servicing of his sources and agents the only thing he was working on that was of any interest was the Walter Reed information. Could that be it? He frowned, drawing hard on his cigarette, then glanced down at the list again. Just what did he have?

According to Scanlon, his file clerk source at the military hospital, Barron had requested information relating to Creutzfeldt-Jakob disease two nights before his "accidental" death. Late the following day the telephone billing computer at Walter Reed listed a Maryland to D.C. call. The number turned out to be that of Hudson Cooper, DDO for the CIA. Digging a little deeper, Travkin had used another source, this one in the telephone company, to get him a printout of any calls made from Cooper's regularly listed number at the Watergate for that same evening.

There were four outgoing calls that could be traced: Two were made to 703-482-1100, the main number for the Central Intelligence Agency, one went to Cooper's office number in D.C., and the fourth to Hollis Macintyre, an old-guard pork-barrel politician who'd been edged out of the Tucker administration. There was clearly a direct connection between Barron and Cooper, but that seemed to be as far as it went.

The oddest piece in the puzzle was Cooper's sudden trip to Barbados with his assistant, Paul Mallory. Unless he was having some sort of oddball gay affair with his assistant, Cooper had gone to the Caribbean island on agency business, and had done so clandestinely, traveling on a bogus diplomatic passport.

There was nothing evidential to tie the Barron telephone call to the brief Barbados sortie, but Travkin had acted on instinct and followed them. The trip had turned out to be almost a total loss, which was one of the reasons he'd been avoiding Koslov's wrath; justifying an overnight flight to the Caribbean on the monthly expense lists sent back to Moscow wasn't going to be easy.

He'd arrived in Barbados fewer than ninety minutes after Cooper and Mallory, catching a direct BWIA flight from Dulles. After discreetly spreading around some hard currency and a few plausible lies, he managed to discover that Cooper and Mallory had arrived in Barbados, then taken a taxi to a mid-price apartment hotel called the Tropicana Court. The taxi driver, a middle-aged Bajan named Leon Blaize remembered his "assified" passengers, although the night manager at the Tropicana did not.

After some delicate prodding about whom the two men might have been visiting, the manager came up with a name and a description: John

128

Duncan, a Canadian. The man had rented two apartments side by side but apparently had made no use of either. According to the manager, Duncan was dark-haired, tanned like someone who'd spent a lot of time in the tropics, in good shape, and probably in his early or mid-forties. He'd paid for both rooms in cash.

More money changed hands, and Travkin was given the keys to units 13 and 14. Thirteen was sterile, but its next-door neighbor was a little more interesting. Travkin discovered the neatly cut hole in the party wall almost immediately and matched it to the pinhole under the electrical outlet next door. Thirteen had been bugged, probably by the anonymous Mr. Duncan. After six hours of dozing in a plastic seat at Grantley Adams and another four on the flight back to Washington, Dmitri Travkin still hadn't come up with an answer that made any sense.

On the other hand, the list he'd picked up from Scanlon's dead drop earlier that day appeared to provide a clue. Travkin stared at the piece of paper on the table in front of him. One name jumped out: Juan José Morazán, chief of Costa Rica's Policia Nacional, a five-thousand man elite force that combined army, federal police, and secret police in one tidy package.

According to the most recent intelligence reports he'd read, Morazán was the chief threat to the semisecret open-port negotiations the Costa Rican government was having with Moscow and the likely figurehead for a CIA-backed coup. According to Scanlon's list, Morazán had been brought to Walter Reed for abdominal surgery and Barron had been the doctor of record.

Travkin lifted his glass to drain the last of the iced tea. He sucked an ice cube from the glass and cracked it thoughtfully between his teeth. Morazán was old, a good candidate for Creutzfeldt-Jakob disease. With its figurehead gone, how could the CIA control the Policia Nacional? A potential problem with a major Central American coup attempt was certainly enough to bring a man like Cooper out of the woodwork, and the Costa Rica connection made Barbados a little easier to understand. But where did the Canadian John Duncan fit in, and why had he seen fit to record his meeting with Cooper and Mallory secretly? The GRU colonel checked his watch. Three-fifteen: time to play the game.

He stood, reached into the breast pocket of his jacket, and took out his wallet. He dropped a five-dollar bill on the table, then began threading his way through the maze of empty tables. Out of the corner of his eye he spotted one of his tails beginning to move. Medium height, well groomed and wearing a neatly tailored gray suit. Mirrored sunglasses and

129

highly polished black dress shoes. Definitely not KGB and too short for
the FBI. Travkin had mentally tagged him as "Brooks Brother." If things
were going true to form, "Seersucker" and "Mustache" would be waiting
in the lobby. The two in the lobby had been driving a dark blue late-
model Thunderbird. If he walked, "Brooks Brother" would follow, aided
by another two-man team outside. Good, but not good enough.

Dmitri Travkin hadn't chosen the Four Seasons randomly. With parking at a premium in the Georgetown area, the hotel offered valet service
for those who could afford it, bringing the cars up from their underground lot. Arriving at the lobby entrance an hour or so before, Travkin
had slipped the driver ten dollars above the parking fee, promising another ten if he brought the car up to the entrance at exactly three-fifteen.
Even if Seersucker and Mustache were right on his heels, it would take at
least three or four minutes to bring their car up, and by then he'd be long
gone. The stunt wouldn't do much in the long run, but at least it would
flush the watchers, announcing that he knew they were there.

The valet parking attendant had been true to his word, and Travkin's
dark green embassy Chevrolet was waiting at the curb, engine running.
He palmed a folded ten-dollar bill into the young man's hand, slid behind
the wheel, and took off, wheeling the car around the brick clock tower in
front of the hotel and cutting into the traffic on M Street. A few seconds
later he bullied his way through the intersection at Twenty-ninth Street
and headed north, making for Q Street and the Dumbarton Bridge over
Rock Creek Parkway. He'd lost them, for now anyway.

# PART TWO

*I HAVE NO ENEMIES. WHY SHOULD I FEAR?*

—William McKinley

# CHAPTER 10

Eric Rhinelander arrived at Miami International Airport on an Eastern Airlines flight from Kingston, Jamaica. He wore a plain dark blue suit, carried two rust-colored canvas-sided suitcases, and used a Canadian passport identifying him as John Duncan. According to the passport, he had been born in Toronto, Ontario, on March 22, 1943, and his profession was listed as "free-lance journalist." The passport had been originally issued in November 1967 and first renewed in May 1972. Since that time, in conformance with Canadian immigration law, the passport had been renewed every five years. The passport and the documents that went with it were authentic. Duncan really had been a free-lance journalist, working out of Saigon. The young man had been killed along with eight other innocent bystanders in a bicycle bomb explosion at a sidewalk café.

Following the established practice of those days, Duncan's hotel room had been cleaned out by professional thieves within a few hours of his death, and his personal effects, including clothes, wallet, a Nikon camera, an Olivetti Lettera 22 typewriter, and a passport, had been put on the black market.

Normally, bureaucratic process rendered personal documentation useless after a relatively short period of time, but in Duncan's case he had neither next of kin nor a full-time employer, so the passport was never canceled by the Canadian government. Rhinelander had purchased the passport and wallet while in Cambodia in 1971, then renewed the passport at the Canadian Embassy in Bangkok, Thailand, in 1972, using the birth certificate from Duncan's wallet as proof of identity and providing a new set of passport photographs, these showing him with a full beard.

Since then he had renewed the passport within six months of the expiration date, always providing new photographs. Rhinelander, who preferred to develop separate identities while working on a project, used the passport only for travel, keeping the Duncan name in abeyance until it was time to leave or in case of an emergency.

Given the present situation, Rhinelander knew that the value of the Duncan persona was just about finished. Mallory had broken his cover in Paris and managed to reach him in Jamaica. Beyond that, the project at hand made the adoption of a new personality imperative. John Duncan, vaporized on a Saigon sidewalk more than twenty years before, was about to vanish again.

After using a hospitality phone to book himself a room at the Fontainebleau, Rhinelander eventually extricated himself from the steady current of people that ebbed and flowed throughout the enormous concourse and reached a cabstand. Fifteen minutes later he was on his way into Miami in air-conditioned comfort. When the driver, a Cuban from Little Havana, tried to start up a conversation, Rhinelander answered in German, and the trip was completed in silence.

Following the Airport Expressway east, they reached the Moore Park interchange, then took Florida 112 to the beach at Stearns Park. The cab joined the heavy traffic streaming onto the Julia Tuttle Causeway to Miami Beach, turned onto the concrete canyons of Collins Avenue, and finally dropped him off in front of the Fontainebleau. The enormous beachfront hotel with its twelve hundred rooms was exactly what Rhinelander wanted: complete anonymity at $150 a night.

He crossed the monumental lobby with its trademark chandeliers, checked in, arranged for a rental car, and went up to his room. It was small, plain, and ordinary, with a view of the Atlantic Ocean and the sunlit beach eighteen floors down. He ordered coffee and a copy of the Miami *Herald* from room service and spent a few minutes unpacking. Most of the clothes had been purchased in Jamaica, and although Rhinelander had long ago taken care to have any identifying tags removed, the clothes, like Duncan's passport, would soon vanish.

The coffee and newspaper arrived as Rhinelander was unpacking the last of his things. He took both to the small table beside the window, lit a cigarette, and got down to work. Turning to the birth and death announcements, he began going through the obituaries.

In Frederick Forsyth's *The Day of the Jackal*, the nameless assassin manufactures a new identity by applying for a passport in the name of a person who has died in infancy. The plot further depends on a variety of bureaucratic oversights and inadequacies as well as some simplistic and naive security measures at a variety of international airports and border crossings. Rhinelander, who had enjoyed the best seller enormously when it was published, realized that the Jackal's days, if they had ever existed at all, were long gone.

To follow Forsyth's scenario for creating a new identity now would be an invitation to disaster; computerization and centralization of records had seen to that. The scenario was also unnecessarily complicated; there were easier and less time-consuming ways of providing yourself with a brand-new name, rank, and serial number.

Rhinelander found three likely candidates in the death notices. The most promising was the obituary of a man named Holt.

HOLT, GAVIN. Suddenly, at the age of forty-three in Miami. Only child of George and Elvira Gavin of Valdosta, Wisconsin, who predeceased him. Friends may call at Baxter and Styles Funeral Home, 3205 NW 11th Ave. Funeral service at 2 P.M. July 17; cremation and interment to follow at Southern Memorial Park Cemetery, NE 151 St., North Miami. In lieu of flowers, donations to the American Heart Association will be gratefully accepted.

Checking the Miami telephone directory, Rhinelander saw only one G. Holt, with an address on Biscayne Boulevard. He dialed the number and let it ring fifteen times without an answer. Mr. Holt was definitely not at home. He turned to the yellow pages, found the number for the Southern Memorial Park Cemetery, and called. According to its directions, the cemetery was a good fifteen miles from the downtown core, almost on the borders of Dade and Broward counties.

Rhinelander glanced at his watch and saw that it was just past 1:00 P.M. The funeral service would take the better part of an hour, and the slow-moving procession would take almost that long to reach the cemetery. He had a minimum safety margin of three hours and a maximum of five. Good enough. Using the phone once again, he called down to the lobby and asked for his rental car to be brought around, then quickly put on new clothes, dressing in a pair of jeans, sneakers, a white shirt, and a lightweight brown leather bomber jacket.

Change completed, Rhinelander stripped the cases from all four pillows on the queen-size bed and packed them into a bright yellow nylon athletic bag he'd carried in his luggage. He added his Nikon F2 camera, a 250 to 500 mm zoom lens, and a pair of thin driving gloves.

Carrying the bag, he left the room, which he locked carefully behind him, then took the elevator down to the lobby. Pausing briefly, he purchased a staple-bound *Trakker's Street Atlas* for Miami, then stopped again in the flower shop, where he bought a dozen long-stemmed tea roses. Packages in hand, he crossed the lobby to the main entrance, where he picked up his rental car, an air-conditioned dark blue Pontiac Tempest.

After tipping the car jockey, he put his packages into the trunk, climbed in behind the wheel, and drove off. He pulled to a stop in the parking lot at Indian Beach only a few hundred feet away from the hotel. Turning the air conditioning up against the blistering heat outside, Rhinelander spent ten minutes examining the detailed street atlas, trying to orient himself.

According to the map, which showed street numbers block by block, Holt's address put him just slightly south of the Dolphin Expressway, facing Bicentennial Park. Using a felt marker, Rhinelander marked the spot, then climbed out into the bright sunlight and opened the trunk. Without haste he undid the ribbon around the box of roses, then emptied the bright red flowers into the trunk. He peeled back the Velcroed mat over the spare tire, lifted out the jack, and put it into the box. After opening the athletic bag, he removed the pillowcases and put them into the flower box with the jack. Exchange made, he retied the ribbon neatly, then got back into the welcome coolness of the passenger compartment.

Rhinelander drove south, following Collins Avenue into the Art Deco district with its old hotels from the thirties and forties, including the Buck Rogers spires of the Plymouth and the tangerine-striped facade of the Essex, all of them gleaming in the bright sunlight. At Fifth Street he turned west and joined the heavy traffic moving across the MacArthur Causeway to the mainland. Twenty minutes later he reached his destination, parked at a meter on NE Eleventh, and opened the trunk again. He shrugged off his jacket, unzipped the athletic bag, and took out the camera, which he fitted with the zoom lens.

Holt's address turned out to be a white-brick condominium called the Foxfire. The building was rectangular, sixteen stories high, with both above- and belowground parking. Toting the Nikon with its long lens, Rhinelander crossed Biscayne Boulevard and stepped into Bicentennial Park. The large area of grass and trees sloping down to the water was being well used, the pathways filled with mothers pushing strollers and men and women in business clothes on their lunch hours. Among the adults, like brightly colored fish darting back and forth, kids in bare feet, bandannas, and electric-hued satin shorts skimmed by on roller skates or twisted through the meandering crowds on skateboards.

In the distance Rhinelander could see the jutting masts of boats at the marina adjoining the park, and farther out in the water he could make out the giant bright white hulls of the cruise ships berthed at the Port of Miami Terminal. After making his way slowly along one of the pathways, he found a park bench and sat down. He spent a few minutes clicking off half a dozen random exposures with the empty Nikon, then turned slightly so that he was facing Biscayne Boulevard and the Foxfire. Bringing a high-powered telescope or binoculars to the park might have excited some interest, but no one paid any attention to a man with a camera.

Squinting through the lens, he adjusted the zoom until it was tight on the main door of the building. He panned back and forth slightly, as though looking for a shot, then hit the shutter release. Unless he was on a break, the Foxfire had no doorman. The entrance foyer was a blank space between two sets of glass doors with the buzzer board and mailboxes on the left-hand wall. Press half a dozen buttons and someone would probably open up, but if anybody asked questions later, it would be remembered.

Rhinelander stood up casually and strolled back up the pathway to the street. He crossed Biscayne, turned left, and went through the main doors. Checking the buzzer board, he found Gavin Holt's name: 1116. Eleventh floor. Turning away from the inner doors, Rhinelander went back out into the stunning heat, feeling the sweat begin to ooze out of every pore. In Jamaica the heat had been dry, offset by the cooling winds from the sea; here the heat was morbidly oppressive, any breath of air leaving the faint smell of rot in the nostrils. Rhinelander frowned; the sooner he was out of Miami, the better.

Returning to the car, he put the camera into the trunk and picked up the beribboned box of "roses." Instead of returning to Biscayne Boulevard and the front of the building, he turned onto Tenth Street and then onto NE First Avenue. He finally reached the wide alleyway that provided access to the rear of the Foxfire. The back of the property was a mess, overflowing Dumpsters waiting to be emptied, the asphalt on the aboveground parking lot cracked and repaired a thousand times. There was a dual ramp, one section leading up to the aboveground lot and one leading down to a battered chocolate brown metal rolling door. A sign over the garage door warned people to use their keys even if the door was open. To the left, halfway down the ramp, there was a pole with a key box jutting out.

Rhinelander walked up the ramp to the aboveground lot, put the flower box down on the ground, and lit a cigarette. Leaning on the guardrail, he smoked and waited. Less than five minutes later a car came down the alley, turned onto the down ramp, and stopped at the key box. The driver rolled down his window, inserted his key, and a few seconds later there was a creaking, rumbling noise as the garage door rolled up.

As the car moved forward again, Rhinelander glanced at his watch and leaned over the railing. The car disappeared into the underground lot, and after a short pause the door began to close again. The whole process took twenty-one seconds—plenty of time.

Ten minutes later another car turned down the alley and headed for the ramp. Rhinelander bent down, picked up the flower box, and began strolling down the upper ramp. By the time he reached the alleyway, the driver of the second car had already keyed the box. Rhinelander turned and began walking down the alley, listening to the sounds of the door cranking upward. He did a slow count to ten, giving the vehicle enough time to get into the garage, then turned on his heel and sprinted for the lower ramp. He reached it with time to spare and ducked under the closing door. Squinting in the sudden darkness, he saw the taillights of the car he'd followed.

He waited in the shadows of a concrete pillar, while the driver parked, then left his car. Rhinelander watched as the man crossed the lot to a bank of elevators, lit brightly from above by a sulfurous high-intensity spotlight. The security light was a joke since the main illumination for the lot was provided by strips of fluorescent bulbs, most of which had burned out.

Rhinelander watched as the elevator arrived and the driver disappeared. He waited another few seconds, then walked forward casually. Anyone coming into the garage now, either from outside or via the elevators, would assume he'd just parked his car. He reached the elevators, punched the up button, and waited. A few moments later the light went off, a bell chimed, and the doors of the elevator on his right opened. He stepped into the empty cage, tapped the eleventh-floor button, and adjusted the weight of the flower box.

He rode up without anyone else entering the elevator, then stepped out into the eleventh-floor corridor. The floors were covered in good-quality dark blue carpeting, and it looked as though the off-white walls had been painted recently. Between every apartment there was a bright globe fixture bracketed to the wall, and there was a faint smell of room deodorizer in the air. The parking lot below was no hell, but someone was keeping the visible maintenance up to scratch.

Holt's apartment was at the end of the hall, directly opposite the stairwell door. Good, Rhinelander thought, nodding to himself, only one adjoining wall. Without hesitation he pulled the ribbon off the box, opened it, and took out the automobile jack and the pillowcases. He formed the pillowcases into two thick pads, lifted the jack, placed it horizontally across the door, the butt end facing the doorframe just above the knob, and slipped the folded pillowcases into position between the jack ends and the metal frame. Holding everything in place with one hand, he worked the crank on the handle until the jack was firmly wedged against the doorframe. Checking the hallway, he began to crank again, grunting with effort as the pressure built.

The technique utilized by the assassin was well known by the security and insurance industries but rarely mentioned to prospective new home buyers. As Rhinelander knew, modern construction methods leave a lot to be desired. To avoid complications and facilitate volume buying of door and frame combinations, the buck, or hole cut for a door, is often made oversize, usually by one or two inches.

When the frame and door are installed, the space between the edge of the buck and the frame are filled with wooden wedges at two or three points, then plastered over. In a relatively short period of time the wedges loosen after repeated opening and closing of the door, and the frame begins to float in the resulting air space.

With the jack the frame is bent outward into the air space, and in the case of Holt's door, only three quarters of an inch was necessary. The Schlage Series B locking unit was quite a good one, with a five-pin tumbler and a dead bolt, but its qualities were irrelevant. Forty-two seconds after Rhinelander inserted the jack, Gavin Holt's door yawned open all by itself.

With another check down the hall, Rhinelander used the side of his foot to sweep the flower box into the apartment, then hit the jack release with the heel of his hand. He pulled the jack out of the frame, threw the wadded pillowcases after the flower box, and stepped into the apartment. He closed the door, holding it shut until the frame settled back into its normal position. He was in. He picked up the jack, pillowcases, and flower box, set them on a low wooden table beside the doorway, then began to explore.

The apartment was large and brightly lit by windows on two sides. To the left of the front door was a narrow galley-style kitchen, and there was a powder room on the right. Beyond the foyer, directly ahead was the living room, complete with a balcony looking out over Biscayne Boulevard to the park beyond. There was a master bedroom with an en suite four-piece bathroom between the living room and the dining room and a short hall leading to the wood-paneled den at the corner of the building.

Except for the bathrooms and kitchen the floors throughout the apartment were covered in short-pile dark gray carpeting. The walls were bright white except for the bedroom, which was a deep, almost institutional green. The furniture was Industrial style: black-enameled pole lamps; leather-and-chrome chairs and couches; a slab of marble resting on a pastel-painted sonotube. The kitchen was done in deep blue Formica, outfitted with half a dozen high tech appliances and a gigantic double-door jet black refrigerator.

To Rhinelander, the most telling of the rooms was the den. Two walls were taken up by floor-to-ceiling bookcases. A third wall held a computer table, a pen-plotter drafting table, and filing cabinets, while the fourth was mostly window. A quick check of the files and the book titles gave him Gavin Holt's occupation: He was an architect, specializing in medium-size and small medical institutions like clinics, rest homes, and walk-in dental suites. Flipping through some of the files, Rhinelander saw that Holt had an office address in the CenTrust Tower. To judge by the quality of the furnishings and the sophisticated at-home computer array, it was clear that he had been doing well.

In a folder tabbed "Personal Banking" he found a neatly typed list of code numbers for half a dozen credit and cash cards as well as up-to-date bank statements and credit card receipts. According to the receipts, all the cards were up-to-date. Rhinelander copied the code numbers down on a sheet of paper from a scratch pad on the desk and slipped it into his pocket. There was also a file marked "Legal," but there was no evidence of a will. If Holt had died intestate, his affairs would be handled by a Dade County public trustee, turning the resolution of the dead man's estate into a lengthy bureaucratic process that could take weeks or even months. Rhinelander nodded to himself, pleased.

Holt's attaché case was stowed neatly between the drafting table and filing cabinets. Opening it, Rhinelander discovered several trade magazines, an address book, several pens, and, in a rear pocket, Holt's passport. Turning to the first page, Rhinelander stared at the dead man's photograph. He was thin-faced with a narrow mustache and balding.

There was no resemblance to Rhinelander, but the description was reasonably close: "Hair—dark brown, Eyes—blue, Height—6'1"." With a new photograph, carefully removed from the Duncan passport, it would do well enough. Rhinelander put the passport back in the pocket of the attaché case, added a few random pages from the filing cabinet and several books from the shelves on the far wall, then closed the case, which he took to the bedroom.

Rhinelander went through the room slowly and methodically, his methods based on long experience. The bedroom cupboard, half the length of the room, with mirrored doors, revealed a dozen tailor-made suits and half that many sports jackets. Shelves above held shirts, folded and wrapped in plastic, printed with the name of a local dry cleaner. Below the hanging suits and jackets was a row of shoes, from Florsheim wing tips to tennis shoes. The cupboard also held a bagged set of golf clubs, a pair of dumbbells, and a leather racquet bag. The racquet bag held a Slazenger squash racquet, a can of balls, and a pair of expensive-looking protective goggles. There was no sign of wear on the racquet handgrip, and the can of balls was still sealed. On the other hand, the golf clubs had obviously seen long use.

He began going through the inner and outer pockets of the suit jackets and hit pay dirt on the second one in from the left: a ring of keys and Gavin Holt's wallet, complete with credit cards, driver's license, Social Security card, library card from the main branch at the Metro-Dade Cultural Center, and the pink slip for a 1957 Austin-Healey sports car. Wallet in hand, Rhinelander turned and looked around the room, remembering the obituary.

Donations to the Heart Association. Holt had probably died in the apartment, victim of a heart attack. Friend, neighbor, or co-worker had discovered the body and made the funeral arrangements. You don't need ID to check into a funeral home, and as far as Rhinelander knew, people weren't buried carrying their wallets. The same was true of the passport. The chances were good that the wallet and its contents wouldn't be missed for some time, if at all.

He shoved the billfold into the hip pocket of his jeans and continued his search. Gold Dunhill lighter with the initials G. H., matchbook from Joe's Stone Crab in Miami Beach, half a roll of spearmint Life Savers and a Cross ball-point done in brushed steel. Rhinelander took them all. Search complete, he pulled out the golf bag and a large black hard-bodied suitcase from the interior of the cupboard.

Rhinelander snapped open the Samsonite and flipped it open onto the bed. He dumped the contents of Holt's other pockets into the suitcase, then went back to the cupboard. Checking the sizes on the shirt collars, he saw that they'd fit and tossed half a dozen into the suitcase. He then went through the man's chest of drawers and added Jockeys, dark socks, two pairs of cuff links, and several folded handkerchiefs. Both handkerchiefs and cuff links were initialed like the lighter.

With his foraging done Rhinelander closed the suitcase and took a last look around the room. Everything was as it had been. Satisfied, he picked up the suitcase and hefted the golf bag, then took both to the foyer. He glanced at his watch. Two-thirty; he'd been in the apartment for slightly more than half an hour—still plenty of time. He went back to the den, sat down at Holt's desk, and rummaged through the drawers until he found a Miami-Dade telephone directory.

According to the phone book, the Florida Department of Motor Vehicles office was located in the Metro-Dade Center on NE First Street. He punched out the number, and after three different referrals he had the information he wanted. In the case of a lost driver's license, a replacement could be provided on the spot as long as you had a birth certificate, Social Security number, and the original number of the driver's license that had been lost. Pleased, Rhinelander hung up the telephone and stood up. If things continued to go smoothly, he'd have usable photo ID before the day was out.

Fifteen minutes later, after another check to make sure that the apartment was in order, Rhinelander left the Foxfire, this time using the front door. He had the suitcase in one hand and the golf bag over his shoulder—just another upscale Miamian starting out on a golf vacation. Reaching the rental car, he opened the trunk, removed the automobile jack from the golf bag, and put it back in its proper niche. He put the suitcase and golf bag in the trunk, closed it, climbed into the car, and started the engine and the air conditioning.

Lighting a cigarette, Rhinelander again consulted the street guide and found the Metro-Dade Center. Marking the location with his felt pen, he put the car in drive and eased out into the mid-afternoon traffic. An hour later, his new driver's license replacing Holt's old one, Rhinelander headed back to Miami Beach and the Fontainebleau Hotel.

The following morning Rhinelander returned the rental Tempest, checked out of the hotel, and took the airport shuttle to Miami International. Using one of the pay toilet booths on the arrivals level, he carefully destroyed all his John Duncan ID, including the passport, then flushed the remnants into oblivion.

He returned to the crowded concourse and went to the Citibank cash machine, where he inserted Holt's MasterCard. He tapped out the code from the list he'd copied and waited. A few moments later two hundred dollars spit obediently out of the slot. Rhinelander put the cash and the card in Holt's wallet. If the MasterCard hadn't been canceled, the other credit cards were probably serviceable as well.

From the cash machine Rhinelander continued down the concourse to the American Express travel booth and purchased three thousand dollars worth of traveler's checks—half the maximum allowed on Holt's gold card. The transaction went off without any problems. With the traveler's checks in his wallet he doubled back to the Hertz counter and rented a black air-conditioned Lincoln Continental.

While he waited for the car to be brought up from the garage, Rhinelander jotted down a detailed set of directions given to him by the reservations clerk, along with a complimentary road map of Florida. Five minutes later he was driving east on the Airport Expressway, and fifteen minutes after that he reached the Highway 95 interchange and went north, heading for the next stop on his itinerary: Palm Beach and the Breakers Hotel.

# CHAPTER 11

Washington's Au Pied de Cochon is an "authentic" French bistro on Wisconsin Avenue between Dumbarton and N Street. There are half a dozen "authentic" restaurants of one kind or another in the same area, including Aux Fruits de Mer next door and the Georgetown Bar and Grill across the street, but Au Pied is the only one open twenty-four hours a day. The food is cheap and reasonably good, the service is adequate, and the quasi-French atmosphere comes complete with a sidewalk patio, zinc bar, checkered tablecloths, and café-crème served up in enormous bowls. It has also been the site of a number of Soviet defections over the years, the fact commemorated by a brass plaque beside the unassuming front entrance.

"The CIA are children," commented Major General Gennadi Koslov. The GRU resident tore off a piece of his croissant, popped it into his mouth, and washed it down with a long swallow of coffee. Squinting in the bright sunlight, he watched the early-morning tourists parading by a few feet away on the sidewalk side of the patio. He shook his head. "Yurchenko and his Central Intelligence escort were having dinner here after his so-called defection and the escort just let him walk away." Koslov laughed heartily and popped another piece of croissant into his mouth. "He actually walked back to Mount Alto!"

Vitaly Yurchenko, Sergei Kuryokhin's deputy in the First Chief Directorate, had "defected" in Rome in August 1985. Three months later he redefected, giving a Washington press conference at which he insisted he'd been kidnapped and drugged by the Americans. The incident had been horribly embarrassing for both the CIA and the FBI and a major "disinformation" coup for Kuryokhin and the KGB.

"I think you underestimate the agency," said Travkin, lighting a cigarette and ignoring the bowl of coffee on the table in front of him. "They simply play by a different set of rules. Yurchenko was supposedly a defector, not a prisoner. The only way his baby-sitter could have stopped him was by main force."

"They were fools!" growled Travkin's bullnecked superior. "The whole thing was an exercise in triplethink. The CIA had spent years trying to track down Kuryokhin's mythical asset within their midst and had come to the conclusion that there was no tapeworm or mole at all. Yurchenko defects, then tells them that they are right. Soon after Yurchenko returns to the fold, thus negating any information he gave to the CIA. Central Intelligence therefore assumes that Yurchenko was lying and that there really is a tapeworm in their midst. The myth is maintained, the CIA's paranoia increases, and more time, money, and effort are wasted trying to track down the nonexistent agent of influence. Absurd!"

"You give Comrade Kuryokhin a great deal of credit," Travkin said.

"Unlimited credit," Koslov replied. "Our friend Sergei has taken the fine art of bullshit to new heights." The old man shrugged wearily. "And why not," he asked rhetorically, "considering the fact that with the Central Intelligence Agency and the FBI he has an audience willing to accept any sort of simpleminded twaddle he produces?"

"What about Cooper?" Travkin asked, bringing the conversation back to the subject at hand.

"You give me nothing but a few unconnected facts and suppositions, Dmitri Aleksandrovich," Koslov answered. "I'll need more if you expect me to act." The old man's bushy eyebrows arched, and he rubbed one white-whiskered jowl with a thick-fingered hand. "And frankly, Dmitri, your recent escapade in Barbados does little for your credibility."

"It was necessary and useful," Travkin insisted. He pushed his coffee aside and leaned over the table. "Recent information bears that out."

"Really?" Koslov replied, acid in his tone. "Is it information I can use on a budget report to explain your little 'holiday'?"

"Cooper and Mallory went to Barbados, where they met with a man named Duncan. The fact that Cooper was personally involved in such a rendezvous is suspect in itself. The operation with Duncan is an important one."

"Who is this man Duncan?" Koslov asked. "Do we know anything?"

145

"According to his passport, he is Canadian, a journalist."

"What does Ottawa have to say about him?"

"I cabled Kamenev; he has illegals in the passport office there as well as their National Revenue department. John Duncan was a free-lance journalist who went to Vietnam during the early part of the war. He has renewed the passport several times since then but has never spent any time in the country."

"So?"

"So this John Duncan has not filed an income tax return since 1969."

"Black-market documents?" Koslov asked.

"Presumably." Travkin nodded. "Whatever the case, the man who met with Cooper and Mallory was no free-lance journalist."

"And where is he now?"

"Here," Travkin answered. "Or Miami at any rate. I checked with Intourist; he came in on an Eastern Airlines flight from Kingston, Jamaica, the day before yesterday."

Tracking Duncan hadn't been difficult; Intourist, the state travel authority operated like any other travel agency and used Pegasus, the International Association of Travel Agents' reservation computer program. Using Duncan's name and the Caribbean as point of origin, Intourist had come up with the Miami arrival almost instantly. Running behind Pegasus was a separate, clandestine program, a worm that effectively blanked out the original request for information.

"So tell me," said Koslov, leaning back in his chair and lighting an Opal, "what is your theory about this man?"

"I think Duncan is a killer, an assassin hired by Cooper. My information from Walter Reed points to Juan José Morazán's having a degenerative brain disorder. We already have information regarding Morazán's connection to the CIA. A coup has been expected for some time now. We are presently in the midst of negotiations with Francisco Cabrera, president of Costa Rica. If the negotiations are successful, we will have an open port in Pacific Central America. Such a port will increase our presence in Central America greatly, consequently lowering United States prestige in the same area. Since the European shift Central America has become strategically key. Highly sensitive. The United States will do whatever it can to delay our intrusion. It could well be another Cuba or even a Vietnam. Such a confrontational situation could be disastrous for everyone."

"There is sense in what you say," Koslov said, nodding. "Go on."

"Cabrera comes to Washington in a month for talks with President

146

Tucker, a state visit with all the trimmings. I think this man Duncan will attempt an assassination."

"You think Cooper has planned this?" Koslov asked.

"Yes," Travkin said firmly.

"No." Koslov shook his large head. "It would be counterproductive. Cabrera is a leftist; he would be transformed into a martyr overnight."

"That worried me, too," Travkin replied, "until I did some research into Cabrera's past. As a martyr he would be somewhat flawed."

"Why?"

"There is a definite link between Cabrera and a man named George Morales, a Colombian drug dealer convicted in Miami. There is also a connection between Cabrera and the Nugan Hand bank. It would take very little to turn Cabrera the leftist into Cabrera the drug kingpin. Costa Rica's wealth, what there is left of it, is controlled by no more than twenty old-guard families, and half of them are involved in the drug trade; Cabrera's murder could reasonably be laid at the doorstep of any one of them. With Cabrera dead, Morazán could justifiably declare martial law, and that would be the end of our Pacific port."

"And you assume such a plot is imminent?"

"Speed is of the essence." Travkin nodded. "Morazán is dying. With Cabrera out of the country there will be no better opportunity. With martial law declared Morazán could step down or be made to step down, and a puppet installed in his place. It wouldn't be the first time the CIA has been involved in such an action. There is even a historical precedent: Cooper was part of the operations group to destabilize the Figueres regime in 1955. He knows the territory."

"It would seem that you've done your homework Dmitri Aleksandrovich," Koslov murmured.

"It fits," Travkin insisted. "It all fits."

"Perhaps," Koslov answered. He stubbed his cigarette out in the buttery remains of his croissant. "But it is not our concern."

"What?"

"It is not our concern," the general repeated. "You are deputy resident for the GRU in Washington. Your job, and mine, is to collect intelligence information of a technical nature which might be of value to the military. Your flight of fancy regarding Señor Morazán and Señor Cabrera does not fall within our mandate. If anything, it is a job for Elder Brother."

"The KGB has had cold feet about Central America since the Cuban missile crisis." Travkin snorted. "Gurenko wouldn't touch this information with a ten-foot pole."

"Nor will I," Koslov replied dryly. "Consider this," the old man continued. "Assuming for the moment that you are right, what should we do? The Central Intelligence Agency hires a killer to assassinate the *presidente* of Costa Rica. The chances are good that they would fail, but fail or succeed, there would be an investigation. What would happen when such an investigation revealed that we were involved, no matter how innocently? You're not describing a potentially valuable GRU operation, Dmitri; you are laying the groundwork for a trip to the incinerator at Khodinka."

"Then what do we do?" Travkin asked.

"Nothing," Koslov answered. *"Pravda ne isvestia i isvestia ne pravda."* The white-haired man laughed, quoting the old joke, a pun on the names of the two state newspapers. "Truth isn't news and news isn't truth."

The general wagged a thick, nicotine-stained finger at Travkin. "But true or not, I don't want to see my name in an American newspaper; I am looking forward to an easy death, pickled in vodka at my dacha in Podolsk."

"There is one other thing," said Travkin. "I'm under surveillance."

"So?" Koslov shrugged. "We watch Gurenko, Gurenko watches us, and the FBI watches everybody."

"It's not the KGB, and it's not Stone's people either."

"Really?" Koslov asked, interested. "Who then?"

"I'm not sure, but at a guess I'd say they're CIA," Travkin responded.

*"Yeb moy!"* said the general, cursing under his breath. "How long?"

"Since I returned from Barbados."

"A caboose?" Koslov asked, using the Russian term.

"Perhaps," Travkin answered weakly. A caboose was an agent who kept a colleague under surveillance from a distance in an effort to see if the man he was watching was being followed by an enemy.

"Of course it was," Koslov said, scorn in his voice. "They set him at the airport there, and he saw you follow Cooper in. Damn it, Dmitri! You should have been watching for something like that!"

"I was in a hurry," Travkin answered, knowing the excuse was laughably weak. Part of his job as deputy resident was training GRU staff to recognize just that kind of procedure. Koslov was right; it was inexcusable.

"Do they know you've flushed them?"

"I believe so, General," Travkin said stiffly, retreating into formality.

"What about your apartment?" asked the grim-faced resident.

"Sir?"

"Has it been bugged?"

"I don't know," Travkin answered, shaking his head.

Koslov sighed. "I want you out of there and into Belmont Road by this evening," said the old man. "You can use the courier's quarters."

"It is only surveillance, General," Travkin countered. "I don't think I'm in any present danger." The thought of camping out in the dingy attic apartment at the Soviet Military Office was enough to make the deputy resident's skin crawl. Dust balls under the bed and battery acid disguised as coffee from the cafeteria.

"To hell with present danger!" Koslov snapped. "This is a question of security. If Cooper is staging some sort of assassination plot, we must be completely removed from it. If I had any sense, I'd insist that you take two weeks' leave at home, just to get you out of the way."

"For how long?" Travkin asked.

"For as long as it takes!" Koslov answered. "At least until this man Cabrera has returned home."

"*If* he returns home," Travkin said.

"The fate of a banana republic head of state is no longer a question that should interest you." Koslov grunted. "Put your time to good use and prepare that report on the New York illegals you've been promising me for the last month."

"Yes, General," Travkin replied, trying to inject a humble note into his voice. The general was letting him off easily and he knew it; a week or so on Belmont Road was a mild punishment compared with what Koslov could have done. On the other hand, there were some unresolved questions Travkin still wanted answered. He banished the thought from his mind and stood up. Koslov might be an old friend of the family, but first and foremost he was a general in the GRU and not someone to cross. If he continued his investigations after being directly ordered not to, the frog-faced old man was capable of inflicting serious damage to his career.

Jamming one hand into his pocket, Travkin made a mildly obscene gesture with his balled fist and bowed tightly to his superior. "I'll pack some things and bring them to Belmont Road immediately," he said.

"Good." Koslov nodded, frowning. "And I'll have none of your impudence, Dmitri," he added. "I was making *figa v. karmane* to my superiors before you were born." Travkin's fist opened in his pocket as though he'd been clutching a hot coal. "If you wish to say something to me," Koslov continued, "say it to my face and not from your trousers; it is most definitely *ne kulturney*."

"Yes, sir," Travkin answered.

"All right." The General nodded. "Enough indigestion for one day." Koslov lit another Opal and made a dismissing gesture with one hand. "Leave me in peace now; I'll see you this afternoon in my office."

"As you wish, General," Travkin answered stiffly. He turned on his heel and threaded his way through the maze of tables to the street. He decided against taking a taxi back to his apartment and turned south; there was still an early-morning freshness in the air, and the walk would do him good. At the very least it might serve to work off some of his frustration.

Seen through the tinted glass of the limousine's windows, the streets of downtown Washington slipped soundlessly by like a smoked gray dream. In the sealed rear passenger compartment of the Kevlar-lined bulletproof Lincoln, Hollis Macintyre listened to Hudson Cooper's report as he relaxed in air-conditioned comfort, oblivious of the heat and humidity being endured by the capital's less fortunate citizenry. The vehicle, complete with driver, was nominally attached to the executive garage, but Joseph Swanbridge, using his authority as secretary of state, had had the car assigned to Macintyre on permanent loan, listing the aging politician as a "senior adviser."

"From what you say it would appear that there are cracks in your security," the enormously fat man said quietly.

Seated across from him, a glass of mineral water in his hands, Hudson Cooper shrugged. "An unfortunate coincidence," the balding CIA executive responded. "We had no idea that the GRU had an asset at Walter Reed."

"Or that the GRU man in question was part of an ongoing watch program by the Rednet group." Macintyre grunted, irritation in his voice. "The skein we've been weaving seems to be unraveling, Hudson."

"It can be gathered in again," Cooper said. He sipped from his glass. The limousine was whispering across the Arlington Memorial Bridge, the distant bulk of the Pentagon squatting like a gigantic bunker to the south. Glancing through the window, Cooper found himself wondering what the massive building would look like in a thousand years: a brooding, dangerous ruin, its history clouded in myth? Or a museum filled with dusty icons from an angrier time?

150

"How much does this man Travkin actually know?" Macintyre asked. The Lincoln came off the bridge and turned north onto the George Washington Parkway.

"Very little in terms of verifiable fact," Cooper replied. "He clearly assumes that one of Dr. Barron's patients at Walter Reed has Creutzfeldt-Jakob disease. He also knows that Barron telephoned you, and presumably he also knows that you telephoned me. He was serious enough to follow Mallory and me to Barbados, so we can assume that he has some information about our man Rhinelander."

"And Stone, the FBI man?" Macintyre queried.

"Ruppelt was very quick to hand off the information," Cooper said slowly. "He's a bureaucrat willing to do anything to keep his job. The last thing he wants to do is stick his face into an agency operation. He didn't come right out and ask, but I'm fairly sure he thinks we're about to catch Travkin."

"A defection?" Macintyre asked.

"Yes." Cooper nodded. "And I didn't say anything to make him think any differently. According to Ruppelt, Stone thinks all of this activity has something to do with Francisco Cabrera."

"The Costa Rican? Why?"

"We've got an ongoing situation with Juan José Morazán, Cabrera's *jefe* of the Policia Nacional. Morazán was in Walter Reed at the same time the President was in for his checkup."

"Morazán was one of Barron's patients?" Macintyre asked, eyes widening.

"Not directly, but as senior resident medical officer Barron was officially in charge of admitting him."

"So Stone thinks that Morazán has the disease?"

"It seems that way." Cooper nodded. "I hope Travkin thinks the same as well."

"What *is* wrong with Morazán?" asked Macintyre.

Cooper laughed briefly. "That's the irony," he said. "Stone and Travkin aren't too far off the mark. There's nothing wrong with Morazán at all. We had him up here for a briefing, and the medical cover seemed like a good idea. From what Ruppelt told me, Stone thinks Morazán has the disease, which is throwing a wrench into our plan to get rid of Cabrera because of his upcoming deal with the Soviets."

"So you think the Russians have the same idea?"

"Probably," Cooper answered. "In which case they'll back off completely."

151

"You think so?" Macintyre asked, one eyebrow lifting.

"Absolutely," Cooper said firmly. "The Central American situation is far too fragile for them to prejudice by involving themselves in a CIA wet operation. They'll stand back and wait to see what happens."

The limousine reached the Fairfax County line and followed the turnpike as it eased to the south. In a few minutes they'd reach the Chain Bridge turnoff to Langley. Macintyre stroked the side of his nose with one delicate forefinger and looked thoughtfully out the window.

"The Russian has the wrong idea, but he's too close. He has to be taken out," the fat man said at last, hand returning to nest with its mate on the broad expanse of gabardine-enclosed gut.

"I agree." Cooper nodded.

"Can it be done safely, without undue exposure?"

"I believe so," Cooper answered. "Ruppelt is expecting a defection. . . . I think we should give it to him."

"What about Travkin's people?"

"We can make it play," said Cooper. "Travkin's an oddball—expensive dresser, very Westernized. Koslov at the GRU might have his doubts, but the KGB will buy it."

"You have a procedure?" Macintyre asked.

Cooper nodded. "It's already in progress."

"Any other problems?"

"None that I can see." Cooper shrugged. "Ruppelt has already taken his people off Travkin, and with the Russian out of the picture Stone won't be able to do anything with the little bit of information he has on hand." The Lincoln reached the Chain Bridge interchange and drifted onto the exit ramp. A large green sign announced that the 123 exit led to the Federal Highway Administration and the Central Intelligence Agency.

"What about your assistant . . . Mallory?" Macintyre asked.

"I gave him the Cabrera-Morazán scenario along with a few extras," replied Cooper, "a drug-related situation that connects the station chief in Barbados to Costa Rica and the Nugan Hand bank scandal." The CIA man drained the last of his mineral water, then continued. "It's thin, but it should hold up while he's staging Rhinelander."

"And then?"

"And then he retires," Cooper replied, his voice cold. "Permanently." The deputy director of operations stared at the man seated across from him. "Don't worry, Hollis. Everything is covered."

"I hope so," said Macintyre, his lips pursed. "For all our sakes."

\*   \*   \*

Paul Mallory, coffee in hand and still dressed in dressing gown and slippers, watched the passing traffic on Alexandria's King Street from his second-floor apartment. Even before he'd become Hudson Cooper's assistant, Mallory had been able to afford better than the one-bedroom apartment above a store on the narrow, bustling street, but it had been his first home after leaving MIT, and moving had always seemed more trouble than it was worth.

To some people at the agency, Mallory's single status so late in life might have been cause for suspicion, but a full-scale investigation by the Human Resources Division prior to the Cooper job had come up with nothing. The search revealed that Mallory had never been particularly good with women and in fact had little real interest in them. He didn't appear to have any gay leanings either, and the investigators finally came to the conclusion that Paul Mallory was exactly what he seemed to be: a highly intelligent man who was a genius with computers and whose only vice was collecting paperback murder mysteries and thrillers.

The balding, slightly stooped man turned away from the high bay window and shuffled along beside the floor-to-ceiling brick-and-board bookcases that filled the side wall of his living room. Sipping at the cooling coffee in his mug, he glanced at the titles on the shelves, enjoying their familiarity.

True to his methodical nature, Mallory's collection was arranged first by genre, then by subject matter, and finally by author, alphabetically. Ludlum and Littell were classed as "Espionage Thrillers/U.S.," Fleming as "Espionage/U.K.," John D. MacDonald as "Action/Adventure/U.S.," and Christie, P. D. James, and Ruth Rendell as "Murder Mystery/U.K." There were a dozen other categories and more than one hundred authors represented in the five-thousand-volume collection, each book carefully logged onto a catalog program of his own invention and stored in the custom-built 386 megabyte IBM system set up on the opposite side of the room.

In addition to simply cataloging the books, Mallory had broken each volume down, listing accurate and inaccurate terminology used, interesting technology and procedure, and any other information he thought might be useful. He'd begun "editing" his books shortly after reading *Six Days of the Condor,* in which a foundation supposedly funded by the CIA actually does go through books looking for information. The novel was eventually made into a film starring Robert Redford.

At first Mallory's breakdowns of the books he purchased had been done out of curiosity, but shortly after he'd begun, he discovered that there were a number of groups involved in role-playing games via computer. Five years ago there had been only a few hundred, and none devoted to spies or mysteries. Now there were more than ten thousand electronic role-playing bulletin boards nationwide, with several hundred falling into the mystery and espionage category. Each member of a group had his own password to log onto the bulletin board and his own role to play in an ongoing game. In the beginning Mallory had logged onto every bulletin board he could find, but now he'd cut himself back to fewer than ten, all of them very sophisticated with some of the games lasting for months.

Frowning, Mallory turned and crossed the room to his work station. The computer was on, the cursor on the amber screen blinking impatiently. Using his free hand, the CIA man pushed his glasses back up on his nose and sighed. He had to confront it and deal with the situation; that's why he'd called in sick after all. But not quite yet.

"One more cup of coffee," he muttered. He left the living room and went down the narrow hall to the galley kitchen. After rinsing out his mug, he poured a fresh dose from the Braun and added cream. Carrying the mug with him, he followed the hallway past the stairs leading down to the ground-floor entrance and went into his bedroom.

It was small, barely more than a cell, with a small window facing the littered alleyway behind the building. Mallory dressed quickly, slipping on a worn MIT sweat shirt and an ancient pair of blue nylon track pants dating back to his high school days. He let out a brief ironic chuckle. What would Mr. Colfax say now? From failed jock to super agent six.

An ex-fighter pilot in Korea, the slab-muscled physical education teacher had laughed at the spindle-legged kid trying out for the track team, calling him a variety of things ranging from four-eyed wimp to needle-shanked nerd. He'd been right, of course, and Mallory didn't make it beyond the first cut, but he'd never forgiven Colfax for judging him before he'd had a chance to prove himself.

Mallory snorted, pulling the drawstring tight around the waist. He picked up his coffee and headed back to the living room. To hell with the past and people like Ernie Colfax. This was beyond name-calling, and the stakes were a lot higher than a place on the team and a letter on his sweater. But the anger was the same; Hudson Haines Cooper had judged him a fool and had done so unwisely.

He sat down in front of his computer, booted up the disk he'd copied from the Langley mainframe, and reviewed the information. Idiotically, as he watched the material scroll by on the amber screen, Mallory wished that he'd taken up smoking when he was a kid; at least now he'd have something to ease the tension. He sipped the scalding coffee and bit his lip instead.

According to Cooper's story, the clandestine employment of QJ/RAIL, aka Eric Rhinelander, was an agency housecleaning operation. The scenario was artfully simple. The Barbados station chief, a man named William Harper, was deeply involved in cocaine traffic from Colombia to the United States via Costa Rica, Jamaica, and Bimini, just off the Florida coast. Harper's Costa Rican connection was a man named Carl Alfonso Hoffman, heir to the Hoffman-Ramírez coffee fortune and also adjutant to Juan José Morazán, head of the powerful Policia Nacional.

The way Cooper told the story, Hoffman was providing safe haven for the aircraft used by Harper and his people, as well as security for transshipment of the cocaine from an airstrip outside San José to the Atlantic port of Limón. It also appeared that Morazán knew about the drug trade and Hoffman's involvement but was turning a blind eye to it for certain "considerations," which included the political and financial backing of the Hoffman-Ramírez consortium.

Since Morazán was also CIA-backed and the State Department's choice to run Costa Rica after Cabrera, Hoffman and particularly his involvement with a CIA station chief were cause for alarm. Rhinelander's job was to "clean house," a bland euphemism for assassinating William Harper and Carl Alfonso Hoffman if it was deemed necessary. The unspoken assumption was that the agency was getting ready to make a move in Costa Rica and Cooper didn't want to leave any dirty laundry where the Washington *Post* could find it.

At first glance it seemed to fit into established agency protocols, but Mallory had spent too long in Threat Analysis to take such things at face value. He also found Cooper's personal involvement suspect. In a situation such as the one the DDO had described, Cooper's first priority would be to distance himself and any other agency people from the project. Hiring a man like Rhinelander was odd as well. Soft file or not, he had been employed by the agency, and God forbid, with enough digging a Senate investigating committee would be able to make a connection. Far easier to co-opt one of Hoffman's own people or at least hire someone out of Costa Rica.

Mallory sat back in his chair, eyes on the screen, the palm of one hand rubbing back and forth across his broad forehead. The story Cooper had given him didn't fit; ergo, Cooper was lying to him, and the story was a cover. Query: Why would Cooper lie to him? Answer: Because the real operation was too sensitive even for the DDO's special assistant.

He poked his glasses up onto the bridge of his nose and nodded thoughtfully. That fitted at least. The real operation was ultrasensitive, so much so that Cooper was handling it himself, taking on the function of Rhinelander's case officer, using his own assistant as a conduit. As deputy director of operations Cooper had enormous power, and releasing money from the various special accounts used by the CIA would present no problem. Covering his trail would be equally simple.

And that was the bottom line and Mallory's real reason for calling in sick. The Rhinelander operation, whatever it entailed and whether it succeeded or failed, was going to need a complete sterilizing procedure. Special accounts would be fiddled, any and all files destroyed, and finally, a double blind team would be hired to remove Rhinelander once and for all. After that there would only be one connection between Hudson Haines Cooper and the operation: Paul Mallory.

Worked up as a cold-blooded assessment for a Threat Analysis, the conclusion would have been obvious: As the liaison between Rhinelander and Cooper he represented the only remaining link between the operation and the agency, and on that basis his life was in jeopardy; if he represented any threat, real or imagined, Cooper would squash him like a bug.

Leaning forward, Mallory tapped out a command, and the scrolling stopped. He sat back, pulling at his lip, examining the screen. It was a detailed description of the Grenada situation in October 1983, showing beyond a shadow of a doubt that there was no strategic reason for the invasion. It also showed clearly that the planning of Urgent Fury had been a disaster, with no cooperation among the various armed services. The report went on to list the real casualties of the operation, including a team of Delta Force commandos who died because no one had thought to check the fuel level of their helicopter. It was damaging material, and compared with some of the other data he'd pulled out of the Langley computers, it was small potatoes.

With his high-level security classification and his computer expertise, downloading the information had been relatively easy, and it would take someone a long time to trace the data theft back to him. The real difficulty lay in a method of squirreling the documents away where no one from the agency could find them.

The whole idea of using computerized data to hold over the agency's

156

head had come from Robert Littell's novel *The Amateur.* In both the book and the movie that followed, the lead character, Charlie Heller, steals data and uses them to force his superiors to allow him to track down and kill the terrorists who murdered his girlfriend. Heller secretes the data in the memory of an electronic horoscope machine located in a restaurant close to the house owned by his girlfriend's father.

A cute gimmick, but even when he'd first read the novel several years before, the question of the horoscope machine had offended his statistician's sensibility. Heller is a computer code specialist, so encrypting the documents presents no problem, but even with the documents ARCed, or compressed, the tiny memory of the horoscope machine wouldn't have been able to hold even a small portion of the data, much less be able to pump them out onto the machine's video screen. Worse than that was the physical vulnerability of the horoscope machine. What if it was taken back to the shop for maintenance? Or simply removed because it wasn't making enough money at the restaurant?

Mallory was sure he'd come up with a better idea. Seated in front of the computer, he began working his way through a set of procedures that he hoped would offer him an escape hatch if the Rhinelander project began to turn sour.

First he used an ARC program in his hard drive to compress the data he'd stolen. The program removed all the spaces between letters and words, allowing the data to take up a smaller electronic "footprint." It was a common program for games and other material being downloaded or uploaded into electronic bulletin boards.

With the data compressed Mallory then ran an encryption program, turning the compressed data into an incomprehensible clutter of letters and numbers. Following that, he added a clock facility tagged with three commands, one to decrypt and another to alert the bulletin board system operator (SysOp). The third command set the time—in this case 4:15 A.M. eastern standard time.

When everything was ready on his own computer, Mallory switched on his modem, pulled his terminal program up out of the hard drive, and then went looking for an appropriate board. It took him the better part of an hour, consulting a printout of active bulletin boards, then dialing them, but he eventually found what he wanted.

The board was called Sherlock's Home, a twenty-four-hour-a-day detective role-playing game operated by someone named David Prados. The address was in District Heights, not too far from Andrews Air Force Base. According to the message board, Prados was off in Europe somewhere for an indefinite time, but Sherlock's Home was on automatic, able to take messages, and also remain on the LODIS WEB.

It was the WEB information that interested Mallory. LODIS stood for "long distance," and WEB was a networking of bulletin boards allowing messages to be transferred over huge distances without incurring line charges. Like an old-fashioned station-to-station telephone exchange, data were bounced from one bulletin board to another close by, which in turn passed them along to the next board on the access route. Messages could be uploaded into the bulletin board, then sent automatically when the WEB went into operation, usually between 3:30 and 4:30 A.M. eastern time.

The way Mallory had set up his commands, his "message," fully decoded, would go out over the WEB, bouncing from terminal node to terminal node, downloading into each bulletin board as it went along. There were thousands of boards on the WEB network, and each one of them would receive the "message," flashing with an urgent command for the systems operator.

To stop the "message" from going out over the WEB, Mallory would have to boot up the Sherlock's Home board and reset the clock function every day, sometime before four-fifteen in the morning. If he didn't reset the clock each day before that time, the damning "message" would automatically begin showing up on thousands of computers across the country.

Satisfied that he'd done everything possible to safeguard himself, Mallory called up the Sherlock's Home message function, then tapped out the send command. The bulletin board asked for a password, and grinning sourly, Mallory logged himself on as Moriarty. The screen cleared, then demanded a file name for his "message." He typed in "Baskerville," then the letters *ARC*, indicating that it was a compressed program. The bulletin board accepted the file name, and the data began to upload.

Letting out a long breath, Mallory stood up and carried his coffee cup back to the kitchen. When the data had uploaded and the floppies been destroyed, he'd be able to relax. For a little while at least. He tipped out the cold brown brew into the sink, poured himself another cup, and found himself thinking about school days again, wondering if his life might have been different if he'd made the track team after all. Mallory shook his head slowly. It wouldn't have made the slightest difference, and he knew it.

*　　*　　*

*Top Secret,* Bob Burton's glossary of espionage terminology, defines "safe house" as a "residence that is used as a meeting place, refuge or network headquarters for intelligence purposes. It is generally deeded to or registered to a 'cleared' person who has no trace." What the book does not mention is the huge volume of such places used by the intelligence community, friend and foe, especially in the Washington area. The twelve major intelligence organizations, which included the FBI, operated almost two hundred accommodation addresses, while foreign embassies and iron curtain agencies such as the KGB, GRU, and the Chinese SAD, made use of another hundred.

The safe house chosen by Stephen Stone as operating headquarters for his Back Door surveillance operation on Dmitri Travkin was a unit in a small condominium complex below the Naval Observatory. The two-story apartment was accessible from an underground parking garage, providing a certain level of security and anonymity, and had been purchased by a fictitious corporation for use by visiting executives. The corporation was actually an element of the FBI Witness Protection Program, and the apartment was occasionally used to interrogate potential customers.

Rather than go through the standard requisition procedures to log out the apartment for official use, Stone simply went down to the Administration Services Division at the Hoover Building, waited until the clerk in the crowded office left her post, then reached over the counter and snagged the keys off their pegboard hook. The chances of anyone else's asking for the apartment over the next few weeks was slim, and even if someone did requisition the safe house, Stone could cite a paper work mixup and bow out gracefully.

Equipping the apartment had been equally straightforward. With the dummy Back Door file as backup, Mort Kessler had stroked Tech Services for everything they needed, including a voice encryption unit, radios, a PC terminal connected to the National Crime Information Computer at the Hoover Building, and night surveillance equipment.

Using Back Door as his authority once again, Kessler had seconded four men he trusted from the Baltimore and D.C. field offices, telling their superiors to contact Stone for the transfer verifications. As deputy director of Rednet Stone had authority enough to satisfy the field office inspectors, and he was careful to remove the related paper work from the interoffice memo circuit before it reached Ruppelt. Back Door had become a ghost project, a Flying Dutchman sailing the bureaucratic seas of the FBI, invisible to everyone except Stone, Kessler, and their little group of agents.

The object of the exercise, at least as far as Stone was concerned, was to maintain a loose surveillance of Travkin and see what they could catch in the net. Stone was interested in seeing whom the GRU deputy resident was contacting on his own, but he was equally curious about anyone else showing an interest in the man.

Since Stone was supposedly off the Travkin assignment and devoting his energies to more mundane matters at the CI-Q offices on Folger Square, he could get to the safe house only sporadically, but so far Mort Kessler had identified two sets of watchers on Travkin. According to Kessler, the first set was obviously KGB, running a surveillance almost as loose as their own. He had yet to identify the second group officially, although he had ruled out another FBI operation. Long-range photography showed a rotation of eight men, two women, and at least six cars, and they were keeping Travkin on a short leash. To Kessler it had all the earmarks of a CIA baby-sitting job, which fitted the defection scenario.

Stone wasn't so sure. If Travkin was going to defect, why hadn't he already done so, and if it was a baby-sitting surveillance, why was it going on for so long? On the other hand, it was equally possible that Travkin was KGB bait and Gurenko was working some kind of sting, playing the GRU man the way the KGB had conned the agency into accepting Vitaly Yurchenko, then pulling the rug out from under it. It was a game of paranoia playing off paranoia, and from the looks of things, no one wanted to make the first move.

At two that afternoon Stone booked out of Folger Square, telling the pool receptionist on the operations floor that he was taking the rest of the day off. After spending ten minutes wrestling with the rag top on the Rabbit, he drove across town, his mood as oppressive as the muggy, cloying atmosphere.

By the time he reached Union Station and the traffic circle around the Columbus Memorial he had it neatly wrapped up in three words: anger, frustration, and stupidity. Anger because of Ruppelt's kiss-ass-the-Company attitude, frustration because the Travkin thing was suffering from chronic gridlock, and stupidity because he should have known better. Once upon a time he had really believed he was doing some kind of tangible good for his country, but that had vanished a few years back along with his marriage. His loss of faith and his separation from Debbie were linked, of course. Over time he'd had less and less in common with his wife, and concurrently he'd grown to doubt the goals and objectives of the bureau, particularly where he was concerned. Like his occasional passionate interludes with Debbie, a few times he had felt good about his work in counterintelligence, but it wasn't enough. In both cases, the commitment just wasn't there anymore.

Lighting a cigarette, he worked his way through the heavy traffic heading west on Massachusetts Avenue. Maybe he could add "self-destructive" to his list of words. Mounting the Back Door operation was an invitation to disaster, and he wondered if he hadn't subconsciously pushed himself out on a limb on purpose. Every instinct told him that there was a connection among Barron's death, Hudson Cooper, and Dmitri Travkin. He also wasn't buying the Morazán and Costa Rica connection either. It was bigger than that, and Stone had a sinking feeling that it was about to blow up in his face. If it did, and Ruppelt discovered Back Door, that would be the end of his career or maybe worse.

Stone crossed Rock Creek Parkway, then turned off Massachusetts Avenue into the small residential enclave below the Naval Observatory. After driving into the dark maw of the underground lot, he parked the Rabbit, then walked the two short flights up to the interior hallway that ran along the base of the complex. He found the door to the apartment and let himself in with a duplicate key Mort Kessler had given him.

Entering the safe house, Stone saw that the red-haired agent was at his control station in the living room, radio equipment piled up on the table in front of him, a pair of oversize headphones hanging around his neck like a horse collar. The agent was chewing his way through an enormous, complicated-looking sandwich and there was a long-necked Budweiser sitting on top of the frequency scanner. Kessler nodded to his superior, then went on with his sandwich.

Stone took off his jacket, enjoying the chilled air circulating through the air-conditioned apartment. He went to the kitchen, found a can of Pepsi in the refrigerator, and snapped it open. He lit another cigarette, then took the open can of pop back to the living room.

The apartment was beige, bland, and anonymous. The furniture was Sears, and so was the pale matching broadloom that covered almost every square foot of floor. The bookshelves were empty, there was nothing on the mantel of the gas fireplace, and the only art on the walls consisted of framed posters from art galleries no one had ever heard of. The main floor was made up of living room, kitchen, powder room, and den, while the second floor contained three bedrooms and a full bathroom. The only interesting thing about the place was the view from the living room. The apartment complex was located at the end of a cul-de-sac, and you could see down into Rock Creek ravine and beyond to the parklands.

"What gives?" Stone asked, sinking down into an upholstered chair, balancing an ashtray on one arm and the Pepsi on the other.

Kessler shrugged, picked up the Budweiser, and tipped it over his mouth. After a long swallow he put the bottle down, belched lightly, and shrugged again. "Not much. He had breakfast this morning with Koslov at Au Pied de Cochon. From there he took a walk back to his apartment. He's been there ever since."

"Anybody watching him?"

"The KGB boys seem to have booked off for lunch," Kessler answered, "probably depending on the bugs they installed to keep tabs on him."

"Ours are still in place?" Stone asked.

"Sure." Kessler nodded. He reached out and flipped a toggle on one of the pieces of radio equipment. A steady hollow hiss began to crackle out of the external speaker set up beside Kessler's Budweiser. "That's the open mike on his phone." Kessler hit the toggle again, and the sound vanished. "He's been pretty quiet since he got back from breakfast. Little bit of slamming and banging, drawers being opened, that kind of thing, but not much else. Oh, he had a shower."

"Exciting stuff." Stone grunted. He took a sip of his drink. "What about our people?"

"Tobias is feeding the pigeons in Lafayette Square; he'll take him if he goes out on foot again. Copeland is parked around the corner." The red-haired agent sat forward suddenly, pulling the headphones up and clamping them around his ears. "Hang on a minute," he muttered, fiddling with the dials in front of him. "He's on his way out, and it sounds like he's carrying something."

"Like what?" Stone asked, leaning forward in his chair.

"Box, suitcase maybe. It's heavy." There was a pause; then Kessler nodded. "That's it, he's out. Locked the door behind him." The agent pulled the large base station microphone in front of him, then switched on the big Motorola transceiver, leaving the speaker open. "Compass One, this is Compass Zero, how do you read?"

"This is Compass One. I read you fine." Compass One was George Tobias, the agent in Lafayette Square. Compass Two was Bob Copeland, waiting in an unmarked car on H Street in front of the Metropolitan Club.

"Little Fox is moving," Kessler informed him.

There was a long pause, and then Compass One responded. "I see him, Compass Zero. Carrying a suitcase."

"Which way is he going?" Kessler asked urgently.

"North. Toward H Street. Do I follow?"

"No," Kessler ordered. "Stay where you are. He may double back." The agent switched channels and called up Copeland. "Compass Two, we have Little Fox coming your way."

"Thank you, Compass Zero."

"Where's he going?" asked Stone.

"Nowhere on foot," Kessler answered. "Closest Soviet address is the maritime attaché, Twenty-first and L."

"A drop?"

"With a suitcase?" Kessler laughed.

"No, I guess not." Stone grinned.

"Compass Zero, this is Compass Two. I have Little Fox getting into a Capital taxi, heading west on H Street."

"Smart boy." Kessler nodded. "He knows he's got Elder Brother on his tail, so instead of calling a cab, he flags one down."

"Where is Elder Brother?" Stone asked.

"He'll be around," Kessler answered. He punched up Tobias and told him to come back to the safe house, then switched channels again and went back to Copeland. "Anybody playing tag, Compass Two?"

"Two baggy suits in a Ford Escort," Copeland answered, the man's voice rising and falling on a sea of static. "They picked him up turning onto Eighteenth. He's heading north now."

"What did I tell you?" said Kessler.

After he put out his cigarette, Stone stood up and crossed the room to the big map of D.C. pinned to the bare beige wall on Kessler's left. Red pins marked Soviet agencies and offices, black pins marked the Back Door people, and a sprinkling of yellow pins marked Travkin's movements over the past few days. Stone's finger followed Eighteenth Street up the map. Beyond Dupont Circle there were half a dozen potential destinations for Travkin. The most likely was the Soviet Military Office on Belmont Road. Ironically, the SMO was almost directly across from the safe house, separated only by the ravine and Rock Creek itself.

"It's the military office," Stone said, turning to Kessler.

"My bet, too." The agent nodded. The two men listened as Copeland kept up a description of Travkin's taxi ride. From Eighteenth the taxi turned west onto S Street, then turned north again onto Twenty-fourth.

The taxi had entered the old Kalorama District, still an enclave of large detached houses dating back to the Beaux Arts era.

"Now I know it's the SMO," Stone said. "There's nowhere else he could be going."

"No evasive moves," Kessler said. "I guess he doesn't care about Elder Brother."

"Maybe he's going to ground for a while," Stone suggested. "That would explain the suitcase."

"Or maybe he's on his way back to Mother Russia," Kessler said.

There was a rush of static from the radio. "Compass Zero, this is Compass Two. We've got a problem."

"Go ahead, Compass Two."

"Bit of a traffic screwup. The taxi turned onto Tracy Place, and there's a truck blocking the street. Gateway Movers. If I get any closer, I'm going to be sitting in the baggy suits' lap." There was a pause. "No, wait, the truck is backing up into a driveway. . . . Shit!" The last word was a barking roar.

"Compass Two, this is Compass Zero. What's going on?" There was no reply. Kessler tried again, his voice urgent. "Compass Two, this is Compass Zero, how do you read me?" Another pause.

"This is Compass Two, Compass Zero." Copeland's voice, panting and angry.

"What the hell is going on, Compass Two?"

"It was a trap, Mort," Copeland answered, breaking code procedure. "The truck pulled back just enough to let the taxi through, then blocked the street again."

"Little Fox?"

"Pinched," Copeland managed to say, still trying to catch his breath. "I tried going around on foot, but it was all over. The cabdriver's unconscious, Little Fox is gone along with his suitcase, and the baggy suits are going crazy."

"Tell him to get the hell out of there," ordered Stone. "We don't want any involvement with the KGB or the local PDs. This one is going to stink bad." The Rednet deputy director turned back to the map and stared at the intersection of Tracy and Twenty-fourth.

Whoever was responsible for the kidnapping had pulled it off within two short blocks of the SMO and done it in broad daylight. There was only one organization with the facilities to work an operation like that. He pulled a drawing pin out of the map and jabbed it down on the intersection.

"Cooper," he said, whispering harshly. "It has to be!"

# CHAPTER 12

If Palm Beach is the last, glitzy, and overpriced refuge of America's not so nouveau riche, then the Breakers Hotel is the castle keep, an ornate fortress in polished pink Tennessee granite, twin towers looking vigilantly out over the Atlantic and also back across the narrow reaches of the Intercoastal Waterway to the uncultured horrors of West Palm Beach, where McDonald's arches grow like golden weeds along the Dixie Highway and motel rooms are equipped with vibrating beds.

The Breakers, originally built by Henry Flagler, co-founder of Standard Oil, had six hundred rooms, two swimming pools, tennis courts, and its own eighteen-hole golf course and was host to the National Croquet Association of America, the lush front lawns of the west-facing courtyard used for the annual championship games. Designed by Leonard Schultze, architect for New York's Waldorf-Astoria, the Breakers used seventy-five European artisans to create more than three and a half acres of ceiling frescoes, reflected in the highly polished pink marble floors and lit by scores of magnificent bronze and crystal chandeliers from Venice and Austria. Used in a thousand fashion layouts and television commercials, the real-life facade of the Italianesque hotel really was imposing. Based on the Villa Medici in Rome, but almost ten times its size, the jutting east and west wings of the building formed an open courtyard, its center punctuated by a gushing fountain, itself an exact replica of one in the Boboli Gardens of Florence.

Eric Rhinelander had no intention of staying at the Breakers, but

165

preliminary reading in Jamaica indicated that the hotel would likely provide him with what he needed for the next step of his plan.

Having steered the rental car across the Flagler Memorial Bridge, the dark-haired man eased onto Royal Poinciana Way, the Breakers Golf Club on his right. He turned onto Breakers Row, followed it south, then pulled into the front entrance of the hotel.

Obeying the sign at the base of the fountain, Rhinelander kept the car to the right and pulled into a vacant spot between a silver Continental and a jet black Rolls-Royce Silver Spur. Dressed in a full set of crisp tennis whites purchased half an hour before in a West Palm sporting goods store and carrying an expensive racket, Rhinelander climbed out of the car and slipped on the Serengeti Driver sunglasses hanging on a cord around his neck. Dressed as he was and carrying the racket, he was the quintessential Breakers guest: middle-aged, athletic, and obviously wealthy.

He lit a cigarette to give himself some time and scanned the open courtyard. Two arch-and-column loggias bracketed the main entranceway, and cars were parked beyond each of them, lined up in front of the tall palms that marked the perimeter of the spacious, neatly groomed lawns, and in the main parking lot to the north. Summers in Palm Beach provided slim pickings for the hotel trade; but the Breakers had enough stalwarts to justify staying open, most of them elderly, and a surprising number of them lived there year-round. The main lot was almost empty, but there were plenty of cars in the area close to the entrance. The automobiles were all luxury class: Cadillacs, Lincolns, Rollses, and Jaguars. There were a few sports cars, but most of the vehicles were large sedans.

Rhinelander began walking casually toward the main entrance, watching for the distinctive Capitol dome symbol that marked a D.C. license plate. He found three without having to check out the main lot: a dark blue Cadillac Seville, a silver Porsche Targa, and a Bentley from the mid-seventies. Ignoring the Porsche, he slid between the Bentley and the car beside it. The driver's side lock button was down. He continued on and stood watching the croquet players on the broad lawns beyond the palm trees. He let a minute or two pass, turned, and went back toward the south loggia, then around the fountain to the northern side of the court and the Seville. The door was unlocked. He placed his racket on the hood of the car next to the Cadillac and bent down as though to tie the lace of his tennis shoe. He knelt, reached up, and pulled open the door. Keeping his head well down, he crawled into the car and pulled open the

166

glove compartment. The registration certificate was tucked into a clear plastic sleeve. Rhinelander pulled it out and scanned it quickly:

JOHN HAMILTON GRAY
1949 CONNECTICUT AVE.
THE WYOMING APARTMENTS
WASHINGTON, D.C. 20009

Rhinelander returned the form to its sleeve, slid out of the car, eased the door closed and stood. The operation had taken fewer than thirty seconds. He gathered up his racket and headed for the main entrance of the hotel. After climbing the short flight of steps to the double-arched doorway, he entered and crossed the cavernous lobby. He reached the main desk and spent a few seconds going through the motions of writing something on a sheet of hotel stationery. He folded the sheet of paper in four, then caught the desk clerk's attention.

"I'd like to leave a message for John Gray," Rhinelander said quietly.

"Of course," replied the reservations clerk. He was young, no more than twenty-one or so, and very serious in a dark suit, white shirt, and dark green bow tie. He tapped at the computer terminal below the counter and frowned. "We have two J. Grays staying with us at the moment."

"John Gray from Washington," Rhinelander said.

The clerk nodded. "Ah, yes. Mr. and Mrs. Gray." He looked up and held out his hand for the message. Rhinelander gave it to him and watched carefully as the clerk put it in the appropriate box. Room 526. He thanked the clerk, then retraced his steps across the lobby and paused at a bank of house telephones near the entrance to the loggia corridor. He dialed 526 and let it ring more than a dozen times. No answer. Fair enough.

Rhinelander went back through the main entrance and headed for his car. With the Cadillac parked in front of the hotel, Mr. and Mrs. Gray weren't far. The classic Breakers high tea he'd read about in the guidebooks wouldn't be served for another hour; that probably ruled out the dining room as well. The beach or tennis. Either way he didn't have much time.

At the rental car he popped the trunk, tossed in his racket, and leaned in to rummage through the bag of things he'd purchased at the hardware store an hour or so before. Keeping his hands out of sight, he took out a five-by-seven rectangle of sheet metal, roughly the size of the paperback book that he'd picked up at a local drugstore and that now lay beside his luggage on the floor of the trunk.

Working the sheet metal with a short-handled pair of tin snips, Rhinelander cut out a semicircle of metal on the long side of the rectangle and a smaller notch farther back. He wrapped the small notch and the entire back half of the device in black electrical tape, leaving the half-moon cut and the rest of the metal bare. Reaching into the bag again, he took out one of the hacksaw blades he'd purchased and wrapped the last three inches in tape as well. When he completed the wrapping, he slipped the sheet metal device and the hacksaw blade between the pages of the paperback and closed the trunk.

Instead of going through the main entrance again, he went through the southern loggia doors and followed the long rattan-furnished lounge to a bank of elevators at the south wing end of the lobby. Paperback in hand, he stepped into one of the elevators, punched 5, and waited. The doors closed, and he went up, alone in the elevator.

The fifth-floor corridor was empty. A sign directly in front of the elevators indicated that rooms 501 to 519 were to the left and 520 to 544 were to the right. Rhinelander went right and found 526 toward the end of the corridor about forty feet from the fire stairs. Getting into the Grays' room wasn't imperative, and Rhinelander wasn't going to risk much for a glimpse of their possessions; but from a quick glance at the locks on the room doors it didn't look as though it were going to be too difficult.

The locks were original equipment, dating back to the reconstruction of the main building after a fire in 1925 and the ornately cast miniature lion's-head escutcheons disguised simple latch bolt mortise locks without latch guards or dead bolts. He wouldn't need the hacksaw blade. Glancing down the hall to make sure the way was clear, Rhinelander removed the sheet metal "key" from the book and eased it between the door and the frame of room 526, just above the lock. After poking it in so that the half-moon was over the lock mechanism, he slowly pulled the device downward, pausing when he felt resistance. The half-moon notch was now over the latch bolt.

Rhinelander checked the hallway again, then curled his right index finger into the taped notch behind the half-moon cutout. Pulling gently toward himself, he began to "walk" the sheet metal device forward. The metal caught the beveled latch bolt, and the door popped open. Rhinelander stepped into the room, closed the door behind him. He put the "key" back into the book and the book into the back pocket of his tennis shorts, then began to count silently. At three hundred he would be on his way out.

The room was relatively small and furnished conservatively. Twin beds with a poorly disguised lockbox safe between them, doubling as a telephone and lamp table. A desk, a chair, and twin bureaus opposite the beds, a club chair, and an upholstered chaise close to the window. The carpeting was pale green, as were the bedspreads, while the curtains were done in a complementary floral print. A clothes cupboard with bifold doors by the door and another beside the bathroom.

Rhinelander worked quickly, going through the cupboards first, followed by the bureaus and then the desk. He'd seen no bathing suits or bathrobes, and there were no large towels in the bathroom. The chances were good the Grays were at one of the two pools or the beach next door. As his count reached 150, he took his haul of personal effects and dumped them on the bed nearest the window.

Mrs. Gray's purse, complete with wallet and credit cards, found hidden inside one of the extra pillows on the cupboard shelf. Mr. Gray's wallet, hidden inside a pair of socks in his bureau. A set of keys from the side pocket of a tweed suit. Passports in the desk along with tickets, vouchers, and a travel itinerary stuffed into a thick folder from Butterfield and Rosen, D.C. travel agents with an address on M Street in Georgetown.

He put the folder aside and opened Mrs. Gray's purse. There was a set of keys inside the bulky leather bag. Rhinelander picked up the set of keys he'd found in Mr. Gray's jacket and compared them. Both rings held a set of keys for the Cadillac, and both had similar but not identical safety-deposit-box keys. There were several small keys on Mr. Gray's ring that looked as if they might fit luggage, two well-worn Medecos and a shiny single-pin key with the name Secor on the tab. Checking quickly, Rhinelander saw that there were also two Medeco keys on Mrs. Gray's ring. House keys. He took one from each ring, as well as the Secor, and slipped them into the pocket of his tennis shorts.

The contents of John Gray's wallet produced a brief history of the man's life. Sixty-two years old, gray-haired with glasses, a semiretired lawyer and senior partner in the firm of Gray, Gladstone & Taylor. Two children, both daughters, both married, both with children, one living in Texas, the other in Colorado. Rhinelander jotted down the man's license number, then removed Gray's Social Security card from a back slot in the card holder; he put it into his pocket along with the keys. He went

169

through the credit cards, removed the Diners Club, and slipped it into his pocket as well. His count was now at two hundred.

Opening the Butterfield and Rosen folder, Rhinelander ignored the tickets and pulled out the computerized itinerary sheet. According to the printout the Grays were to remain at the Breakers for another ten days, then travel to Miami, where they were booked overnight at the Hilton. The following day they were scheduled to board the *QE2* at Port Everglades for a round-the-world cruise. According to the schedule, they would be gone for months.

The only other thing of interest in the folder was a folded carbon copy of a receipt from a Washington company called Housecalls Inc. According to the carbon, Housecalls would have someone in to water the plants and collect the mail every third day for the duration of the Grays' extended vacation. Rhinelander frowned. A problem certainly, but nothing serious. He took down the telephone number of the company, then replaced the carbon in the folder. His count was up to 250; time to be on his way.

He went around the room, returning everything to its proper place, finally reaching the hotel room door as his count reached three hundred. Rhinelander stayed for a few seconds longer, his dark eyes scanning the room to make sure he hadn't overlooked anything. When he was satisfied, he opened the door, checked the corridor, and stepped outside, easing the door shut behind him.

Pleased with the way things had gone, Rhinelander left the hotel and returned to his car. A few moments later he was on his way back to the mainland. He'd been prepared to spend much more time developing his Washington position, but the Grays had given it to him in one neat package. At best he'd expected his side trip to produce an address in D.C. for a week or ten days; the three-and-a-half-month world cruise was an unexpected bonus. Even the Housecalls Inc. receipt was more of an asset than a liability; it would be easy enough to call and cancel the service, and the fact that Mr. and Mrs. Gray had employed the company at all meant that they weren't on particularly intimate terms with their immediate neighbors.

Given his success at the Breakers, Rhinelander decided to move his plan up a day. Instead of booking in at the Holiday Inn, as he'd originally intended, he drove the car south on Olive Avenue to Okeechobee Boulevard, then north on Tamarind to the Amtrak station. After a quick change of clothing in the parking lot he went into the station and purchased bedroom accommodations on the northbound Silver Star, paying

170

for his passage all the way to New York. According to the ticket agent, the train would arrive in West Palm Beach at 6:35 P.M. and depart ten minutes later. After traveling up through the southern states during the night, the train would reach Washington in the early afternoon of the following day.

Returning to the parking lot, Rhinelander spent the next twenty-five minutes going over the rental car. He took the unused material from the hardware store to a Dumpster beside the station, then added the tennis outfit, the racket, and finally, Gavin Holt's set of golf clubs. He kept the sheet metal key and the book, slipping them into the single suitcase he'd removed from the dead man's apartment in Miami. Chores done, he took the suitcase into the station and checked it with the baggagemaster, adding a five-dollar tip to ensure that it reached his bedroom on the train in good order. He ate a mediocre meal at a greasy spoon on the other side of the street and returned to the station just as the train pulled in.

After boarding, he found his bedroom, spent a few moments with the sleeping car steward, making his preferences known, then sat down in one of the folding club seats that would disappear when the bunks were lowered. The steward reappeared a moment later, carrying a tray with the cup and carafe of coffee that had been requested. Rhinelander tipped the man, poured himself a cup of coffee, and lit a cigarette.

At six forty-five the train jerked, moaned, and then began to move. Coming out of the station, Rhinelander could see Clear Lake on his left, ringed by high rises, windows coppered by the lowering sun. As the train rocked ponderously through Riviera Beach, the conductor appeared and collected Rhinelander's ticket, punching it neatly and returning it with a nod. When that was done, Rhinelander closed and locked the door. He sat by the window, watching the scenery pass by while he smoked and drank coffee. He stayed at the window until it was dark, and then he buzzed for the steward to come and make up his bed.

Later Rhinelander sat on the edge of the bed, the lights of his compartment extinguished, his window blind up. He smoked a last cigarette, watching the fleeting lights of the small North Florida communities scattered along the snaking path of the old Seaboard Coast Line. Finishing the cigarette, he carefully stubbed it out in the wall-mounted ashtray, then pulled down the blind.

Naked, he lay on top of the crisp sheets, eyes wide open and seeing nothing. Listening to the stuttering rocking of the train, he allowed himself to think about tomorrow and Washington and what he had been asked to do and why, in the depths of some darkly shrouded well within

171

his soul, he already knew he'd go through with it, no matter how great the risk of failure and its consequences or how pitiful the odds of his success and its rewards. Finally, having reached no real conclusions, Rhinelander turned on his side, closed his eyes, and fell into a deep and dreamless sleep.

As Eric Rhinelander slept, Dmitri Aleksandrovich Travkin was slowly regaining consciousness and becoming aware of his surroundings. He came out of the darkness in stages, groping his way out of absolute nothingness, following the trail of clues left by his awakening senses. The medicinal smell of a hospital, reassuring at first, then frightening. What was he doing in a hospital? Why couldn't he see or hear? Then the foul taste in his mouth he'd last experienced after having his appendix removed. General anesthetic. Jesus Christ! They'd operated on him! Who?

Sound and sight at last. The faint whirring of an air-conditioning unit, white acoustic tiles overhead, and an inset fluorescent panel, dimmed. He lifted his head from the pillow, wincing as pain stabbed at his temples. Small room, pale green walls, and a single, narrow window, uncurtained. Darkness beyond. Night.

Groaning, Travkin eased his legs out over the side of the bed and pushed himself into a sitting position. The pain in his temples was followed by a sweeping wave of nausea combined with vertigo. Gritting his teeth, he swallowed hard, keeping the rising bile in his throat at bay. He waited out the nausea, and after a minute or so it began to recede.

Definitely a hospital bed in a hospital room. He was wearing an openbacked hospital gown, tied once just above his buttocks. The floor was cool gray tile. No intravenous, no catheters, no obvious pains. Surgery seemed unlikely. Why would they operate anyway?

Why would who operate? Splintered shards of memory began to form. He'd been in a cab on his way to the SMO. No more than a block or two from the military office the taxi driver had turned down Tracy Place instead of continuing up to Kalorama Road. He'd started to say something, but there'd been a huge crashing noise and he had a vague recollection of a large red, white, and blue postal van smashing into the side of the taxi. And that was it until now.

He forced himself to take a long series of deep breaths, trying to bring himself out of the threatening panic he was beginning to feel. He'd been snatched; that much was clear. His own people? Remotely possible but highly unlikely. Why kidnap him when he was on his way in to the SMO anyway? That left Gurenko and Elder Brother, Central Intelligence, or Stephen Stone.

Pushing himself up off the bed with both arms, Travkin staggered over to the window. There were no bars on the outside, but the glass was embedded with steel mesh. He cupped his hands around his eyes and looked outside. He could just make out an open playing field-like area directly under the window and the dark, shadowed shapes of a forest beyond. No lights twinkling, no reflected glow of a nearby city. He made his way back to the bed and sat down wearily. Gurenko and the KGB had nothing like this in the Washington area, and neither did Koslov.

Gently, using only the tips of his fingers, Travkin began massaging his temples, willing the terrible pain to go away so that he could think clearly. He closed his eyes and tried to concentrate but opened them again almost instantly as the vertigo returned.

Not Gurenko, not Koslov. Stone or the CIA? Stone had neither the mandate nor the authority to organize a kidnapping, and if it leaked to the press that the FBI was going around snatching foreign diplomats, the bureau's good guy public image would disintegrate. On top of that, his intuition from the beginning had told him that Stone really *was* one of the good guys, even if he was a counterintelligence officer.

That left Central Intelligence. Obviously the most probable, but still astounding, considering the circumstances. For one thing, the CIA was forbidden to operate domestically, and more important, the kidnapping violated the unwritten law that you didn't physically interfere with agents in each other's capital cities. Clandestines and illegals were fair game, but as a registered member of the Soviet Embassy staff Travkin should have had immunity. If that immunity had been violated, someone, almost certainly Hudson Cooper, was very worried.

If he assumed the kidnapping had been a CIA operation, that meant he was in one of two places: Camp Peary, the Farm, as it was known in the annals of spy fiction, or the less publicized Bowie Institute. The Farm was used to train potential agents in the basics of tradecraft and field operations, and it was also more than a hundred miles from Washington, just outside Williamsburg, Virginia, a risky long-distance transport problem. The institute, on the other hand, was fewer than forty miles from where he'd been snatched, occupying a small corner of the gigantic and absolutely secure National Agricultural Research Center just north of the town of Bowie, Maryland.

The institute, built in the early thirties as the Maryland State Refor-

CHRISTOPHER HYDE

matory for Girls, had been taken over by William Donovan's OSS early in the Second World War. Used then as a training center for agents about to be sent overseas, it languished unused for a number of years after the war, its function usurped by the newly built facilities at Camp Peary. In the late fifties it was decided that the fledgling Central Intelligence Agency needed its own medical facilities close to Washington, and the interior of the old reform school was renovated.

The east wing, once a dormitory, was turned into a ward, with the two common rooms used as nurses' stations. Several classrooms in the center block were transformed into operating rooms, and a number of other alterations were made, including a special surgical suite for plastic and reconstructive surgery. The pool in the west wing was rebuilt, while the gymnasium was transformed into an auditorium and theater.

During the middle and late sixties a number of the CIA's infamous MKUltra and LSD experiments were carried out at the Bowie Institute, but by the seventies its role had become that of a rest and recuperation center for agents in from the field, a discreet drug and alcohol detoxification clinic for selected agency employees and their wives, and an occasional debriefing unit for high-ranking defectors like Vitaly Yurchenko.

It was the KGB's Yurchenko who had provided most of what was known about the institute, and even that had been sifted down through a number of GRU "sympathetics" within Elder Brother. According to Yurchenko, he'd been taken to the institute on three different occasions, each session lasting several days. Perhaps because of his high rank within the KGB, drugs hadn't been used on him, but he reported seeing several interrogation rooms equipped with drug-related paraphernalia, including gurneys fitted with leather restraints, pharmaceutical cabinets, and intravenous equipment. His debriefers had tried hypnotism, but according to Yurchenko, he was a poor hypnotic subject and unable to go into a trance.

The KGB man had very little to say regarding a physical description of the institute and its location other than the fact that it was a single extended building running along an east-west axis, that it had brick exterior walls and a slate roof. By his estimation the building was about 350 feet long by 50 to 75 feet deep, and was located on a slight rise in a large clearing surrounded by thick stands of coniferous trees, none of which appeared to be more than 35 or 40 feet high. He had no information at all regarding perimeter security, fences, or electronics.

Travkin tried standing up again, one hand gripping the bed sheets. He edged slowly around to the end of the bed, then shuffled across the room

174

to the door. It was locked, of course, and there was no knob on the inside. He kept moving around the edge of the room, propping himself up with one hand and ignoring the mild waves of dizziness. The closet was empty except for a pair of paper slippers and some extra bedding. No clothes. The bathroom was just as bleak: pedal flush toilet with handgrips for wheelchairs and a large stainless steel sink. Thin towels and a face-cloth on a rod, a still-wrapped bar of soap, three rolls of toilet paper on a metal shelf.

After finishing his inspection, the GRU major guided himself back to the bed and sat down gratefully. Whatever drugs he'd been given were wearing off, and he was slowly regaining control. He mentally pushed away the stabs of panic; long before becoming an officer within the GRU, he had been *spetsialnoye nazhacheniye,* graduate of the Spetsnaz training school at the Lenin Komsomol Higher Airborne Command Facility, 175 kilometers southeast of Moscow. If he could survive the birch swamp horrors at the special forces unit in Ryazan, he could survive anything, even the Bowie Institute.

Travkin heard a faint electronic click and turned, frowning. The door to his room opened, and he saw two men, both dressed in the loose-fitting white fatigues used by hospital orderlies. The men were medium height, one more muscular-looking than the other, but both obviously fit. The muscular one was blond, while his slimmer companion was dark-haired and heavily bearded. The blond stood behind a wheelchair.

*"Preyezieu moy,"* ordered the dark-haired, slimmer man. The Russian was bland and unaccented—freeze-dried language from an American university.

"Why should I come with you?" Travkin asked, replying in English. "I don't know who the hell you are or where I've been taken."

"You have no need to know," the dark-haired man answered, still speaking Russian. "I repeat, come with me."

Travkin thought for a brief moment. To resist now, in his condition, would be foolish. He nodded, then stood up slowly. The dark-haired man stepped aside, allowing the blond to push the wheelchair into the room. He brought it around to the side of the bed, and Travkin sat down. The blond man fastened heavy rubber restraints around Travkin's wrists, then turned the wheelchair around. The dark-haired man held the door open, and Travkin was wheeled out into the hall.

They went down a long, brightly lit corridor, turned left, and took a shorter passage to a small elevator. They went down one floor, exited, then followed a broad, marble-floored hall to what had once been the offices of the Bowie Reformatory nurse. A full set of Travkin's clothing had been laid out across the old-fashioned leather examining table.

"Get dressed," the dark-haired man ordered, speaking Russian. "When you're ready, go through that door." He pointed to the other side of the room. The blond man undid Travkin's restraints and stepped back. A few seconds later they left, locking the hallway door behind them.

Travkin pushed himself toward the examining table and then stood up. The clothes had come from the suitcase in the taxi. Dark blue lightweight suit, pale gray shirt, underwear, socks, loafers, and a blue-and-red-striped silk tie, one of his favorites. He dressed, sitting down to put on the socks and shoes, then went to the connecting door.

Opening it, he paused, startled for a moment. The room beyond wasn't at all what he'd expected. Instead of a bleak interrogation chamber, he found himself looking into a well-furnished sitting room. He stepped inside and closed the door behind him. A rattan sectional couch dominated the room. In front of it was an ornate marble-topped coffee table, its surface scattered with magazines.

Two upholstered chairs were arranged across from the couch, and behind them an antique writing desk stood against one wall. To the left of the couch and chairs there was an Art Deco-style fireplace, several logs burning cheerily in the hearth. The walls were painted a warm oyster white and hung with a variety of well-framed mid-nineteenth-century oils. The whole room was lit discreetly by recessed pots in the ceiling.

A paneled door beside the writing desk opened, and a man stepped into the room. He appeared to be in his late forties or early fifties, his gray hair thick and curly over a broad forehead and large hazel eyes. He was wearing suede desert boots, dark trousers, and a brown tweed jacket over a light blue shirt. No tie. In his right hand he carried a clipboard, and in his left a thick file folder.

"Mr. Travkin?" the man asked, extending a hand. "My name is David Cook." Bemused, Travkin took the hand and shook it. Cook's grip was cool and dry. He gestured toward the couch, and Travkin sat down. Cook followed suit, taking one of the chairs across from him. He opened the file folder on his lap and consulted the clipboard.

"Let's get the formalities out of the way first, shall we?" Cook began. "Your name is Dmitri Aleksandrovich Travkin?"

"I'm not saying anything," the GRU major answered.

"You were born in Ljalovo, a small town on the outskirts of Moscow." Cook went on blithely. "Your father, Aleksandr Antonovich Travkin, died of a heart attack six years ago. Your mother, Maria Fyodorovna

Travkina, presently lives at Twenty-six Ulyanov Prospekt between Sokolniki Park and the Riga Station, is that correct?"

Travkin remained silent. He had always assumed that Central Intelligence had a complete dossier on him, but hearing his mother's address coming out of this man's mouth made his stomach twist. After a few moments he decided to go along with the odd interrogation and nodded.

"Yes, that is correct," he said finally.

"Good, thank you." Cook smiled, pleased. "You presently hold the rank of major in the GRU, working under General Gennadi Koslov, yes?"

"I am senior economic adviser to the Soviet Trade Mission in Washington, and I have been illegally kidnapped by the Central Intelligence Agency," Travkin replied. "I am now making a formal request to contact the Soviet ambassador immediately."

"Of course." Cook nodded, smiling again. "I wonder if you could tell me at what point you decided to defect to the United States."

"I have not defected," Travkin answered calmly. "As I just said, I was kidnapped by the CIA."

"Would you say that your defection was politically motivated?" Cook asked, ignoring Travkin's interjection.

"I did not defect," he repeated.

Cook kept on smiling. He turned, looking back over his shoulder. The door beside the writing desk opened, and the blond man who had guided Travkin's wheelchair appeared. He was now dressed in a white steward's jacket with small brass buttons. He was carrying a tray loaded down with a silver tea service and a platter of small pastries. The blond man put the platter down on the table between Travkin and Cook, then retired.

"Refreshments!" Cook beamed. He closed the folder and leaned forward, putting it down on the table beside the platter. He set out two cups and poured. "If I remember your file, you take lemon and sugar, is that right?"

"Yes." Travkin nodded. The whole thing was insane. It was the middle of the night, and he was drinking tea!

Cook handed him the cup and swept a hand over the tray of pastries. "Help yourself," the CIA man said. Realizing just how hungry he was, Travkin took two small meringues and placed them on the edge of his saucer. He stirred his tea and took a swallow of the hot, tart-sweet brew. Holding the cup and saucer in one hand, he took one of the meringues and bit into it, letting the piece dissolve on his tongue. The institute apparently had an accomplished pastry chef on its staff. He took an-

177

other bite and stared across the table at his interrogator. The questions continued.

Dressed in evening clothes and nursing a glass of scotch, Hollis Macintyre stood at the floor-to-ceiling living-room window in Hudson Cooper's Watergate apartment, staring out into the darkness. It was well past midnight, and he was tired. Before coming to the deputy director's home, he'd spent several hours at his monthly Gourmet Society dinner in Georgetown, but his interest had been distracted by his need to know the progress of the Travkin operation, so the meal and the evening had been wasted.

The huge man turned away from the dark night outside, frowning as another stab of pain surged through his massive gut. On the far side of the room Hudson Cooper sat at the ornately carved desk, speaking softly into the telephone. Breathing heavily, Macintyre walked slowly across the large Oriental carpet and sat down in one of several leather chairs arranged around Cooper's fireplace. He took a small sip of his drink, then set the heavy glass down on the table beside him. A few moments later Cooper hung up the telephone and joined him.

"Well?" Macintyre asked as the deputy director seated himself.

"Everything is going as planned," Cooper answered, staring at the cold hearth of the fireplace a few feet away.

"Your man at Bowie knows nothing?"

"No more than necessary." Cooper sighed. "I was careful to double-blind the operation. The pickup crew was from Covert Ops. Cook is a psych expert from the Office of Soviet Analysis. Tech Services is handling the rest. It's set up to look like a variation on the honey trap. Travkin is taken by main force, but everything after that is set up to resemble a defection."

"Will it work?" Macintyre asked.

"It should," Cooper replied. "The debriefing suite at Bowie has half a dozen hidden cameras and microphones everywhere. By the time Cook is finished we'll have at least two hours of both video- and audiotape to work with. The questions are set up to elicit responses that can be re-edited to suit our requirements. The end result will be a ten- or fifteen-minute segment that will make Travkin look like a grateful defector. We don't even have to make the defection public. A copy sent to Koslov or Gurenko will be more than adequate."

"They'll believe it?" Macintyre asked skeptically.

Cooper shrugged. "Perhaps not, but they'll have to accept it," the deputy director replied.

"Repercussions?"

"Some harassment of our people in Moscow, possibly an expulsion, nothing more. If we don't try to make political points with the Travkin tape, they may simply choose to ignore it. For the time being, the political climate requires us all to act like the best of friends, at least in the public eye. There may well be no repercussions at all."

"You mentioned before that Travkin was trained at Spetznaz," Macintyre said slowly. He picked up his glass and took a short swallow. "Is there any chance of his escaping from Bowie?"

"Unlikely," Cooper responded.

"But what if he does?" Macintyre pressed.

"We've learned our lessons," Cooper said, smiling bleakly. "Unlike the unfortunate affair with Comrade Yurchenko, we will have proof that Major Travkin was a willing defector to this country." Cooper shook his head. "No, Hollis," he continued, letting his head fall back against the chair. "I think we've effectively defused Dmitri Aleksandrovich Travkin. Even if he did manage to get out of the Bowie Institute, he'd have nowhere to run. I can assure you that his own people have already written him off."

"So the project continues," Macintyre murmured softly, twirling the remnants of ice in his glass.

"It would seem that way," Cooper answered.

"When do we hear from Mr. Rhinelander?"

"Within the next two or three days if there aren't any difficulties. He'll contact Mallory and give him a yes or a no on the feasibility of the operation."

"And if his answer is yes?" Macintyre asked quietly.

"Then presumably we call the committee together and make the final decision one way or the other," Cooper answered.

Macintyre put his glass down on the side table and stared thoughtfully at his host for a moment. "You don't really approve of this, do you, Hudson?" he asked finally.

"The question of my approval is irrelevant," the deputy director responded. "I am a member of the Romulus Committee. That position holds inherent responsibilities, one of which is to ensure that this nation doesn't find itself with a lunatic at the helm of the ship of state." Cooper paused for a moment, ducking his head and pinching the bridge of his

179

nose with thumb and forefinger. He looked up again and continued. "If you're asking me if I approve of the assassination of the President and the Vice President of the United States, then the answer is no, I find the idea abhorrent. On the other hand, I recognize the efficacy of such a plan and have no hesitation in recommending it."

"That's clear enough," the fat man answered, allowing himself a small smile. Grunting with effort, he levered himself up out of the chair. "I must be on my way," he said, extending a hand to Cooper. The CIA man stood up and shook the proffered hand briefly, then led Macintyre to the front door of the apartment.

"I'll keep you advised about Rhinelander," Cooper said, opening the door.

"I'd appreciate that," Macintyre told him.

The two men shook hands again, and then the fat man was gone. Cooper closed the door after him and let out a long breath. It was past one in the morning now, and he was exhausted; but there was still more to do. His steps weary, he went back to his desk and picked up the telephone.

It was just after 9:00 A.M. in Moscow, and the gray slate floors of Sheremetyevo Airport's Terminal 2 were awash in arriving and departing passengers. Small groups of militia were scattered here and there along the low-ceilinged concourse, and Sergei Yulevich Kuryokhin also noticed a number of green-uniformed KGB border guards.

Carrying a single small bag, the old man turned off the concourse down a narrow corridor leading to the VIP lounge, the burning stump of a Lucky Strike clamped between his thin lips. He disliked long-distance travel, especially by air, but the trip to Warsaw was unavoidable. His only consolation was that he would travel to the meeting on Aeroflot, not LOT, the Polish state airline.

There was a score of people waiting in the lounge, luggage gathered around their feet, and all of them looked up as he came through the automatic doors. As quickly as they looked up they looked down again, intuitively sensing the power that hung like an invisible mantle across the old man's stooped shoulders.

Kuryokhin frowned as one of the people stood up and approached him. It was Baklinov, the Washington desk controller from Teply Stan. The burly middle-aged man stopped a few feet from his senior officer and bowed stiffly.

"This is a surprise," Kuryokhin said. He handed his overnight bag to

Baklinov and let the younger man lead him to a pair of seats away from the rest of the waiting passengers. Kuryokhin sat down, pushing his cigarette into the sand-filled ashtray beside him. He adjusted his wire-rimmed glasses and stared at Baklinov. "Well?"

"We've had a report from Gurenko in Washington," the broad-shouldered man said hesitantly. "It came in last night. I got here as quickly as I could."

"Report on what?" Kuryokhin asked. He reached into the pocket of his thin brown raincoat and took out a package of cigarettes. He lit one and waited.

"Travkin, the GRU major we were discussing."

"What about him?" Kuryokhin asked, puffing out a cloud of blue smoke.

"It would appear that he has defected."

"Explain," Kuryokhin demanded, his voice soft.

"He has disappeared. Our surveillance was broken off. Apparently it was quite a sophisticated operation. Gurenko is positive that Travkin had help."

"In other words it was planned," Kuryokhin said.

"Yes." Baklinov let out a long, whistling breath. "There may be some problem with Koslov. He insists that Travkin was kidnapped."

"Foolishness. He is trying to save face. Travkin was his protégé, and the lecherous old bastard used to be his mother's lover."

"Whatever the case, Gurenko would like some direction."

"Tell him to do nothing, at least for the moment," Kuryokhin said after a moment's thought. "If Travkin has defected, the news will eventually leak out even if the Americans try to keep it quiet. Their security is like cheesecloth about such things. Gurenko should assume the worst."

"And if Travkin reappears?"

"Tell Comrade Gurenko that from this moment on, his Major Travkin no longer exists," Kuryokhin said, smiling gently. "If he surfaces again, it only means that he has been turned by the CIA or cut loose by them. In either event he is no longer of any use to us. His only value now is the embarrassment he is causing Gennadi Koslov."

A young and clearly nervous stewardess in a beige Aeroflot uniform appeared, bearing a tray of smoked salmon and squares of black bread. The tray also held a small carafe of tea and two small glasses. She placed the tray down on the small table in front of Kuryokhin and then vanished. Kuryokhin extinguished his cigarette, then took a piece of the salmon, placed it on a square of bread, and put it into his mouth. He

181

chewed slowly. Baklinov ignored the food, knowing that if Kuryokhin wanted him to eat, he'd offer.

"Is there anything else?" the white-haired old man asked, peering up at Baklinov.

"No, sir. I think Gurenko will be pleased. *Spasiba.*"

"*Nyeh probleme,*" Kuryokhin answered, startling Baklinov with his use of current slang. "Now let me get on with my food."

"Of course, sir." Baklinov stood up, bowed again, and left the VIP lounge. Kuryokhin made himself another bite-size sandwich, this time arranging a few pickled capers on the salmon. He popped it into his mouth, then poured himself a glass of tea.

Sipping the hot liquid, he stared across the lounge at the mural on the far wall: broad-shouldered women gathering wheat to their expansive bosoms; muscular men sweating over forges. God, it was boring! Trying to ignore the industrial art, he thought about Travkin and found himself wondering if there wasn't more going on in Washington than he'd first assumed. It was worth checking on when he returned from Warsaw.

# CHAPTER 13

In 1885 Henry Adams, novelist, historian, and presidential descendant, together with his close friend John Hay, statesman, built adjoining houses on the north side of Washington's Lafayette Square at Sixteenth Street. Situated only three hundred yards or so from the front door of the "President's House," the Hay-Adams residences became a focal point of capital society, with Theodore Roosevelt likely to drop in for afternoon tea, only to find that writer Henry James had already beaten him to the fresh biscuits.

The historic houses were demolished in 1927 to make way for a new hotel, properly named the Hay-Adams, in honor of the two famous men. The hotel's location so close to the White House guaranteed a certain cachet, but by the 1970's the Hay-Adams, although still a landmark, was certainly not on the A list of Washington hotels.

The interiors of the lobby and public rooms were darkly paneled and dimly lit, the rooms were shabby, and the service was arthritic. By the early eighties the hotel had become a ghostly old lady, maintaining a certain dignity because of its proximity to power but sadly down at the heels.

In 1983 that suddenly changed when the Hay-Adams was purchased by David Murdock, a California financier, and transformed by his wife, Gabriele. Within a year of the purchase the Hay-Adams had regained its grandeur, rooms and suites brightened and refurbished, lobby lit with chandeliers, spring colors to eat breakfast by in the Henry Adams Room, rich reds and lavish carpeting in the John Hay restaurant and bar. The exterior of the building was cleaned, the brass polished, and new pale blue stationery printed with the address "One Lafayette Square," even though the main entrance and the real address were on Sixteenth Street.

Eric Rhinelander, although mildly curious about the illustrious building's past, was far more interested in the fact that south-facing rooms on the fifth, sixth, and seventh floors of the hotel had clear views of the north facade of the White House and the White House grounds. Utilizing the small cherry-wood breakfast table in his room, his Nikon fitted with a 300 mm telephoto lens and a low tripod, Rhinelander had been taking photographs since his wake-up call at 6:00 A.M.

To avoid arousing suspicion about his interest in the presidential residence, he was using Polachrome 35 mm Polaroid slide film, which he would later develop himself, using the inexpensive processing kit he had purchased the day before, soon after his arrival in Washington.

During a career as a professional killer that spanned almost three decades, Rhinelander had been presented with assignments offering varying degrees of difficulty, ranging from hand-to-hand butchery in the jungles of Laos and Cambodia to surgically accurate removals on the platforms of the Paris metro. He had killed KGB agents asleep in their beds, South American military leaders in the arms of their lovers, a British research scientist in his laboratory, and a Turkish arms dealer in his private aircraft at nineteen thousand feet above the Aegean.

But this, he knew, was very different. Any head of state, by the nature of his occupation, was a "hard target," and the President of the United States was the hardest of all. Compounding that fact was Hudson Cooper's requirement that the assassination take place within the White House. At first glance it appeared not only fantastic but insane.

Not once in the building's history had an assassination attempt taken place in the White House or on the grounds and since the killing of John Kennedy and the multitude of attempts on the Presidents who followed him, the White House had been steadily transformed into an impregnable fortress; there was even a rumor about a ground-to-air missile installation hidden on the roof of the Treasury Building.

On the other hand, he saw Hudson Cooper's point. To assassinate the President and the Vice President in the White House would be a strike at the very core of American mythology. You might not approve of the man in power, but like the Constitution, the flag, and the Liberty Bell, the White House and the office it represented were symbols fundamentally sacred to the vast majority of Americans. Tamper with them, and you risked the rage of an entire nation.

184

That, of course, was precisely what Cooper wanted. If the plan was successful and Nezar Assad, the terrorist, took the fall, Cooper and whoever he was fronting for would be able to change the focus of foreign policy in the Middle East. Qaddafi could be bled dry overnight, and domestically the specter of international terrorism let loose in America would be the leverage and justification needed for enormous budget increases within the intelligence community.

Not that the political ramifications were any of Rhinelander's concern; he was here to find out if the plan was workable. He leaned forward and again put his eye to the viewfinder of the camera.

The north fence had two openings: the northeast gate and the northwest gate. Each gate had a small guardhouse manned by two uniformed Executive Protection Branch officers. Every ten minutes or so the roving plainclothes Secret Service agents patrolling the north lawn used the guardhouses as rest stops. Scanning the expanse of lawn with the camera, Rhinelander had counted an even dozen uniformed guards on patrol and six Secret Service agents.

Focusing on the White House itself, Rhinelander could see two uniformed officers at the east wing gatehouse, two Secret Service agents walking the curving drive between the gate and the east wing portico entrance, two more uniformed officers walking back and forth along the length of the east wing, two more at the north portico entrance, and six Secret Service agents visibly present around the west wing and the Press Office entrance.

In all he counted thirty-six people. If he assumed that there were at least an equal number of agents and officers in the southern quadrant, it meant he was dealing with almost seventy people involved with external security.

In addition to the human security forces, there was a considerable number of electronic countermeasures in place. Pushing the telephoto to its most extreme, Rhinelander could make out the slowly moving turrets of closed-circuit cameras hidden behind the louvers of the rooftop ventilating units, and there were still more cameras nestled under the eaves, their wide-angle lenses focused down on the grounds and driveways directly in front of the mansion.

Coming in tight on the fence close to the northwest gate, he could also see the corner of a small gray box, partially hidden at the foot of one of the stone gate columns. A thick cable was just barely visible, snaking out from the box, down the gate column and into the ground; almost certainly the control box for a microwave security fence. A closer inspection

185

would probably reveal half a dozen identical boxes in place around the perimeter of the grounds. Linked together, the buried cables would create an invisible barrier of ambient microwaves capable of detecting anyone climbing over the fence and walking across the grounds.

Rhinelander took another few exposures, then leaned back and lit a cigarette. At that sophisticated level of security he could also expect ground sensors in the lawn, infrared capability from the closed-circuit cameras and possibly an intruder radar setup. Along with all the manpower and electronics there were the physical barriers. The big concrete obstacles put in place after the Beirut catastrophe had been removed long ago, but Rhinelander could see the telltale lines in the asphalt just inside the gates. Try to make a high-speed entrance onto the grounds, and a spike-studded barrier would rear up out of the ground, puncturing your tires and ripping the belly out of any vehicle short of a tank.

The dark-haired man sighed, blowing out twin wisps of smoke through his nostrils. He picked up the three-ring binder from the small table in front of him and began jotting a few things down, roughly diagramming what he'd observed.

To a big-game hunter this would be called a difficult lie, to Rhinelander it was far from impossible. Even the most cursory examination of White House external security showed that the focus of the efforts was on the fence-climbing lunatic or the car-bombing fanatic. The implication seemed to be that no one in his right mind would want to kill the President of the United States.

To Rhinelander, who had seen the results of terrorist activity from Dublin to Dubrovnik, that kind of thinking was incredibly naive. He reached out and picked up the Fodor's Washington guidebook he'd purchased in the train station. Turning to the section on the White House, he used a yellow highlighting pen to underscore the visiting hours: 10:00 A.M. to noon, Tuesday through Saturday.

He tossed the book back onto the table, butted his cigarette in the crystal ashtray, and lit another. In an era of death squads, cassette player bombs in jumbo jets, and the slaughterhouse politics of South America, the private residence of the President of the United States was open to the public five days out of seven.

Rhinelander shook his head, trying to imagine groups of tourists tramping through 10 Downing Street or regiments of camera-toting Japanese and Germans fanning out through the echoing corridors of the Élysée Palace in Paris. It was absurd, yet here in Washington it was accepted as the norm, as commonplace as a ride through the haunted house at Disneyland or a climb to the Statue of Liberty's crown.

He leaned forward and put his eye to the viewfinder again. The White House. Beyond the symbolism what was he actually seeing? A four-story mansion, the ground floor almost invisible from this side because of a slope in the terrain, the fourth floor hidden behind the protective wall that ringed the roofline. From the east and west sides of the building, columned porticos connecting the two-story annexes, the east and west wings. All this in a parklike setting of trees, lawns, and fountains. Impressive perhaps, but there were bigger mansions on more lavish grounds within an hour's drive, and that was going to be the key to his approach; it was simply a question of degree. Every lock had a key; every problem, a solution.

Taking his eye from the camera, Rhinelander picked up his notebook again and carefully penned a series of headings and subheadings, setting out areas of research that needed to be completed before he continued with the project at hand:

Schedules
• Secret Service
• Executive Protection Branch (uniforms)
• services (food?)
• shift changes
• lights?/surveillance?/radio frequencies?

President/Vice President
• daily routine/is there one?
• kids/relatives
• vehicles/where?
• food again

Tucker/Teresi
• bios
• habits

Building/grounds
• history
• floor plans?
• books/periodicals
• maps/plans

- accidental documentation

Blair House/floor plans

Weapons
- silent
- probably nonmetal (security/metal detectors?)
- lethal
- poison/fléchette ?
- $CO_2$?

Mallory
- shopping list

Rhinelander dropped the pen, massaged his eyes briefly with thumb and forefinger, then yawned. Enough for now; there was no point in getting too involved in the research until he was settled in John Gray's apartment at the Wyoming. He began packing away the photographic equipment; it was time to check out of the Hay-Adams.

By noon the assassin had left the luxurious hotel, taking his single suitcase by taxi to the more modest lodgings offered by the Connecticut Avenue Holiday Inn. He checked in, using John Gray's name, offering the man's Diners Club number as security against a proposed two-week stay at the hotel.

Rhinelander was not a man who placed much value on the concept of luck. Finding the Grays at the Breakers and discovering that they would be gone from their apartment for such an extended period made for a pleasant surprise, but no more than that. To treat it as a stroke of good luck would be a mistake. Depending on that sort of happenstance could be disastrous, hence the fallback position at the Holiday Inn. If he had to bail out of the Wyoming quickly for some reason, the hotel was only a few hundred yards away.

After carrying his bag up to the room, Rhinelander let himself in and locked the door behind him. The room was plain and functional with two single beds, a desk, and a chest of drawers. After placing the suitcase on one of the beds, Rhinelander went to the small rectangular window and pulled back the heavy pale green curtains; as he had requested, the room overlooked Connecticut Avenue.

Directly across from the window was the white gull-wing shape of the Washington Hilton, its main entrance on T Street. Slightly to the left, facing the rear of the Hilton, was the Wyoming. Originally the three linked seven-story blocks had a clear view across Columbia Road and out over southwestern Washington, but the Hilton, three stories higher, had usurped the splendid panorama for its own guests.

Rhinelander unpacked his camera, then returned to the window, where he used the Nikon's long lens for a closer inspection of the building. At a guess, and on the basis of the heavy-handed architectural detailing, he put the building's construction date around 1900 or slightly later. From the look of the large, deeply inset arch facing Connecticut Avenue, it had once been the main entrance to the building, but it had been long since filled in with a small window and an air-conditioning unit. Panning to the right, he focused on the side of the building facing Columbia Road.

There were three sets of double doors, modern glass and steel, one set for each of the three connected blocks. Rhinelander put the camera down on the chest of drawers and lit a cigarette. He stood looking across at the Wyoming, working it out.

With three main entrances it was unlikely that any one of them would have a doorman. Considering the building's age, the deep courtyards between the blocks presumably gave access to servants' entrances along the connecting corridors of the buildings. The three entrances all faced Columbia Road, but the registration certificate in Gray's car gave a Connecticut Avenue address, which probably meant their apartment was in the first of the three blocks. The way things looked, getting into the building would be relatively easy.

And it was. Wearing jeans and a short-sleeved blue knit shirt and with the Nikon slung over his shoulder, Rhinelander left the hotel. He crossed Connecticut, pausing in front of the equestrian statue of Civil War General George B. McClellan to take a photograph, then took the crosswalk the rest of the way across the avenue to Columbia Road.

Casually he went up the short walk to the front door of the Wyoming's first block and pulled open the door. Making a show of fumbling for his keys, Rhinelander glanced around quickly. The foyer was a fairly recent addition, probably for security reasons. There was a buzz board on the right and a double row of mailboxes on the left. Only fourteen names on the buzz board, two apartments per floor with the Grays listed as number 502. Directly ahead was a heavy glass door and beyond it the original lobby, complete with marble floor and a curving staircase bracketed by old-fashioned cage elevators on either side. No security desk.

Rhinelander removed the keys from his pocket and tried the first

189

Medeco. It turned, and the door opened. Moving quickly, he crossed the lobby, pulled open the left-hand elevator door, and stepped into the cage. He pressed the fifth-floor button, and the cage began to rise. A few moments later he reached the fifth floor and stepped out into a small public hall that mimicked the larger main-floor lobby. There were two doors, 501 on the right, 502 on the left. Using the second Medeco key and with the single-pin Secor key ready in his hand, he let himself into the Grays' apartment.

The front door opened onto a small reception hall. At eye level on the right-hand wall was a small gray alarm box with three pin lights, two green and one red. The two green lights were labeled "Monitor" and "Enable," while the red was labeled "Arm/Disarm." Below the lights was a lock switch. Rhinelander fitted the Secor key into the lock switch and turned. The "Arm/Disarm" light went from red to green. Pocketing the keys, he closed the front door.

The apartment was enormous, and from the furnishings and accessories it was obvious that John Gray's career as a lawyer had been lucrative. To the left of the reception area a high oak-trimmed archway led into a living-room area at least forty feet long and twenty feet wide. The room was divided into two distinct sectors by a pair of trifold black lacquer Chinese screens, decorated elaborately with etched gold-leaf cranes and dragons. On one side of the screens several leather-covered chairs were arranged around a deep-hearthed fireplace, while the long end of the room was furnished more lavishly with couches, upholstered chairs, small rosewood tables here and there, and a magnificent sixteenth-century marquetry English lady's writing table. The carpets scattered across the pegged dark oak floors were antique Persian, while the individually lit and ornately framed paintings on the pale yellow walls were nineteenth-century American. There were four large windows on the long side of the room, looking down onto Columbia Road, and two windows on the short side, overlooking Connecticut Avenue.

Brass-trimmed oak and leaded-glass pocket doors opened onto an equally opulent dining room. Here the walls were covered in light peach moiré silk. A Wedgwood chandelier lighted a long Chippendale dining table with matching chairs, which rested on a large, brightly colored Kazakh carpet.

An archway on the far wall of the dining room gave access to a long hall running the length of the apartment. Both walls of the hallway were filled with framed photographs, most of the family album variety: Gray with his wife; Gray with his children at various stages in their lives; Gray in U.S. Navy uniform; Gray with Presidents from Eisenhower to Reagan.

The rooms on the right side of the hall were utilitarian: a pantry, a large but very outdated kitchen, a small servants' elevator, a bathroom, a storage room tucked in beside a rear staircase, and two small rooms that might once have been used as servants' quarters but had now been changed into a guest room and a sewing room.

On the left side of the hall, directly across from the kitchen, was a den-office, one wall filled with books, while the one across from it held glass-fronted display cabinets filled with golf trophies. There was a wood-burning fireplace in the wall facing the drapery-covered windows and a highly polished twin-pedestal mahogany desk. At odds with the rest of the room was the work station to the left of the desk, within easy reach of the wood-and-leather swivel chair.

A modern steel table held an Everex 386 computer with a large-screen color monitor and a stand-alone Toshiba fax machine. On a shelf under the table there was a laser printer, and on the desk there was a complex-looking telephone console that appeared to be connected to the computer. The credenza nestled behind the desk and underneath the two high windows was crammed with software boxes that included three different accounting data base programs, a legal billing program, and the manuals for PC Link, InfoNet, and half a dozen other networking services. Gray might have retired, but he hadn't put himself out to pasture.

There were two more rooms on the left side of the hall, both of them with en suite full bathrooms. Both were furnished as master bedrooms, the room adjoining the den fitted out with a single bed, the room beyond containing a queen size. The far room was done in blues and greens, the floor covered with thick dark blue wall-to-wall carpeting. The room close to the den was more masculine, the walls white, the wood floors bare except for a rattan mat at the foot of the bed. Apparently Mr. and Mrs. Gray slept apart.

Back in the den Rhinelander took a small address book out of his jeans, sat down behind the desk, and picked up the telephone receiver. He placed two calls. The first was to Housecalls, the apartment sitters. Posing as John Gray, he told it that because of illness, its services would no longer be required and that he would be sending one of the lawyers from his firm to collect any accumulated mail and the key to the lobby mailbox. His second call was to the number given to him by Hudson Cooper in Barbados. On the third ring the connection was made, fol-

191

lowed by the tone-beep of an answering machine. Speaking quickly but clearly, Rhinelander read off the number of a telephone booth in the National Visitors Center at Union Station and a time—ten-thirty the following morning. Mallory was to be there, waiting to be contacted.

The calls made, Rhinelander left the apartment and returned to his room at the Holiday Inn. It was one-thirty, still time to do some shopping for a new wardrobe and pick up the mailbox key from Housecalls. After that the rest of his day would be spent browsing through some of Washington's better antiquarian bookstores doing preliminary research. By evening he would be settled in at the Wyoming.

Rhinelander smiled to himself, feeling the familiar tension gripping the pit of his stomach. Standing in the middle of the anonymous hotel room, he closed his eyes briefly, visualizing the White House as he'd seen it that morning through the lens of his camera. The stalking ground had been chosen; now the hunt could begin.

# PART THREE

A *PRESIDENT HAS TO EXPECT THESE*
*THINGS.*

—*HARRY TRUMAN,*
*commenting on the Blair House assassination*
*attempt*

# CHAPTER 14

As Rhinelander prepared to set out on his shopping expedition, Stephen Stone was finishing a late lunch at the Hotel Washington's rooftop restaurant, the Terrace. Seated across from him was Lyall Spencer, head of the Secret Service's White House detail. A light breeze was blowing, but both men had removed their suit jackets against the hazy heat of the early-afternoon sun.

Spencer was in his late forties, a twenty-five-year man with Treasury, more than half of it spent as a Secret Service agent. He'd been promoted to head of the White House detail almost three years before, and Stone knew he was just about ready for rotation to another field office or to Secret Service headquarters on G Street. He was a tall man, broad-shouldered and thick-necked like a football player. His hair, or what there was left of it, was close-cropped and grizzle gray. When he took off his standard-issue aviator sunglasses, his eyes were a rich brown, the warm color offset by the piercing, stone-faced gaze referred to as the Look by Secret Service insiders.

Stone watched as Spencer stabbed his fork into the remains of his Sacher torte. He'd come in contact with the man several times when Spencer was working out of the Washington field office and socially on two or three occasions, but he knew little about him beyond the fact that he was divorced with two teenage children living in California.

Studying him as he attacked his dessert, Stone saw a man who lived a life of total, nerve-racking concentration combined with numbing boredom. Constantly alert and personally responsible for the well-being of the

195

most important man in the nation, he spent every day in an endless series of drills and false alarms. It was an occupation tailor-made for heart attacks, alcoholism, and divorce. On the other hand, no one had drafted him; the choice of job had been his own.

As Spencer finished eating, Stone hailed a waiter for coffee, and when it had been served, both men lit cigarettes and got down to the real business at hand.

"Discreet lunches at the Terrace aren't too common for the FBI and the service," Spencer said. "From your phone call it sounds as though you're on a private fishing expedition." His voice was a surprisingly cultured baritone. "What's on your mind?" he asked bluntly.

"I'm just trying to cut some red tape," Stone answered. "A few quiet words early on could save us both a lot of paper work in the future."

"As long as both of us don't bother to mention the 'few quiet words' to our respective bosses," Spencer retorted.

"Well, it's not as though your guys and mine are on particularly good terms." Stone shrugged.

Both men were well aware of the long-standing and ongoing difficulties between the bureau and the service. Partially because of the domestic security guidelines introduced in 1976, the FBI had placed most of its working emphasis on crimes that had already taken place, rather than accumulate information that might stop the events from happening. Considering the curtailment of the FBI's domestic intelligence work, the quality of the information it actually did provide to the Secret Service had deteriorated simply because of its second-drawer priority. Half a dozen congressional hearings over the past decade hadn't done anything to solve the problem.

"All right. Screw procedure for the moment," Spencer said. "You ask your questions, and I'll get my jollies at the irony of the bureau coming to *us* for information."

"Francisco Cabrera," Stone said carefully, watching Spencer's expression. Nothing changed; the man was a cyborg in a gray flannel suit.

"What about him?" The Secret Service agent took a swallow of coffee and stared blankly across the table at Stone.

"I'm chasing down a few rumors about his visit."

"Don't play games with me, Stone. I don't have the time," Spencer answered. "He's the president of Costa Rica; he's coming here next month to open the new embassy building officially. That's all public information. You're sniffing around my ass like a bitch in heat. Why?"

"Any threats against him?" Stone asked, pressing. "Anything come

196

up from OPI?" OPI was the Secret Service's Office of Protective Intelligence.

"This is pay to play," Spencer replied. "Why do you want to know?" There was a long pause. Stone finally spoke. "We've got a Russian who took a powder," he said, juggling the facts slightly. "A GRU high-end type. He's been making noises about Cabrera."

"What kinds of noises?" asked Spencer, suddenly interested.

"A possible assassination attempt," Stone answered.

At the word "assassination" Spencer's eyes flickered slightly, and then the expression on his face hardened even more. "How good is his information?" the Secret Service man asked.

"Very good," Stone answered.

Spencer sat back in his seat. "The obvious question then," he said after a moment. "Why isn't this going through normal channels?"

"I've been asked to back off," Stone said quietly. "I've been told the situation is outside the bureau's mandate." The implication was clear: If Stone was being muzzled, the orders had come from an agency on a higher rung of the intelligence ladder, and if a Soviet defector was involved, that meant the senior organization was the CIA.

"Shit," said Spencer. "Just what I need, more political bullshit!" He stubbed out his cigarette in the last remnant of Sacher torte, then lit another.

"You really haven't heard anything?" Stone asked.

Spencer shook his head. "Not a damn thing," he said. "How long did you have your pigeon before they took him off your hands?"

"Long enough to know that he was on to something," Stone responded cautiously. Make the lie too complicated, and he'd wind up tripping over it.

"Anything substantial?"

"No," Stone answered, shaking his head. That was true enough. So far all he had was a trembling web of circumstantial evidence. Christ! If only Travkin had really defected to him!

"All right." Spencer nodded. "I'll check it out. Last time I looked we had about forty thousand potential freaks logged onto the computer. Maybe one of them is a Costa Rican expatriate with a bone to pick."

"What about professionals?" Stone asked.

"Sure. Those, too." Spencer sighed. "Where do I get in touch with you if something rings a bell?"

"Here," Stone answered. He took a ball-point out of his shirt pocket and jotted the safe house telephone number onto his napkin. He folded it

197

once and handed it to Spencer. The Secret Service man stood and took the napkin, which he put into the pocket of his trousers. He pulled his suit jacket from the back of his chair and shrugged it on.

"Thanks for the lunch," he said, nodding. He put on his sunglasses, turned, and headed for the exit, threading his way between the empty tables. Stone watched him go, then leaned back in his chair, looking out across the city. Over the roof of the Treasury he could see the White House and beyond it Blair House, the presidential guest quarters. In a few weeks it would be used as Francisco Cabrera's residence while he was in Washington.

Resisting the urge to light another cigarette, Stephen Stone frowned. Glancing over the low wall beside him, he watched the slowly moving traffic work its way up Pennsylvania Avenue toward the Capitol, a heat-rippled white dome a mile away, barely visible in the murky air.

"I must be nuts," he whispered to himself. He'd put his career on the line by deliberately disobeying Ruppelt's orders, and now he'd compounded it by involving Spencer and the Secret Service. The worst thing about it was not having anybody to talk to about it. He felt a sudden tug of loneliness and realized that he was thinking about Debbie.

And that was a waste of time, of course, because she was still away at that conference in Paris. He shook his head, bemused, and allowed himself the cigarette. Somewhere along the line his life had come completely off the predictable rails of existence, and now he was hurtling down some bizarre spur line populated by kidnapped Russians, Central American heads of state, and a wife more desirable now that she was an ex.

With an irritated grimace Stone stood up abruptly and put on his jacket. That kind of thinking really *would* drive you nuts. The only cure was work, and one way or the other that meant Dmitri Aleksandrovich Travkin. The beleaguered counterintelligence agent dipped into his wallet and pulled out a handful of bills. He slipped enough to cover the check under his water glass and followed Spencer's route out of the restaurant.

To Sergei Kuryokhin Prague represented everything that was wrong with Central Europe, past and present. Architecturally the dark city on the banks of the Vltava River was a paean of praise to the baroque sensibilities of the Hapsburgs, its steep, winding streets and looming hilltop fortresses acting as a constant reminder of its feudal origins. Politically it was a city based on a philosophy of entrepreneurial corruption from pencil-stealing office clerks to senior officials renting out holiday time in their country homes. The food was invariably bland and starchy, hotel accommodations were appalling, and the summer dust on the streets irritated his sinuses. As far as Kuryokhin was concerned, the only thing good about Prague was the quality of its beer.

Still, it had been part of his circuit of agent contacts for the better part of four decades and required his personal attention from time to time. His twice-yearly trips also served notice to the Young Turks of the KGB that he was still a force to be contended with, not simply an aging has-been. This trip, however, was more than just a public relations gesture; his agent in Prague was the access point of his pipeline to the West and a necessary element for setting up a contact with Osin.

The system had been in place almost from the time Osin had been activated. His Prague agent, part of an established KGB network, was linked to a secondary cutout, supposedly an illegal run by the man in Prague. The cutout in turn provided Kuryokhin with a connection to a free-lancer headquartered in Amsterdam. The free-lancer, a man named Tetar van Elven, ran a wholesaling company and came to Prague regularly to purchase glassware.

The Prague agent knew nothing of Van Elven, and Van Elven knew nothing of the Prague agent, so the connection was clean. The complex system also ensured that Osin's true identity was safe from a thousand-and-one prying eyes at Teply Stan. The deep-cover agent in the American intelligence establishment was the crowning achievement of Kuryokhin's career, and he'd gone to great lengths to ensure that the identity of his most valuable asset would never be compromised.

At seven-thirty that evening, after a mediocre meal in the Hotel Ambassador's Pasaz Café, the elderly intelligence officer stepped out onto Wenceslas Square and began walking south toward Opletalova Street and the looming equestrian statue of the square's namesake, King Wenceslas.

The square was actually an eight-hundred-yard-long boulevard, its broad sidewalks shaded by trees, the tumbled skein of rococo buildings on either side outfitted with every amenity, including restaurants, airline offices, clothing boutiques, antiques stores, and galleries. On summer nights such as this one the sidewalks themselves were an obstacle course of ice-cream vendors, sausage stands selling bloated *kolbasy* to anyone who dared purchase one, and wandering crowds of local citizenry, dirndl-costumed peasants from the outlying provinces, and roving squads of German tourists.

Ignoring it all, Kuryokhin continued on his way. At first glance the square looked like the Prague version of Manhattan's Fifth Avenue, but in reality the long boulevard bore the stamp of a violent history. The

199

republic had been declared here in 1918, and Red Army tanks had made their triumphant way down the broad avenue in 1945. They had returned in 1968 to choke the Dubček-inspired uprising, and the philosophy student Jan Palach had incinerated himself at the foot of the Wenceslas statue in 1969.

None of which mattered to Kuryokhin in the slightest. To him, at seventy-seven, history, like sex, was a thing of the past. As the white-haired old man threaded his way through the meandering crowds, he could feel every day of every year in his bones and every beat of a heart that by now had probably reached the consistency of tissue paper. He'd fought wars no one had ever heard of, screwed women from Murmansk to Melitopol, and witnessed the rise and fall of everyone from Beria to Andropov. The only lesson learned through all those years was that power was the only pleasure and survival the only law. To him, life had devolved into an intricate game played out one day at a time without nostalgia for the past or hope for the future. For Sergei Yulevich Kuryokhin there really was no time like the present.

His musings took him to U Natrovski Alley, a narrow lane running off Wenceslas Square, its entrance almost invisible to the casual passerby. Kuryokhin turned up the deeply shadowed walkway, ignoring the darkened, grime-encrusted windows of the tiny shops on either side. Fifty yards down the alley he reached his objective: the dimly lit window of Antikvariât Masaryk.

The old man glanced at the meager selection of volumes on display behind the dirty glass: a long-out-of-date French-language guide to Prague, a fan of early Penguin editions of P. G. Wodehouse, and two Stephen King novels in German. Peering beyond the stained felt of the display shelf, Kuryokhin could see a cubicle now more than a few meters on a side, the walls filled with awkward-looking homemade bookshelves, the shelves themselves half empty. A middle-aged man with dark slicked-back hair sat behind a scarred desk at the rear of the cubicle, a curtained doorway at his back and an enormous marmalade cat asleep on the desk in front of him. The man was looking at a battered copy of *Penthouse* magazine. Masaryk at work, a moth-eaten gray cardigan buttoned over his fat belly, studying the black-market wares that kept him in business.

Kuryokhin pushed open the door of the tiny bookstore, pleased by the brief look of fear on the pornographer's face as he made his entrance. Seeing who it was, Masaryk settled back in his chair, exhaling loudly. Kuryokhin closed the door behind him and took three brief steps to the desk.

"I thought perhaps you might not be coming tonight," the bookseller grumbled, looking up at Kuryokhin. He spoke in English, the only language common to them both. Masaryk was incapable of learning Russian, and Kuryokhin refused to force his larynx around the impossible convolutions of Czech. The KGB man grimaced, his nose wrinkling. The smell of stale beer hung over Masaryk like a pall.

"I said I would be here," Kuryokhin answered. "I am here."

Masaryk nodded dully and put down the *Penthouse*. He pushed himself back in his chair and opened the center drawer of the desk. Reaching into it, he withdrew a thin manila envelope. He handed it to Kuryokhin and waited. The KGB man examined the package carefully, his gnarled fingers playing over the closure and all four edges of the envelope. In the old days courier material had been secured with wax, but the "flaps and seals" technology of both East and West had made such procedures useless. Years ago Kuryokhin himself had suggested coating the edges and flaps of envelopes with a thin layer of rubber cement. The method was cheap, tamperproof, and still in use.

Ignoring Masaryk, the old man opened the envelope. Inside was a single sheet of thin paper and a rail ticket dutifully stamped with the official seal of approval from Cedok, the Czech State Travel Office. The ticket was dated for midnight the following day and would take him from Prague to Berlin and then on to Amsterdam. In all the trip was almost twenty hours long.

By air the journey could be made in a tenth of that time, but the old man preferred to keep away from the myriad eyes and ears of both Ruzyně and Schiphol airports. Turning his attention to the sheet of paper, Kuryokhin tilted his eyeglasses up on his nose, squinting in the dim light as he read the brief message: "CANAL HOUSE 148 KEIZERSGRACHT. TEL. 262-231 ON ARRIVAL."

There was no signature, but the addition of the figures in the telephone number ensured that both the train ticket and the hotel address had come from Tetar van Elven. Kuryokhin slipped the sheet of paper and the railway ticket back into the envelope, then put the envelope into the inside breast pocket of his suit jacket. From the opposite pocket he withdrew another envelope, this one filled with well-used German marks, Masaryk's currency of choice. He handed the money to the bookseller, who then placed it in the drawer of his desk. From the expression on his face Kuryokhin knew that Masaryk couldn't wait for him to leave so he could count it.

"Our business is concluded," the KGB man said, making no effort to conceal his contempt.

The money in hand, Masaryk offered a thick-lipped smile. "Until next time." He nodded.

Kuryokhin made no reply; instead, he turned away and left the bookstore. Walking back down the alley to Wenceslas Square, he wondered how long it would be until one of the currency squads from the SNB raided Antikvariåt Masaryk and dragged the oily little shit off to the cells at the Bartolomejska Police Headquarters. The old man shook his head slowly, mouth pulled down in a frown. He'd seen enough of the world to know that it didn't matter who ruled, Marxist, martinet, or mushroom, every state, every city had its version of Lars Masaryk, and the trade which he enjoyed. The East bloc had no corner on the market in filth and depravity. Kuryokhin spit onto the pavement. In his youth such men would have been rooted out like vermin. Now it was the order of the day; he'd even seen such goods on the metro back home. He shook his head again; he'd lived too long.

Reaching the boulevard, he began trudging up the gentle slope, taking deep breaths of the cool night air. By the time he reached the main entrance to the Hotel Ambassador he'd managed to purge the sour stink of Masaryk's store from his nostrils, his thoughts concentrated on the upcoming journey to Amsterdam. An hour later the white-haired old man had fallen into treasonous sleep, coiled dark dreams of old battles won and lost rising from memory to contradict his present tense philosophy.

Dmitri Travkin lay on the bed in his room at the Bowie facility, leafing through a month-old copy of *Newsweek*, trying to ignore the constant itch of frustration caused by his enforced inactivity. Earlier that day they'd moved him out of the hospital wing, but his new quarters weren't much better. His room was small, with a narrow mesh-glass window. The floor was hardwood, freshly sanded and glossy, the walls white over aging plaster. The room was furnished with a single bed, a straight-backed wooden chair, and a nondescript chest of drawers. A closet on the left-hand wall had been converted into a tiny bathroom with a sink and toilet. The only decorative touch was a framed government-issue official portrait of Richard Milhous Nixon.

Dropping the *Newsweek* onto his lap for the twentieth time in as many minutes, Travkin stared at the picture of the former President, wondering at the exigencies of fate that had made it his only companion. The GRU agent grimaced. It was oddly fitting since both men had been trapped in a trembling, far-flung web of lies, counterlies, illusion, and deceit, but there the similarity ended. Tricky Dicky was making six-figure publishing advances for his peccadilloes while Dumb Dmitri was getting three bland meals a day and a monk's cell for his best efforts.

By now, he knew, Gennadi Koslov would have written him off like a bad debt. Travkin didn't hold it against his boss; the old man wouldn't have any choice, no matter what his personal feelings were. The fact that he'd been kidnapped was irrelevant: Once taken, he was compromised; returning, he would be suspect. It was the Yurchenko scenario in reverse, and Travkin found himself wondering if his kidnapping by the CIA might be in reprisal for the KGB man's infamous and highly embarrassing double defection in 1985.

The origins of his plight didn't really matter to Travkin one way or the other. His concerns were much more immediate. Following the preliminary interrogation, he'd spent almost all his time trying to formulate some sort of plan. So far he had identified his problem as having three stages: escape from the Bowie facility; somehow gathering evidence to prove that his kidnapping had been just that, not a defection; then finally, and most important, convincing Gennadi Koslov of his innocence. For all his Western affectations and affections the thought of being marooned in the United States, unable ever to go home again, was unbearable.

His bitter train of thought was broken as the door to his room opened. It was the Mutt and Jeff pair who'd escorted him to his previous interrogation, this time minus the wheelchair. Once again it was the slim dark-haired man who spoke to him, this time in English.

"Come with us," he said briefly. Travkin made no attempt at a reply. He simply nodded and stood up, allowing the two men to fall in on either side as they went down the maze of half-lit corridors to the pleasantly furnished room where he'd spoken with David Cook, his bland and strangely vague interrogator.

His two escorts opened the door to the room and allowed Travkin to enter. They withdrew, closing the door behind them, leaving the GRU man to himself. There was no sign of Cook, but there was an oddly familiar smell in the air. Cigarette smoke certainly, but neither the tart-sweet odor of a blended American tobacco or the acrid fug of a European Tabac-Noir. Travkin sniffed, frowning. A green raw scent, almost like a cigar.

There was a large cut glass ashtray on the coffee table between Cook's upholstered chair and the couch. To judge from its position, the ashtray had been used by someone sitting on the couch. Travkin went around the table and picked up the ashtray, examining the half dozen or so butts ground into the gray-brown ash. One of them was long enough to read the brand name: Coronado. Mexican? Cuban? Why here and now? A Latin American defector being debriefed? Silliness. Or . . . His mind did the necessary hop, skip, and jump to the obvious conclusion: Francisco Cabrera. Not a defector, but perhaps an assassin, or someone chosen to play an assassin's part.

He took the cigarette butt and dropped it carefully into the breast pocket of his jacket. There was still no sign of Cook. Putting the ashtray back on the table, Travkin began to roam the room, desperately trying to gather more information. Reaching the antique writing desk, he paused, tilting his head toward the doorway beside it. Still no sound. He went through the drawers quickly. Pads, ball-point pen, book of matches from a restaurant on H Street called Big Wong. Travkin knew it; basement dim sum all day long with an atmosphere like an opium den. He pocketed the matches and kept on going. Nothing, nothing, nothing. Wait!

The surface of the desk was protected by a large buckskin-colored felt blotter in a leather frame. The telephone stood at the lower-left-hand corner, and there was a Parker pen set in a marble base at the upper center. For the most part the blotter was clean, but the area around the telephone was scored with a variety of doodles and scrawls. One in particular caught Travkin's eye. A single word in ball-point, deeply inscribed and boxed, then struck out, with a telephone number beneath it:

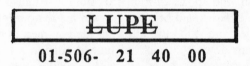

"Lupe" was Spanish for "wolf." A code name perhaps? The 01 prefix meant that the telephone number was international, but he had no idea what country the 506 number represented. Working as quickly as possible, Travkin jotted down the name and number on a sheet of notepaper. After folding the slip of paper into a small square, he bent down and slid it into his shoe, praying that it would be overlooked if there were a snap search.

He checked the desk to make sure everything was as it had been, then went back to the couch and sat down. Picking up a magazine from the coffee table, he willed himself to relax, trying to slow the hammer rhythm of his heart. The name and number might mean nothing at all, but they could also represent the first faint crack in the door he'd been looking for.

"He took the dangle," said David Cook, watching Travkin on the monitor screens. Beside him, Hudson Cooper nodded silently, lips pursed in concentration. Cook had given the evening observation room shift a dinner break, and the two men were alone in the dimly lit surveillance suite. While Cook went back to the list of questions he'd been given for the next "interrogation," Cooper kept his eyes locked on Travkin.

Taking the GRU deputy resident had been a calculated risk but an unavoidable one. Now, it seemed, the risk was paying dividends. Initially the kidnapping had been a quickly devised solution to the unexpected problem of Rednet's snooping. Almost by accident Travkin had stumbled on to Rhinelander, and with Stephen Stone and his people keeping the Russian under surveillance the possibility of the real conspiracy's being uncovered grew with each passing day.

The fact that both Travkin and Stone had misinterpreted the information and were following the red herring involving the Costa Rican situation was a bonus, but Cooper knew he couldn't depend on the cover story forever. Without some additional input by the agency, either Stone or Travkin would have gone beyond it eventually. Hence the kidnapping.

With Travkin removed as an element in the chess game Stone's source of information dried up overnight. Augmenting this was Cooper's thinly veiled intimation to Ruppelt that Travkin was an agency asset, which in turn lent weight to the idea that the kidnapping had actually been a defection. To Ruppelt the Travkin case was out of his hands and good riddance. For Cooper, the required result had been obtained, and the leak plugged.

The only remaining problem had concerned the GRU man's final disposition. At first Cooper had considered simply removing him like Dr. Barron, but the kidnapping itself and the time spent at Bowie had exposed Travkin too broadly. Keeping him on at the facility indefinitely was also out of the question.

It was at this point in his thinking that the deputy director saw the opportunity for another improvisational stroke. If Travkin could be neither killed nor kept, then he would have to be released. By now the GRU man was persona non grata both to his own people and to the KGB. Eventually Travkin would come to the obvious conclusion: To stay alive, he would have to defect, and he would almost certainly defect to Stone at the FBI Rednet office. In the final analysis Cooper didn't really

205

care if Travkin went over to Stone or was picked up by the KGB. Either way he would be debriefed and the "dangle" information relating to the Cabrera scenario would come out, giving it even more credibility and building a false and winding trail away from Rhinelander.

According to Mallory, the assassin had finally called the secure number earlier that day. The message had been straightforward, and Mallory had been given access to the DDO's special account at the agency's proprietary bank in Miami, which had electronically transferred the required amount to a dummy account in New York. Equipped with ID to match the dummy account, Mallory had left for New York on the shuttle earlier that evening and would be back in time for the contact call at the Visitors Center the following morning. The plan, it seemed, was unfolding as it should.

Watching Travkin on the screens in front of him, Cooper allowed himself a small, bleak smile. With the knowledge of President Tucker's progressively destructive ailment and the possibility of Vice President Teresi's assumption of power, the decision to develop an assassination plan had been necessary and inevitable. Even so, it had depressed Cooper profoundly, leaving him with a cold sense of foreboding that ate at his bones like a winter wind. Travkin's intrusion had only made the feeling worse. But now, with the plan actually in motion, Travkin compromised, and Stone effectively blocked, Cooper found himself beginning to believe that it all might work out after all. His smile broadened slightly as he tried to imagine which senior senator would be appointed to head the committee to investigate the assassinations.

"Mr. Cooper?" David Cook's voice invaded his thoughts. Cooper turned and looked at the man.

"Yes?"

"These questions . . . from the looks of it, I'm supposed to be homing in on what he knows about GRU activities in Central America, particularly Costa Rica, is that right?"

"Yes."

"I was just wondering if we had something on down there. The questions are kind of vague."

"Treat it as a fishing expedition, Mr. Cook, nothing more," Cooper answered. He stood up, taking a last look at Travkin, seated on the couch in the interrogation room. "Get the transcript to me when it's done."

"Of course."

"I'll be in administration if you want me," Cooper added. "We're having Comrade Travkin transferred to the Farm tomorrow and I want to

206

make sure the paper work is in order." He nodded toward Cook. "Good night."

"Good night, sir."

The deputy director left the observation room and turned down the wide corridor leading past the old auditorium to the east wing of the facility. If Travkin was half the ex-Spetznaz commando his records indicated, he'd be safely sprung and wandering the streets of Washington, D.C., by this time tomorrow night.

# CHAPTER 15

The night had cooled the baking, humid dome of air shrouding the nation's capital, leaving long, ragged sheets of mist that lay close to the ground, clinging damply to every tree and lamppost, dew beading on each blade of grass for a few brief moments before the sun climbed wearily above the pale stone monuments of the inner city, announcing the beginning of yet another day.

Eric Rhinelander, dressed in a dark blue Nike jogging outfit, pedaled the old-fashioned three-speed bicycle down Connecticut Avenue toward Farragut Square, tires hissing softly on the damp roadway as he piloted the machine through the thin early-morning traffic. The bicycle had been purchased secondhand the day before from a sporting goods store on P Street off Dupont Circle along with the Paragon lock and the custom carrying case welded and bolted behind the seat.

Skirting Farragut Square, Rhinelander guided the bike past the national office for the U.S. Chamber of Commerce, crossed H Street, and coasted down Jackson Place to the intersection at Pennsylvania Avenue. He dismounted at the end of the street, then walked the bicycle into Lafayette Park. He locked the bike securely to the bicycle rack almost directly across from Blair House on the corner. Fifty yards away on the far side of the street he could see the twin cut-stone guardhouses and the heavy double gate that blocked off West Executive Avenue.

Using a key on a chain around his neck, Rhinelander opened the lock on the metal carry case and took out a small red nylon knapsack. At the same time he pushed the start button on the Kyocera KD3030 video cam-

208

era that had been hidden under the knapsack. With the camera running he closed and locked the box, opened the knapsack, and withdrew a lightweight windbreaker to match his dark blue jogging outfit. He put on the windbreaker, slipped the straps of the empty knapsack over his shoulders, and jogged across to the Rochambeau statue. He spent five minutes doing warm-up exercises, casually glancing across Pennsylvania Avenue from time to time as he went through his workout.

His preliminary surveillance at the Hay-Adams and the reading he'd done the day before after making the rounds of Washington's bookstores had taught Rhinelander a number of things, the most important of which was timing. Even the few hours he'd spent at the Hay-Adams showed that everything at the White House was done on a fanatically tight schedule. Shifts changed right to the minute, patrols were made on a strict routine, and people came and went to a time clock's beat.

What he didn't know yet was the complexity of that rhythm—how the patterns of activity meshed together into an overall system. That was the reason for the video camera hidden in the bicycle's carry case. He'd chosen the Kyocera because of its time-lapse function, then added a tiny fiber-optic lens and battery-powered light source, telling the salesman he was a teacher and wanted to record insect activity for his high school biology classes.

Later, in the basement parking garage of the Holiday Inn, after checking out the camera thoroughly, Rhinelander had used a metal punch to poke a small hole in the rear of the metal carry case. He placed the camera and light source in the case, threaded the flexible lens cable into the freshly punched hole, and secured it with a seam of clear nail polish.

Finally, in the early evening, Rhinelander took a taxicab down to Lafayette Square and spent some time trying to identify the best location for the bicycle the following day. From his time at the Hay-Adams he knew that virtually no one except visiting diplomats entered by way of the south portico and that virtually all official traffic entered via the closed-off West Executive Avenue or the east and west entrances on Pennsylvania Avenue.

He eventually settled on the bike rack because he could leave it there safely without arousing suspicion and because it gave the best overall view, including the west entrance on Pennsylvania and the more heavily used West Executive entrance. The nickel cadmium batteries for the camera and the light source pack had a record life of two hours, more than enough for Rhinelander's purposes. In the time-lapse mode the camera was only in operation for two seconds out of every minute, recording twenty-four frames of videotape every thirty seconds. Over a twelve-hour period the camera would take 1,440 individual images, catching any and all traffic going in and out of the two entrances, compressing it into twenty-four minutes of tape.

With his athletic bona fides firmly established in the minds of the Executive Protection Branch guards on the far side of Pennsylvania Avenue, Rhinelander finished up his stationary exercises and began jogging, heading west past Blair House, then north toward Washington Circle. Turning up Nineteenth Street, he made his way to the Presidential Hotel, then caught a taxi back to the Wyoming.

He showered, changed, then spent the two quiet hours going over more of the research material he'd gathered the previous day. By 9:00 A.M. he was having breakfast at the Holiday Inn, and by 10:00 he was on his way to the Visitors Center at Union Station, the envelope containing his instructions to Cooper safely hidden in the inside pocket of his sports jacket.

Sweating in his wilted blue and white seersucker suit, Paul Mallory leaned against the telephone booth partition, the dead receiver to his ear. It was almost exactly ten-thirty, and he'd kept the phone occupied for the last fifteen minutes, ensuring that he'd have possession of it for Rhinelander's call. The Visitors Center was thronged with tourists as well as the ebb and flow of traffic from Union Station and the metro.

He poked a finger under his glasses and swept the pooling beads of stinging salty perspiration away from his eyes. He had a splitting headache, his stomach was hyperacidic and tied in a knot, and his scalp itched. For the twentieth time since he'd climbed out of bed that morning he found himself wishing he'd gone into some other line of business.

The last few days with Cooper had been agonizing. It took every ounce of concentration he had just to keep up the appearance that everything was normal, sending out budget memos, reminding the DDO of meetings, and keeping the filing up-to-date. Thankfully Cooper had been spending most of his time dealing with another project involving a defector out at the Bowie facility, but even that didn't bring any relief from his tensions. For Mallory, given what he knew and what he surmised, imagination was his worst enemy. The day before, on the New York shuttle, he'd come up with a dozen different ways for Cooper to get rid of him and another dozen on the way back.

The more time that passed, the more Mallory's concerns about the

Rhinelander operation solidified, especially considering his own close involvement. To someone with a mind as logical as his, the conclusions were inescapable. Assassination was an outlawed method within the agency, by policy and by law, yet Rhinelander was a professional assassin. By definition, then, the operation planned by Cooper was ex officio, so anyone close to it would be scrubbed.

"Shit," the balding, bespectacled man whispered. He blinked more sweat from his eyes, listening to the whispers and crackles emanating from the dead telephone receiver in his hand. His backup plan using the computer bulletin boards was fine and good, but to be effective as insurance, Cooper would have to know that it existed, and Mallory didn't have anything like enough courage to confront his boss with what he knew. Once again logic came into play because when you got right down to it, he didn't really know anything at all; his suppositions were logical, but they were still just suppositions.

"Shit," he repeated. Every involvement, every bit of contact and information just took him deeper down, and there wasn't a damn thing he could do about it. He let out a long breath and tried to apply his logic and experience as a threat analyst in an optimistic light. The only thing he could come up with was the fact that he was still alive. He glanced at his watch. Ten-thirty on the button. He hung up the receiver, then wiped his palms on his pants legs. A few seconds later the phone rang, and he picked it up.

"Mallory," he said, trying to keep his voice firm.

"What's my name?" The tone was cool, unhurried. Rhinelander.

"QJ/RAIL," Mallory replied.

"What's your slug?" Slug was the agency word for a person's designated office and position.

"Operations," said Mallory.

"Five-one-six Tenth Street Northwest," Rhinelander instructed, "across from Ford's Theater. There's a green refuse container with a swinging lid at the foot of the stairs. Drop what I want into the container. What you want will be stuck to the inside of the lid. Take the metro from Union Station to Metro Center. Take the G and eleventh exit. You have an outside limit of twenty minutes. Go." Suddenly Mallory was listening to a dial tone.

It took Mallory fourteen minutes to reach the address on Tenth Street, which turned out to be the residence where Lincoln was taken after being shot. It was a narrow brick building, three and a half stories high, sandwiched in between a gray office building and a nightclub. A curved staircase led up to the front door above the half-story basement. True to Rhinelander's description, there was a green metal refuse container at the foot of the steps.

Pausing at the stairway, one hand on the wrought-iron railing, Mallory dropped his envelope into the garbage bin, then tipped up the swinging lid and peeled away the envelope Rhinelander had left for him. There were a few people on the street, but no one appeared to be paying any attention to him. If Rhinelander was anywhere close, he was well hidden.

Mallory slid Rhinelander's envelope into his pocket, then headed down Tenth toward E Street and Pennsylvania Avenue. There was a metal pay phone kiosk bolted to the wall of the office building next door to the refuse container, but Mallory ignored it, even though he knew he should be calling into the office as soon as possible after the pickup. At the intersection at E Street his view was overwhelmed by the massive fortress architecture of the J. Edgar Hoover Building, which made him feel even worse. Here he was surrounded by official Washington, contemplating an act of what amounted to treason.

At Pennsylvania Avenue he paused and sat himself uncomfortably on the edge of a large concrete pot containing a fountain of bushy flowering plants that were rapidly shriveling away under the hot late-morning sun. Mallory reached into his pocket and took out the envelope. It appeared to be standard business size. There was no special seal that he could see except for the gummed flap, and the front of the envelope was blank. It had been stuck to the inside of the lid with loops of masking tape, leaving two one-inch-square areas on the flap side that were still a little sticky.

Frowning, he slipped the envelope back into his jacket. He squinted across at the old National Revenue Building on the other side of Pennsylvania Avenue, trying to figure out his best course of action. Cooper's only scheduled event for the day was a reception at Blair House for the Canadian prime minister, and that wasn't until 7:00 P.M. As far as Mallory knew, the DDO was booked out to the Bowie facility for the day, and that gave Mallory some leeway. Even so, Cooper was well aware of the midmorning contact, and if he had any suspicions about Mallory's loyalties, he could scan the computerized security log to find out when he'd checked in. At best Mallory assumed he had only a few hours, no more.

It was enough. Mallory nodded, making up his mind at last. The risk was worth the reward. The worried-looking gangly man climbed to his feet and went to the curb. He hailed a cab, ducked into the battered vehicle, and gave the driver his address in Alexandria.

\* \* \*

Rhinelander, less than two minutes behind Mallory, picked up his envelope from the refuse container, then retraced his steps to Metro Center and played subway tag for half an hour just to make sure that Cooper's man hadn't set him up with a tail. Finally, satisfied that he hadn't been followed, Rhinelander took a taxi back to the Holiday Inn, then walked across Connecticut to the Wyoming Apartments.

As requested, the envelope contained a Citibank passbook from a New York branch with a complete history of deposits and withdrawals and a current balance of two hundred thousand dollars. There was also a Citibank Visa, encoded to a James Smythe, a cash card in the same name, and a New York driver's license with a fuzzy photograph that could have been Rhinelander or anyone else with the same color hair.

Rhinelander went into the study, sat down, and lit a cigarette. In front of him on the desk were stacks of books and magazines he'd picked up on his tour of Washington bookstores. Even for someone used to doing a great deal of research, Rhinelander had been amazed at the massive amount of information about the White House that was freely available. Putting the cigarette aside in Gray's cut crystal ashtray, he flipped open his three-ring notebook, uncapped a felt pen, and got down to work.

The White House, formally known as U.S. Federal Reservation 1, was the first official building erected in Washington. It was designed by an Irish architect named James Hoban and based on the plans for an English country home. The cornerstone of what was to become the quintessential American residence was laid in 1792. Located on a slight ridge and overlooking a swamp that led down to what was then the Tiber Creek, the building was drafty, damp, and uncomfortable.

Thomas Jefferson occupied the White House in 1801 and made the first major additions: the east and west wings, which concealed workshops, wine cellars, and the presidential stables. In 1812 the city was occupied by the British, and the White House was left a gutted ruin. It was reopened in 1818 by President Monroe, and in 1824 and 1829 respectively, the south and north porticos were added. Over the next 120 years succeeding Presidents added, removed, altered, and fiddled. Executive offices were tacked onto the west wing, bomb shelters were dug, and tunnels were bored. One tunnel led from the basement of the east wing to the Treasury Building, another went from the west wing to the headquarters of the Department of War, which eventually became the Ex-

213

ecutive Office Block, and a third was put in from the basement of the mansion to the basement of the west wing offices.

By Truman's time the building was on the verge of collapse, and the pragmatic little man convinced Congress that problems would arise if the ceiling of the Diplomatic Reception Room collapsed onto a visiting dignitary. Funds were allocated, the Trumans moved into Blair House, and the entire building was gutted. Two subbasements and air-conditioning vaults under the north lawn were added; then a steel framework was constructed to support the new floors and walls. The original woodwork—doors, mantels, and cornices—had been carefully preserved, and when the renovations were complete, they were returned to the appropriate places. The work was finished in 1952 after four years' work and an expenditure of almost six million dollars.

There were other alterations made after Truman, although none so complex. Roosevelt's swimming pool in the west wing annex was reopened by Kennedy, ignored by Johnson, then closed and transformed into a press conference room by Nixon. It had only recently been reopened by the Tucker administration. Kennedy also opened up the third-floor attic rooms as well as added a brand-new and supposedly atomic-weapons-hardened bomb shelter, which was now used as headquarters for the White House Communications Agency.

The Communications Agency was interesting in itself. According to the information Rhinelander had assembled, the WHCA was the largest and necessarily the most secret White House support group. Made up of a rotating unit of almost eight hundred elite military professionals, it operated the signal board that connected the President to the nation's diplomatic and military communications nets all over the world.

On a smaller scale, but of more use to Rhinelander, was the knowledge that the WHCA central radio console also connected the White House staff car radios and was in charge of supplying the Secret Service with its communications, including hand-held voice-secure walkie-talkies. The WHCA also operated the White House paging system, which was capable of reaching any staff member in the D.C. area.

Finding accurate information about the Secret Service and other White House staff had been a little more difficult than tracing the building's history, but not impossible. After skimming a dozen or so books, Rhinelander was beginning to build a reasonably complete profile of the executive residence and how it operated.

There were ninety-three actual staff members working within the White House, although none lived in the mansion. They included carpenters, plumbers, upholsterers, cooks, waiters, and elevator operators, all under the supervision of the chief usher, who was effectively the White House manager. As well as the house staff there were thirty-six National Park Service officers to maintain the grounds and manage the greenhouse and storage warehouse.

The Secret Service, Rhinelander discovered, had 1,800 agents within the D.C. area, 800 of whom, in shifts, were assigned to the President and the Vice President. At any given time of the day or night 40 plainclothes agents were in position in and immediately around the President, their location, and the chief executive's, constantly monitored by the White House detail communications center located directly below the Oval Office in the west wing. There were also an additional 125 uniformed members of the Executive Protection Branch on duty on the outer perimeter of the grounds and at the entrances. Both uniformed and plainclothes members were equipped with radios and with a variety of weaponry that went from sidearms and automatic weapons to shoulder-fired Redeye antiaircraft missiles that were stored for possible use.

As well as the Secret Service protective detail, there was a hundred-person Technical Security Division, located in the White House area, which regularly swept the White House looking for bugs, radioactive material, or anything else that might harm the President and his family. The TSD was also responsible for the perimeter security system, which included a buried microwave fence, just as Rhinelander had expected, as well as infrared cameras, motion detectors, and antipersonnel radar within the building and seismic sensors buried under the lawns to detect intruders. All these were augmented in turn by a complex array of panic buttons, locator boxes, metal detectors, and X-ray scanners as well as zoned identification procedures.

Using floor plans and blown-up views from a *National Geographic* article as well as comparative plans from a *Life* magazine special on the presidency, Rhinelander began to sketch out a schematic diagram of the White House and grounds, detailing in the security with a set of colored pens. At first glance it appeared to be an impregnable target, but from long experience Rhinelander knew it was just such a fortress mentality that led to oversight.

Castle walls and palace guards hadn't stopped an intruder from reaching Queen Elizabeth's bedroom, and the most stringent security measures in existence hadn't prevented Stauffenberg from placing a briefcase bomb within a yard of Adolf Hitler's knees. Glancing at the wealth of research material spread out on the desk before him, Rhinelander knew that

215

within it and the steadily unreeling videotape he would find the logistic flaw, the chink in the armor, the single, simple error that would give him entry through the battlements of this particular Troy.

Paul Mallory held the envelope up to the glaring fluorescent light in the bathroom of his Alexandria apartment, trying to see if Rhinelander had taken any special precautions with his message to Hudson Cooper. The worried-looking CIA man squinted up at the rectangle of cream-colored paper, checking the translucent interior with extreme care. After five minutes, still nervous, Mallory took the envelope out into the living room, hesitated for a minute, then slipped the sharp end of his letter opener under the flap. Inside was a single sheet of lined paper. The message was brief and hand-printed in the terse telegraphic style common to agency reports:

IN MY ESTIMATION PROJECT IS FEASIBLE AND I WILL ACT ON THE ASSUMPTION THAT IT IS ONGOING UNLESS I AM OTHERWISE IN-FORMED.

TO EXPEDITE COMPLETION SUBJECTS MUST BE IN POSITION AS PER OUR DISCUSSION. FURTHER, INFORMATION REGARDING CROWN SECURE VOICE COMMUNICATIONS MUST BE RELAYED TO ME WITHIN 72 HOURS OF RECEIVING THIS MESSAGE.

YOU WILL BE INFORMED OF PROCEDURES FOR PRELIMINARY PAY-MENT WITHIN THE NEXT SEVEN DAYS. IF PROCEDURES ARE NOT COMPLIED WITH, THE PROJECT WILL BE TERMINATED.

The message was unsigned. Frowning, Mallory read through it again, trying to decipher its real meaning. Apparently Rhinelander had done enough preliminary work to conclude that he was capable of doing the job, whatever it was, but the use of the word "subjects" indicated that there was more than one person involved. The line about Crown secure voice communications was also confusing.

One thing was certain: The use of the word "subjects" almost cer-tainly ruled out Cabrera as a target, as did the mention of "preliminary payment." While setting up the bank account for Rhinelander, Mallory had assumed that the two-hundred-thousand-dollar Citibank deposit rep-resented at least part of the assassin's fee, but according to this message, the preliminary payment was still to be paid. The largest CIA "free-lance" fee on record was fifty thousand dollars paid to the three-man team hired to assassinate Trujillo in May 1961, and even with inflation taken into account, any payment over and above a slush fund of almost a quarter million dollars would be wildly exorbitant, especially for the removal of a minor player like Cabrera.

But if not Cabrera, who? At least two people—the subjects—to be in a specific place at a specific time and rating a secure voice communications network with the code name Crown. Mallory shook his head; it had occurred to him that so far he'd been assuming that Rhinelander-QJ/RAIL's targets would be killed inside the United States. What if that wasn't the case? Maybe Crown was Queen Elizabeth or Prince Charles. It was no use; he simply didn't have enough information.

Mallory glanced at his wristwatch. With traffic it would take him at least an hour to get back to the office. He refolded the message carefully and slipped it back into the envelope. Shrugging on his wrinkled jacket, he headed for the stairs. There was a quick-print shop at the corner where he could get the message photocopied and probably pick up a new envelope as well. If he was lucky, Hudson Haines Cooper would never find out that someone had been tampering with his mail.

Dressed in his jogging clothes once again, Eric Rhinelander retrieved his bicycle from the rack in Lafayette Square at almost exactly 6:00 P.M. After returning his windbreaker to the carry case, he switched off the camera, relocked the case, and rode off. Half an hour later he reached the Holiday Inn on Connecticut Avenue, locked the bicycle to the rack in the basement parking lot, and went up to his room.

He showered, changed into the clothes he'd set out on the bed an hour before, then returned to the basement parking lot. After making his way to the bicycle rack on the main level, he unlocked the carrycase, took out the camera, and left the garage through the main entrance. Carrying the camera by its handgrip, he crossed Connecticut Avenue and entered the Wyoming.

It took another twenty minutes to cross-cable the VCR in John Gray's study to the 8 mm format video camera, but finally Rhinelander found himself watching the comings and goings through the gates of West Executive Avenue. He ran through it quickly once, then replayed it, using the remote control to adjust the speed.

Most of the activity involved staff automobiles and the occasional limousine, but there were other vehicles as well, including several delivery vans and a Park Service truck. All but one were stopped and checked by the uniformed guards at the gate. The exception was a plain white twenty-four-foot box cube van with government plates that arrived at seven-fifteen in the morning, according to the elapsed time counter in the corner of the frame. Rhinelander ran the sequence back and forth several times, picking up details, including the fact that the front of the box above the cab appeared to be fitted with a refrigeration unit.

Smiling, Rhinelander paused the tape at the point where the van was being waved through the gate by the guards without challenge. Lighting a self-congratulatory cigarette, he began poking through neat stacks of research material in front of him. He found what he was looking for and leaned back in the chair behind John Gray's desk, flipping through the pages of the magazine he'd picked out of the pile.

He was reasonably sure he had it now, the secret of the way in, held on the paused videotape across the room, his exit discovered on page 486 of the April 1935 issue of *National Geographic* magazine.

# CHAPTER 16

Sergei Kuryokhin made his way carefully down to the main floor of the small hotel, one hand firmly on the railing. The Canal House had no elevator, and the stairs were very steep. Still, alpine stairway aside, it had a wonderful little dining room which served a rijsttafel comparing favorably with that of some of the better-known Indonesian restaurants in the city.

The old man crossed the tiny lobby and stepped out into the cool night air. He buttoned his tweed jacket, then dipped one hand into his pocket and pulled out an almost empty package of Lucky Strikes. He lit one, looking out over the dark slash of the Keizersgracht to the glittering lights of the narrow buildings on the far side. He smiled around the cigarette; to him Amsterdam was Venice without Italians and, outside Moscow, his favorite city in Europe.

He turned south toward the Herenstraat, enjoying the sights and sounds, on both the cobbled street and the canal beyond. The street was alive with bicycles and cars, most heading in the direction he was going as the crowds of both tourists and locals converged on the Centrum, or downtown area of the city, its center marked by Dam Square.

Just before the bridge spanning the canal at the Herenstraat Kuryokhin turned into a small café adjoining Shaffy, a progressive theater company. After choosing a table outside under the narrow awning, the KGB man ordered an Amstel and settled back in his chair. His objective lay less than fifty feet away—a houseboat barge moored to the canal side with the somewhat unappealing name of D'Vijf Vlieghen (Five Flies).

219

Kuryokhin's beer arrived, head almost overflowing the sides of the large glass tankard. He sipped, then wiped the aromatic mustache away from his upper lip. From where he sat he could just make out the thin insulated wire that snaked down from the slightly bowed roof of the houseboat, then found its way to a nearby utility pole onshore. Tetar van Elven, Kuryokhin's agent in Amsterdam, was more than just an amateur spy; he was also a thief of electricity.

The white-haired man took another sip from the tankard, then lit a cigarette. For the next twenty minutes he sat calmly, smoking and drinking, his eyes roving over the café tables, the few cars angle-parked on the far side of the street, and people passing by on the sidewalk. Finally satisfied that there was no direct surveillance of the barge, he drained the last of his beer and went inside the café to use the telephone.

"Hallo! Tetar van Elven." The voice was hale and hearty, filled with the casual bonhomie common to salesmen in any country.

*"Heeft u iets in zwart?"* Kuryokhin replied, using his identifying phrase.

*"Ya. In Naylon."*

*"Binnen tien minuten,"* the KGB man ordered. He went back to his seat under the awning, lit another Lucky Strike, and waited. Well short of the ten-minute limit, Tetar van Elven appeared at the top of the cabin companionway on the *Five Flies*. In his late forties the glassware salesman was going to great lengths to look younger. His blond hair was too long, his thinly handsome face too tanned, and his clothes just a little too up-to-the-minute. Still, he knew his business and followed orders. Kuryokhin stubbed out his cigarette in the Amstel ashtray on the table. Marxism might work for the masses, but after more than half a lifetime in intelligence he'd learned that the better an agent was paid, the more he produced; spying, it seemed, was fundamentally a capitalist affair.

Van Elven stepped over the low gunwale of the barge and crossed the sloping gangplank to dry land. He ran a long-fingered hand through his hair, then turned and headed toward the Herenstraat and the Dam. For Kuryokhin, Van Elven's leaving the barge served two purposes: It gave him privacy, and if there were any surveillance, the Dutchman would draw it off.

The old man waited for another few minutes, then slipped a five-guilder note under his empty beer glass and left the café. He crossed the narrow street, stepped onto the gangplank, and cautiously edged his way aboard the *Five Flies*.

There are close to three thousand houseboats afloat on the canals of

220

Amsterdam, fewer than half carrying any official registration. They come in all shapes and sizes, from huge ten- and twelve-room affairs to simple loftlike cabins built onto old barge hulls. The barges were welcomed as an alternate form of housing during the shortage after World War II, but by the sixties they were considered an eyesore. The city made several halfhearted attempts to have them banned, but nothing ever came of it; the floating homes had become as much an integral part of Amsterdam's atmosphere as Rembrandt, the red-light district on Oudezijds Voorburgwal in the Old Town, and the marijuana bars of the Haarlemmerstraat.

The *Five Flies* lay somewhere between a New York loft and an antiques store. The interior of the cabin had been rebuilt into a single room, the floors highly polished, the open beamed ceiling fitted with four large skylights. The high clerestory windows running along the port and starboard sides of the cabin were done in modern stained glass, and the kitchen, fitted into the far corner, was state-of-the-art, complete with a Jenn-Air range. The furniture was an eclectic mixture of everything from Bavarian woven-vine chairs to a Louis Quinze sideboard, and dozens of shelves carried an astounding collection of glassware and crystal from every conceivable nationality and period.

In the center of the room was a surprisingly simple dining table Van Elven used as his desk. On it, surrounded by stacks of papers, invoices, and orders, was an IBM clone. There was a medium-size padded envelope balanced on the keyboard. Kuryokhin sat down at the desk and peeled open the envelope. Inside were a microcassette tape and a 3.5-inch computer floppy disk—not compatible with Van Elven's 5.25 disk drive.

The KGB man reached into the inside pocket of his jacket and took out a Phillips memocorder microcassette machine, popped it open, and inserted the cassette from Osin. He picked up the floppy disk and slipped it into his jacket, ignoring it for the time being. As usual the disk would contain various documents and reports of possible interest, scanned into the agent's computer and dumped onto the disk. The microcassette would hold the flash, or highly current information.

Kuryokhin inserted the tiny earphone from the recorder, adjusted the volume slightly, and leaned back in his chair, eyes closed. There was a brief, hissing silence, and then he heard the gravelly, mechanically altered voice of his prize agent.

"... As you requested in your last transmission, the bulk of the material I've gathered for you on the computer disk relates to agency studies regarding the installation at Ivanovo and transshipment of finished mate-

221

rial to the new base at Kohtla-Jarve. On the basis of several conversations with agency personnel at a high level, I think we can safely assume that the initial cover story has been accepted by Defense Intelligence and the Pentagon. Central Intelligence, however, is maintaining an on-off watch over Kohtla-Jarve utilizing a one-in-three pass ratio with the KH-eleven satellite. With regard to this I would advise maintaining the camouflage routine until such time as even such limited surveillance is ended.

"I thought you might be interested to know that I was recently given a courier assignment by Hudson Cooper. As you are aware, I'm on the list as a regular messenger for the agency as long as it doesn't conflict with my own work, so I wasn't entirely surprised when he called, but the substance of the assignment is odd and might bear investigation.

"For some reason Cooper wants me to purchase two million dollars' worth of gem-quality emeralds and bring them to him at the agency. Just as interesting is the fact that I'm to use funds drawn from the triple-zero account at Crédit Suisse. In case you're not aware of it, the three-oh account is a discretionary slush fund for the DDO's European operations, and using it isn't going to show up on the books for a long time, if ever.

"In terms of project budgets the two million isn't particularly large, but the gem purchase is suspect. It sounds like an attempt at making an untraceable payoff to some group. The other point of interest is the fact that I can't get any kind of line on this through regular channels. The only recent thing Cooper is devoting time to is a GRU defector named Travkin they're been holding at Bowie.

"If you want to look into this more deeply, the purchase is being made from Mouwes and Van der Loon, Number eight Albert Cuypstraat. Cooper gave me identification as a representative of a Swiss-Dutch consortium called Ashengruppe Juwelen. I assumed that it was an agency proprietary company, but it's not listed anywhere. Frankly the whole thing stinks. Anyway, I thought you might want to pursue it. If you have any questions or instructions, please transmit them in the usual way." The cassette drifted into hissing silence.

The KGB man pulled out the earpiece and stopped the tape. Once more the ubiquitous Dmitri Travkin made an appearance, this time in connection with the CIA's deputy director of operations and a covert purchase of gemstones, probably for some kind of payoff, according to his tapeworm agent. There were no hard facts, but Kuryokhin had learned long ago that even the vaguest intelligence analysis by Osin was uncannily accurate. The old man made a small snorting sound. There was

222

even a long-standing theory at Teply Stan that the high-quality information provided by his mysterious agent of influence came about because
Osin was actually a double agent working for the Americans.

Kuryokhin popped the tape out of the machine and put both into his
pocket. He checked his watch. It was late—time for an old man with
creaking bones to be in his bed. He pushed back the chair and stood up,
sighing. One more day in Amsterdam and then home again. Much as he
loved the *rodina* and Moscow in particular, the thought of returning to
the Gordian knot of bureaucracy in the woods of Teply Stan didn't en-
courage homesickness. Turning away, he climbed the companionway to
the deck of the *Five Flies,* then crossed the gangplank to the bank of the
canal. With slow steps, lost in thought, he headed back to his hotel.

Like the four adjoining houses in the Beatles' movie *A Hard Day's
Night,* Blair House, the President's official guest quarters, is actually four
separate addresses, 1653 and 1651 Pennsylvania Avenue and the last pair
of row houses around the corner on Jackson Place. Built in 1824 for Dr.
Joseph Lovell, the Pennsylvania Avenue addresses became a favorite
haunt of President Andrew Jackson and his cronies, eventually leading to
the coining of the term "Kitchen Cabinet" to describe their vital but in-
formal meetings.

The two houses were purchased by the federal government during the
Franklin Roosevelt administration to be used as the President's official
guest quarters, and during the Truman administration they were used as
the President's home while the White House was undergoing its massive
renovations. During the Nixon years the last two Victorian row houses on
Jackson Place were purchased and joined through their interiors to connect with 1651 Pennsylvania Avenue. These two houses were designated
for the staffs of visiting dignitaries.

In 1982, as badly in need of repair as the White House had been forty
years previously, Blair House was given a complete overhaul at a cost of
more than five million dollars. Security was beefed up, including the installation of bulletproof glass, and a large room for entertaining guests
was added to the rear of the building, as was a courtyard backing onto
the new Executive Office Building. Platoons of the nation's best-known
interior designers were hired to upgrade all 112 rooms, and warehouses
full of antiques were raided to furnish them. According to the resulting
article in *Architectural Digest,* the net effect of the renovation, restoration, and redecorating was "stunning."

Hudson Cooper thought the whole thing was a waste of money.

Arriving at Blair House for the reception honoring the Canadian prime minister, the CIA's deputy director of operations handed his car over to the marine in charge of valet parking and crossed the wide sidewalk to the twin wrought-iron gates. A Secret Service man opened the gateway for him while a second agent stood under the columned porch at the head of the low flight of steps leading to the main entrance.

Cooper knew that both men were armed, and he was also aware that part of the restoration of Blair House had included the installation of a custom-designed Meteor weapons detector in the hollow doorframe. Glancing at the multipaned windows on both sides of the door and above it, Cooper was willing to bet that the sheer curtains drawn behind the bulletproof glass were weighted at the bottom and made of a bombproof fabric designed to prevent shattered window fragments from exploding into the room.

The second agent opened the broad white front door, and Cooper stepped out of the muggy late-evening air into the air-conditioned coolness of Blair House's ornately wallpapered entrance hall. He endured the formal greeting from Maggie Scarfe, the Blair's official hostess, then followed the sound of chamber music and the smell of expensive perfume. It led him left through the drawing room to the much larger Dillon Room with its twin fireplaces and French doors opening onto the garden.

To Cooper the "prettiness" of the Dillon Room summed up his feelings about Blair House and his required attendance at so many of its official functions. For him, pale green hand-painted Chinese wallpaper had no place in a room supposedly designed to represent the United States of America to foreign visitors. Neither did delicate porcelain, bonsai, fans spread out in the fireplaces, and an obstacle course of rosewood occasional tables, knickknack pedestals, and silk-upholstered chairs. In the first place, it was like stepping into a furniture showroom, and in the second place, it was far too effeminate. Frowning, Cooper threaded his way through the chattering crowd garbed in black ties and evening dresses standing around the large, rectangular room, then made his way to the gold upholstered couch in front of the French doors. He nodded in the direction of a few people he vaguely recognized, then slipped behind the couch and out through the doorway into the courtyard garden.

Glancing at his watch, the tall, balding man noted that it was just past eight o'clock. The reception had been under way since six. Fifteen or twenty minutes of well-considered mingling would guarantee that his presence had been noted, and then he could go home to the Watergate and await the outcome of the Travkin business.

The courtyard was cool, shaded by the high red-brick walls of the new Executive Office Building. Lines of magnolia trees softened the looming perimeter, and a raised rectangular bed of flowers and shrubs, bounded by a stone retaining wall, gave color to the center of the garden. Guests meandered along the pathways marked by urns containing more flowers, and here and there waiters cruised like white-jacketed pilot fish, palms loaded with trays holding drinks and canapés.

Cooper snagged a champagne flute from a passing tray and eased himself into the fray. At the far side of the courtyard he could see the lantern-jawed Canadian prime minister posing for an official photograph with his wife, Braithewaite, the Canadian ambassador, and Vincent Teresi. The CIA man turned away, keeping the stone wall of the flower bed between himself and the Vice President.

Meandering slowly through the knots of Washington's murmuring elite, Cooper was aware that no more than half of the invited guests had any idea who he was, and the majority of those who did recognize him tended to turn away at his approach.

With the director a semi-invalid for the past year and a half because of a worsening heart condition, Cooper as his "social designate" was required by protocol to attend most functions honoring a head of state, but attending, he was a pariah because of the nature of his work. He was the gray man, keeper of the nation's nasty secrets and professional Peeping Tom. Not your first choice for idle cocktail party chatter. The fact that he had the general appearance and demeanor of a slightly stooped mortician didn't help the situation either.

He chose a spot at the corner of the stone wall and watched the ebb and flow of elegantly dressed people, catching snippets of their conversations. All of it was meaningless, words from another world. For Cooper there was nothing now but the terrible reality of Rhinelander's presence in the city.

It was like a slow-motion film of frost growing on a wintery pane of glass—the razor edge of crystals joining, spreading, and climbing in rigid geometric patterns until the pattern was complete. It had been Hollis Macintyre's own cold breath that had begun the process and the senior members of the Romulus Committee who had approved it, but if Rhinelander failed, Cooper knew it was his head that would roll.

"Mr. Cooper." Startled, the CIA deputy director looked up and found himself staring into the media-perfect features of Vincent Teresi.

"Mr. Vice President." Cooper nodded stiffly, ancient instincts assert-

225

ing themselves as he placed his champagne glass on the retaining wall, keeping both hands free in the face of an enemy.

"Both doing our duties in the absence of our superiors, I see," the Vice President commented. The smile flashed, but it had a wolfish edge. "How is Director Maitland doing these days?"

"Not well," Cooper answered, angered by the question. Both men knew that Maitland would almost certainly resign within the next few months, giving the Tucker-Teresi people an opportunity to place one of their own men in the key position. The CIA man couldn't resist an oblique dig of his own. "How is the President?"

"Touch of the flu," Teresi answered easily. "He and the First Lady are spending a few days at Camp David while he gets his strength back." The smile flashed again. "Frankly our friends from the north didn't really warrant interrupting his recuperation."

"I see," Cooper said. He watched Teresi carefully, wondering how much, if anything, he knew about Tucker's real illness. Probably nothing. Teresi wouldn't be the first Vice President to be in the dark about a serious illness in the White House. Thomas Marshall, Woodrow Wilson's Vice President, was completely unaware of his superior's neurological problems, and Lyndon Johnson assumed that Kennedy's back problems had to do with his naval exploits, not with JFK's long battle with Addison's disease.

"This may not be the time to bring it up," Teresi said, still smiling, "but I'm concerned with your request for new satellite appropriations regarding the report you filed on activities at Kohtla-Jarve."

"Oh?" Cooper replied calmly. It sounded as though Teresi had spent time memorizing the proper pronunciation of the Russian naval installation on the Baltic coast.

"We're trying to ease relations with the Soviets," the Vice President explained, his tone chiding. "The President and I agree that doubling up satellite surveillance of a base manufacturing a prototype coastal patrol boat radar system seems counterproductive."

"The radar story is a cover," said Cooper, trying to keep the irritation out of his voice. "The fact that they left the appropriate equipment out in plain sight during a KH-eleven pass wasn't an error; it was bait."

"Presumably you have proof of this?" Teresi asked.

"The Soviets have been using a modified *Mayakovskiy*-class trawler called the *Odissey* as a chemical warfare factory ship." Cooper answered coldly. "Up until six months ago she was using Kiev as her home port, now she's coming in to Kohtla-Jarve."

226

"That doesn't prove anything," said Teresi. "And I was under the impression that the ghost ship scenario had been debunked."

"You were under the wrong impression," said Cooper. "The *Odissey* is very real, unlike the Ivanovo installation."

"Where the radar system is being manufactured," interrupted Teresi.

"A major factory would leave an infrared signature," explained Cooper. "The Ivanovo plant is almost cold. It's a warehouse for inventory coming out of Kohtla-Jarve, not into it. Given enough time on the KH-eleven, I'll prove it to you; all we need is a pass when the ship is in port and off-loading."

"I'm afraid that won't be possible," said Teresi. He'd been keeping the best until last. This was the reason he'd instigated the conversation in the first place: the payoff. "Your request for increased time has been denied, although you can bring it up at the next joint intelligence meeting if you wish."

The CIA man shifted slightly, then picked up his half-empty champagne glass. He lifted it to his lips and drained the crystal flute. His face devoid of any expression, Cooper stared at the Vice President without saying a word. He let a silent thirty seconds pass, then nodded, returned the empty glass to its place on the stone wall, and walked away. There was no doubt in Hudson Cooper's mind that Vincenzo Santino Michelangelo Teresi had paid his professional dues, but he lived in a world of politics and bright promises, while Cooper's world was one of much darker realities.

The last of the sun had stained the walls of Blair House an uneasy sulfur, and on the other side of Pennsylvania Avenue the White House was pooled in shadow. Cooper reached the front gate of 1651 and handed his ticket to the waiting marine. The young man spoke into a walkie-talkie, reading off the number on the ticket to one of the drivers waiting in the underground garage of the new Executive Office Building around the corner on Seventeenth Street. The CIA man waited, hands clasped behind his back, thinking about Teresi, thinking about Rhinelander, and thinking about Dmitri Travkin.

"Christ, I hope this works out," Stephen Stone muttered. He sucked up the last dregs of shake from the McDonald's cup and stared moodily out into the darkness of the National Agricultural Research Center. The car he sat in was parked on a narrow access road a little more than half a mile from the front gates of the Bowie Institute.

"Relax, Stef," Mort Kessler, seated behind the wheel, said placatingly. "The plan's foolproof."

"What time is it?" Stone asked, dropping the empty cup onto the floor.

"Nine forty-five," the red-haired FBI agent answered. "It's not due to go down for another fifteen minutes."

"*If* it goes down." Stone grunted. He reached out and pulled a Camel Light out of the pack on the dashboard. He lit it, closing his eyes as the lighter flared, protecting his night vision.

"Relax," Kessler repeated. "The information is good." Tapping every available FBI source, which included one of the kitchen stewards at Bowie, the apple-faced agent had discovered that a "unit" was being moved that evening at ten. Ferreting a little deeper, he discovered that the Bowie Agricultural Research Institute had filed a flight plan out of the nearby Beltsville Airport for ten-thirty. The destination was logged as Patrick Henry International at Newport News, but Kessler was fairly sure that the real objective was the restricted field at Camp Peary a few miles north on the York River.

"I should have my head examined for approving anything as harebrained as this," Stone said. He dragged deeply on the cigarette, then exhaled, letting the smoke drift out the open window beside him. Outside, there was nothing but the rich scent from the pine woodlot surrounding them and the never-ending rattle of crickets.

"It's not harebrained." Kessler laughed. "It's just tit for tat. You know as well as I do that all these so-called high-level rumors about a defection are a crock of shit. Everything about the Travkin snatch was illegal. The CIA kidnapped a Soviet diplomat and is holding him against his will. That violates a whole bunch of established protocols, not to mention a few laws as well. How can the CIA complain when we just reverse the process?"

"Because we're not KGB. We're agents of the Federal Bureau of Investigation, no matter what your fancy license plates say, and the Company is supposedly a brother organization."

"Horsepuckies." Kessler snorted.

Within a few minutes of discovering that Travkin was about to be moved from the Bowie facility, Mort Kessler had jury-rigged an operation to get him away from the CIA. Stone had to admit that the plan, harebrained or not, was elegantly simple.

Using three pool vehicles from the Baltimore district office and diplomatic plates "liberated" from the Special Services branch of the D.C.

Department of Motor Vehicles, the entire six-man Back Door contingent would box in Travkin and his keepers on the way to Beltsville Airport and benevolently rekidnap the GRU officer.

In a best-case scenario the CIA would assume that the kidnappers really had been KGB retrieving one of its countrymen, while in a worst-case situation the CIA might suspect Stone and his people but would have no way to prove it and, more important, no official way to do anything about it.

Stone knew that Ruppelt would inevitably discover what had happened, but he hoped the material gained from debriefing Travkin would soften his anger. He was also sure that Travkin would cooperate, even if grudgingly. Travkin's own people would now assume that he was tainted and the Russian would have no choice but actually to defect. Hudson Cooper was a powerful enemy, but the defection of a major player like Dmitri Aleksandrovich Travkin would provide a virtually unassailable bulwark against any attack mounted by the aging DDO.

The FBI man stubbed out his cigarette in the dashboard ashtray and stared out into the night, feeling the perspiration dampening the armpits of his windbreaker. The whole thing had sounded perfectly reasonable being discussed in the air-conditioned confines of the safe house overlooking Rock Creek Park, but out here in the hot, humid night he wasn't so sure. If they pulled it off, they might be able to stop a political assassination and reel in a top-grade intelligence coup into the bargain. If they failed, and he missed his grab at the ring, his career would be over.

He reached down on the seat and touched the walkie-talkie beside him. One wrong move, one man out of place, and the whole thing would go down hard. Stone had been on enough operations to know that things never went exactly according to plan and that something could easily go wrong. Christ on a crutch! Anything could go wrong. *Everything* could go wrong.

"If anyone's out of place, it'll screw up," Stone warned.

"No one's out of place, Stef. Sinclair's in the woods across from the front gates, Putnam has the spiked chain at the intersection, and Midbrook and Dofney do the block on the Springfield-Hillmeade Road. Fifteen seconds to pick up Sinclair will put us about a minute behind. We make up half that on the way to the intersection of Powder Mill and Springfield. Midbrook gives us the word as soon as he sees their lights, and we close it up."

The red-haired agent reached out and popped open the oversize attaché case that lay between them on the seat. It contained a Smith &

Wesson antiriot kit complete with 37 mm gas gun, Tru-flite penetrating projectiles, rubber ball gas grenades, and half a dozen pepper-gas projectiles.

"Ka-boom!" The agent grinned. Stone smiled back; the man's optimistic mood was infectious.

"Dmitri's going to be POed even if we do save him from the evil clutches of the Company." Stone laughed. "This stuff will have him crying for a week."

"Better to shed tears than blood," Kessler answered. There was a crackling sound from the walkie-talkie. The two men stiffened. Stone picked up the radio, and Kessler leaned forward, turning on the ignition.

"*Es ist grün.*" Sinclair, giving the "green" code, speaking in German just in case anyone was listening in.

"*Ich verstehe,*" Stone answered crisply. Beside him Kessler was counting.

"Five, six, seven, eight . . ."

On nine he put the specially equipped hot-pursuit vehicle in drive and began to move, headlights dark. Stone switched channels on the walkie-talkie and alerted the rest of the Back Door crew.

"*Zündung.*" Ignition.

Dmitri Travkin sat between his two keepers in the front seat of the car and wondered if he was going for the proverbial last ride. If he was, Mutt and Jeff weren't telling him the final destination. Mutt, the blond with the biceps, was behind the wheel, guiding the dark green GMC van along the Bowie Institute's long, curving drive, while Jeff, his dark-haired partner, sat between Travkin and the door. The windows were wound up, and cold air was blowing from the dashboard vents.

"Don't tell me," the GRU officer said brightly, breaking the silence. "You're taking me to the Eddie Murphy concert at Wolf Trap."

"Shut the fuck up," Jeff said coldly. They reached the end of the treelined drive, and the high gates slid back on their rails, monitored by closed-circuit video cameras from the main building.

"*Esvaynya,*" Travkin muttered. Pig. A humorless one to boot.

"What did you say?" snapped Jeff, the dark-haired one.

"Nothing," Travkin answered, then lapsed into silence once again. Mutt, the blond driver, turned south onto Powder Mill Road. It was full night, the world collapsed to a narrow tunnel bored into the darkness by the van's headlights. Travkin had brief glimpses of plowed fields and forests but nothing more.

230

The Russian eased back in his seat, wishing he had a cigarette but knowing that Mutt and Jeff were unlikely to give him one. He willed himself to relax and considered both his future and his options. At that moment, as he stared through the windshield at the dark, unraveling road, neither seemed very promising. The interrogation by the bland Mr. Cook had been superficial, no more than a fishing trip to find out how much he knew about the Costa Rican project. Now things would get nasty: hard questions and rough treatment, perhaps even drugs.

"Company," said Mutt softly, eyes flicking to the van's side mirror.

"Where?" asked Jeff. The dark-haired man reached under his jacket and came up with a short-barreled S&W .44 revolver.

"Behind us, two hundred yards and no lights."

"Shit." Jeff leaned forward and peered into the mirror on his side. "Speed it up," he instructed.

Mutt accelerated on command, the sudden increase in speed pushing Travkin back against the bench seat. The Russian sat stiffly between the two men, muscles tense; sudden movement with a nervous man beside you holding a gun was a definite no-no. As he sat motionless, his mind worked furiously; he realized that he was being given an opportunity but was not sure how to take advantage of it. It all depended on who was coming up behind him. If it was one of Vladimir Gurenko's KGB goon squads intent on "rescuing" him, he preferred to take his chances with the CIA; at least with the agency there was a chance of coming out of the whole thing alive. With Gurenko the question was moot.

Mutt, tensed behind the wheel of the van, took the long curve at speed and came into the intersection of Powder Mill Road and Spring-field-Hillmeade at close to seventy miles an hour. Rocketing out of the T crossing, he was suddenly aware of two things: There was a vehicle approaching in the wrong lane with its headlights on high beam, and all four of his tires had blown out, the rubber cut to smoking shreds by the razor-sharp carbon steel of the spiked chain laid across the intersection only a few moments before. Mutt's driving was further encumbered by the fact that the forty-foot length of security chain had now entangled itself in both front axle and drive shaft. The flailing ends gutted the brake lines, fuel line, and ignition system, while a two-foot length sliced through the floor of the van and hacked through Mutt's right shoe, severing his Achilles' tendon and turning his ankle into a pulped mass of bleeding flesh, bone chips, and shredded shoe leather.

While Mutt began to scream and the van went into a long, broadside drift, the vehicle coming up from the south erupted in a retina-peeling

231

blaze of light as its grille-mounted custom-built halogen floodlights burst into life. Stone and Kessler, in the darkened vehicle following Travkin, sped up at the last moment. The heavy-duty all-steel police bumper slammed into the van broadside and pushed it into the shallow ditch on the right side of the road.

Travkin, blinded by the floodlights, was hurled against Jeff, now choking on his own blood, his right cheekbone smashed from its impact against the window. The CIA man's finger jerked spasmodically, firing the revolver into the seat beside him. The Russian grappled with his keeper, trying to turn the weapon away from himself, while on his left Mutt was still screaming, coiled up on the seat, his hands desperately trying to reach the partially amputated remains of his right foot.

The GRU man was vaguely aware of a stuttering series of sharp, barking sounds, and then every window in the van was shattered as the Back Door team began firing tear gas penetrating projectiles, followed by a popping hail of number fifteen rubber ball tear gas grenades. Within a few seconds the van's interior was filled with a choking fog of chemical smoke. Before he passed out, larynx burning and eyes streaming, Travkin was sure he heard voices speaking in German but was not quite as certain of a goggle-eyed rubber-covered face peering at him through the shattered remains of the windshield. After that he didn't care, unconsciousness a blessed relief from the nightmare inside the van.

# CHAPTER 17

For most people a city is a place of tall buildings, dense traffic, and crowded sidewalks. Few urban dwellers realize that beneath their feet is a monstrously complex system of tunnels, conduits, and chambers outstripping anything conceived of by Dante for his infernal underworld. Below the familiar surface lies a city in itself, a Hades of forgotten rivers, abandoned pipes and passages, sunken sewers, tubes, crypts, and cellars.

The city of London has fifteen hundred miles of sewers, a hundred miles of covered rivers, eighty-two miles of subway tunnel, twelve miles of subterranean government passages, and a hundred thousand miles of cable and pipe. New York has gigantic aqueduct tunnels more than eight hundred feet below the pavement, and Chicago has an all-but-forgotten system of freight tunnels running forty feet under the surface and covering more than sixty-two miles.

Washington, D.C., is no exception to this labyrinthine rule, and after discovering his first clue hidden in the pages of the aged *National Geographic* magazine, Eric Rhinelander focused the next stage of his research on the underground history of the city. The information was readily available, and after going to several municipal offices and making a return visit to one of Georgetown's antiquarian bookstores, he had everything he needed in the way of text.

The article in the 1935 issue of the *National Geographic* was entitled "Wonders of the New Washington," and a portion of it described the newly built central heating plant at Twelfth and D streets, next door to the Bureau of Printing and Engraving Annex. A quick check assured

233

Rhinelander that the heating plant, expanded and modernized, still existed in the same location a few blocks west of the L'Enfant Plaza Hotel.

In 1935 the heating plant provided warmth to seventy-one buildings in the Federal Triangle area, including the White House. The giant steam pipes were carried through more than three miles of huge concrete-lined tunnels branching up along Twelfth Street and beneath Pennsylvania, Maryland, and Constitution avenues. The article's author, a man named Frederick G. Vosburgh, was on his way to the Treasury after his tour of the heating plant, and his guide, one of the plant engineers, informed him that he could walk underground to his destination at Fifteenth Street and New York Avenue.

A visit to the D.C. Planning Office and an hour spent at the Public Works Information Office gave the assassin a general history of the city's waste and storm sewer system since the Civil War, and his trip back to the bookstore on M Street provided him with several arcane civil engineering textbooks relating to Washington that the bookseller was only too pleased to see leave the premises. Collating the material back at the Wyoming, Rhinelander quickly built up an overview of the city's belowground environment.

Prior to its elevation to the status of national capital, Washington had been a malarial patch of swamp on the banks of the Potomac just below the river port of Georgetown, Maryland, and just above Alexandria, Virginia. The marshy ground was kept eternally soggy by the outflow of Rock Creek to the west, emptying into the river at the foot of Georgetown's Greene Street, and by the various branches of Tiber Creek. The two main branches of the Tiber originated in springs at what is now roughly the intersection of V Street and Fourteenth Street, then flowed through central Washington, skirting the elevated areas around the White House and the Capitol, and eventually reached the James Creek estuary at Buzzard Point and Fort Lesley McNair as well as an outfall close to what is now the Washington Navy Yard, both on the east branch of the Potomac. Another, more sluggish course turned just in front of Capitol Hill, curving north and then following the line of what is now Constitution Avenue.

During the capital's early years the various creek branches were used for both water and sewage, worsening the health hazard and giving Washington the reputation of being a highly dangerous city to live in. In 1802, in accordance with the grand plan for the city envisioned by the French architect Pierre L'Enfant, the western branch of Tiber Creek was excavated and turned into a canal. The hope was to connect the Tiber with

234

the Chesapeake and Ohio Canal in Georgetown, eventually bringing it up to within sight of the Capitol steps. It was not to be, and by 1860 the canal was a stagnating open sewer, albeit a stone-walled one.

Following the Civil War the first attempts were made to create a proper sewer and water system in Washington. The meandering branches of the Tiber were covered over, an aqueduct was built to bring fresh water from the north, and the Tiber Canal was partially filled, then covered, forming the first rude version of what is now Constitution Avenue. Most of the sewage and runoff still approximately followed its original course, but at least now it was out of sight. For the next half century, as the city grew, so grew its underground system of water tunnels and sewers.

In 1897, as part of an enormous landfill operation, the Tidal Basin was created. While most people today view the basin as a recreational area and a fitting backdrop for the Washington, Lincoln, and Jefferson memorials, it is also a feat of hydraulic engineering. A system of locks and pumps captures rising tidal water in the basin, water that is later flushed out into the Washington Channel, thus ensuring its cleanliness. At the same time the central storm sewer running below Constitution Avenue was renovated and given a "water gate" to control the flow of waste water into the Potomac a few hundred yards north of the Arlington Memorial Bridge. There was also a storm sewer outfall directly into the Tidal Basin at the foot of Seventeenth Street and a waste outlet at the O Street pumping station down by the navy yard.

From the civil engineering texts Rhinelander learned that the first sewers had been brick-lined and egg-shaped in cross section, always following the slope of the land, no matter how convoluted the course. Later sewers and water conduits were constructed of clay or concrete pipe. Out of necessity the old and new systems were interconnected, and all were vented to the surface at intervals through manhole shafts and storm drains.

At 11:30 P.M., slightly more than twenty-four hours after Stephen Stone's Back Door rescue of Dmitri Travkin, Eric Rhinelander parked his rented minivan beneath the Twelfth Street Expressway overpass and slipped into the rear compartment to change clothes for his late-night excursion. He peeled off his T-shirt and jeans and pulled on a black one-piece Lycra dive skin, then shrugged on a pair of D.C. Public Works coveralls he'd liberated from a truck in the heating plant parking lot earlier that day. Donning a battle-scarred hard hat from the same source, he added an equally battered doctor's valise and a clipboard, then left the van, which he locked carefully behind him.

Carrying the valise, he crossed the Conrail tracks, then climbed the embankment to D Street. A few moments later he walked through the open gate of the heating plant parking lot, then boldly pulled open a service door and stepped into the main boiler room. The chamber was enormous, a broad central aisle lined on both sides with looming furnaces, several stories high, each heavily insulated and joined together by a twisting, seemingly random web of heavy pipes and spidery catwalks.

The boiler room was brightly lit by scores of overhead lights dangling from the girders overhead and empty except for two maintenance men working silently in the distance, ears covered by protective headsets against the constant, thunderous boom of the furnace blowers. Even in 1935 the plant had been almost totally automated, and now, with the advent of computer controls, the entire operation could be handled by fewer than twenty men. Beyond that during the summer season the heating plant was working with fewer than half its normal complement.

Ignoring the men working at the far end of the giant room, Rhinelander walked casually across the central aisle, trying to visualize the design specifications for the plant he'd viewed on microfilm at the Planning Office. The clerk there had provided the plans without question, nodding pleasantly but without interest at Rhinelander's story about creating a historically accurate model railroad layout of the Conrail yards as they existed in 1917.

He found the access door leading to the northern service tunnel, opened it, then took the winding metal stairway beyond down to the heating plant's lower level. Once there, he simply followed the directions stenciled in dark green against the pale yellow walls. After going down several more sets of echoing stairs, he eventually found the tunnel entrance and went through a heavy, counterweighted door. The tunnel itself was slightly more than nine feet high and almost twenty feet across, lit by a string of caged lights that vanished into the distance. Down the center of the arched corridor was a strapped bundle of eighteen-inch steam pipes, each wrapped in thick insulation with bolted expansion joints at hundred-foot intervals. Bunches of smaller pipes and cables were bracketed to the walls, snaking down the gloomy passageway into infinity.

Keeping to the raised concrete walkway on the left of the tunnel, Rhinelander began to make his way northward. Here and there along the way the main steam pipes dipped below the level of the floor, allowing access to branch passages on the eastern side. Rhinelander also noted that there were heavy manholes set into the concrete floor at regular intervals, their code numbers and positions stenciled on the wall: "DCWW#234/12TH /IND. JUNCT, PW#5/FREER SUB #3, PW #8/ JEFF."

After walking for ten minutes, he reached a niche carved into the western wall of the tunnel. Sealing it was a small gray-painted metal hatchway marked "CONSTITUTION AVE. INTERCEPTOR/WATERGATE OUT-FALL." From his reading Rhinelander knew that an interceptor was a main floodway for either a sewer or storm drain and sometimes for both, acting as a collection point for secondary sewers and providing emergency flood control in the event of a major storm. The location of the access door put him somewhere below the intersection of Constitution Avenue and Twelfth Street. From the look of the old-fashioned lever and bar-locking mechanism the door hadn't been opened in decades.

Rhinelander put down the clipboard and valise, then looked both ways along the tunnel: empty and silent except for tiny, faintly echoing creaks and the steady sound of his own breathing. Gripping the big locking lever in both hands, the assassin dragged downward with a steady motion. The sixty-year-old mechanism turned with surprising ease, the cam wheel and bars pulling back the locking pins from their slots. He picked up the clipboard and bag, pulled open the door, and stepped across the threshold.

Beyond was nothing but darkness, and before he closed the door, he opened the bag, withdrawing a compact Ikelite halogen diver's flashlight. He closed the door, pushed the inside lever to lock it, then turned on the light. In its brilliant beam he saw that he was standing in a small semicircular chamber lined with damp, crumbling concrete. The room was no more than eight feet across and barely six feet high. In the center of the floor was the opening of a shaft some thirty inches across.

After placing the light upright on the floor, Rhinelander unzipped the coveralls and removed the hard hat. Dressed now in nothing but the one-piece diver skin and thick-soled sneakers, he sat himself on the edge of the narrow shaft, feet dangling over the side. Opening the valise again, he took out the same red nylon knapsack he'd used during his brief career as a jogger in Lafayette Square. This time it contained a mask, insulated diver's gloves, a utility belt, a strap-on Ikelite compass, and half a dozen nine-inch Spare Air bottles, each one of the miniature emergency tanks giving five minutes' breathing time. The zippered compartment on the side of the bag also contained a spray can of glow-in-the-dark yellow paint, a short-handled rock climber's pick, fifty feet of ultrathin nylon rope, and an assortment of pitons.

Poised on the edge of the dark hole in the floor, the muscular dark-haired man wrapped the utility belt around his waist, then loaded it with the flashlight, still on, the Spare Air bottles, the rope, and the pick. He rolled up the coveralls and pushed them down into the bottom of the knapsack, then strapped the wrist compass onto his left arm, snapped on the diver's gloves, and finally threaded his arms into the knapsack harness. He stuffed the clipboard and the hard hat into the valise, closed it, and dropped it down the hole between his dangling feet. There was a faint echoing thud when the bag reached bottom a few seconds later.

Rhinelander edged out over the hole, feeling for the ladder with his sneakered feet. Finding it, he reached out with one hand, the twisting light giving him a gyrating glimpse down into the yawning shaft. Getting a firm grip, he pushed off and planted himself securely on the ladder. He descended, careful not to put too much weight on any rung before he'd tested it. A few minutes and thirty feet later by his own estimation, he reached another chamber identical to the one he'd just vacated, although damper and in poorer condition. After dropping the bag a second time, he descended once again, the air growing noticeably cooler, thick now with a deep, musky odor.

Suddenly, without warning, he found himself in the main interceptor tunnel, a brick-walled crumbling vault at least thirty feet across and half as high. Stepping off the final rung of the iron ladder onto a narrow masonry ledge, Rhinelander swung the light across the broad channel. This was the last, buried remnant of L'Enfant's "American Venice," a foul-smelling Styx, its flow the consistency of soup, its color a putrescent brown so dark it seemed to swallow up the beam of the assassin's light. Thin, dangling stalactites oozed from the mortar of the bricks in the curving roof, and the walls were coated in a glistening film of subterranean mucosa. Rhinelander sneezed, and the sound rebounded up and down the vault, the echo changed to a short, barking laugh.

He clipped the light back onto his belt, slipped off the knapsack, unzipped the main compartment, and rummaged around in it, finally coming up with the spray can. He popped the top, shook the can briskly, then sprayed a large yellow X beside the shaft entrance. The paint ran slightly before it set, leaving a glowing twin track on the crumbling wall, like the cold leaked blood of some underground creature.

Rhinelander put the knapsack back on, then checked the dial of his compass. He turned until he was facing west, the same direction as the

238

almost invisible flow in the dank waterway to his right. Leaving the battered valise at the foot of the shaft, he began to move, the light held before him, keeping to the center of the walkway. If there were no obstacles or interruptions, he calculated it would take him no more than fifteen minutes to travel the three quarters of a mile to his next destination.

At intervals along the way the beam of his light picked out the openings of secondary sewers angling into the main stream, always on the far side of the tunnel; these were the northern collectors, bringing waste water down from Brentwood Heights and Columbia Park through the complex descending maze of passages below the city.

Because of the weather, most of the sewers were dry, but a few added small trickles to the main interceptor. Rhinelander also noted that some openings were much larger than others and fitted with damlike weirs and counterbalanced gates to hold back all but the most serious flows. Setting aside the grotesque environment, the assassin was able to appreciate the engineering genius of a system entirely dependent on gravity for its operation.

Twenty minutes after reaching the base of the interceptor shaft, Rhinelander found himself in a cavernous chamber at least thirty feet high, crowded with buttresses, pillars, and cross-connected weirs. The water was deeper here, sheets of thick liquid topping the broad patchwork dams, waterfalls from upper-level drains splashing down into the central pool. There were nine separate openings, high and low, on both sides of the chamber, the tunnels angling off in all directions. Except for the roving beam of his light it was brutally dark, and the air was foul, a rotted, choking stench that burned into the dark man's nostrils and set his stomach churning.

Resisting the urge to hold his breath, Rhinelander consulted his wrist compass again and turned, following the needle until he was facing north. His foray down the abyssal tube had taken him to a point almost directly beneath the Ellipse; according to his information, the heating and air-conditioning vaults jutting out from the subbasement below the north portico of the White House were exactly 2,851 feet away.

There were three man-high storm sewers on the far side of the chamber, one angling northwest, the other northeast, and the middle one on a heading approximately two degrees east of due north. Thankfully, all three appeared to be almost completely dry.

Rhinelander shuffled forward along the slick walkway, branching himself with one gloved hand against the sloping wall. Reaching the main weir across the channel, he stepped outward carefully, arms outstretched.

On his right was the low water tunnel he had been following, while to his right, twenty feet below, on the far side of the wedge-shaped dam, was the lower interceptor, its bed no more than a muck-laden path etched with a snail track tracing of streamlets.

Behind him, four feet above the crest of the weir, was an overflow conduit; in extreme conditions, if the flow topped the weir by more than that amount, the excess water would be drawn off and carried to an outfall at the northern edge of the Tidal Basin almost directly below the statue of John Paul Jones.

Rhinelander reached the far side of the weir, then climbed a short rust-covered iron ladder to the north side walkway. Arm muscles tensing, he boosted himself up onto the lip of the center tunnel. He crouched, pausing for a few moments as he waited for his breathing to steady, then stood, head bent low under the low, arched roof, the beam of his flashlight playing on the dank walls of the passageway ahead. Hunched over, he began to move, his sodden sneakers making small sucking noises as he walked.

After half an hour he paused again and dropped to his knees, using his gloved hands to work the stiffening muscles of his neck and shoulders. He'd kept a rough count of his steps since entering the passage, and by his count he'd come almost twenty-five hundred feet. He treated himself to a few long breaths from one of the Spare Air bottles, then continued up the gently sloping tunnel.

Rhinelander's distance estimate had been close; a hundred yards farther along the passage he saw the first evidence that he was nearing his objective: a patch in the left-hand wall of the tunnel, the gray, pocked surface of the fifty-year-old slab of concrete showing its rusty chickenwire skeleton. In the center of the patch was the open end of a ten-inch-diameter clay water pipe. During the Truman renovation, which involved the complete gutting of the White House interior as well as the addition of two new basement levels, all the plumbing and wiring had been replaced. The clay pipe and the concrete patch in the storm sewer wall were clearly from that period. Thirty feet beyond that the beam of his light picked up a second and far more important clue overhead.

At some time in the past the arch of the tunnel roof had begun to collapse, forced downward by pressure from above. When he shone the light upward, the cause of that pressure was clearly visible. A section of the roof had collapsed completely, the broken bricks and mortar swept away by some long-forgotten storm. The bright beam from Rhinelander's flashlight illuminated the resulting cavity and revealed a six-foot section of eight-inch-diameter cast-iron steam pipe, a feeder branch from the main conduit in the heating plant tunnel. The pipe ran at right angles to the storm sewer, putting him directly opposite the north portico heating and air-conditioning vaults. The only question now was one of distance. How far was the tunnel from the vaults?

According to the original site plan for the White House, U.S. Federal Reservation 1 on the federal government's planning files, listed as one of Tiber Creek's countless tributaries, ran within sixty feet of the southeast corner of the building. For freshwater the occupants of the White House used a well dug in the basement of the southwest corner of the building, but the stream was used originally for waste water and eventually for sewage. The storm sewer had been built conforming to its drainage pattern.

The first vaults beneath the north portico had been constructed during Theodore Roosevelt's time, when storage space in the building was at a premium. At that time the underground chamber had been used for furniture, china, and a hoard of gifts from visiting dignitaries. During the all-encompassing Truman renovations everything in the storage area was removed, and during the excavation of the two basement levels the vaults were expanded to accommodate a brand-new heating and air-conditioning system.

From various descriptions in *First Lady* and other assorted White House biographies Rhinelander knew that the Roosevelt vaults jutted out 10 feet beyond the portico and 15 feet on either side of it. The mansion building was roughly 60 by 110 feet, and on the bases of the dimensions of the portico itself, this meant the original vault wall would have been roughly 20 feet from the sewer; the Truman expansion would have decreased that distance.

No matter what the plans showed or the biographies described, Rhinelander knew there was only one real way to find out his exact location. He slipped the pack off his shoulders, unzipped the side pocket, and took out the rock climber's pick. Choosing a spot where the mortar between the bricks looked particularly soft, the assassin began to dig.

The dark anvils of the thunderclouds had been building steadily since the late evening, rising over the hills above the Appalachian Trail, blotting out the stars in the night sky from Charlottesville, Virginia, to Harrisburg, Pennsylvania, creating a roiling lightning-slashed front that threatened to break at any moment. As the ominous mass of clouds slid down into the triangular depression containing the District of Columbia,

241

the first rain began to fall, fat droplets slapping the dusty rooftops and windows of houses in Randolph Hills, Springbrook, and Calverton. Within ten minutes the storm had broken completely, the pounding sheets of rain preceded by an advance guard of cracking thunder and jagged, blinding forks of lightning.

In Washington there had been no relief from the stupefying heat for almost three weeks, and the ground was parched. Both the McMillan and Georgetown reservoirs were low, and the normally energetic flow of Rock Creek had been cut in half. A hundred thousand thirsty lawns in Montgomery County drank in the torrential downpour as it careened blindly toward the Chesapeake, and everywhere suburban gutters filled with foaming, racing streams.

Within minutes of crossing the D.C. line just south of Seminary Road the concrete trash traps in the first storm drains overflowed, and water began to flood through the storm lines, scouring out a season's worth of silt, twigs, broken bottles, and all the other garbage that finds its way into the sewers. Secondary lines filled, then spewed furiously into mains, spreading beneath the city, pressed forward by gravity and the force of new water from the continuing rain.

Eric Rhinelander had been working in the storm sewer tunnel for almost an hour and a half when he first realized that something was wrong. By then he'd opened a yard-square hole in the brickwork of the sewer wall and dug another two feet into the heavy claylike soil beyond. So far there was no sign of the vault wall.

Dragging back yet another load of dirt into the already half-choked passage, Rhinelander paused and looked northward up the tunnel. It took him a few seconds to identify what had caught his attention, but then he had it. The fetid, still air was moving, creating enough of a breeze to fan his cheek. He tensed, listening. The sound was faint, distant, and echoing, but he recognized it immediately: rushing water, Niagara Falls through cotton.

He acted instantly, scooping up the knapsack and slinging it over his shoulders. He scrambled around the pile of dirt he'd created, unclipping one of the Spare Air bottles as he fled, hunched over, down the passage. The assassin knew exactly what had happened, and he cursed himself silently for not checking the weather reports.

The water struck when he was still a thousand feet from the interceptor chamber. Clamping the Spare Air mouthpiece between his teeth and hanging on to the bottle with one hand, he curled himself into a ball and

242

used the other arm to shield his face. Within an instant he was swallowed by the fuming water, then carried downstream with it. With a diver's instinct he tried his best to keep to the center of the current, but even so, he found himself being slammed back and forth against the tunnel walls, his only protection coming from the knapsack and the thin Lycra suit.

Forty seconds later the hammering current reached the Constitution Avenue chamber and spewed Rhinelander out into the stinking pool at the foot of the weir. For a single, horrifying moment the struggling man was sure he'd be trapped in the foul quicksandlike ooze, but with the foaming trash-laden water rising quickly around him, he managed to un-clip the rubber-covered flashlight from his belt, then flailed his way to the opposite side of the tunnel and the iron ladder bolted to the slimy brick.

Reaching the walkway ledge, he dropped onto his hands and knees, panting. He was bleeding from a dozen scrapes, and his dive skin was torn to ribbons; but he knew he was lucky to be alive. He forced himself to stand up and then examined his position. Shining his light around the chamber, he saw that the pool behind the weir was filling quickly, and the eastern channel, virtually dry a few hours before, was now filled almost to the level of the walkway. In another few minutes the dam would be topped and the lower interceptor would begin to fill as well.

Rhinelander quickly saw that any attempt to retrace his steps could easily end in disaster, and following the lower route was probably even more dangerous, especially if the rise in water level continued. His only choice was the overflow tunnel leading down to the Tidal Basin. Wasting no time, he walked unsteadily to the weir, then boosted himself up onto the lip of the southern passage. It was oval, like the northern channel he'd just been flushed out of, but wider and high enough for him to stand upright without any trouble. Because it was used only for emergency out-flow, the floor of the tunnel was dry and clear.

Rhinelander worked his way down the passage, one ear cocked for any sound of water coming from behind. Twenty uneventful minutes later he reached the tunnel exit. As he'd expected, the last few yards of the passage angled down sharply, ending in a smooth, slightly oily pool of water. For both safety and security, the open end of the outfall was lo-cated underwater, probably closed off by a grate.

After allowing himself a five-minute rest, Rhinelander took the still-intact mask out of his knapsack, cracked another Spare Air bottle, and slipped into the pool, using the flashlight to guide him. Breathing easily and ignoring the growing pain from his cuts and bruises, he pulled himself down to the base of the outfall. The only trace of a grate covering the

243

opening was the rusted remains of a linch bolt. Unopposed, he grasped the lip of the outfall pipe and pushed forward. A few seconds later he reached the surface, stripped off his mask, and lifted his face into the pouring rain.

He treaded water, taking huge, grateful gulps of the wonderfully fresh air, then swam the few strokes needed to take him to the quarried stone shore. Not surprisingly, considering the hour and the weather conditions, the entire Tidal Basin area was deserted. Rhinelander lifted himself up onto the path at the edge of the basin, then slipped under the abutment of the East Basin bridge. Shivering now, he quickly stripped off the tattered remains of the dive skin, then put on the coveralls.

He put the utility belt, flashlight, and clothing into the knapsack, weighted it with a few pieces of broken concrete from under the bridge, then dropped the telltale parcel into the water. Even with his wallet and ID safe in the coverall's zippered side pocket, it would be difficult to explain what he was doing out before dawn in the middle of a downpour, but if a cop stopped him with the knapsack, it would be impossible. There was nothing in it that couldn't be replaced anyway.

Rhinelander reached the minivan half an hour later, changed into fresh clothes, and drove to the underground lot at the Holiday Inn. Ten minutes after that, just before 5:00 A.M., he was stepping into the shower of John Gray's apartment at the Wyoming.

As the professional killer washed away the sweat and grime of his night's labors, there was an unseen event taking place deep in the now-sodden earth below the White House grounds, and although Rhinelander was no believer in fate, luck, or coincidence, he would have seen the irony immediately.

The force of water thundering down the narrow storm tunnel had pushed away everything in its path, including more of the brickwork from Rhinelander's excavation. The continuing current began to erode the earth behind the sewer wall, eventually bringing down a section more than fifteen feet long, including the ceiling. By dawn, with the rain over and the surface water beginning to recede, a new chamber had been created almost twenty feet on a side. In the southeastern corner of the low-ceilinged cave there was an obviously man-made structure. It was the wall of the north portico vault.

# CHAPTER 18

Dmitri Travkin used the remote control to switch off the VCR, then levered himself out of the comfortable upholstered chair. He'd watched the *Eddie Murphy: RAW* tape three times in the past forty-eight hours, and he was getting sick of it. He'd also watched *Good Morning, Vietnam, Robin Williams Live, Howie Mandel's Hawaiian Special,* and eleven *Fawlty Towers* episodes. At first he'd been intrigued at this off-the-wall procedure for softening up a prisoner, but now he was simply bored by it. He was also bored with the endless succession of pizzas and fried chicken dinners he was being served and the bland Holiday Inn decor of the two-room suite he was occupying.

The sitting room was rectangular, the floor covered in deep-pile cream-colored wall-to-wall carpeting. It was furnished with an oval eating table set with four "caned" chrome-and-plastic chairs, a couch, a coffee table, a scattering of upholstered chairs and a "media center" against one wall, containing a television, VCR, and stereo. A sliding glass door led out onto a narrow balcony; but the door was locked, and during daylight hours all Travkin could see were the bushy tops of half a dozen trees poking up above the solid cedar balcony railing.

The bedroom was equally sterile: double bed, dark blue vase lamps on each side of it, chest of drawers, and walk-in closet with nothing in it and mirrored doors that discreetly *didn't* reflect the bed when you were lying on it. There was a large en suite bathroom with a Jacuzzi bathtub, but no window. Travkin went to the bathroom, urinated, flushed, then splashed cold water on his face. As he dried himself off with a small,

245

fluffy, and very pink hand towel, it struck the GRU man that his brief ablutions were undoubtedly going to be the high point of his day.

Sighing, Travkin left the bathroom and dropped onto the bed, hands clasped behind his head. His captors had taken away his watch, but by the color of the sky on the other side of the balcony door he put it at early evening. Next would come the big question: pizza or chicken? Brought to him by the spooky, silent redheaded man with the almost invisible eyebrows. He'd unlock the door and enter the room, carrying a cloth-covered tray on one raised palm.

After placing the tray on the table in the sitting room, he'd step back and give the Russian a brief half-smile, then glance at the tray mysteriously. Travkin knew it was only a psych move, but it worked every time. After the redhead left, he'd lift the cloth on the tray, never quite sure if he was going to find food or a writhing mass of pit vipers. Staring up at the ceiling, he spoke out loud, doing his groaning imitation of an Uzbek comedian impersonating W. C. Fields.

"Tovarich Dmitri, you have the stepping made into kaka exceedingly deep." It wouldn't get a laugh in the big room at the Rossiya, but under the circumstances it was the best he could do. "Frankly, my friends, I'd rather be in Novosibirsk." Better, but still not up to scratch.

Except for the bursting light, the tear gas, and the muffled German voices behind rubber masks he couldn't remember very much about his second abduction. In the last few seconds before he blacked out he remembered thinking that the Germans had probably been hired by Gurenko, but now he wasn't sure. Gurenko wouldn't have provided him with comedy tapes, and bland or not, the suite of rooms was far too decadent to be used as a KGB debriefing center. Capture by Gurenko would have meant being doped, stuffed into a trunk, and shipped back to Moscow on the next Ilyushin out of Dulles.

Travkin heard a faint knock on the door and frowned as he swung his legs off the bed. The redhead never knocked, and the door was always locked anyway. He stood up and walked into the sitting room. The knock came again, louder this time. Travkin stepped forward and tentatively put his hand on the knob. He turned it, and the door opened.

The man on the other side of the door was dark-haired, the temples flecked with gray, and good-looking in a craggy, rough-cut way. He was wearing a wrinkled blue and white seersucker suit, light blue shirt, and a dark blue tie. His penny loafers were scuffed, and it looked as though he'd neither shaved nor slept in the past two or three days. Travkin recognized him immediately; it was Stephen Stone, his opposite number at Rednet.

"Mr. Stone," Travkin said, the pieces of his puzzle clicking into place. He stood aside and let the tired-looking man into the room. He closed the door behind Stone and gestured toward one of the flower print club chairs. "Please sit down." The FBI man nodded and dropped into the chair. Travkin sat down on the couch across from him and took a cigarette from the wooden box on the coffee table. He lit it and sat back against the cushions, staring at Stone with unabashed curiosity.

"I trust you're being treated well, Major Travkin?" Stone asked, speaking Russian stiffly and with obvious unease.

"Well enough," Travkin replied. He smiled. "And please speak in English. Your vocabulary is fine, but the accent makes my teeth ache."

"Sorry," Stone said.

"I appreciate the effort," Travkin responded. *"Spasibo."*

The two men sat silently together for a long moment, watching each other and wondering who was going to make the first move. They'd been playing espionage hide-and-seek for the last year and a half, but sitting face-to-face was something different, especially under the present circumstances. Both Travkin and Stone had things to gain, and neither of them was about to give up something for nothing. In the end it was Travkin who broke the silence and the ice.

"I gather it was you who snatched me from the gaping jaws of the Company. Many thanks."

"Don't thank me yet, Comrade Major. Now that I've got you, I'm not sure what I should do with you."

"Call me Dmitri," the Russian said.

"All right, Dmitri. And you call me Stephen." The FBI man paused, hesitated, and finally reached out and took a cigarette from the box on the coffee table. They were unfiltered Chesterfields with as much tar and nicotine in one as in an entire pack of Camel Lights. Stone lit the cigarette and dragged happily.

"A question," said the Russian.

Stone nodded. "Shoot."

"You rescued me from Central Intelligence. Why?"

"Kidnapping is a federal offense," Stone answered glibly. "That's what the FBI does."

"Please," said Travkin, frowning.

"All right," said Stone wearily. "In the first place, what they did was

247

illegal. Kidnapping is a capital crime, and beyond that, the CIA has no mandate for domestic covert action. In the second place, they were poaching in my territory, and last but not least, I want to know why they snatched you at all."

"It was definitely a breach of protocol," Travkin said, nodding. "Can you imagine what it would be like if we went around plucking each other off the streets just for the hell of it?"

"So why take the risk?" Stone asked. "What do you know that would make them do something like that?"

"I don't have the faintest idea." Travkin shrugged.

"Bullshit," said Stone. "You must have an opinion."

"Perhaps."

"And you're going to keep it to yourself?"

"Perhaps." The Russian nodded.

"Now who's playing games?" Stone retorted.

"Let's get something clear," Travkin said, leaning forward. "I can call you Stephen and you can call me Dmitri, but the fact remains that you're an FBI counterintelligence officer and I'm a major in the GRU. I didn't defect to the Central Intelligence Agency, and I haven't defected to you either. I am a registered agent of a foreign country being held against my will." There was a long silence. Stone stubbed out the half-smoked cigarette and sat back in his chair.

"Okay," he said finally. "Then go." The FBI agent glanced over his shoulder. "The door's not locked. You can walk out. I'll even give you cab fare. You can be at Mount Alto in twenty minutes." He cocked an eyebrow at the blond man seated across from him. "I'm sure General Gurenko of the KGB will greet you with open arms."

"Touché," Travkin answered bleakly.

"Face it, Dmitri," said Stone. "You're screwed. After Cooper snatched you, Koslov can't take you back, and Gurenko would like nothing better than to see you swinging in the wind. Step out that door, and you'll have the GRU, the KGB, and the CIA all over you."

"So what do you suggest?" the Russian asked.

"Cooperate."

"With the FBI?"

"With me. I pulled this off on my own."

"I was wondering about that," Travkin said, nodding thoughtfully. "Stealing me from Cooper's people didn't seem like an operation your Mr. Ruppelt would have sanctioned."

"Ruppelt wouldn't sanction wiping his own ass unless he had a signed memo from someone higher up the ladder."

"So this isn't a formal debriefing?" asked Travkin.

"No," Stone answered, shaking his head emphatically. "No tapes, no nothing."

"Then why am I here? You didn't take me away from Cooper out of some Good Samaritan impulse."

"Barron," Stone replied. "Cooper and Mallory going to Barbados. Cabrera. All of it."

"Good grief!" Travkin said, affecting mock surprise. "You've had me under surveillance."

"No shit." Stone laughed. "You've been my main project for over a year now."

"I'm flattered." Travkin grinned.

"Cabrera," Stone repeated.

"Wait," said Travkin, raising a hand, palm outward. "We talk, but on one condition."

"What condition?" Stone asked.

"We share information. I cooperate, you cooperate. The only way I'm going to get back into Gennadi Koslov's good graces is by pulling some kind of diplomatic rabbit out of the hat. We work together. Agreed?" The Russian blew a long feather of smoke into the air.

Stone wasn't sure there was any rabbit in the world Travkin could produce that would ensure his reinstatement, but that was neither here nor there at the moment. After a reasonable interval he nodded. "Agreed."

It took almost two hours of back-and-forth conversation for the two men to complete their stories. Midway through the exchange they were joined by Mort Kessler and a large pizza from Armand's on Wisconsin Avenue. While the men talked and ate, Kessler used a thick pad of yellow paper to take notes.

"Okay," said the redhead, seated to one side of the coffee table. "This is what we have so far." He cleared his throat dramatically and looked from Stone to Travkin. The FBI man lit a cigarette, and the Russian took a slug of Pepsi from the can beside the open pizza box.

"Fire away," Stone said. "Dmitri and I are all ears."

"I'm doing this in chronological order, so jump in if I leave anything out." He cleared his throat again and began. "First we have Barron's telephone call. He makes it to Hudson Cooper, deputy director of opera-

249

tions for the Central Intelligence Agency, and a little while later Cooper makes one to Hollis Macintyre, *éminence gris* of Capitol Hill and beyond. He—that is, Dr. Barron—has previously requested material from the library at Walter Reed that relates to a relatively obscure illness called Creutzfeldt-Jakob disease—apparently a nasty sort of Alzheimer's. It appears that any records of that request have now been scrubbed. Anyway, within a day or so of making his phone call to Cooper and Cooper's making his call to Macintyre, Dr. Barron winds up getting himself killed."

"Murdered," said Stone, interrupting. "The autopsy was pretty clear about that. In view of the time of death, the water in his lungs should have had a higher salinity count since it was high tide when he died. He was drowned, but it was in low-tide water. Took the ME a little while to figure it out."

"Fine." Kessler nodded. "Anyway . . . Barron is murdered. Shortly thereafter the erstwhile Mr. Cooper and his assistant, Mr. Paul Mallory, take off for a very brief visit to Barbados. They meet a dark-haired, dark-eyed man of medium height calling himself John Duncan. Duncan appears again in Miami, getting off a flight from Jamaica, and that's the last we see of him. Meanwhile, the word comes down from above that we're to red-flag the surveillance of our man Dmitri here, and in fact, we're told to drop everything and anything that has to do with him. But we're doing some snooping around, and we pick up on the Costa Rica thing. Then bam! Dmitri gets snatched. He spends time at Bowie, and during a preliminary interrogation a lot of the questions are about Central America. On top of that we have the Spanish cigarette butt clue and the Costa Rican telephone number. We rescue Dmitri from Cooper, and that's the end of the story. Did I leave anything out?"

"What do you think?" Stone asked.

Travkin was now lying down on the couch, his head propped up on a pillow. The Russian reached out and plucked a cigarette from the emptying box on the coffee table. He lit it and blew another expressive stream of smoke toward the ceiling. To Stone it appeared that the GRU man was incapable of thinking without a cigarette in his mouth.

"I think it has holes," Travkin said after a few more thoughtful drags.

"Where?" asked Kessler, pencil poised over a fresh sheet.

"For one thing," the Russian asked, "why does Barron call Cooper?"

"You have a contact at Walter Reed; why shouldn't Cooper?" Stone answered.

250

"Okay," said Travkin from the couch. "Why does Cooper call Macintyre?"

"Maybe there's no connection," said Kessler, tapping the rubber end of the pencil against his chin.

"Let's assume there's a connection," said Stone. "Barron to Cooper, Cooper to Macintyre."

"I don't know much about this Macintyre person," said Travkin.

"Power behind the throne," Kessler explained. "He backed Tucker for the presidential nomination, but not Teresi. He's been put out to pasture ever since the inauguration."

"Forget about Macintyre for the moment," said Stone. "What about Cabrera?"

"It is all supposition," said Travkin, swinging his legs around and sitting up.

"Explain," said Stone.

"Thanks to Mr. Cooper and yourself, I've had a lot of time to stare at the ceiling," the GRU man replied. "The more I stare, the less sense this all makes."

"You mean Cabrera?" Stone asked.

"All of it," Travkin replied. "If this were a KGB operation, I'd say we were being given disinformation. We assume Cabrera is involved because of the visit to Barbados and because Barron was Morazán's attending physician at Walter Reed."

"It makes sense." Stone shrugged. "If Morazán has Creutzfeldt-Jakob, then the CIA has to act quickly to get rid of Cabrera. Cooper hires Duncan to do the job."

"Perhaps." Travkin nodded. "But what if it is all makeshift? A cover. Cooper is no fool, yet I have the Spanish cigarette and the telephone number in Costa Rica given to me on a platter."

"Go on." Stone prodded.

"Assume that Cooper has an operation in place, but also assume that he wasn't expecting my involvement," the Russian continued. "That would explain the kidnapping. He feeds me the cigarette and the telephone number to corroborate what you were already thinking—that Cabrera is the target—and then he lets me go, knowing that my only sanctuary lies with the FBI."

"You think the whole rescue thing was a setup?" asked Kessler.

"A fortuitous coincidence." The Russian shrugged. "Cooper has a file on me, he knows I was Spetznaz, yet he sends me off into the night with

251

only two men in a van. Presumably I was being taken to Camp Peary for more intensive interrogation. Proper procedure would call for a helicopter to take me from the Bowie facility directly there."

"He's right," Kessler said. "Flying out of Beltsville was a little strange."

"It all revolves around Cooper," Stone mused. Without thinking he took another cigarette from the box and lit it. "He's the focus."

"Which brings us to the Barbados trip," said Travkin. "If we assume that the trip was to employ the services of Mr. Duncan, then he was acting outside established procedure once again."

"In other words, deputy directors of the CIA don't do their own fieldwork," said Kessler.

"That one's bothered me right from the start," said Stone. "Not only is Cooper doing his own fieldwork, but he's also hiring a free-lance, presumably out of Jamaica, if Duncan's flight into Miami is any indication."

"Do you have anything at all on Duncan?" Travkin asked.

"No," said Stone, shaking his head. "He's a blank page."

"*Chyorny,*" murmured Travkin. "A black file."

"What's that?" asked Kessler.

"An asset you keep to yourself," explained the Russian. "Duncan will be someone with no obvious connection to Cooper."

"Why not a Costa Rican national?" Stone asked rhetorically. "If you want Cabrera taken out without its coming back on you, that would be the obvious way to go."

"He is operating outside normal channels," said Travkin, "and assuming a great deal of risk. This is what makes no sense."

"So what are you saying?" Stone said.

"He's saying the result doesn't justify the risk," Kessler answered. "Cooper wouldn't put his career on the chopping block for a two-bit like Cabrera. We've been working on the Costa Rica angle because it's been made to look like the right one."

"I agree." Travkin nodded. "It is like the aluminum foil window dropped from bombers to obscure radar."

"Okay," Stone said, frustrated. "If Cabrera isn't the target, then who is?"

"It all goes back to Dr. Barron," Kessler said, riffling through his notes. "He knew something, and it got him killed."

"Then the real target is another one of the patients under his authority," Stone added. "Who?"

"I think I know," Travkin answered quietly. He stubbed his cigarette out in the cut glass ashtray on the coffee table. He looked at the two men carefully. "I think Cooper's target is the President of the United States."

In Georgetown, less than a mile away from the FBI safe house, the four senior members of the Romulus Committee were meeting at Hudson Cooper's request. Cooper had arrived first, followed by Hollis Macintyre, then Joseph Swanbridge, the secretary of state, and finally Stuart Shrenk, President Tucker's attorney general. Shrenk, although new to the position of attorney general, was a longtime Washington lawyer and a close colleague of Swanbridge's. In view of Shrenk's authority as attorney general and his relationship with Swanbridge, the Romulus people had decided to tell Shrenk everything about the Tucker situation and their plan for its resolution. The secretary of state had briefed him privately several days before.

Shrenk, Macintyre, and Swanbridge were seated in the living room of the town house while Cooper stood in front of a wheeled stand containing a large video monitor and VCR. The CIA deputy director inserted a videocassette, reached behind him to turn off the lights in the room, then sat down in a vacant chair to the left of the video stand. A few seconds later color bars appeared on the screen and the room was filled with the monotonous hum of an audio tone. Using a remote control, Hudson Cooper fast forwarded the tape.

"This is an edited tape made from a variety of sources," Cooper explained, his voice hollow in the darkened room. "Pieces of it are from security cameras in the White House, dining room, corridors, elevators, some of it is from broadcast sources, and there is also some material we've managed to 'appropriate' from Mike Kaufmann."

"The fellow doing the Tucker documentary?" asked Swanbridge out of the gloom.

"That's the one," Cooper replied. "All the material on this tape was taken within the last ten days."

The color bars vanished and were replaced by a high-angle shot of the State Dining Room. In the corner of the screen a digital counter began to move. The main table in the expansive pale green room was set for twenty-five, with the President seated at the north end of the table. The camera, discreetly located in the northwest corner of the ceiling, showed a half profile of the husky, balding man. To his right there was a somewhat doughy woman in her fifties wearing a dark blue evening dress, while on his left there was a young woman in her late teens, pretty, but with the same pudginess as the woman on Tucker's right. Clearly mother

CHRISTOPHER HYDE

and daughter. Cooper hit the pause button on the remote control, and the picture froze.

"The dinner was held in honor of the new German chancellor, Johann Schiller," Cooper explained. "The President is in the center of the picture. The woman beside him is Annalise Schiller, the chancellor's wife; the teenager is Angelika Schiller, his daughter. She's eighteen. Halfway down the table you can see Gail Tucker, the First Lady, directly opposite Secretary of State Swanbridge. The chancellor is seated at the far end."

"They barely spoke English," commented Swanbridge, his cigar end glowing in the darkness. "The whole evening was boring as hell."

"Not for some people," said Cooper. "Watch."

The CIA man fast forwarded again, and the dinner progressed in a Chaplinesque frenzy. White-jacketed stewards came and went, heads bobbed back and forth, plates emptied, and glasses filled. Cooper tapped the pause button again, followed by the zoom control. The screen filled with a grainy picture of the President's back and the space between his chair and the young woman beside him.

"State-of-the-art video technology," Cooper said. "Japanese," he added apologetically.

He hit the slow-motion button, and the three other men in the room watched, fascinated, as the President's arm snaked out of his own lap and into that of the chancellor's daughter. The hand, showing just the right amount of starched white cuff at the wrist, moved up and down the young woman's thigh, then paused, fingers splayed, directly over her pubis.

"My God!" Shrenk whispered from the couch. "What is he doing?"

"Just what it looks like," said Cooper. "It goes on for two or three minutes. Then he pulls his hand away as though he'd been burned."

"I never noticed a thing," said Swanbridge.

Cooper sent the tape forward. The scene changed. This time the President and the First Lady were walking along a wooded pathway. In the background were two Secret Service men. Tucker was dressed in blue jeans and a dark green cable-knit sweater. Gail Tucker was wearing a denim skirt and a light brown suede jacket. A couple in late middle age, out for an evening stroll.

"Camp David, the President recuperating from the 'flu,'" Cooper narrated. "This is footage from the Kaufmann documentary."

The scene unfolded as the chief executive and his wife continued along the path. Just as they reached the camera position, Tucker paused. Cooper stopped the tape. The President's expression was one of childish bewilderment. The CIA man let the tape play again. Tucker turned and

254

looked back at the Secret Service men, then spoke to his wife. She took him by the arm, but he resisted, insisting on going forward. Tucker spoke again, and it didn't take a lip-reader to make out the words "fucking bitch." Tucker shook his wife off, then walked out of the frame, the expression on his face now one of furious anger.

"He's getting worse," said Swanbridge.

"Indeed," murmured Hollis Macintyre.

There was another twenty minutes of tape, each segment showing the deterioration of the President's condition. Most of the episodes were subtle, but if you knew what to look for, it was clear that the man's mental health was declining. When the tape ran out, Cooper switched off the machine and turned on the lights in the room.

"Using a third party cutout, I had a blind prognosis done for a man of the President's age with Creutzfeldt-Jakob disease," Cooper said. "According to it, Tucker is in an advanced state. His next faux pas could be politically fatal."

"Surely his wife must be getting suspicious," said Shrenk. "It isn't every day that the President hauls off and calls the First Lady a fucking bitch."

"According to my information, she's worried about exhaustion," Cooper answered. "I don't think she's taken it any further than that."

"What about his doctor?" asked Swanbridge.

"Which one?" replied Cooper. "The White House physician or the senior man at Walter Reed?"

"Either," said the secretary of state.

"Barron's replacement is a man named Eganthaler. He doesn't know anything, and there's nothing in the files to alert him. As you're aware, the White House physician is Charlie Moorehead. A general practitioner, old friend of the family. He wouldn't know Creutzfeldt-Jakob disease if you struck him on the head with it."

"Being made White House physician is a sinecure," said Macintyre. "We're all aware of that."

"How long until the press catches wind of this?" asked Shrenk.

"It could be any time," Cooper replied. He lit a cigarette, something he rarely did in public.

"This situation with the Russian," Macintyre interjected. "Has it been dealt with?"

"Yes." Cooper nodded. "He was picked up by the Rednet group. When Ruppelt is informed, Stone will almost certainly be suspended. Travkin no longer has any credibility with his people. With Stone's protection removed he'll go to ground. Both of them are still operating on the Cabrera theory anyway; it doesn't present a problem."

"I hope not," said Macintyre.

"The question is," Swanbridge said calmly, "how do we proceed?"

"As planned," Cooper replied. "Nothing has changed appreciably. Frankly, we have very little choice in the matter since communication with our man is a one-way affair. At the last contact he said that the operation was feasible. I've taken steps to see that the first payment is made."

"Will there be further contact?" Macintyre asked.

"Yes."

"He should be notified that speed is now of the essence," ordered the huge white-suited man.

"And if he asks for more money?" said Cooper.

"The question is moot," said Macintyre, "since he'd have to be alive in order to collect it." He turned to Shrenk. "What about the succession?"

"As we discussed," the Attorney General replied, smoothing his tie under the lapels of his blazer. "Both the speaker and the president of the Senate have letters of disability on file because of their questionable health. Since the Twenty-fifth Amendment doesn't cover the simultaneous deaths of both the President and the Vice President, I'll invoke the 1947 succession legislation. It was last ratified in 1979, so I don't see any trouble. Secretary Swanbridge could be sworn in immediately."

"President Swanbridge," intoned the florid-faced man. He'd obviously been drinking prior to his arrival at the meeting. "That has a nice ring to it."

"We won't let it go to your head, Joseph," Macintyre said coolly. "Rest assured."

Hudson Cooper listened as the three men discussed the logistical problems resulting from the assassination. He was bemused by the bland ease of their conversation. Had Brutus and his conspirators been so calm in the last few days before the Ides of March? Had there been an evening like this before Kennedy's fateful visit to Dallas? This was a terrible moment in the history of the United States, unfolding in the well-appointed confines of a Georgetown home. It was insane, and the CIA man suddenly felt the desperate weight of his own history, decades lived in a phantom world where trusts were meant to be violated and truths turned into lies.

Once upon a time, or so they all believed, intelligence had been a game for gentlemen, played by gentlemen's rules. In his mind's eye Cooper saw the bronze statue of Nathan Hale standing guard at the front entrance to the CIA's Langley headquarters. The perfect gentleman spy, at least to Allen Dulles and the early espionage establishment in Washington, but to the British he was just another traitor, with no more honor than a Blunt, Philby, Burgess, or Maclean.

And there is no pretense of honor here in this room tonight, he thought. None of us is Nathan Hale, regretting that he has but one life to give for his country, and Geoffrey Tucker is no tyrant to be deposed by men history would eventually deem heroes. The deputy director looked from one man to the other. Certainly not heroes or even gentlemen and definitely not a game. To Cooper that was the cold, dark terror of it. For these men the deaths of Geoffrey Tucker and Vincent Teresi were merely expedient, the rectification of a political error, a balancing of the nation's books. Business.

Five thousand miles and eight time zones away dawn was breaking over Moscow, its first pale rays putting a red-gold blush on the onion domes of Ivan the Great's bell tower in the Kremlin. Across Red Square, a few blocks to the north on Zhdanova Street, Sergei Yulevich Kuryokhin was already awake and preparing for another day.

Carrying his morning coffee to the main room of his apartment over the Sardine Café, the old man noticed a new pain, this one running from his left shoulder down to his hand. He sat down at his scarred ancient desk and used his right hand to massage the aching shoulder joint. The arthritis was getting worse, and the cortisone treatments didn't seem to be having very much effect anymore.

Kuryokhin lit a Lucky Strike, sipped the hot sweet coffee, and looked thoughtfully down at the file folders spread out on his desk. The folders were bright yellow, each bearing a crimson horizontal band and a firmly stamped notice in black: "SOVERSHENNO SEKRETNO" (completely secret). By rights the files should never have been removed from the Central Registry at Teply Stan, but Kuryokhin's seniority and rank gave him special privileges.

He'd worked on the files until the early hours of the morning, taking notes and watching as a faint pattern slowly began to emerge. Gurenko, his resident in Washington, had long ago infiltrated Koslov's GRU operation and through that connection had come up with an overview of Dmitri Travkin's recent activities, including a copy of his computer logs.

This in turn led to Barron, the Walter Reed doctor, his death, and Travkin's follow-up work.

Initially Kuryokhin had accepted the scenario involving Cabrera, the Costa Rican, and Morazán, his police chief, but the more he examined the possibility of Morazán's possible illness, the less likely it all seemed. Following his instincts and the odd tidbit of information from Osin, the elderly intelligence man began working in another direction.

Hudson Cooper's telephone call to Hollis Macintyre and the deputy director's anomalous visit to Barbados intrigued him. Requesting and immediately receiving Gurenko's logs, he'd followed the snakes and ladders course of Cooper's movements over the past two weeks. People of Cooper's stature were subjects of regular surveillance, and tracing him wasn't particularly difficult. Interestingly, Hollis Macintyre kept coming up, as did Joseph Swanbridge and in the last few days, Stuart Shrenk, the attorney general.

Meetings among Cooper, Swanbridge, and Macintyre had taken place at Macintyre's country estate as well as a small town house on Cherry Hill Lane in Georgetown. The town house was owned by Delaware Real Estate Holdings Ltd., which turned out to be a CIA proprietary corporation. In other words, the Cherry Hill Lane address was a safe house.

According to the research information plucked from the fifteen million files on hand in the KGB Central Registry, the enormously fat man had figured in every administration since Roosevelt. A powerful figure certainly, but retired now and with no ties except social ones to Joseph Swanbridge and Stuart Shrenk and no connection at all to Hudson Cooper. There was also an unverified report that at one of the early meetings on Cherry Hill Lane, the deputy head of the Joint Chiefs of Staff and the secretary of the treasury had been in attendance.

Kuryokhin squinted, a trail of smoke drifting up under his glasses from the short end of his cigarette. He frowned, flipping through the pages of his lined yellow pad. A cabal of Washington's elite, a multimillion-dollar purchase of gemstones presumably to be used as a payoff, Cooper's out-of-character trip to the Caribbean. Not for Cabrera or Morazán, that much was certain. If either one was a target for assassination men like Shrenk and Swanbridge would distance themselves from the operation, not embrace it.

The old man felt another bolt of pain in his arm and grunted with the fresh ache. Perhaps a visit to the pool on Volchonka Street was in order. An hour in the *parilnya*, the steam room, instead of paper work. The huge sports complex on the Kropötkin Embankment was only a few stops away on the metro, and even with a steam he could be at Teply Stan before most of his colleagues. He put out his cigarette and pushed himself up from the desk. Enough of this.

The pain was enormous, worse than anything he'd felt in his life, the razored talons of some enormous vile bird tearing into his chest. He knew immediately what it was: At last his heart had failed, each blood pulse pounding through the frail organ wreaking the inevitable vengeance of time.

*"Ya umirayu,"* he whispered softly, amazed at the simple truth of his statement. "I'm dying." Turning, he took a single stumbling step toward the glass-doored cabinet on the far side of the room, his eyes fixed on the bottom shelf and a small, brightly painted wooden *matryoshka* doll. They would find it certainly, but would they see it, and seeing it, would they know what they had found? A good riddle to die with, and enough to make him smile, even with the terrible pain. The smile vanished then, the blood draining from his face.

*"Maht!"* he whispered, a child again, and Sergei Yulevich Kuryokhin, son of Zinaida Kuryokhina, took a final gasping breath and died.

Exhausted and mentally drained by the Travkin debriefing, Stephen Stone went down the short dark hall and let himself into his ex-wife's apartment on South Capitol Street. He knew that Debbie wasn't due in from Paris until the following day, but he hadn't been able to bear the thought of his own bleak and un-air-conditioned bachelor. The conclusions they'd reached in the Rock Creek safe house were numbing, and even the faint aura of Debbie's presence in the vacant rooms was better than facing those conclusions on his own.

The apartment took up the main floor of a gentrified brownstone tucked in behind the Rayburn Building just north of the Conrail tracks. It was an old-fashioned high-ceilinged railway flat, the entrance hall opening onto a long corridor with the rooms all in a line to the right. The living room and dining room looked out onto the street, while the bathroom, kitchen, and bedroom faced a narrow alley between Debbie's building and the one beside it. A rear doorway at the far end of the hall next to the bedroom led out to a tiny rear garden.

Reading Deborah Stone's résumé, replete with degrees in European languages and history, someone without any real knowledge of the woman would have expected an apartment decorated with dark, heavy furniture, carpets in various dour shades, and Polish hunting prints lined

259

up neatly on the walls. In reality the apartment was anything but dark and dour.

In what Stephen Stone knew was a deliberate attempt to separate her work and home lives, the entire apartment was done in Art Deco splendor. The living room was furnished with Frankl Chinese-style chairs, an ebony gilt-wood-and-marble commode, and a 1925 Paris Exposition rounded display cabinet inlaid with ivory in a floral motif. The dining room was filled with furniture that looked as though it had been taken from an early twenties transatlantic liner, and there was Fauré enameled glassware everywhere.

Ignoring it all, Stone went down the short hall to the bathroom, stripped off his clothes, and climbed into the shower. Standing under the noisy lukewarm spray, he let the water play over his face and body, faintly hoping that it would wash away his frustration and confusion.

Even if Travkin's assumption was wrong, the FBI man knew there was enough circumstantial evidence to take action. The hiring of an assassin by Cooper was in direct contravention of a standing presidential directive irrespective of the target. At the very least the Secret Service had to be notified so it could initiate an investigation, but the ramifications of that were enormous.

Cooper was almost certainly acting outside normal CIA channels, but Travkin was right: His "rescue" by the Back Door group had been equally illegal, and any information gained from it was tainted. If he went to Ruppelt, the Rednet director would have no choice but to suspend him and return Travkin to Cooper and the CIA. As it stood now, Stone would be perceived as a frustrated FBI agent with a questionable Soviet asset as his only backup. Not even the Washington *Post* would go for a conspiracy story like the one he and Travkin had jigsawed together.

Stone stepped out of the shower, dried himself roughly, and wrapped a towel around his waist. Standing in front of the medicine cabinet, he wiped the condensation off the mirror and stared at himself. Whom was he trying to kid? Questions of belief were irrelevant. If Travkin was right and Cooper's target was the President of the United States, the CIA deputy director would use any means to keep the operation secret, including murder.

Frowning, Stone left the bathroom and padded barefoot down the hall to the bedroom, his rumpled clothes in his arms. He stopped in the doorway, openmouthed. Debbie, his ex-wife, was sitting on the edge of the bed, peeling off her pantyhose. A black canvas suitcase lay open on the floor in front of her.

"Enjoy your shower?" she asked, smiling.

He nodded from the doorway, suddenly embarrassed by the intimacy of the moment—he in a towel, she with her stockings down around her ankles. Bizarrely he found himself becoming aroused. It was like getting a hard-on in your high school math class.

"Yeah, thanks," he muttered. She really was beautiful in a strange, plain way. Standing, she was close to his height with a model's legs but large, almost lush breasts. Her hair was cut shoulder length, framing a wide, intelligent face. Once upon a time the hair had been chestnut, but now it was faintly streaked with lines of gray she made no effort to conceal.

"I caught a late flight out of Paris," she explained, yawning. She stood up, pulling the dark green dress up over her head. Beneath it she was wearing an almost sheer cream-colored bra and panties. The undergarments were as Art Deco as the furniture in the room. The embroidery on the bra was paisley, and there was a delicately curved see-through panel across the front of the panties showing the dark mass of her pubic hair. "What are you doing here, by the way?" she asked, reaching up and unclipping the bra. She tossed it toward the suitcase.

"I needed someone to talk to," he answered. "I knew you wouldn't be here but . . ." He let it dangle, unsure of how to explain himself and trying not to look at her breasts.

"You sure you want to talk?" she asked, nodding toward the towel wrapped around his waist.

"Force of habit," he said, smiling weakly.

"Bring your habit over here." She laughed.

He crossed the room, then paused in front of her. "Look," he said, "you must be exhausted. I'll just put on my things and let you unpack."

Debbie Stone shook her head, then put her arms around his neck. "I'm glad you're here," she said quietly. "It's a nice surprise even if you are trespassing." She leaned forward slightly, taking his lower lip between her teeth and nipping gently. "We may not be married anymore, but cohabitation isn't everything." She let one arm drop between them and slid her hand under the towel. He closed his eyes at the warm enclosing touch of her fingers, but instead of its arousing him further, he saw a vision of the Zapruder film from the Kennedy assassination, frame by frame to the horrible image of the President's brains spraying upward and back over the trunk of the Lincoln in garish 8 mm color. He softened instantly.

"Sorry," he said, opening his eyes and staring into hers.

261

She looked concerned. "Problem?"

"Nothing I can talk about." He sighed.

"Don't be silly," she answered. "This is your ex-wife, Deborah Basti Stone, last of the Magyars." Her hand milked him rhythmically, and he began to thicken again. She paused, then used both hands to push him toward the bed.

"I think this goes beyond anything even the last of the Magyars can handle," he said, the towel falling away completely as he fell back onto the soft down comforter.

"I wouldn't be so sure of that." She laughed, dropping down on her knees between his outstretched legs.

An hour later Debbie Stone, nude, slipped out of bed, careful not to wake the sleeping man beside her. Despite his doubts, she'd managed to handle both his physical and mental requirements, but while his gushing confession of the situation had allowed him to fall into an exhausted sleep, it had left her stunned and wide-awake.

The long-legged woman tiptoed to her closet, draped a pale green shantung robe over her shoulders, and left the bedroom. In the kitchen she found an open bottle of Riesling in the refrigerator, poured herself a glass, and took it to the living room. She sat down in the floral print upholstered chair next to the telephone, took a few sips of wine, then took a cigarette from the zigzag enameled box on the side table. She lit it, then leaned back in the chair, staring up at the ceiling.

After a decade of work at the European Studies Institute Debbie Stone had analyzed virtually every important intelligence operation mounted by both East and West since the end of World War II. Her particular field focused on the Russians and the Eastern bloc countries, but she was also an expert on the British, French, Italians, and West Germans. Nothing in all she'd read and studied came close to the scenario Stephen had outlined to her.

Ironically, the only other piece of intelligence information with as much crucial importance as Stephen's was that of her own identity. She sat forward, took a last, long drag on the cigarette, then crushed it into the ashtray on the side table. Deborah Stone, on file with the European Studies Institute and the Central Intelligence Agency as Deborah Basti and in the files of the Hungarian Allavedelmi Hatosag (the State Security Agency) as Anna Danilla Rakozi, picked up the telephone, tapped out an almost forgotten number, and waited. When her call was answered, she spoke a single word.

"Autumn."

262

# Part Four

---

*I'M GLAD TO BE GOING . . . THIS IS THE LONELIEST PLACE IN THE WORLD.*

—WILLIAM HOWARD TAFT,
on leaving the White House at the end of his term

# CHAPTER 19

During the course of his researches Eric Rhinelander had amassed an impressive library of books relating to the White House, including half a dozen formal histories, several architectural critiques, and at least a score of tattletale biographies. He'd discovered detailed floor plans and cutaway drawings in both *Life* magazine and *National Geographic,* pieced together security information from several Secret Service exposés, and built up a comprehensive photographic study of the Oval Office, using various magazines and a number of books. Combining personal observations and the minicam videotape, he had been able to construct an accurate overview of White House personnel and the daily activities.

The working day at 1600 Pennsylvania Avenue began at 7:15 A.M. with the arrival of the food delivery truck. The vehicle was an unmarked white refrigerated cube van on a Ford Econoline chassis, and from his reading Rhinelander knew it was driven by a U.S. Marine driver from the executive garage, with a Secret Service agent riding shotgun. Entering the White House grounds from Executive Avenue, the truck stopped briefly while the driver's pass was checked by one of the gate guards. At the same time a second guard used a long-handled mirror to check the underside of the truck. After passing inspection, the truck drove to the rear of the White House, where the food was unloaded at the basement kitchen entrance.

Rhinelander knew that all food delivered to the White House was security-vetted on a regular basis—a high tech version of the food tasters employed by a variety of suspicious pharaohs, kings, queens, and heads of state for thousands of years. In the case of the White House, foodstuffs from more than twenty different longtime suppliers were delivered to McCreery's Provisioners, a security-cleared catering company in Georgetown, where the various orders were consolidated into a single shipment. Under the Secret Service agent's supervision, the shipment, already on skids, was loaded onto the truck, then delivered to the executive mansion.

Following the van on three separate occasions, Rhinelander noted that on arriving at the rear entrance to McCreery's, both the driver and the Secret Service agent left the empty truck unattended for almost fifteen minutes each morning, presumably while they enjoyed a cup of coffee and a cigarette with the catering company staff. On his third visit to McCreery's Rhinelander crossed the narrow alley at the rear of the building and climbed up into the truck.

His thirty-second inspection confirmed his initial observations after viewing the minicam tape. The truck was brand-new and equipped with a Thermo King 9,000 BTU flush-mounted reefer unit. The refrigeration box was fitted over the cab, with nothing but a vent inside the Kemlite insulated cube. He'd been given a guided tour of an identical vehicle on a truck-leasing lot in Alexandria the day before and knew what to expect.

According to the salesman at the leasing company, the flush-mounted units worked well as long as the truck wasn't loaded tight to the rear wall, blocking the vent and letting the frozen goods thaw. Enough space had to be left all around to let the cold air circulate; hence, most trucks with flush-mounted units each had a wooden baffle added to the front wall of the box to prevent the skids from being pushed up against the vent.

The Secret Service cube van was no exception. The plywood box was four feet high and eight feet long and jutted out approximately sixteen inches. Rapping it with his knuckles, Rhinelander could tell that the baffle was hollow, fitted with a vertical brace in the center. The end pieces, also plywood, were fastened down with six Phillips screws. Lots of room to hide and more than enough time to remove the screws. Rhinelander took out a pocket tape, took some accurate measurements of the cratelike structure, then left the box unseen. He'd now dealt with the initial phase of his entry. The second phase was equally straightforward and took place the day after his last visit to the catering company.

Using the truck was one of three options Rhinelander had devised as a way of getting into the grounds, but getting in was only a small part of the battle. For the operation to succeed he needed to be able to remain within the White House undetected for roughly five minutes. To accomplish that, he needed protective coloration—a disguise.

The simplest would be to impersonate a Secret Service agent since each agent wore no uniform beyond a color-coded pin in the jacket lapel, but the White House detail was a relatively small group, the members of which knew each other well. SS staff was occasionally called in from other field offices, but usually only for special events. A better choice was to dress as an Executive Protection officer.

His name was Paul Axworthy. At forty-four he had been with the EPB for seven years. For eleven years prior to that he had been a uniformed officer with the Metropolitan Police. His scores on the sergeant's examination had been well above average over a four-year period, but eventually he realized that a combination of factors, including ethnic quotas and internal politics, was clouding his chances of advancement within the force, so he opted for the Executive Protection Branch and was accepted.

During his time with the Washington police Axworthy had married, fathered three girls, and divorced. Most of his regular EPB paycheck and all his overtime went to support his ex-wife and children in Fort Myer, and what was left barely covered his personal living expenses and the rent on his one-bedroom apartment in Columbia Heights.

During his preliminary surveillance from the Hay-Adams Rhinelander was unaware of Axworthy's background, but he had marked him as being roughly the right physical type. Following the White House policeman home after shift end, the assassin had discovered his address and name. The following evening, with Axworthy safely on duty, Rhinelander had let himself into the man's apartment.

It was tiny and immaculately clean. Framed photos on the white walls of Axworthy and his girls at Disney World, a picture of Axworthy in his EPB uniform, a class photo from the Washington PD Academy. Furnishings were sparse: foldout bed, coffee table on a Sears rug, chrome-and-Formica dinette set in the kitchen area, and two flea market upholstered chairs. Student's desk under the picture of his kids.

Rhinelander went through the desk drawers quickly, building an image of Axworthy's past. Satisfied that he knew enough, he moved on to the large closet on the wall between the foldout bed and the kitchen area. Like the rest of the apartment, the closet and its contents were a study in meticulous order.

Footwear was arranged by type and color along the floor, while caps and hats were lined up on the shelf above the chrome hanger bar. The bar itself was completely filled: sport shirts on the far left, followed by dress shirts in solid colors, then white uniform shirts. Suits and ties followed the shirts to the center of the pole. The right side was filled with uniforms: five standard EPB uniforms, four of them in plastic dry-cleaning bags and a set of dress whites; two Washington Metropolitan Police uniforms; three U.S. Marine uniforms, still fitted out with corporal's stripes, a Vietnam-vintage set of tropicals, and a set of Marine dress whites.

From his research Rhinelander knew that the EPB uniform was much like that of the D.C. police. The only real differences were the gold stripe on the legs of the EPB trousers, the badge, and the shoulder flashes. He'd been prepared to simulate the uniform and its accessories, but Axworthy's wardrobe saved him the trouble.

From what he could see, the White House policeman wore his uniforms in order, from right to left, probably at the rate of one a week. When he was down to the last one, he took the others in to be dry-cleaned. Given the narrowing time frame of his operation, Rhinelander felt it was worth the small risk of the man's noticing that one of the uniforms was missing. He took the uniform on the far left, then let himself out of the apartment.

The question of weaponry was next on the assassin's list. In works of fiction there was usually a brilliant gunsmith or weapons master for the hero to visit; but Rhinelander was well aware that in reality such men didn't exist, and if they once had, their clients had long ago removed them. Anyone involved in the business of professional murder would hardly put his identity and whereabouts into the hands of a stranger, and anyway, there was rarely the need. Forsyth's Jackal and Fleming's Bond aside, the real assassin tended toward cheap but efficient means of carrying out his assignments.

Hence, you had Stauffenberg's satchel of explosives for killing Hitler, Ramón Mercader's ice ax for Leon Trotsky, Booth's derringer, fired less than a foot from Lincoln's head, and six men with automatic rifles and machine guns attempting to kill De Gaulle at Petit Clamart. The truth of professional killing was rarely, if ever, as intriguing and romantic as its fictional counterpart.

In this instance, Rhinelander's weapon of choice would probably have been a hand grenade, but he knew that blood and brains smeared all over the walls of the Oval Office wasn't what Hudson Cooper was looking for. The CIA man and his ghostly conspirators were looking for something that would play on the evening news: murder most foul, but relatively palatable to the television audiences of the world.

Obviously a rifle was ridiculous, and using a shotgun at such close range was also out of the question, both technically and aesthetically. Some sort of handgun was an obvious choice, especially if he was wearing an EPB uniform, but getting off at least two accurate shots under the conditions he was envisaging was highly unlikely. After considering every aspect of his plan, Rhinelander concluded that he needed a quiet semi or fully automatic weapon capable of inflicting fatal injury at close range.

Ironically, the criteria he established for his weapon eventually led him to a real-life "armorer." Unlike the bow-tied Q from the Bond books or Forsyth's dapper little Belgian, this weapons man was barely twenty, had shoulder-length hair tied back in a ponytail, wore a Def Leppard T-shirt, and operated openly out of a mall on the outskirts of Baltimore.

The young man's name was Willis Johnson, and he managed a store called the Gasworks. The store supplied weapons, ammunition, and designer clothing for something variously known as paintball, the survival game, and action pursuit. As far as Rhinelander could tell, it was actually a high tech and expensive version of cowboys and Indians. According to Willis Johnson, the first paintball gun was actually designed to mark trees for logging companies. A forestry surveyor could choose a tree to be cut and mark it from a distance with the $CO_2$-powered handgun. The "bullet" was actually a gelatin ball filled with a mixture of paint and mineral oil.

Over time, the weaponry and its accessories had become highly sophisticated, as had the game itself. Instead of using old-fashioned single-shot marking pistols and chasing after one another through the trees, organized teams now stalked one another on playing grounds complete with mock Vietnamese villages and dummy tanks and palisaded forts, using constant air machine guns with brand names like the Terminator. They wore full camo outfits, hand-loaded their own paintballs, and took their wives to competitions all over the country.

On a range in the basement of the store Willis Johnson demonstrated the technology with his own custom-designed weapon—a short-barreled machine pistol fed by a small tank of $CO_2$ clipped to his belt and connected to the hard plastic butt of the Uzi-style weapon by a loop of rubber tubing. The air powered a spring, which in turn forced the paintballs along the barrel of the gun at about six hundred feet per second. Not fatally rapid, but well below the speed of sound, it kept the gun quiet.

The range was made up of three fifty-foot-long lanes, each one sepa-

269

rated by head-high walls made of sheet plywood. At the end of each lane was a black-painted silhouette of a man. According to Willis, the targets, also made of plywood, were hosed off at the end of each day.

"Just like a real weapon," said the young black man, pulling on a pair of safety goggles and flipping a switch to light up the middle lane on the range. "You got three settings: safety, that's the red dot on the lever; then single shot; then full auto." Willis set the paintball gun on single shot and squeezed the trigger. There was a brief cracking sound, and a blood-red stain three or four inches across appeared on the head of the silhouette. "Sound comes from the ball smackin' into the wood." Johnson smiled. "Quieter out in the bush." He flipped the lever to full auto, adopted a pained Charles Bronson expression, and squeezed the trigger again. There was a stuttering roar, ending abruptly as the twenty-round magazine emptied in under two seconds. Johnson had stitched a line of red from the crotch of the target up to its neck.

"Impressive," said Rhinelander.

Johnson handed him the weapon and pulled a fully loaded tubelike magazine from his fatigue jacket. He showed Rhinelander how to load the ball bearing-size paintballs, then stepped back. Rhinelander slipped the six-inch-long black plastic air bottle into the pocket of his jacket, then settled himself into a firing position. He fired five rounds: left eye, right eye, heart, stomach, and groin.

"You've used guns before," said Johnson, peering downrange at the stitched line of paint splatters.

"Now and again," Rhinelander said. "What would you say is the optimum range for a gun like this?"

"For real?" Johnson asked.

Rhinelander nodded. "Yes."

"Fifty feet, sixty at the outside," the young man answered. "Trajectory's pretty flat, but the balls are light, and the barrels are smoothbore."

"I see," said Rhinelander. He hefted the weapon in his hands. "The CO-two bottle is plastic, and so is the gun. How much metal is involved in the manufacture?"

"Hardly any," Johnson answered. "It sounds kind of silly, but one of the problems they used to have was cleaning these things, so now they're dishwasher-safe. Almost anything not plastic is made out of ceramic. The spring is probably the biggest piece of metal in the gun."

They went back upstairs, and twenty minutes later Rhinelander left the store, leaving Willis Johnson with a sketch of the weapon he wanted the young man to build for him. The gun, stripped down to barrel, trig-

270

ger, and frame, looked more like a fat-handled nightstick than a pistol. According to Johnson, it would take three days to create.

Rhinelander made two more stops before returning to Washington. Using the yellow pages, he found a discount plumbing and heating store, where he purchased two dozen secondhand residential thermostats. From the plumbing store he went to a hobby shop and bought three model-maker's syringes, normally used for putting glue in hard-to-reach areas. His out-of-town shopping complete, the assassin returned to the capital and dropped his packages off at the Wyoming. Consulting his detailed notes on the upcoming operation, he was pleased to see that there was only one thing left on his list.

Wearing a suit and tie, Rhinelander crossed to the Holiday Inn and rented a car, using the James Smythe Visa. He drove out of Washington, heading south on the Maryland side, to the small town of Indian Head. There he found the marina mentioned in one of the guidebooks he'd purchased, and using the Smythe credit card, he rented a twin-pontooned houseboat. The vessel was at least ten years old, was painted a non-descript pale blue, and offered only the barest essentials. At twenty-eight feet it had sleeping accommodations for six, a small galley-dining area, and a head with a shower stall. It was powered by twin inboards, and according to the manager of the marina, it was capable of six knots upstream and eight downstream if the tides were running in your favor. It suited Rhinelander perfectly. He took the boat for two weeks, put down a five-hundred-dollar deposit, and told the manager he'd pick it up in the next day or so.

During the early planning stages Rhinelander had thought of something a lot faster than the houseboat; but the assassin knew he'd overstayed his welcome at the Wyoming, and the boxy vessel he'd rented was just the kind of anonymous living quarters he required for the last few days before the event. Satisfied with his progress, he drove back to Washington, dropped off the car at the Holiday Inn, and returned to the Wyoming.

He spent the next few hours going over every detail of the operation, checking and rechecking each move and countermove. Access, exit, and escape all had been dealt with; the question of weaponry and ammunition was in hand; he'd even chosen the date: Saturday, August 12, with the Beach Boys performing on the floating barge at the water gate and the

271

President of the United States celebrating his birthday at the White House. The only thing necessary now was his final telephone call to Mallory. Rhinelander glanced at his watch. The last few minutes of Wednesday, August 9, were ticking away. If all went well, seventy-two hours would see the operation to its conclusion. Rhinelander gathered his notes into a neat pile on the desk, turned out the light, and went to bed.

# CHAPTER 20

Stephen Stone sat in the coffee shop of the Old Town Holiday Inn in Alexandria, drinking stomach-souring coffee, smoking Camel filters in an unending chain, and contemplating his future as a defrocked FBI agent with an out-of-date law degree and a fugitive Soviet spy on his hands. It didn't look promising, especially since Ruppelt was threatening criminal action unless he coughed up Travkin's whereabouts. So far the Rednet director had only put him on indefinite suspension, but Stone knew it was only a matter of time. Cooper would pressure Ruppelt for Travkin's bolt-hole, and Ruppelt would pass the pressure along.

A bored waitress filled Stone's cup for the fifth time that morning, then moved down the row of injection-molded booths to the front of the coffee shop. The FBI man followed her with his eyes, then looked beyond her to the lobby, hoping for a glimpse of Mort Kessler. The red-headed agent was his only link to the Rednet office now, and even that was tenuous: Stone had been under suspension for the last five days, and right from the start Kessler was sure that he was being tailed.

Stone sighed, added three cream capsules to the coffee, and lit yet another cigarette. Thanks to Debbie, Travkin was safe, at least for the moment. It had taken her awhile to absorb the scenario he'd laid out for her that night in her apartment, but eventually she'd accepted it. They both knew she was putting her own career on the line by helping him, but she'd brushed aside his attempt at thanks and got down to the business at hand.

The following morning Debbie returned to work at the institute, and

273

before lunchtime she'd organized a new safe house for Travkin. She'd spotted a typed advertisement for a summer home rental on the bulletin board in the administration office and discovered that the owner was one of the Georgetown professors she'd done a research project for the previous year. She gave the woman a deposit, and the professor gave her a set of a keys and a map. The cottage was on Lake Anna, a few miles west of Bowling Green on the Virginia side of the Potomac.

That evening, using Debbie's car and after making sure they weren't being followed, they drove Travkin to the cottage, pausing briefly in the little Civil War town of Spotsylvania to stock up on food. The cottage had turned out to be quite lavish—a four-bedroom log house with its own beach, dock, and boathouse. The house was surrounded by trees, accessible only by a narrow, winding drive leading down from the main, graveled road. After settling the Russian in, Stone and Debbie returned to Washington and parted company, the FBI man insisting that she have no more involvement in the affair. The next day he'd been suspended. He hadn't seen his ex-wife or Travkin since.

Mort Kessler appeared in the coffee shop just as Stone was butting his cigarette. The red-haired agent slid into the booth across from Stone and frowned.

"You look like shit," he said. The waitress drifted by, and Kessler ordered a large tomato juice.

"I feel like shit," Stone answered. "Anyone on your tail?"

"That's one of those dumb questions like 'Are you asleep?'" Kessler grinned. The tomato juice arrived, and he took a sip. "If I'd been followed, I wouldn't be here, I'd still be dodging the tail."

"Don't be irritating." Stone sighed. "Did anyone try to tail you?"

"Not today, not that I could see." Kessler shrugged. That was good enough for Stone. Mort was a ghost when it came to surveillance, and he knew every trick in the book.

"Okay," Stone said. "What's been happening?"

"You've got leprosy as far as the bureau is concerned," the red-haired agent told him. "Anybody working with you has been shit-listed."

"You?" Stone asked.

"Bet your life." Kessler snorted. "I've got two weeks' leave, and then I'm off to the Seattle field office."

"Cooper." Stone grimaced.

"Some of it," Kessler said. "The Roop is pretty ticked all on his own, though. The big piss-off is that you won't tell him where you've got Dmitri stashed."

"I told him I didn't know anything about Travkin," Stone said. He lit another cigarette. "I told him the last I knew about it, he'd been kidnapped by persons unknown."

"He knows you're shitting him," Kessler answered, sipping his juice. "I think one of the guys we picked up in Baltimore must have talked. They tore up the Rock Creek place a couple of days ago."

"Cooper again," Stone murmured.

"I think so." Kessler nodded. "They've had two sniffers going through your office the past couple of days, loading everything into boxes and lugging them out."

"Have they got anything on you?"

"Nothing but my association with you," Kessler answered. "No hard evidence about sporting Dmitri away from the Company. I think the Roop is suspicious, though. He keeps on giving me these nasty looks when I run into him in the hall." Kessler grinned. "And to make it worse, I just told him I was taking my two-week leave early."

"To follow Mallory around?"

"That's the plan, isn't it?" Kessler asked. "He's got to be the link to our killer."

"If there really is a killer." Stone grunted.

"What's the matter? Losing faith in Comrade Dmitri's hypothesis?"

"No," the weary FBI man responded. "But you have to admit the whole thing sounds pretty crazy. We're sitting on a conspiracy to assassinate the President of the United States, a deputy director of the CIA is deeply involved, and our best witness is a Russian military intelligence officer."

"We've been over it a hundred times," Kessler answered. "Travkin's information is backed up by our own surveillance of him, and it fits in with Cooper's visit to Barbados. So does the telephone call from Cooper to Hollis Macintyre. Those two have been thick as thieves for years, and Macintyre was one of the back room boys who got Tucker elected in the first place. Now he's been put out to pasture."

"It's still hard to imagine." Stone sighed. He butted his cigarette and lit another. The coffee in front of him was mud brown and cold. He could feel his stomach beginning to protest. There was no antacid made that could take on indigestion brought on by an assassination.

"I don't have any trouble with it." Kessler shrugged. "You know as well as I do that this country was built on conspiracies and assassinations. And Cooper's not so far out of whack either; don't forget, he works for the same boys who tried to murder Castro with a poisoned cigar."

275

"All right," Stone said finally. "How do we work it?"

"Like we said before," the redhead answered briefly. "There has to be a link. Cooper's not going to expose himself if he doesn't have to. Mallory went with him to Barbados, so he's the most likely."

"Did you manage to find anything on him?"

"Not a lot. Smart, our age. Heavy math background. Used to work in Threat Analysis. A computer whiz."

"Doesn't sound like your average Company cutout," Stone commented.

"Maybe not, but he makes the perfect fall guy. When this is over, Cooper could remove him without making any waves. His slate is so clean it squeaks: no immediate family; no close friends at the agency; nothing in our files at all."

"Presumably Cooper is working him blind," Stone mused.

Kessler nodded.

"It's a good bet. All he knows is that he's servicing a covert agent for his boss," said Stone.

"He's got to realize it's an illegal operation," said Kessler. "Company agent operating within the country?"

"Don't be naive," said Stone. He gave a dry laugh. "You know as well as I do that the Company's got at least a dozen proprietary operations ongoing in Florida alone. Miami is one big recruiting station."

"Still, maybe we can turn him."

"On what grounds?" Stone snorted. "Do we appeal to his patriotism?"

"Self-interest," Kessler replied. "If this really is a plot to kill Tucker, and if Mallory is running as a cutout, you and I both know Cooper's going to off him as soon as the operation is over. Let him run *that* through his Threat Analysis computer."

"Not yet," Stone murmured. "Let's watch him and see if we can get a lead on Travkin's man from Barbados."

"What happens if we do find him?" Kessler asked. "We can't go to the Roop, that's for sure."

"If we have enough real evidence, I can take it to Lyall Spencer at the Secret Service."

"Okay." Kessler nodded. "We put a hot watch on Mr. Mallory."

"All by yourself?" Stone asked.

The redheaded agent shook his head no. "Putnam and Dofney are still in as long as I can let them take the after-hours shifts. Where will you be if something comes up—home or uh . . ."

"Debbie's?" Stone smiled, filling in the slightly embarrassed blank. Mort Kessler was the only one of his co-workers at Rednet who was aware of the on-again-off-again affair with his ex. He shook his head. "No. I'll be at the safe house at Lake Anna with our Russian friend, at least for tonight. You've got the number."

"Okay." Kessler nodded, standing up. "I'll call you if anything breaks."

Stephen Stone watched his friend leave the coffee shop. He pushed the cup and the overflowing ashtray away and leaned back against the sticky vinyl upholstery of the booth. His stomach was churning, but that didn't account for the dull, deep ache in his guts. Somehow, perhaps bred by the instincts and paranoias of his profession, he knew they were running out of time.

General Vladimir Gurenko, KGB resident in Washington, leaned back in his chair, eyes closed, hands clasped behind his neck. His deputy, Major Valentin Ivashutin, sat on a low couch on the far side of the room, browsing through the welter of teletype tearsheets and handwritten notes on the birchwood table in front of him. Behind Gurenko the large picture window was slashed with streaks of rain. The shower had begun early that afternoon and showed no signs of stopping. The rain was a false promise, though, and was doing nothing to offset the sweltering heat of the capital.

"Go through it again," the dark-haired KGB resident murmured, his eyes still closed. "As much as we have so far."

"Our colleagues at Moscow Center followed procedure when General Kuryokhin did not appear at his normally scheduled morning briefing." Ivashutin repeated the sequence of events outlined in the first of the teletype messages received at the Mount Alto complex. "A two-man unit was sent to his apartment. They entered and found the general dead, apparently of a heart attack."

"There is no doubt of the cause of death?" Gurenko asked mildly. Within the ranks of the KGB "heart attack" was a well-worn euphemism that covered a lot of ground.

"Not at this point," Ivashutin responded, neatly avoiding a firm opinion. "Once again following procedure, the men sealed the apartment after the body was removed and a team of 'janitors' was brought in. In addition to the notes General Kuryokhin was making at the time of his death, the janitors discovered a wooden key hidden inside one of the general's collection of *matryoshka* dolls. It took some time, but they

277

eventually discovered that the handmade key opened up a small compartment behind one of the bookshelves in the room. The compartment contained a number of journals written in code."

"Ignore the logistics of our intrepid comrades," Gurenko ordered. "Get to the meat of it."

"The code was one that hadn't been used since the Great Patriotic War," Ivashutin continued, his voice even. "It was easy enough to break. At any rate the journals have given us the identity of Osin among other things." Ivashutin leafed through the papers on the table and pulled out a stapled sheaf of hastily prepared notes. He hesitated for a moment, his small, bright eyes scanning over the rough dossier he'd prepared.

"Go on," Gurenko ordered. He opened his eyes and sat forward in the chair, his small, long-fingered hands playing over the surface of the desk in front of him.

"She was born Anna Danilla Rakozi in Budapest, August seventeenth, 1951. Her father was Dr. Lutz Rakozi, a professor of history at the university. Her mother died in childbirth. In 1968 at the age of seventeen she obtained a scholarship in languages and history from the University of Moscow. We recruited her in 1970, and after her father's death in 1971 she returned to Budapest and continued her education while monitoring student activities for us at the same time."

"What was Kuryokhin's interest in her?" Gurenko asked.

"After we lost Sasha in 1964, the general and other ranking members of the Foreign Directorate were looking for ways to reinfiltrate the Central Intelligence Agency. Given the CIA's own recruitment methods, generally utilizing its so-called Ivy League universities, the general thought placing students within their educational system seemed a likely path. He left standing orders with the secret police in Budapest to alert him of any possible identity switches that could be made.

"According to the general's journals, an opportunity presented itself late in 1973. A Hungarian couple who'd emigrated to the United States long before the '56 revolution returned to Budapest on a holiday. They died in an unfortunate automobile accident."

"Indeed," Gurenko murmured softly. "Automobile accident" was as much a euphemism as "heart attack."

"Yes," Ivashutin answered. He paused, trying to find his place in the notes, then continued. "The couple's name was Basti, Sandor and Danuta. He worked for a plumbing supply company in New York, and she was a housewife. They had no children. Technical gave her a passport identifying her as their daughter, and she accompanied the remains of her

278

'parents' back to the United States. From what we understand, there was no other family."

"Of course not," said Gurenko, smiling wanly. "There wouldn't be."

"Rakozi, now known as Deborah Basti, enrolled at Columbia University and obtained a degree in European history and Russian. Considering her education at the University of Moscow and her language facility, it isn't surprising that she was granted a postgraduate scholarship to Georgetown University. From there she was recruited by the European Studies Institute."

"The CIA," said Gurenko.

"Precisely." Ivashutin nodded. "In 1979 she was handpicked by Hudson Cooper, deputy director of operations. He's employed her as a strategic analyst and a high-level courier ever since. She's been sitting in on every major project and debriefing for the last seven or eight years."

"All the while being run by Kuryokhin," said Gurenko, impressed despite himself.

"She is obviously the source of the general's so-called magic touch," said Ivashutin. "According to his notes, she was even hired as a consultant for the counterintelligence program."

"I'm intrigued by the connection to Stephen Stone, the Rednet man at the FBI."

"A fortuitous twist of fate by all appearances." Ivashutin shrugged. "They met at a conference and had an affair. One thing led to another. It's not too unreasonable when you think about it. They both were in the same field, a great deal in common. We don't have a psychological file on the woman, but one presumes there was some guilt on her part. It was a small bonus for the general; through her he could keep some kind of watch on the bureau's counterintelligence activities."

"A watch he saw fit not to share with us," Gurenko responded. He tapped his fingers on the desktop. "The general's conspiracy theory?" he said after a moment.

"It relates to the last notes he was making before he died," Ivashutin answered, his tone hesitant again. Both men knew they were on dangerous political ground here. Kuryokhin was dead, and there was no telling who his successor would be; by rights the man, whoever he was, would inherit Osin and the current delicate situation.

"He made contact with the Rakozi/Basti woman in Amsterdam," Gurenko said.

"Yes." Ivashutin nodded. "Not directly, but an information exchange was made. This fits with what we know of Deborah Basti's movements at

279

the time. She was in Paris at a conference and took the last three days in Holland. They were there at the same time. According to the notes, she was making a large gemstone purchase on behalf of Cooper, using an 'invisible' Swiss account. It was her opinion that the gemstones, emeralds, I believe, were to be used as an agent payoff. The size of the purchase indicated a major operation."

"That was as far as she took it?"

"Yes." Ivashutin cleared his throat. "General Kuryokhin developed the scenario further."

"Using our logs?"

"According to our transmission records, yes. He connected Travkin's suspicions with information relating to Hollis Macintyre, Secretary of State Swanbridge, and Stuart Shrenk, the attorney general. Apparently there were a number of meetings at a town house on Cherry Hill Lane. The house turned out to be owned by a CIA proprietary company."

"Such men meet all the time," Gurenko pointed out. He pursed his lips. "You've checked the logs on this?"

"It's being done right now," Gurenko's deputy answered.

"And the last meeting?" the KGB resident asked.

"Macintyre, Swanbridge, and Shrenk, also the deputy head of the Joint Chiefs and the secretary of the treasury. That was two days after Osin had given Cooper the gemstone consignment."

"According to our own information and what I discussed with Koslov about Travkin's disappearance, the man had come up with a theory regarding Costa Rica."

"Kuryokhin discounts it in his journal," answered Ivashutin, leafing through his notes. "A blind."

"What do you think?"

"It isn't my place to offer opinions," the deputy answered calmly.

"Nor mine," Gurenko parried, allowing himself a small, wolfish smile. "Our duty requires that we deal in facts, not flights of fancy."

"Yes."

"So what are the facts?" Gurenko asked rhetorically, leaning back in his chair again. "Travkin vanishes but does not defect, at least according to Koslov. Cooper has an unprecedented meeting in Barbados. Cooper then requests Comrade Rakozi, Basti, Stone, Osin, or whatever you want to call her, to obtain a large gemstone consignment, presumably to pay off the man in Barbados for services to be rendered." Gurenko paused. "Just for the record, Tovarich Valentin, tell me again what did General

280

Kuryokhin conclude a few moments before his unfortunate and untimely demise?"

"The conclusion has no basis in operational information," the pale, thin man replied uneasily.

"The conclusion is a documented fact," Gurenko said softly. "They amount to being the general's last words."

"It was Comrade General Kuryokhin's theory that such a group of men, such a large amount of money for an operation, and such an extraordinary juxtaposition of events indicated a major political assassination being planned."

"And not the assassination of a Costa Rican police chief or even a Costa Rican head of state?"

"No, Comrade General."

"Whom did Kuryokhin think the target was, Valentin?"

"The President of the United States."

"The situation complicated by the fact that a senior officer of the GRU and a deep-cover illegal for the KGB are intimately involved in the plot."

"Yes, sir," Ivashutin answered, acutely aware that he had been outmaneuvered by his superior. Any record, either his own testimony or that of the hidden tape recorder undoubtedly spinning away somewhere in the room, would show that technically it had been he who had uttered the fateful conclusion. *Glasnost* or not, the bearer of bad tidings was still a universally unloved figure.

"We must develop some course of action," Gurenko said. He glanced at his deputy. "Any suggestions?" he asked blandly.

"No, sir," Ivashutin answered.

Gurenko smiled. "You should show more initiative, Valentin," he said, chuckling. "You will go stale."

"Yes, sir," the pale man replied coldly from across the room.

"I want Osin found, then followed. She is to have a twenty-four-hour watch."

"No action?" asked Ivashutin, obviously hoping his boss would overstep his bounds.

"Not yet," Gurenko said, shaking his head. "Not unless there is need. At this point we are dealing with a conspiracy, not an actual assassination. If it appears that she is directly involved with Cooper's plot, then I will ask Moscow Center for permission to eliminate her. In the meantime, nothing but a day and night watch. The same goes for Cooper's little band. I want all of them put under surveillance, discreetly, and I want a permanent watch on the Cherry Hill Lane house."

"That's a lot of manpower," said Ivashutin.

"We have a lot of manpower," Gurenko answered. He had two hundred legitimate agents to call on in the Washington area, and more could be brought up out of the East bloc embassies.

"Nevertheless . . ." Ivashutin began, then let the thought dangle.

"Let us drop the pretense," Gurenko said, breaking the silence, weary of the semantic dance that seemed to be part of his job. Beyond anything else, he saw himself as a soldier, and for a soldier, problems were there to be solved, not evaded, while obstacles were to be surmounted, not avoided. "We both are aware that General Kuryokhin's death will inevitably create a power struggle at Teply Stan. So be it, and eventually that power struggle may impact on us both. For the moment we have a dangerous situation here that must be addressed. It is quite possible that there is a conspiracy under way by a group of high-ranking Americans to assassinate their own President. Two of our agents appear to be in some way involved. You realize, of course, that this is intolerable. We must in no way interfere with the Americans' internecine squabbles, but by the same token, we must interfere enough to remove our own people."

"Remove?" said Ivashutin, cocking an eyebrow. He began gathering up the papers on the table in front of him.

"Remove," Gurenko repeated, his voice firm. "One way or the other. Both Travkin and Osin. Before it is too late."

"And if Stone or the CIA is in the way?"

"That will be their misfortune," said Gurenko. "The relationship between our two nations used to be very simple. We were each other's most feared enemies. Now we must pretend a friendship that is equally imaginary. The slightest hint that we were somehow involved in a plot to assassinate President Tucker would bring the world down around our ears. If he is to die, then so be it. We must remain like their symbol of justice: blind."

He swiveled around in his chair and stared out through the rain-etched window. Behind him Ivashutin pushed the papers into a single pile and gathered them up under his arm. A few moments later he left the office and shut the door quietly behind him.

The full roster of Romulus Committee members began arriving at the Cherry Hill Lane house in Georgetown as dusk fell over Washington. The

282

rain that had begun earlier in the day persisted, the slow, warm drizzle turning the entire city into a steam bath. By 9:00 P.M. all the members had entered the town house, unaware that each of them had been photographed and videotaped by a team of damp and disgruntled KGB surveillance operatives on the roof of a house under renovation on Cecil Place, a few hundred feet away.

By nine-thirty the three stewards from the CIA catering department had set out coffee and water carafes around the long burled walnut table in the dining room and then withdrawn. The members of the Romulus Committee then sat down, and the meeting began.

As usual, Hollis Macintyre sat at the head of the table, with Hudson Cooper at the far end opposite him. To Macintyre's left sat General Marcus D. Andrews, deputy head of the Joint Chiefs of Staff, and Elaine Goodhouse, the hard-nosed, honey-tongued southern belle in her sixties who was the assistant secretary of the treasury. Across from Andrews and Goodhouse were Joseph Swanbridge, the secretary of state, and Stuart Shrenk, the attorney general. The meeting began with Macintyre's request for an update from Hudson Cooper.

"It would seem that things are coming to a head," the balding, hawk-faced man said, speaking slowly. "Our man has requested his payment and wants a final meeting before he proceeds."

"Do we have a date?" Stuart Shrenk interrupted.

"Yes." Cooper nodded. "Sometime during the President's birthday festivities."

"That's the day after tomorrow," drawled Elaine Goodhouse. The gray-haired woman seemed surprised. "This is all happening very quickly." Goodhouse had been the last of the committee to be told of the plan, and even then it had been over the objections of the others, mostly because few of the men at the table knew her. In the end Hollis Macintyre had insisted; like Swanbridge and Shrenk, she was in direct line of succession and had to be informed.

"What about the Russian Dmitri Travkin? At our last meeting you said the matter was well in hand." Macintyre made a delicate bridge of his fingers, then touched it to the tip of his nose.

"As I informed you, Travkin was going to be released anyway. Initially I assumed he would be picked up by his own people. This was not the case; instead, he was 'rescued' by Stephen Stone, deputy director of the FBI Rednet program. Stone has since been suspended from duty because of the unauthorized operation."

283

"Do we know where Travkin is hiding?" asked Shrenk, the attorney general.

"Yes. A cabin on Lake Anna. We have the cabin under surveillance."

"How did he find the place?" asked Andrews, the army general.

"Through Stone's ex-wife. I suggested it to her in fact."

"I beg your pardon?" Swanbridge asked. "You suggested it to her?"

"Mr. Cooper is having his little joke with us," murmured Hollis Macintyre. "Deborah Stone works at the European Studies Institute. She is also in the employ of the Central Intelligence Agency."

"I'll be damned." General Andrews laughed. "In other words, you've got him all tied up with a ribbon and a bow."

"Precisely." Cooper nodded.

"And having him all wrapped up," said Macintyre, "it's now simply a question of to whom we give the package."

"Frankly," said Shrenk, "from a legal position, the less we know about Comrade Travkin's eventual fate, the better."

"From a legal position, all of us could be charged with conspiracy to commit murder, honey." The Secretary of the Treasury smiled. "But you're right. This Russian fellow is a detail I think we can leave to Mr. Cooper. What we need to know is the procedure . . . um, after the dirty deed is done, so to speak."

"Indeed." Swanbridge nodded. "A smooth transition is necessary. We can't have any embarrassments like the Haig affair." The secretary of state turned slightly in his chair. "Hollis?"

"There will be no embarrassments," Macintyre said soothingly. "With the exception of myself and General Andrews, all of you will be at the birthday party, is that correct?" There was a silent chorus of nods. Macintyre smiled. "Good. Then it will be up to Joseph." Macintyre tilted his huge, leonine head in Swanbridge's direction.

"As soon as we know that the President and Mr. Teresi are no longer with us, I'll speak with Jack Reynolds and Charles Whittaker. Both of them will be at the party. Their letters of direction are already on file with Attorney General Shrenk, I believe."

"That's right." Shrenk nodded. "After that succession is automatic. Joseph doesn't even need to be sworn in. He simply becomes the President of the United States by default."

"I didn't know that," drawled Elaine Goodhouse. "What about LBJ being sworn in on Air Force One after the Kennedy assassination?"

"Window dressing." Hollis Macintyre grunted. "The old goat was doing some hard-core public relations and he knew it at the time."

"All right," said General Andrews. "Then what?"

"We bring out our window dressing," said Hudson Cooper. "The media will want something to chew on; we'll give them our mythical terrorist."

"We want to take the focus away from the actual assassination as quickly as possible," Macintyre put in. "If that's done properly, we can have the media and the public screaming for revenge against Libya instead of calling for a Senate investigation into the assassination itself."

"And we certainly don't want that." Elaine Goodhouse smiled.

"No, indeed," said Macintyre. "At any rate, we will have Joseph installed as President within forty-five minutes to an hour after the event. From then on it should be relatively smooth sailing. With all the attention on our Libyan assassin, we should be able to clear up any loose ends."

"Like a Cabinet shuffle, Mr. President?" asked the attorney general.

"Among other things, Stuart." Swanbridge laughed.

"A question for Mr. Cooper," said General Andrews.

"Yes?"

"For our man to accomplish his aims, both the President and Mr. Teresi must be in the Oval Office at the same time. Granted, both President Tucker and the Vice President will be in the White House for the birthday celebration, but how are you going to manage having them both in the Oval Office without arousing suspicion, either at the time or later?"

"That's been taken care of, General," Cooper responded. "I have already made the appointment through Rumsford and the chief of staff's office. Nothing has been stated specifically, but the implication is that I will be using the opportunity to tender my resignation unofficially to the President. Teresi has wanted me out right from the beginning. With both me and Maitland out of the picture he'll press for one of his own people to get the director's slot. He won't pass up the opportunity to gloat. Rumsford is Teresi's man; he'll make sure the Vice President knows."

"What time is the appointment?" Swanbridge asked.

"Ten P.M." Cooper said.

"You'll be President of the United States by ten-fifteen," decreed Hollis Macintyre.

"Unless something goes wrong," the elderly, bespectacled man warned.

Macintyre waved a dismissing hand. "Nothing will go wrong, Joseph," he said firmly. "I guarantee it."

285

\* \* \*

Deborah Stone sat in the silent living room of her Washington, D.C., apartment and stared at the plain gray-painted metal box on the coffee table in front of her. It was twelve inches long, eight inches wide, and six inches tall, a combination lock inset into the hinged top. The container's plainness was in striking contrast with the Art Deco surroundings, but all of her being was concentrated on it.

Her initial call to the long-sleeping cutout agent after learning about her ex-husband's hypothesis had led her to the shattering news of Sergei Kuryokhin's death. That news culminated in the unearthing of the lockbox now sitting in front of her on the table. Stephen's incredible story and the savage story of her own involvement through Hudson Cooper were difficult enough to deal with, but Kuryokhin's death was almost too much to bear.

She had only physically met her control once, in Moscow, shortly after her recruitment into the KGB; but he had been a continuing presence in her life for more than a decade, and in a real sense, he was the man responsible for the day-to-day identity she had assumed over all that time. Somehow, she knew, he had also represented truth. Her own life, her marriage to Stephen, her friendships with co-workers at the European Studies Institute, her work for Central Intelligence—all of it was subterfuge, a tissue of lies. Kuryokhin had given her purpose, a reason for it all, and even if it was done only through tape-recorded messages, she could talk to him. Now that was gone, all that remained of her relationship with the old spymaster was contained in the small metal box that lay before her.

She had known of the box's existence from the beginning, and its location, buried at a dead drop close to the mouth of the bypass tunnel at the National Zoological Park. Her cutout, the man who'd informed her of Kuryokhin's death, knew the combination but not the location. Finding and digging up the box had been easy enough, accomplished that evening after she'd left Stephen and the Soviet defector at the Lake Anna cabin, but now she wasn't sure she wanted to know what it contained.

Debbie Stone, Kuryokhin's "Osin," stood up, found her cigarettes, and lit one. She moved nervously around the room, touching and shifting the Art Deco knickknacks she'd collected over the years. Lies, just like her name, her work, her world—icons to flesh out a character that didn't exist. She turned and stared at the box again, her thoughts feverishly trying to give her some kind of answer.

She sat down on the couch, puffing hard on the cigarette. There were three basic ways she could go, none of them without risk. She could follow official protocols on the death or removal of a control, reporting either to the Washington, D.C., resident or to Moscow Center. But the Washington resident was an unknown quantity; all she really knew about him was his name. Reporting to Moscow Center was equally a shot in the dark. There was no way of knowing who would take over as head of the First Chief Directorate or where that person's loyalties would lie.

Her second choice was simply to do nothing and become a sleeper. In many ways this seemed to be the most palatable, but she knew that eventually the strain of living in such a vacuum would become intolerable.

The third option was to defect, but except for her own activities over the years she had little to offer in the way of KGB information. And whom would she defect to? Hudson Cooper, or her ex-husband?

She ran a combing hand through her hair and shook her head; she'd be more valuable as an agent in place to both of them, but she had no stomach for it. She had allowed herself to be recruited by Kuryokhin because she sincerely believed that the Soviet way was inherently better than that of the West, and she still believed it: Soviet social democracy was a more equitable and humane philosophy than American monopoly capitalism; she'd seen the proof of that with her own eyes for more than a decade.

Debbie stubbed out her cigarette in the ashtray on the end table. Balancing political philosophies was fine, but she had to deal with the harsh realities of both nations' intelligence organizations. The fact that she had operated virtually as Kuryokhin's private spy would be equally embarrassing to both the KGB and the CIA. The general's successor to the head of the First Chief Directorate would be unsure of her loyalties, and Hudson Cooper would be the laughingstock of the American intelligence community if it became known that an adviser and special courier he'd chosen and vetted personally turned out to be a KGB illegal.

Finally, she opened the box, turning the stiff dial carefully through the combination. She pushed open the lid, leaning forward to see what was inside: a sealed envelope; two passports, one Canadian, the other Swiss; a bank passbook with the gold stamping of the Banque Crédite Internationale de Genève; a small brass key on a leather thong; and a standard-size tape cassette. There was no label on the cassette, but since all her communications with the general had been recorded, she assumed the cassette held a message from him.

Pulse pounding, she got to her feet, went to the bedroom, and took her Walkman from the top of her chest of drawers. She set it down on the

287

coffee table, put on the headphones, then inserted the cassette from the box into the machine. She pressed the start button and waited. After a few moments' silence she heard Kuryokhin's firm, measured voice, speaking in his Moscow-accented Russian. She blinked, startled, as she listened to the general use her real name.

"My dear Anna Rakozi, the fact that you are listening to this recording means that either I am dead or I have finally run afoul of that octopuslike bureaucracy known as the KGB. One way or the other, the time has come for us to say farewell.

"We have worked well together over the past years, and I have taken every precaution to keep your identity a secret. However, if I am dead or in the less-than-gentle hands of my colleagues at the Lubyanka, your identity will not remain a secret for long. In consideration of this fact, and I hasten to repeat that it is or soon will be a fact, you are now faced with several decisions, which must be made as quickly as possible.

"First, there is the question of your work and your loyalty to the organization that employs us both. You have proved to be an outstanding intelligence asset, and you have every reason to be very proud. On the other hand, as you are certainly aware, the KGB, like its counterparts in other countries, is an organization much given to internal politics. An agent who was an unimpeachable asset to one man can be a terrible liability to another.

"Secondly, the question of your personal survival. If, for any reason, you doubt your welcome at Mount Alto in Washington or at Moscow Center, do not hesitate to remove yourself altogether. To facilitate this, I have enclosed two passports as well as a passbook for a Swiss bank. The account there is in the name of Monique Le Clerc, which is also the name on both the Canadian and Swiss passports. There is enough money for you to live comfortably for the rest of your life.

"Thirdly, the final disposition of my work as head of the First Chief Directorate. Over the last twenty-five years I have been making careful notes concerning my work. Initially I wrote them as an exercise in memory and later with a possible eye to someday writing my memoirs. As time passed, however, I realized that the very act of writing the notes was dangerous and could easily be misconstrued by my superiors within the KGB and a number of enemies outside it. Rather than destroy the notes I chose to hide them, using my regular trips abroad to secrete them in a safety-deposit box. Strangely I found myself continuing to keep notes, perhaps out of willful mischief or perhaps to give myself some sort of immortality—I'm really not at all sure even now. At any rate I continued to write and continued to remove the complete notebooks. They are in box number forty-nine-seventy-nine, at the Saint-Mandé branch of the Banque Nationale du Paris on the outskirts of Paris. The key to the box is on the leather thong. You may do whatever you wish with the notebooks: Read them or not; distribute them or not; perhaps even use them as a bargaining chip of last resort if you need to. Their disposition is up to you, my dear.

"Lastly, a final act for both of us if you choose to take on the role. There is an envelope with the passports, key, and bankbook. Within it is a list of every illegal in the United States, Canada, and the United Kingdom. It also includes a list of our assets in NATO. In all there are some six hundred and fifty names, each with recruitment date and the initial of the recruiting officer. Some of them go back more than forty years, and some, obviously, are more highly placed than others.

"Sometime ago, after a thorough check of their status, I realized that the vast majority of these supposed agents of influence, each with his own dossier, case officer, and interior budget, were in fact noneffective at least in terms of intelligence. Some, like yourself and a few others, were and continue to be extremely valuable, but the rest could stand a good sweeping by an old broom like myself.

"My suggestion is this: Defect, choosing your 'guardian angel' with due care, and let the Americans have the list, giving the names to them slowly, over a period of time, perhaps a year. At first glance this might seem to be a gigantic coup for the Americans, but in fact, it might well deal their intelligence apparatus a crushing blow in much the same way as the Philby-Burgess-Maclean defections. In that case, like this one, the agents concerned were either under suspicion, and therefore of limited value, or past their time of usefulness anyway. The result of their stories' being made public was the complete disruption of British intelligence to the point where its reputation has been forever stained. No other agencies trust the British; no other agencies will give them access to sensitive material.

"You are in a position to accomplish the same thing: a single agent bringing about the downfall of a country's entire intelligence establishment. It would guarantee your place in the history books, and mine, for that matter.

"At any rate, my dear Anna, these choices are all yours to make. In closing, I can say only that the choices should be made quickly, while they are still yours to make. *Dasvidanya,* my child, and may God go with you."

The general's voice fell silent, but listening, Debbie Stone could hear the faint creaking of his chair as he leaned forward to turn off the tape recorder. It sounded like a leather chair, old and worn, and the image of the old man in his chair made her shiver with a strange emotional force. She pulled the earphones way and let them fall to the table. The general was right: Her defection, coincidental with the revelations of his list of illegals, would rock the U.S. intelligence establishment to its very foundations. She shook her head; it was as though her entire career had been leading to this culminating moment.

Lighting another cigarette, she laughed, then reached for the sealed envelope in the box. Not only would she give them herself and the general's list, but she would give them Dmitri Travkin and an internal conspiracy to kill their own President. For that they should give her a medal!

She tore open the envelope eagerly and pulled out the stapled pages which made up the list. She scanned the closely typed names slowly. Each was followed by his or her occupation and then by a date and the name and position of the recruiting officer. They were listed by the date of recruitment rather than alphabetically, the earliest going back to November 1945, the subject in question being an American army major stationed in Berlin. Debbie nodded to herself, recognizing the name; the man had gone quite a long way since the end of the war.

The KGB deep-cover agent continued reading over the list, recognizing some names, not others. From what she could tell, the majority of the people on the list had been recruited shortly after graduation from the university; almost all were professionals, and the bulk of them were men.

She made her way through the names, finally coming to the last page. Halfway down it her eyes fell across a name, and she felt her mouth go suddenly dry. The date of recruitment was July 1969, and the place was Washington, D.C. Still not able to believe it, Debbie turned back to the beginning of the list. The date in the upper left-hand corner was April 1986, the year in which the dead drop box had been buried, seventeen years after the agent had been brought under the wing of the KGB. Hands shaking, she turned back to the last page, her eyes drawn to the name once again.

"He couldn't have known," she whispered softly, and then realized that she was speaking Hungarian. It felt as though the familiar name on the list were being burned into her brain. "He couldn't have known."

# CHAPTER 21

Standing at the helm console, Eric Rhinelander guided the squat forty-foot houseboat up the Potomac channel, keeping the throttles back and making little more than two or three knots against the steady current running down to the Chesapeake, fifty miles behind his back. It was early morning, the sky above a pale steel gray, the river dark, and cold wisps of fog hovering a few inches over the surface, torn and tattered like old cloth, dissolving into nothing as the blunt prow of the old C-Drifter slid almost silently upriver.

For the first time since leaving Jamaica he felt at ease and at peace with himself. The water, the boat, the silence, and the solitude all contributed to his feeling, but he also knew that it was his subconscious at work, calming him, easing his mind into a narrow cone of concentration where there was no reality except for the job ahead.

With one hand on the small wheel he glanced at the chart spread out on the map table on his left. According to his calculations, he was a little more than twenty-five miles below Washington, coming up on someplace called Hogbow Island. The notation on the chart said it was owned by the National Park Service, as were most of the dozens of Potomac islands scattered across Chesapeake Bay to the Virginia highlands.

He eased off on the twin throttles even more, barely making headway as he peered through the windshield, searching for his landfall. In any other class of vessel he might have worried about running aground, given the treacherous convolutions of the channel and the hidden, constantly shifting sandbars on either side of it, but the C-Drifter had a draft of less than two and a half feet, and the twin 270 horsepower Chrysler inboard-outboard engines were capable of pulling the slightly V'd hull off anything but the biggest bar.

The C-Drifter suited his needs perfectly. It was an old boat, dating back to the sixties, with none of the flash and filigree of more modern craft. The helm console was comfortably located on the starboard side of a spacious main saloon with a large dining area and lounges directly behind him. To the port side were more lounges arranged against the cabin wall and, behind them, an efficient galley with a propane stove, oven, and refrigerator.

Two steps led down to the midships section, which contained a large storage locker on the port side and a full head to starboard, complete with a shower. The aft section contained a private stateroom with a double bed and dressing table. Beyond that a small door led out to the engine hatch. The floors were carpeted in dark blue, while the walls were paneled in teak. There was even a flying bridge with another steering console located in the opening above the main saloon.

Technically the houseboat was fitted out with a reasonable cross section of gear, including a basic radar facility, a radio, and a sonar unit that was really nothing more than a glorified fishfinder. The boat could do ten knots if necessary, cruised comfortably at six, and had a range of almost two hundred miles with full tanks. More than enough for his purposes.

The island appeared suddenly as the last of the mist burned off with the first warming rays of the sun. Seen from half a mile downriver, it looked like a small tree-shrouded hump in the middle of the channel, but as Rhinelander swung the wheel a few points to point, he saw that it was actually quite large, complete with two rocky projections guarding a narrow-necked bay almost a hundred yards across.

Keeping his eye on the little sonar screen perched on top of the console, he pushed the C-Drifter across the unseen current, bullying his way across the surge until he was positioned just above the entrance to the bay. He cut the throttles almost to nothing, letting the bargelike vessel drift back down the river, then pushed both handles forward. The engines rumbled powerfully as he tucked the houseboat in between the two house-size boulders and into the protected bay.

Once out of the current, he idled the engines and let the boat's inertia carry it toward the narrow strip of gravel beach. The sonar screen was showing five feet of water almost to the shore. At the first wet crunching of the hull on the bottom he reversed the engines for a moment, backing off, then killed them entirely. The boat came to a full stop less than ten feet from the shore, and taking his time, Rhinelander went out onto the forward deck and dropped the single cleat anchor off the bow, warping it in tightly. He went to the stern and stepped off the boat, carrying a line, which he snugged around the broad trunk of a willow.

He went back into the main saloon, picked up his binoculars, and went out on deck again, sliding around to the catwalk railing on the port side. Using the glasses, he scanned the entrance to the bay and the river beyond. The opening to the small, hidden landfall was on the lee side of the channel, and even if there were boat traffic, the houseboat would be hidden from view, protected by the two large rocks at the entrance. Not that it mattered; he wasn't going to be here for long.

Rhinelander went back into the main cabin, ducking through the midships doorway. He gathered up the small KLM flight bag containing the custom-built paintball gun from the shop in Baltimore, as well as an empty knapsack from the storage compartment. Carrying both bags, he went forward to the galley. He opened the refrigerator and removed a large plastic bag from the vegetable crisper and a much smaller one from the freezer compartment. He put the plastic bags into the knapsack, slipped it over his shoulders, and then went topside, the flight bag in his right hand. At the stern he dropped down onto the earthen bank, sidestepped the willow tree, then headed along a sloping path that led up through the trees.

According to his chart, the entire island was tilted upward to a narrow ridge running along a north-south line. There were no buildings marked on the chart as navigation aids, and from what Rhinelander could see as he made his way up the path, the bulk of the island was covered in a mixed forest of sycamore and sweet gum. The path itself seemed to be a dry streambed running down from the ridge, its gently sloping banks choked with fireweed and buttonbush. The leaves and branches were dark with rain from the night before, and Rhinelander found himself wondering if the area around the sewer junction and the north portico vaults had been eroded even more. He'd been through his subterranean escape route several times since his first visit, entering the system through an alleyway manhole off F Street and Thirteenth rather than the longer walk from the Twelfth Street heating plant. With the exception of a few small details and the package he'd ordered Mallory to bring to their next ' meeting, everything was in place for the event.

Rhinelander reached the open meadow marked on his chart and looked around. Silent except for the angry hammering of an unseen woodpecker hard at work and invisible from the river; ideal for what he had in mind. He spotted the rotted stump of an old tree on the far side of the small clearing and walked over to it, shrugging off the knapsack as he approached. He opened the pack, removed the large plastic bag, and eased its contents out onto the stump. The bag contained a goat's head he'd purchased from a Greek butcher in Alexandria, kept cool in the houseboat refrigerator until it was needed.

He reached into the knapsack for the smaller bag and then turned away from the stump. He paced off a large oval in the damp grass. For Rhinelander, worst-case scenario would put the President behind his desk in the Oval Office, offering the poorest target. The goat's head was lower than Tucker's position, but approximately at the maximum range from which Rhinelander would be required to shoot.

Rhinelander positioned himself on the left side of the oval, roughly at the position of the entrance to the Oval Office from the private secretaries' office and directly across from the bulletproof French doors leading out to the Rose Garden. From where he stood the goat's head was in profile—unlikely for Tucker at the actual moment, but a better test now of the ammunition he had created for the job.

The assassin squatted down, unzipped the flight bag, and took out the custom-made weapon and a small red-handled hatchet. Putting the hand ax aside, he examined the gun. With the exception of the trigger mechanism and spring, the pistol was made entirely out of flat black plastic and looked very much like a small buttless sawed-off shotgun. The upper barrel was actually the magazine for the gelatin paintballs, while the lower barrel held the spring mechanism that actually powered the weapon. A constant-air $CO_2$ tank was attached to the rear of the gun. When the trigger was pulled, a brief burst of compressed gas was released, blowing a plunger down the barrell and forcing out the paintball at a rate of between 450 and 600 feet per second.

In the case of the weapon Rhinelander had ordered, the mechanism had an automatic blow-back cocking system, which meant that it could be fired automatically, pumping out twenty of the ball bearing–size spheroids in fewer than two seconds.

The barrel and cocking mechanism was eleven and a half inches long, and when he wore it beneath the stolen EPB uniform, the weapon fitted comfortably and invisibly along Rhinelander's arm from wrist to elbow, secured by two Velcro strips. The air feed tube snaked back to his armpit and down to the $CO_2$ tank secured to his belt.

From the small plastic bag from the freezer compartment Rhinelander took out a dozen gelatin balls and fed them into the upper magazine of

294

the weapon. He secured the magazine lock, flicked the toggle on the trigger mechanism, setting the weapon on single shot, then let it dangle loosely in his hand. He took several breaths, let them out slowly, then lifted the weapon and fired in a single smooth motion.

There was a hard, coughing sound as the $CO_2$ charged the piston chamber and ejected the ball. A split second later the macabre target on the stump jerked slightly, the clouded, sightless eye of the severed head showing no reaction to the impact. After placing the weapon and the attached gas cartridge carefully on the empty knapsack, Rhinelander picked up the hatchet, walked across to the stump, and examined the head.

Unlike his fictional counterparts in spy novels written over the years, he knew that a roast beef on a fence post or a melon in a string bag was no test of a weapon's utility; the human body was more than meat, and the rind of a watermelon was no substitute for the hard bone matter of a human skull. Hence the goat's head.

Kneeling, Rhinelander saw the impact point of the gelatin ball. It had struck half an inch below the left eye, creating a ragged hole an inch across. Using one hand, the assassin turned the head around on the stump. There was no sign of an exit, and he smiled, pleased with his work. Lifting the hatchet, he sighted along the center of the skull and brought his hand down in a single hard stroke. The head split open neatly, and Rhinelander examined the interior; he'd purposely told the butcher to leave the brain inside the head so he'd have an honest measure of the weapon's value.

The hatchet had sliced the brain into two pieces, revealing the damage done by Rhinelander's reconstructed ammunition. Using his index finger, the assassin could follow the track of the "bullet" as it chewed through the dark gray brain matter. Slamming through the cranium, the paintball had flattened out and broken apart, bits and pieces spinning at odd angles into the brain, slashing it into a stewlike, watery mass of tissue. He nodded, pleased once again; if it worked on a goat, it would certainly work on the President of the United States.

The standard load for a paintball gun consists of a thick gelatin ball filled with a mixture of water-based paint, usually red, and cod-liver oil. On impact the gelatin ball splits open, and the oil-and-paint mixture splatters over a six- to eight-inch area of the target's clothing, thus "killing" him. In essence, the whole paintball/action pursuit game is an updated and expensive version of cowboys and Indians.

Instead of the regular balls, Rhinelander had purchased several hundred empty gelatin "bullets," which would normally have been filled with special paint, often fluorescent for use in night games. Using mercury from the surplus thermostats he'd purchased and the modelmaking syringes from the hobby store, he had injected the empty gelatin capsules, using half mercury and half ordinary tap water. The water and liquid metal separated as cleanly as oil and water and, after freezing for twenty-four hours, gave him a projectile half ice and half solid metal. He had tested the balls once in the Wyoming apartment, putting a splintered hole in a quarter-inch-thick piece of plywood at twenty feet.

The ballistics were relatively simple. Fired almost silently from the air gun with a muzzle velocity of four or five hundred feet per second, the ball spun with the heavier metal section ahead of the lighter half sphere of ice. On impact the frozen metal would maintain the integrity of its shape briefly as it punched through plywood or bone, forced onward by the ice, which, like water, cannot be compressed at any velocity. With the impact friction dissolving the gelatin skin, the brittle frozen mercury would shatter, tiny splinters of it cartwheeling through the brain tissue like pellets from a shotgun. As the goat's head proved, the effect was violent and clearly fatal. A secondary benefit was the neatness of the wound since the below-the-speed-of-sound velocity guaranteed that there would be no exit hole. Tucker and Teresi would lie in state with their coffins open, and the walls of the Oval Office wouldn't have to be repainted.

After jamming the two pieces of the head back together, Rhinelander retrieved the paintball gun, then walked back across his foot-stamped firing range and took up a position occupied by the fireplace in the Oval Office, some thirty-five feet from the President's desk. He set the weapon on automatic, lifted the barrel a second time, and squeezed the trigger. There was a dull, ripping cough as the machine pistol vomited a hail of frozen projectiles toward the remains of the severed head on the stump. All nineteen balls left in the magazine struck the target, smashing through jawbone, skull, nose, and cheek. In a silent, bloody flurry, bone chips, brain matter, fur, and fluid fountained into the air. Within three seconds of his squeezing the trigger, the goat's head had vanished, leaving little more than a thick dark stain on the low stump. At no time had there been a sound louder than the popping of a paper bag.

The woodpecker he'd heard before began its hammering again, somewhere on the far side of the clearing, breaking the morning silence with much more force than Rhinelander's weapon. The assassin glanced at the gore on the stump, smiling.

"Excellent," he said quietly.

*  *  *

There are a hundred different vantage points in Washington where tourists and other visitors can view the Capitol dome. The most famous is probably the postcard scene taken from the Mall, showing the dome and Congress in all their marble white glory. The least known is almost undoubtedly the view over the cement works on the banks of the Anacostia River, in the wasteland between the Frederick Douglass Bridge and the Washington Navy Yard Annex. Seen from the river, the dome rises, heat-shimmered, above an apocalyptic assembly of rusting tanks, graffiti-decorated warehouses, flyblown shacks, and piles of industrial rubble. The area is bounded by the bridge, Potomac Avenue, O Street, and the river. There is constant truck traffic around the cement plant, and once in a very long while a police car makes its way along the rutted dirt roads that meander through the trash tips and rubble, but for the most part it is a vast weed- and rat-infested vacant lot.

This is a Washington rarely seen, far from the looming monuments and broad, inspiring avenues, a dead zone, nestled like a dark sore in the city's flesh. By its very nature it is a place for criminals and conspirators to meet, a place where deals are made and payoffs paid.

Paul Mallory waited uneasily beside the nondescript blue Ford from the Langley pool, horribly aware of the small flat pistol in the waistband holster beneath the idiotic Hawaiian print shirt he was wearing. Hudson Cooper had suggested arming himself for the meeting, supposedly to inspire confidence, and the armorer from the Tech section had told him to wear something loose to cover the bulge of the gun and to give him quick access. Instead of confident, he felt like something out of an old episode of *Hawaii Five-O,* and the thought of drawing a weapon on someone like Rhinelander was nauseating. Grimacing, he pushed his glasses up onto the bridge of his nose and squinted over the wasteland surrounding him. If it came to that, he could use the gun to kill himself, since pulling it on the assassin was tantamount to suicide anyway.

So where the hell was he? The telephone message from Rhinelander had been specific about time and place; but it was already half an hour past the appointed time, and there was still no sign of him. There were no cars in sight, and he hadn't seen a soul since arriving at the riverside rendezvous. He glanced into the open window of the Ford. Two packages, both wrapped in brown paper, were on the seat. The smaller one contained a shoebox, which in turn contained Rhinelander's gemstone payoff, padded with wads of cotton batting. The larger held the specialized Motorola transceiver the assassin had requested, as well

297

as the 2.5 kilogram warhead from an AT3 Sagger antitank round. The Sagger was an obsolete Soviet weapon, now widely deployed in the Middle East.

"Mallory." The voice came out of nowhere. No warning, no plume of dust from the dirt tracks crisscrossing the junkyard acreage. Nothing except the white bright sun and the voice. Rhinelander's.

"Yes?" Mallory answered. He let his hands reach back and touch the hot metal of the car door, wondering if the killer knew he was carrying a weapon. He blinked and then swallowed hard. The voice had come from somewhere directly ahead of him, close to the heap of reinforced concrete at the river's edge.

"You have what I want?" Definitely the riverbank. Shit! The son of a bitch had come in off the water!

"Yes. Everything you asked for." Mallory swallowed again, mouth dry.

"Good," the ghost voice answered. "Take it out of the car, bring it to the edge of the road, then leave."

"Yes," Mallory responded. He turned slowly, keeping his hands away from the pistol in his belt. Opening the door, he reached in, picked the two parcels up off the seat, and took them to the edge of the road. For an instant he thought he spotted something in the choke of weeds and garbage: A point of sun, splintered on what? The barrel of a gun? Lens of a binocular? Eyepiece of a telescopic sight? Crosshairs like an invisible rune upon his chest? His fear took him back to Jamaica and the first split second after he had been discovered by Rhinelander. The dead, cold eyes—dead and cold because of what they had seen over time. Frighteningly dark, capable of anything.

Mallory followed his instructions to the letter. He walked back across the road to the Ford, climbed in behind the wheel, and drove away, his retreat marked with the dust flag thrown up by his wheels as he sped toward O Street. A few moments later he had gone, the two packages on the weedy verge of the road were the only sign that he'd ever been there. The sun burned down, and the dust of his passage drifted over the rubble and rubbish like the fading smoke screen on a battlefield.

"What the hell is going on?" Mort Kessler asked, peering through the binoculars. "He waits for half an hour, and then he drops the packages by the side of the road and rabbits."

"We're missing something," Stephen Stone answered, looking through his own powerful Zeiss glasses. Both men were discreetly hidden in a musty abandoned warehouse two hundred yards from where Mallory

298

had parked his car. The warehouse was filled with an odd mixture of faint smells that ranged from horses to human urine, the urine explained by the rusting sign above the half-ruined loading dock identifying the warehouse as being owned by a polyurethane varnish manufacturer. God only knew where the horse aroma came from.

"There," Kessler said, excitement in his voice. The redheaded FBI man leaned forward slightly. "The right-hand side of the road."

Stephen Stone turned his binoculars slightly to the right. Through the lens he saw a lone figure clamber quickly over the pile of reinforced concrete that lay between the road and the river's edge. Beside him Mort Kessler droped his binoculars and put his eye to the viewfinder of the Nikon on its tripod next to him. He focused quickly and hit the motorized shutter release, catching a dozen exposures of the man as he dropped down from the rubble and gathered up the parcels.

"Shit!" Stone muttered. "He came up from the river; that means he has a boat. Why didn't we think of that?"

"Because we didn't have time." Kessler grunted, snapping more photographs. "We barely got to put the tap on Mallory's telephone."

"Where would he get a boat?" Stone muttered, watching as the figure retreated back up onto the pile of rubble.

"Eastern Power Boat Club or the Anacostia Boat Dock. Both of them are only five minutes upriver."

"All right." Stone nodded, stepping away from the grimy window. "Get the pictures developed and then go sit on Mallory. I'm going to take a run at this guy and see what I can turn up."

"Nothing heroic, I hope," Kessler said.

"Surveillance from a distance." Stone grinned. He lifted a palm. "Nothing more, I swear."

"Contact?" asked the red-haired agent, slipping his binoculars back into their case.

Stone thought for a moment. Somewhere safe, with no chance of surveillance.

"The Key Bridge Marriot Hotel," he said finally. "The main entrance parking lot."

"Good enough," Kessler replied.

General Vladimir Arkadyevich Gurenko rode the elevator down from his office in the main building of the Mount Alto complex, contemplating his fate and planning his future. Brains, talent, and drive had taken him to heights achieved by few without benefit of *nomenklatura* connections, but now circumstance threatened to take it all away. His career and perhaps even his life now depended on how he handled the situation with Osin and Dmitri Travkin, his every move scrutinized by the Weasel, Ivashutin.

Before his death Kuryokhin had patched together a theory about a possible presidential assassination, and both Debbie Stone, Kuryokhin's deep-cover illegal, and Travkin, the GRU officer, were directly involved. In the aftermath of such an assassination, the Soviet connection would almost certainly surface, mangling the concepts of *glasnost* and *perestroika* for a generation. Gurenko, like Kuryokhin and most senior KGB people, thought Gorbachev's philosophies were madness, destined to bring the worst kind of *besporyadok* (social disorder) to the Soviet Union, but the KGB was not the omnipotent power it once had been. The Politburo was unlikely to cast a benevolent eye on those involved in an American assassination plot.

By the same token, Osin was a valued agent and Travkin was a military officer; removing them, at least in political terms, would not be an easy feat. Koslov, Travkin's commanding officer in the GRU, was a fool, but a fool with friends in high places, and Osin had been Kuryokhin's "sparrow." Even on the embalmer's table the old bastard still had power—power that would continue to be a force within the KGB even after he was buried in the Kremlin wall. The "janitors" who'd gone through his effects in Moscow had come up with detailed operations journals going back over forty years, and there was always the possibility that he'd made copies. Gurenko shook his head wearily; now there was a rumor that would circulate for decades!

The elevator reached the third subbasement, and Gurenko stepped out into a narrow corridor. The cinder block was thickly painted in yellow, and the floors were covered with a dull brown linoleum. Gurenko was sure the decor had been chosen to remind the building's occupants of the Lubyanka, lest they become too enamored of the glitz and glamour of Wisconsin Avenue, a few hundred yards to the east.

At the end of the corridor he pushed through a heavily padded door, and his ears were instantly assaulted by an irregular madhouse roar of gunfire as he stepped onto the underground firing range. The Soviet diplomatic corps and even embassy security personnel weren't allowed to bring weapons of any kind into the United States, but that obstacle was easily surmounted simply by purchasing necessary armament at any of several dozen local sporting goods stores. The range also served as a

300

testing laboratory for newly designed American armed forces ordnance that happened to come their way.

He found the man he was looking for in the stall at the front of the third firing lane. His name was Artyom Roginsky—dark hair shot with gray, fists like hams wrapped around a Swiss Rexim-Favor submachine gun. As Gurenko approached him, Roginsky tucked the wooden butt of the weapon into his hip and began triggering a series of short bursts down the firing line, his movements as studied and bored as a worker hammering rivets into a sheet of steel.

"Roginsky," Gurenko called, raising his voice over the booming echoes of the cavernous range. The large man turned, his expression blank. He recognized Gurenko but showed no deference to his rank. On the U.S. State Department files Roginsky was listed as a junior attaché in the Cultural Services Division. In fact he was squad leader of a rarely used ten-man Spetznaz commando, the only one of its kind in North America. In the previous two years the commandos had been used only four times, and on each occasion they were used to track down missing embassy personnel. Two of the assignments had led to the Metro Police drunk tanks, one had involved a homosexual tryst, and the last had been a bona fide defection.

"Good afternoon, Comrade General Gurenko," Roginsky said, putting the submachine gun down on the bench to his right.

"The scenario given to you by Comrade Ivashutin is now operational," Gurenko said crisply. "Gather six of your men, and meet me in the briefing room in an hour."

"Certainly," Roginsky answered. "Is there anything else?"

"Nothing else," Gurenko replied. He turned away and headed back to the padded door.

"Good," said Roginsky. He picked up the Rexim-Favor, banged in a new magazine, and stared at the dangling target fifty feet away. The target was man-shaped, silhouetted in black. Most of the chest was missing, a ragged hole blown through the target. The head was relatively free of "wounds." Roginsky pulled back the slide, toggled the safety off and slipped his right index finger over the trigger. He let out a short breath, lifted the weapon, and squeezed. The head of the target vanished. The commando belched lightly. Time for a beer or two in his room before the briefing.

# CHAPTER 22

The three-man team moved through Paul Mallory's Alexandria apartment with methodical efficiency. All three wore dark blue windbreakers with "Capitol Courier Service" printed on the back in white letters. Two of the three distributed the contents of two large suitcases throughout the rooms while a third worked at Mallory's computer. The project file on Mallory indicated the possibility of classified material being misappropriated, and the man sitting at the terminal was a highly trained specialist in reprogramming and computer ciphers. So far he had located the embedded backup signal containing Mallory's information on Rhinelander, and he was now unraveling the time code that would broadcast the information over a nationwide bulletin board network.

Ever since the Philip Agee and Victor Marchetti fiascos of the late sixties and early seventies, followed by the advent of a federal Freedom of Information Act, the agency decided that steps would have to be taken to ensure the CIA's internal security. By the mid-seventies a "ghost" department within the Operations Division had been formed, blandly referred to in budgetary submissions as the Historical Analysis Group. The HAGs, as they were called, supposedly worked out of a suite of offices in Georgetown but were actually based at Camp Peary—the Farm.

Their mandate, far from analyzing history, was to rewrite it. When an agent or an operation went sour, the HAGs went to work, removing or replacing public files, changing identities, and otherwise skewing events so that they conformed to approved agency policy. In a case like Mallory's, given to them by the DDO himself, their job was to cloud, corrupt, and besmirch the subject's character, thus stripping him of any credibility. Although the DDO hadn't gone into detail, it was clear that Mallory was about to go public with material garnered while working as Cooper's special assistant.

To prevent him from doing this, the team at work in his apartment was reestablishing the man's personal history, staging evidence that would mark him as a particularly nasty type of homosexual with definite leanings toward young boys. In addition, they were also giving him a fully constructed background of love letters and other correspondence graphically proving him to be untrustworthy, greedy, and potentially a threat to national security. Once in place, the evidence was photographed *in situ,* providing an evidence package that might eventually be handed over to the Justice Department for espionage and treason prosecution unless the subject cooperated.

It took the HAGs two hours to complete the project. They left the apartment, carrying the two empty suitcases with them, climbed into an unmarked van, and began the long drive back to Camp Peary. The apartment had been appropriately "salted" with damning evidence, the computer had been cleansed of damaging information, and all that remained was for a second and completely separate transportation team to arrest Mallory and bring him in for interrogation.

Lyall Spencer, head of the Secret Service White House detail, followed one of the paths that meandered around the north lawn, hands jammed into the pockets of his suit jacket, trying to ignore the sour pain in the pit of his stomach. After fourteen years in the service and three as head of the White House detail he was seriously thinking of bailing out. He was forty-seven, divorced, verging on alcoholism, and utterly jaded about government, the presidency, and any kind of public service.

In other words, he was burned out and ready for rotation. On the other hand, he was pretty sure that staying on in the Secret Service as a field director in Des Moines or some other godforsaken place wouldn't cut it after three years at the White House. The job was a pain in the ass most of the time; but it had its perks, and it stroked the ego from time to time, not to mention other body parts. There were ladies in singles bars all over the world who'd do just about anything after you flashed your tin at them.

None of which was important right at the moment; he had the job to consider. And that was always the excuse—the job. It covered everything from proscrastinating about his future to catching up on his reading. The job. Nothing in the world was more important than protecting the President of the United States, and he was the man responsible for doing just that. It was his favorite gripe to the other guys on the detail, and he'd harped on it so much they made him a T-shirt that said: "The Buck Doesn't Stop There—It Stops Here." It was true in a way: The President was responsible for the country, but he, Lyall Spencer, son of George Spencer, the New Jersey plumber, and Marie Spencer, apple-crisp maker and part-time bookkeeper, was responsible for the safety of the President.

The Secret Service chief dropped down onto a bench beside the path and lit his fifty-first cigarette of the day. The rules said he wasn't really supposed to smoke on duty, but then again, the rules also said he was working the eight-to-four shift, which made it three hours into overtime. Spencer's personal rule about smoking on the grounds was simple: Don't let the tourists see you, and pocket the butt once you're done.

It was the worst time of day for Spencer, the hours before dusk when shadows lied and the light flattened, throwing perspective off. In Vietnam they'd called it the killing hour, and even now the last hours, neither light nor dark, still made him nervous.

That was ridiculous, of course, especially here. From the other side of the fence on Pennsylvania Avenue the White House was a symbol of American strength, ubiquitous, appearing on everything from dollar bills to CNN broadcasts. Spencer knew better. The lawns where kids rolled eggs at Easter were actually minefields of motion sensors. The fence itself was reinforced by buried microwave cables, and the glass in the windows was armored. The President might be at risk coming out of hotels or gladhanding crowds, but if he could be considered safe at all, it was here. Harry Truman had known the score when he referred to it as the big white jail.

Spencer took a drag of the cigarette and let the smoke drift up into the still, humid air. Being nervous might be ridiculous, but it was part of the job. For all the motion sensors, metal detectors, interior radar, and panic buttons, there was no real guarantee of safety for the Man, even here. You didn't need a high-powered rifle to take out a President; a loose brick or a paperweight could be just as deadly.

Tomorrow's birthday party for Tucker was a case in point. He and the other members of the detail had taken every possible precaution. All the guests had been screened, extra catering and cleaning staff vetted, even the cake batter checked for poison. None of it meant a thing. All it needed was a crazed guest who'd slipped through the psych profiles and a carving knife. Still, they'd done the best they could.

The lunch he'd had with Stephen Stone still bothered him, though, and he frowned, recalling the conversation. If Cabrera was at risk, so was the Man. But even after checking, he'd come up cold. He'd tried to call Stone; but the number he'd given was dead, and when he called the FBI man's office number, he'd been cold-shouldered until he dug around and discovered that Stone had been suspended indefinitely.

Sighing, Spencer pinched out the glowing tip of the cigarette, grinding the hot ash into the gravel of the walkway. He dropped the butt into his jacket pocket, dusted his fingers off, and stood up wearily. Stone had appeared to be a straight shooter, even though the Secret Service man didn't know him well. The suspension, coming on the heels of their conversation, was a weird coincidence, but there was nothing he could do about it now. Tin pot *el Presidentes* could wait until next month. Right now he had a birthday party to organize.

Flipping back the tail of his jacket, Spencer used his left hand to pull the walkie-talkie out of its belt holster. He tapped the send button and checked in with the command center in the East Wing basement.

"Dungeon, this is Dragon One. What's our status?"

"Clean and clear, Dragon One," replied the tinny voice of the duty watchman.

"Where's Diamond?" Spencer asked, using the President's radio call sign.

"Having dinner with Emerald in the family dining room." Emerald was the First Lady.

"All right," Spencer answered. "Let me know if anyone goes for a walk."

"Will do, Dragon One."

Spencer returned the walkie-talkie to its holster, then continued down the gravel path, heading for the guard post at Pennsylvania and West Executive. He walked slowly, head bent, going over the security precautions for the following day, wondering if there was anything he'd overlooked, and trying not to think about how good an ice-cold beer would taste.

Returning to the Wyoming for the last time, Eric Rhinelander made himself a cup of tea, then took his packages to the den. Setting the box containing the gemstones aside for the moment, he slit open the heavier package with a penknife and carefully removed the contents. He placed the oblong antitank warhead on the desk and examined it carefully. The 2.5 kilogram charge was made up of ammonium picrate and was fitted with a spring-loaded contact percussion primer. Triggered by a simple clock mechanism delay he'd already constructed, the warhead would provide a suitably loud explosion when the time came.

Rhinelander had already picked out the point where the main electrical and communications cables came into the vault, and he would cut power from inside, but the detonation of the charge would serve as a distraction after the fact and would also open up his escape route into the sewer system. The hollow charge, capable of blowing a hole in three-inch armor plate, was more than enough to open up the relatively thin concrete of the vault.

Next, the assassin removed the Motorola walkie-talkie from the package and placed it beside the box of gemstones. The radio was the exact model used by the Secret Service on the grounds of the White House and set to its private frequency. He would have been able to find the secure frequency himself, using a modified scanner from Radio Shack or any other electronic supply house, but it seemed a needless waste of energy and time when it could be just as easily provided by Cooper.

The last item in the package was a flat sealed manila envelope. Rhinelander checked to make sure that Mallory hadn't tampered with the seal, then used his penknife again to slit the upper edge of the flap. There were two documents inside. One contained a list of call signs used by the Secret Service White House detail, complete with their designations, while the second, made up of several sheets stapled together, gave a schedule of events for the presidential birthday party. Rhinelander went over the call signs first, committing them to memory:

| | |
|---|---|
| PRESIDENT | DIAMOND |
| VICE PRES. | COBALT |
| 1ST LADY | EMERALD |
| SEC. STATE | FLINT |
| SEC. DEF. | GARNET |
| HOUSE SPKR. | GOLD |
| NAT. SEC. ADVSR. | GRANITE |
| WH PHYSICIAN | HELIOTROPE |
| PRES. SEC. | JADE |
| WHITE HOUSE | CROWN |
| AIR FORCE ONE | ANGEL |

306

| MARINE ONE | BLADE |
|---|---|
| PRES. LIMO | STAGECOACH |
| VP RESIDENCE | SHIELD |
| U.S. CAPITOL | SWORD |
| ANDREWS AFB | HELMET |
| CAMP DAVID | CORRAL |
| SS DETAIL CHIEF | DRAGON |
| SS COMM. HQ. | DUNGEON |

Rhinelander turned his attention to the typed schedule for the party, complete with a list of invited guests as well as a full menu. The schedule was a photocopy of an original produced on White House stationery. After quickly glancing over the list of guests, he flipped to the page with the actual schedule on it.

6:30 P.M.
*
GREETINGS IN THE DIPLOMATIC RECEPTION ROOM
SOUTH PORTICO ENTRANCE
*
7:00 P.M.
*
COCKTAILS IN THE EAST ROOM
"HAIL TO THE CHIEF"
*
7:45 P.M.
*
DINNER IN THE STATE DINING ROOM
*
9:00 P.M.
*
CAKE AND COFFEE
THE LIBRARY
"RUFFLES AND FLOURISHES"
*
9:45 P.M.
*
FIREWORKS ON THE NORTH LAWN

There was a small notation on the schedule, printed neatly in pencil: "8:50–8:55." According to his research, dinners at the White House were inevitably punctual. The meal would begin at 7:45 precisely and end exactly an hour later. There would be a fifteen-minute break in the festivities while the guests made their way to the Library, some discreetly making use of the toilet facilities on the way. During the quarter-hour break the President and Vice President would make a brief detour to the Oval Office at Hudson Cooper's insistence. The assassin unrolled his enlarged floor plans of the White House.

The State Dining Room was on the state, or second, floor of the mansion on the west side of the building. To go from there to the Oval Office meant that the President, the Vice President, and Hudson Cooper would use either the back stairway leading off the main corridor or the private elevator. With two Secret Service agents in attendance the small elevator would be somewhat crowded, so it was more likely that they would use the stairs. From the stairway they would walk west along the corridor on the ground floor, passing the kitchen and the housekeeper's quarters.

If the weather was good, they would probably then take the colonnaded walkway to the Oval Office via the Rose Garden, and if it was bad, they'd use the corridor that ran beside the newly reopened swimming pool. From the floor plans he knew the exact distances involved and had paced it off several times. At an average walk it would take four and a half minutes to reach the Oval Office.

There were four entrances to the Oval Office: a pair of French doors to the right of the President's desk, leading out to the colonnade and the Rose Garden; an almost invisible doorway set into the wall to the left of the desk, which led to the President's study; a doorway to the right of the fireplace at the north end of the room, leading to the secretaries' office; and a doorway on the left of the fireplace, which was the formal entrance to the room, leading out to a narrow hall.

Except for the French doors and the exit to the President's study, the entrances were comprised of heavy oak doors, painted white. The doors swung in both directions, closed with vertical bolts, top and bottom. The doors were fitted with dead bolt locks with a knob turn on the inside and a key cylinder on the outside. The glass on the doors, like all the windows in the Oval Office, was bulletproof, and the draperies over the three tall windows behind the President's desk were lined with a bombproof synthetic fabric.

With the President and Vice President in the office there would be two Secret Service agents on the outside, one at the French doors and another patrolling the area around the south windows. A third agent would be on guard at the hall doorway, and there would be a fourth on duty in the secretaries' office.

For Rhinelander, the placement and number of people directly protecting the Oval Office and its occupants had been the project's major stumbling block. To get to the President, he would have to confront at least one Secret Service agent. After a great deal of thought he had eventually decided that access to and egress from the Oval Office would be made through the Cabinet Room. The long, narrow chamber adjoined the President's secretaries' office as well as the colonnade and the hallway running along beside the swimming pool.

Approaching the west wing from the rarely used basement tunnel, he would come up the stairs to the main floor in plain sight of the Secret Service agent at the outer door of the President's study, but he would then appear to be walking away from the Oval Office as he headed for the colonnade. He would then turn right into the colonnade hallway and enter the Cabinet Room, using one of the two small doors flanking the chamber's fireplace. He would remain in the room until the appropriate moment, then enter the secretaries' office through the connecting door. After eliminating the agent on duty, he would proceed into the Oval Office. His work done, he would exit the same way he had entered.

At that point the explosion in the north portico physical plant vault would douse the lights in the mansion as well as the west and east wings. Since the vault also contained the mansion backup generator, the main house would remain dark. The entire security system for the White House and grounds had its own backup, but there would be a brief period while "Dungeon," the west wing communications and security headquarters, was deaf, mute, and blind. It would be during this time that Rhinelander would make his way back to the north portico vault.

Standing orders required that when there was a potential executive threat, agents on the White House detail would immediately cover their assigned people. With the President and Vice President in the Oval Office, the entire detail, with the exception of the four-man group protecting the First Lady, would rush to the west wing, forming a tight protective perimeter, both inside the building and outside.

Within ninety seconds of discovering the assassination, every Secret Service agent and EPB officer would be alerted, and the White House grounds would be locked up tight, making escape impossible. As the minutes ticked by, the perimeter would be expanded, and the Metro Police and the FBI would be alerted. Bus stations, the railway station, Dulles,

National, and Baltimore airports would be secured. Eventually they might even resort to roadblocks.

And none of it would do any good at all.

The Key Bridge Marriott Motel is located on the Virginia side of the Francis Scott Key Bridge between the George Washington Memorial Parkway and the Lee Highway. To the north is the Potomac, with Georgetown University on the D.C. side. To the east is the wooded bulk of Roosevelt Island, and to the south there is the cluster of apartment buildings, high-rise offices, and hotels that make up the suburb of Rosslyn. Farther south, hidden by the wall of buildings, is Arlington Cemetery, and beyond, the low fortress of the Pentagon.

Smoking, Stephen Stone stood by his car in the Marriott parking lot, watching as the lights blinked on at the Kennedy Center, the dignified structure just visible over the trees on Theodore Roosevelt Island. Beyond the JFK Center the rest of the city was lost in a dusky haze of heat and air pollution. It was cooler on the Virginia side, or at least it seemed that way to the FBI agent, and he'd slipped back into his wrinkled seersucker jacket.

His search for the assassin had led to a frustrating dead end. It had taken him and Mort Kessler almost ten minutes to reach their cars and five more to reach the Power Boat Club on the far side of the Anacostia Bridge. Another ten minutes were lost while he established his bona fides with the club management, and by then it was too late. In the end all he had to show for his trouble was a list of boats rented and returned that afternoon. There were seventeen names, and because of his suspension, he had no way of checking them quickly.

Waiting for Mort at the Marriott, he'd tried Debbie's number at work and then at her apartment. No answer. There was no reply at the cabin either, and that made him even more nervous; even if Debbie wasn't there, Travkin was. The only thing he could think of was that the Russian was out of earshot, perhaps down by the dock.

He stubbed out his cigarette and lit another, ignoring the acid bite in his throat as he dragged deeply. If Travkin was right, there was a plot to assassinate the President in progress, and by the looks of things, there wasn't a goddamn thing he could do about it. Both he and the Russian had been cut out of the system with surgical efficiency, robbed of their powers, stripped of their credibility. Christ! He didn't even have a weapon. He normally didn't carry one, and the Smith & Wesson automatic he'd been issued was on the upper closet shelf in his apartment.

310

Mort Kessler's tan Ford turned into the lot. The red-haired agent found a spot, pulled into it, and parked. He climbed wearily out of the vehicle and walked over to Stone. Boosting himself up onto the low retaining wall at the edge of the parking lot, he looked expectantly at his colleague.

"Well?" he asked.

"Diddley-shit," Stone answered. "A list of names for you to check out on the NCIC."

"They took out Mallory," Kessler replied baldly. "I watched the whole thing go down from across the street."

"Shit!"

"Right." Kessler grunted. "I guess they had a team inside. I followed Mallory back to Alexandria. He goes up to his apartment, and ten minutes later an ambulance pulls up. Two guys in paramedic uniforms go up with a gurney and come back down with Mallory, sheet up to his chin, blood on his face. The ambulance splits, and a couple of minutes later a trio of heavies comes down, all dressed in blue windbreakers and carrying suitcase-size briefcases. They climb into an unmarked van and disappear. All they needed were stencils on the back of the jackets that said CIA."

"Cooper's got a cleanup going," Stone responded, his voice dull. He flipped his cigarette butt into the growing darkness. "He's closing all the doors."

"You think it's getting close?" Kessler asked.

"Has to be," Stone replied. "Duncan, or whatever his name is, wouldn't risk a meet like that unless it was almost time to make the play."

"So what do we do about it? Go to Spencer?"

"With what? The suspended Rednet loony with a defrocked Russian as his only evidence? I don't have a single fucking fact to give him, Mort. It's all conjecture and hypothesis. If I went to him, the only person he'd arrest would be me."

"So?" Kessler shrugged. "We've only got one other option."

"Such as?"

"Find Duncan. Take him down."

"Easier said than done," Stone answered. He reached into the inside pocket of his jacket and took out the folded sheet of paper with the Power Boat Club list on it. "This isn't much to go on."

"It's better than nothing," Kessler said.

"While you're at it, see if you can get a rundown on what Tucker's

311

going to be doing for the next few days. Any gladhanding, speeches, that kind of thing. If he's slated to be out of town, find out where he's going."

"That should be easy enough." Kessler nodded. "The Protocol Office at State should have it. Anything else?"

"A weapon," Stone replied. He paused and gnawed his lower lip, a worried expression on his face. He thought about Travkin, alone up at the cabin, and of Debbie. Both of them were terribly vulnerable. "Maybe you should get something for the Russian as well," he said finally. Kessler looked skeptical but nodded. He dropped down from the low wall, brushing dust off the seat of his pants.

"What's the obscure rendezvous this time?" Kessler asked, laughing.

"Here again. Say around seven-thirty tomorrow morning."

"Okay," Kessler said. "Maybe we can do something civilized like have breakfast."

"One more thing," Stone asked. "Take a run past Debbie's and see if she's around. I haven't been able to get in touch all day. She's probably up at the cabin with Travkin, but I'm starting to get a little worried. Her office said they hadn't heard a thing from her." He looked at his colleague. "And be careful, they might have the place being watched."

"Done," Kessler said, and they parted company for the second time that day.

"I've always felt that you looked somewhat out of place in this decor," Hollis Macintyre commented, glancing around Hudson Cooper's living room at the Watergate. The drapes were drawn over the picture window that looked out over the Potomac, and except for two table lamps the large room lay in darkness.

"Miriam liked antiques," the CIA deputy director answered softly. "Especially American Victoriana; she said it reminded her of her mother." Cooper nodded toward the large, ornately framed oil painting over the fireplace. The portrait showed a plain-faced woman, severely dressed in black from throat to toe. Below the painting, the mantel was choked with dozens of tiny metal picture frames, all filled with aging photographs.

Macintyre bobbed his head in polite appreciation while Cooper climbed to his feet and made his way across the room to his desk. He gathered up half a dozen file folders and returned to his chair across the glass-topped coffee table from Macintyre. The fat man lowered his Wedgwood cup and saucer and placed them carefully on the glass. He sat back

312

against the sofa cushions, his expression blank, tiny pale pink hands crossed over the bulging vest of his suit.

"Presumably we're still on schedule," he murmured.

"Yes." Cooper nodded. He flipped open one of the folders and glanced at it briefly.

"From what you said on the telephone I gather that your feelings about Mr. Mallory were not unfounded."

"He fulfilled his role," Cooper answered. "He's been dealt with."

"Good. No loose ends?"

"He came very close," the Deputy Director answered. "He had some information embedded in a computer program as a safeguard. It's been removed, and Mallory has been given a completely revamped legend for the official record. Closet pederast, depressed, potentially vulnerable."

"Not entirely original," Macintyre commented.

"Perhaps not," Cooper responded. "But safe enough. He has no family."

"All right." The fat man acquiesced. "What about the rest of it?"

"The dinner begins at seven forty-five tomorrow evening. I haven't been invited, but I insisted that my appointment be scheduled for that night. Dinner ends at eight forty-five; coffee and cake will be served at nine. I'll have five minutes in the Oval Office—eight-fifty to eight-fifty-five."

"At which point your man will strike."

"Our man," Cooper replied pointedly. "Yes."

"Grounds for suspicion there," Macintyre murmured. "We've already discussed the possibility of an assassination hearing after the fact. How would 'our' killer know you were going to be in the Oval Office with the President?"

"Mallory will have told him," Cooper answered coolly.

"I'm afraid I don't see."

"Nezar Assad," Cooper answered, "our terrorist from the Abu Nidal group."

"Explain."

"The legend that was developed has Assad co-opting Mallory through sexual favors; doctored photographs can be produced if necessary. Using Mallory as a pipeline to me, Assad develops his assassination plot."

"And how does a terrorist get into the White House?"

"A Secret Service oversight, using Mallory again. An extra notation

313

in the security file. Assad will be logged as part of the service staff at the dinner."

"It sounds vague," Macintyre interjected.

"It's meant to," Cooper answered. "A back story that's too complete is suspicious in itself. Fewer facts, more hypothesis; more hypothesis leads to even greater confusion."

"I see," Macintyre said, nodding thoughtfully. "The grassy knoll."

"Precisely," Cooper replied. "The Kennedy affair is a perfect example. The knoll, extra gunshots, the motorcycle policeman's exchange, the doctored photos of Oswald, even Ruby's connection with the Dallas police. All we need are a few pivotal points; public opinion will take care of the rest."

"What about our people?" Macintyre asked.

"That's been taken care of as well," answered the gaunt CIA man. He leaned forward and fanned out the file folders across the coffee table. "Just as you requested—complete dossiers on everyone in Romulus, including Swanbridge. They should be enough to quell any sudden pangs of conscience."

"And is there a file on me?" Macintyre asked, smiling lightly.

"We're each other's best defense," Cooper answered, returning the fat man's look with a smile of his own. "We know enough to hang each other ten times over." He gathered up the files and pushed them into a neat pile. He picked them up and dropped them in front of the huge white-haired man. "My last act for Romulus. After tomorrow I'm finished, Hollis. I really will be handing my resignation to Tucker."

"That's absurd." Macintyre frowned. "Leave the agency if you wish—you've certainly earned your retirement—but you know perfectly well that you must remain with Romulus. Even if you're inactive."

"Don't threaten me," Cooper answered, weariness in his voice. "I'm too old and too tired."

"It's not a threat; it's a fact," said Macintyre. He grunted as he sat forward on the sofa. "On three occasions over the past forty years, people have tried to take information about Romulus to the public. Two were members of the committee, and the other was a journalist with connections to a third member. All four individuals were eradicated before they could do any damage beyond promulgating the odd rumor or two."

Cooper leaned over and opened the carved box on the coffee table. He took out a cigarette and lit it with his dead wife's silver lighter. For a moment Macintyre looked surprised. For Cooper, smoking was a rarely practiced vice. The thin, hawk-nosed man took a careful drag on the cigarette, staring at the huge-bellied man seated across from him.

"Listen to me, Hollis," he said finally, his aging voice flat and deathly cold. "I've spent virtually my entire adult life working in the field of intelligence. I've made the art and craft of deception my profession. I've seen the smallest, most inoffensive of white lies turned into a towering conspiracy, I know things about this country and its recent history that would make your soul shrivel and turn black. So don't give me any lectures on the consequences of remorse." He stabbed out the cigarette and looked back at Macintyre. "Right here, Hollis, in this room, you and I are discussing treason and blandly planning the aftermath of assassination."

"Do I detect a note of guilt?" asked the fat man, unmoved by Cooper's speech.

The deputy director let out a short, barking laugh. "Guilt?" he asked, eyes widening behind his eyeglasses. "Guilt is for people who have consciences, Hollis, something you and I dispensed with many, many years ago."

"That may well be true, but it doesn't alter the fact that I have no intention of spending the last few years of my life in prison. I merely wish to make sure that nothing has been left to chance, including the confessional urges of the people involved."

"Then you have nothing to worry about," Cooper answered. "At least on my account. My sins are my responsibility, and if I feel the need to atone for them, I will do so alone."

"Good enough then." Macintyre nodded, then smiled pleasantly. He eased himself upright, using the arm of the sofa for support. Standing, he tugged down the tails of his vest, then brushed away an imaginary crumb. "One last thing," he said as Cooper stood up on the other side of the table.

"Yes?"

"The Russian and our friend from the FBI. Still a problem?"

"Travkin has gone to ground," Cooper answered. "Stone has been suspended. He's powerless. If he presents a problem, he'll be removed."

"Good." Macintyre smiled. He headed for the foyer of the apartment, and Cooper followed. The fat man paused, one hand on the doorknob. "If all goes well, we won't be seeing each other for some time."

"No," Cooper answered. "Except for normal day-to-day meetings all the members have been advised not to see each other. Not that there will be much time for socializing in the near future."

315

"True enough," Macintyre said, his voice somber. "A few dark days ahead, I suppose." He opened the door and stepped into the hall. "I'll be at Stoneacres if I'm needed."

Cooper nodded good-bye and closed the door, which he locked securely. He walked back to the living room, glancing at the heavily shadowed portrait over the fireplace, and then at the cold hearth itself. He'd burned no fire there since Miriam died.

"Dark days indeed," he said quietly.

After leaving Mort Kessler, Stephen Stone drove south through the last of the evening traffic, taking the Jefferson Davis Turnpike to Fredericksburg, then turning west into the hills on State Highway 208. Night had fallen, and the road ahead was almost empty as he drove toward Lake Anna and the cabin safe house Debbie had provided.

Staring through the windshield down the long twin cones of brightness cast by his headlights, the FBI man seemed caught within a single cycle of thought. A chance piece of information given to a Russian spy had led them link by link down a chain of events designed to culminate in the murder of a President. Stone had played the game of plot and counterplot for years, but for all its seriousness he knew it was just that; he and Travkin and all the others were players on a board with well-defined borders and rigid rules. Some days you won, on others you lost, but the game went forward. This was different, and he knew that he was traveling uncharted ground; dark as the road ahead and much more dangerous.

He reached the Lake Anna exit and turned onto the narrow gravel road that led down to the water and meandered around the shoreline. The cabin Debbie had borrowed was at the far end of the lake, isolated from its neighbors by almost ten acres of screening pine and bracken. According to Debbie, it had been built in the late twenties by the parents of her professor friend from Georgetown University.

Ten minutes after he turned off the highway, his headlights picked up the cabin mailbox, the name Sleeman on its side in reflective tape. Slowing, Stone turned down the narrow drive, pine boughs slapping at the windows and brushing against the sides of the car. He tapped the horn three times to announce his arrival—the signal they'd worked out to separate the good guys from the bad. A few moments later he reached the end of the narrow lane, his lights flashing across the cabin. There was no sign of Debbie's late-model Subaru wagon, and there were no lights on in the cabin. Stone killed his engine, switched off the headlights, and

316

climbed out of the car. Once again he found himself wishing he had a weapon.

He stood by the car, waiting for his eyes to adjust to the darkness. The cabin was located at the top of a gentle slope leading down to the water. There were two entrances, the one facing him on the side of the cabin and the main entrance through the screen porch facing the lake. A winding set of flagstones went from the bottom of the porch steps to the dock and the boathouse fifty yards away. Peering into the darkness, Stone could hear the lake, but he couldn't see it. He sniffed. Woodsmoke. There was a fire going in the cabin stove. Pine gum. Grass in the small clearing. Nothing but ordinary night sounds and the ticking of his engine as it cooled. Lots of stars in a pure black sky, but no moon. Safe?

Maybe. But where was Travkin?

"Here," said a voice, reading his mind. Stone whirled, dropping into a crouch, heart pounding. Dmitri Travkin stepped out of the darkness, palms up to show that he was unarmed. "I heard the horn, but I didn't want to take any chances."

"You scared the living shit out of me!"

"My apologies." Travkin smiled.

"Any sign of my ex-wife?" Stone asked, rising out of his crouch.

"She brought some supplies yesterday. Nothing since," the Russian answered politely. The GRU officer hadn't shaved since his abduction by Cooper and was now sporting a reddish blond beard. Either the beard or the circumstances had aged him.

"Let's go inside," Stone said. Travkin nodded, and the two men walked to the front of the cabin and climbed the steps to the screened porch. Bypassing the comfortable-looking array of white-painted wicker furniture, they crossed the porch and went through a doorway into the main room.

It was a living memory for anyone who'd ever spent summers in a cottage by a lake. Couch made from the rear seat of a Model T, wind-up Victrola, scarred table, children's watercolors roughly framed and hanging from the wall, silhouettes of fish caught during some long-lost July, their imprints outlined in pinholes through shelf paper. Small fire crackling in the wood stove, taking off the chill, casting flickering shadows over honey-colored floors glazed by ten thousand barefoot passages. Stone dropped down onto the automobile seat couch and let his head fall back against the cracked ancient leather. Travkin sat down on a straight chair,

317

closer to the stove. Beyond him, stairs rose to dark bedrooms on the second floor.

"Bad?" Travkin asked.

"Worse." Stone grunted. He sat forward, rummaging around in his pockets for a cigarette. Travkin tossed him one from a package of Marlboros on the table to his right, followed by a box of wooden matches.

"How so?" the Russian queried, lighting a cigarette of his own.

"Cooper's taken out Mallory."

"His assistant?"

"Yes. Just after he made a drop to our Mr. Duncan. I tried to follow him, but I lost him. Kessler followed Mallory and watched him get picked up by one of Cooper's teams."

"So what are our options?" Travkin asked, scratching at the new beard along his jaw.

"Kessler's following up some leads on Duncan. I'm going to meet with him tomorrow."

"I wish to come with you," Travkin said slowly.

"Out of the question," Stone answered firmly, shaking his head. "Set one foot in D.C. and you're a dead man, you know that."

"I must talk to Koslov, explain the situation. Perhaps—"

"What?" Stone asked coldly. "Koslov's an old man. You know it's almost certainly out of his hands now. Gurenko's people will be looking for you everywhere by now."

"Still—"

"Still nothing!" Stone barked. "Right now you're the only piece of hard evidence that I've got. So you sit tight." The FBI man took a deep breath, then let it out slowly. "Sorry," he said after a long moment. "I'm going a little crazy, I guess."

"Understandable." Travkin shrugged. "Neither of us is in the most comfortable of positions."

"Quite the understatement," Stone answered, laughing bleakly. Outside, there was the faint sound of a horn. Three beeps. "Debbie," he said, standing up, relief in his voice.

"Quiet," Travkin murmured. He slid past Stone, motioning for him to follow. The Russian padded quickly into the kitchen, then out the side door. The FBI man went after him into the darkness. Together they crouched down by the side of the cabin, hidden in the deep shadows. In the distance Stone could hear the sound of a car engine. "Keep your face down, look from the top of your eyes," Travkin ordered. "A white face is like the moon, reflecting any light available. When she parks, make sure

318

that she is alone in the car. If there is someone with her, we leave. There will be no heroics. Understand?" Stone simply nodded. The Russian was in full command, and the FBI man knew that Travkin's Spetznaz training went far beyond anything he'd learned at Quantico.

The car appeared finally, and Stone smiled, recognizing the utilitarian shape of the station wagon and catching a glimpse of Debbie's face behind the wheel as she swung past and parked beside his own vehicle. He began to stand up, but Travkin's hand gripped his forearm painfully. Stone was five inches taller and fifty pounds heavier than his companion, but the Russian's grip was like iron.

"Wait," Travkin whispered.

Stone did as he was told, watching as she climbed out of the car, slamming the door easily behind her. She took a few steps toward the cabin, then paused. She turned then and went back to the Subaru. After opening the passenger side door, she leaned down, then stood again, this time holding a briefcase. Gripping it tightly, she made her way toward the cottage once more. Travkin let out a short, sharp whistle, then stood up and stepped out of the shadows. Stone followed suit, then brushed past Travkin, moving toward her at a trot.

"Stephen!" she called out, stopping halfway between the car and the screened porch. "What are you doing out here in the dark?"

"Playing commando with Dmitri." He grinned, looking back over his shoulder as the Russian came forward. He turned back to Debbie. She looked exhausted. She was pale, and there were blue-gray shadows under her eyes. "Here," he said, reaching for the briefcase. "Let me take that for you."

"No!" she said, pulling back quickly.

Stone jerked his hand back as though it had been burned. "Relax," he cautioned. "I'm not going to steal anything."

"I'm sorry," she said, nodding toward Travkin as the Russian approached. "I guess I'm just a little on—"

A single round from the Finnish-made Valmet assault rifle caught the chestnut-colored dark-haired woman at the base of the neck, exiting just below the jaw and finally coming to rest in one of the wooden porch supports. A split second later Stone and Travkin heard the sound of the weapon and watched, horrified, as Debbie Stone lurched forward, eyes bulging, when a second round struck her in the back, blowing out most of her diaphragm in a gory fountain of cloth, blood, and bone.

Screaming, Stephen Stone threw himself toward the dead but still standing woman. As a third round took off the upper portion of her skull,

319

Travkin gripped the FBI man by the back of his collar and pitched him backward, away from the line of fire. Stumbling, he managed to drag Stone back into the shadows, his other hand jerking him toward the ground at the base of the porch steps. The Russian pushed Stone's face into the dirt as a ragged volley of shots struck the crumpled form of the woman ten feet away.

The Spetznaz-trained intelligence officer made a quick, intuitive analysis of the situation. Too many shots, too quickly, but with no rippling hammer of automatic fire. Several shooters, all firing from the left, hidden in the trees. A run for either of the two vehicles would be fatal; their best bet lay in the woods behind.

"Low," he commanded in a whisper, his hand tight on the back of Stone's neck.

"Debbie . . ." Stone's voice was anguished, choked with tears.

"Dead," Travkin said harshly. "Unless you want to die as well, you must follow my instructions."

"Who are—"

"Quiet!" Travkin ordered. He listened. Silence, not even the snap of a twig. Very professional. Waiting for them to make a move. "Keep with me," the Russian whispered. His hand still on Stone's neck, he began to shuffle backward, keeping the porch between himself and the vehicles. If they were lucky, the cars and the porch would mask their movements. Hugging the ground, they reached the corner of the cabin, and Travkin paused, listening again, eyes and ears focused on the dark curtain of trees twenty feet away. If one or more of the killers had split from the main group and come this way, he and Stone would make perfect targets as they tried to cross the open space.

Still crouching, his hand on Stone's shoulder now, Travkin crab-walked along the side wall of the cabin. He stopped at the stacked pile of firewood on his right. His eyes were fully adjusted to the darkness now, and he could make out the hard-edged shape of a hatchet sticking up from one of the logs. He reached out and pried the tool loose, hefting it in his hand. Better than nothing.

"Stay here," he whispered, turning to the man crouched on his left. "Count to ten slowly; then follow. Straight into the trees." Stone nodded, and Travkin stood and began to run, his movements smooth and silent. Numb, the image of Debbie burning in his mind, Stone watched the Russian melt into the shadows along the line of trees. He began to count, and on ten he lurched upward and began to run, nerves wire-taut.

Halfway across the clearing there was a blast of sound, and he was almost positive he felt the sharp passage of air as the bullet creased his shoulder, then smacked into the side wall of the cabin a few yards behind. Without thinking, the FBI man dropped and rolled, then scrambled the last few feet into the trees. Travkin was there to meet him, a banana-clip Valmet rifle hanging limply from one hand. He motioned with his free hand and then slipped farther into the trees. Stone followed, stumbling over the body of one of their attackers. The man was on his knees, head bent forward like a Muslim at prayer. The hatchet from the wood-pile was buried deeply in the flesh of the man's neck, half severing the head. To the dead man's left was a small collapsible shovel, blade embedded in the soft earth, and further left a neatly dug firing position, twelve inches deep and just large enough for a man to lie prone.

"Jesus!" Stone whispered. He clenched his teeth, fighting off the overpowering urge to vomit.

"Listen to me," Travkin said, his voice clipped. "I spent my first day here walking the terrain. We are thirty meters from the beach—a hundred feet. From there the ground breaks at the beach. Ten meters to the right is the dock and the boathouse. There is a powerboat, a dinghy, and a canoe. When we reach the edge of the beach, we will be exposed to fire from the cabin. Therefore, we will go into the water rather than move along the sand. Do you understand?"

"Yes." Stone nodded. Fear had frozen out every other emotion. The universe had collapsed into a tiny frame of reality that included no one else but the Russian. Right now Travkin was squad leader, commanding general, and God all rolled into one.

"Head for the boathouse. Go around to the end of the dock. Keep the boathouse between you and the cabin. We'll take the powerboat. You are familiar with outboard engines?"

"Yes."

"Good. You will start the engine, but not until I am in the boat. Try to leave me behind, and I will kill you. When we come out of the boathouse, turn left sharply and follow the waterline until we are out of range. Then head for the far side of the lake. On the map I saw in the cabin there is a town, yes?" The Russian's English was deteriorating, and Stone had to concentrate.

"A town. Yes." He tried to think of the name and couldn't. Finally, absurdly, he remembered. "Cuckoo," he said. "The town is called Cuckoo."

"Then it becomes our objective."

"All right," Stone said, and began moving off. Stone took a last look at the man with the hatchet and followed. The Russian slid through the forest like a wraith, his sneakered feet hardly seeming to touch the ground. Stone kept close behind him, heart slamming in his chest. Behind them and to the left he could hear voices now, the words unintelligible. There was a deep, coughing sound and a muted thump, followed almost instantly by a gouting flare of light. They were burning the cabin.

Travkin and Stone reached the lakeshore and paused. The FBI man watched as Travkin took off his shoes, tied the laces together, and hung them around his neck. Stone was wearing slip-ons, but he did his best, shoving them into the pockets of his jacket. While he was doing that, the Russian vanished for a few moments, then returned, carrying a charred piece of wood. He rubbed his hands over the charcoal, then stroked the sooty ash first onto his own forehead and then Stone's.

"Like before," Travkin instructed. "Go into the water up to your neck. Head down, nothing but the eyes and bottom of nose above water. Do not look toward cabin. Yes?"

"Understood." Stone nodded.

Travkin smiled and clapped his companion on the shoulder. "Boy Scout shit." He grinned, then turned and headed into the cool water of the lake.

It took them fewer than five minutes to reach the boathouse, with Travkin leading, the Valmet held rigidly in his hands, level with the water. The Russian paused in the lee of the dock, motioning with his chin for Stone to join him. From the corner of his eye Stone could see the blooming caldron of the cabin fire, and for an instant he saw Debbie again, eyes wide and throat torn open as she died. Chilled and shivering, he swallowed hard, joining Travkin at the edge of the dock. The Russian handed him the Valmet.

"They may have someone posted here. Wait." Stone nodded, holding the weapon out of the water, and Travkin slithered off. He returned a few moments later. "All clear." He took the rifle from Stone, then urged the FBI man forward.

They entered the boathouse from the open lake side, and Stone dragged himself up onto the narrow floating walkway. The dinghy was hanging on the wall, supported by half a dozen thick wooden pegs, and the canoe was strung through the rafters overhead. The powerboat was nothing more than an aluminum rowboat fitted with a twenty-five-horse-power Evinrude.

Dripping, Stone stepped down into the rear of the boat, settling himself at the transom. He gripped the pull rope and waited for Travkin to

322

join him. The Russian took a few seconds to check the back window of the boathouse, then undid the bowline and dropped onto the forward seat. Holding the Valmet ready across his chest, Travkin turned and nodded to Stone. Gritting his teeth, the FBI man put all his strength into his shoulder, ripped the starter rope, and twisted the throttle wide open. The engine caught instantly, and they surged out of the boathouse, the sudden acceleration almost throwing Stone out of his seat. He hung on as they thundered forward, bow rising, then snapped his throttle arm hard to the right.

Engine howling, the small boat careened along the lakeshore. Stone prayed desperately that there were no deadheads of hidden rocks in his path and kept the throttle open. In front of him, Travkin turned in his seat and leveled the assault rifle. There was a roaring stutter that rose above the engine noise, and Stone saw the dazzling pulse of the weapon's muzzle flash. He was vaguely aware of dense trees looming up on his left and then saw Travkin toss the now-empty rifle over the side. A minute went by as they tore along the foreshore, and then Travkin motioned with his arm.

"Turn!" he bellowed, raising his voice over the screaming outboard. "Cross the lake!"

Stone nodded, pulling the throttle lever toward him. The bow spun around, and then he straightened, pointing them toward the invisible shore more than a mile away.

"Who were they?" Stone called out, his voice torn away by the wind. He squinted forward, spray pounding upward over the gunwales as they raced across the dark, unruffled water.

"My people!" Travkin answered, fury in his voice. "They were damn fucking Spetsnaz!"

"How can you be sure?" Stone yelled. "Why not Cooper's men?"

"The little shovel for one!" Travkin explained, half turning on his seat to look back at Stone. "It is a trademark. And also the fact that the man in the woods cursed me into eternity as he died. In Russian."

"Jesus!" the FBI man moaned. He wiped the spray out of his eyes with the back of one hand. "We've got everyone after us now!"

"It could be worse, tovarich!" Travkin answered, breaking into a death's-head grin. "At least we have each other."

323

# CHAPTER 23

At six on the morning of President Geoffrey James Tucker's sixty-third birthday, Eric Rhinelander pedaled his bicycle through the dawn streets of Washington. He was wearing a blue and green lightweight wet suit, cut down to look like a form-fitting bicycler's outfit, and carried a knapsack on his back. The pack contained some small tools, black heavy-soled lace shoes, Paul Axworthy's carefully folded Executive Protection Branch's uniform, and the broken-down components of the $CO_2$ powered weapon built for him by the Baltimore paintball store. A side pocket of the knapsack held the small short-range detonating mechanism for the explosive he'd installed on the sewer side of the north portico vault late the previous night and the dedicated frequency radio that would be fitted onto the uniform web belt.

At six-fifteen he reached the silent, empty intersection of Wisconsin Avenue and M Street in Georgetown. He pedaled through the intersection and continued down toward the Chesapeake and Ohio Canal. Thirty feet through the crossing he slowed, then dismounted and pulled his bicycle up onto the sidewalk. Looking around casually, he checked to make sure that he wasn't being observed, then turned down a narrow lane, its entrance posted with a No Parking in Lane sign.

Walking the bicycle over the dew-damp cobblestones, he went past the Blues Alley jazz club, crossed a small open square, and turned up a second, even narrower lane that ran parallel to Wisconsin Avenue. Fifty feet farther on the second alley ended in a T intersection with a service alley running behind M Street. Just before the T a large dark green

324

Dumpster squatted heavily at the rear of a Wisconsin Avenue delicatessen.

Overhead the pewter-colored sky was lightening to blue, and Rhinelander could hear the growing traffic noise from the Whitehurst Freeway, which ran between the canal and the Potomac only a few hundred yards away. It was going to be another heat-wave day in the nation's capital, and Rhinelander was pleased that he'd be spending most of it within the air-conditioned confines of the White House.

He parked the bicycle behind the Dumpster and slipped into the darkened rear service doorway of the deli. He'd checked the hours of business and knew that it didn't open until ten each morning, by which time he'd be long gone.

He stripped off the knapsack, opened it, and assembled the pieces of his weapon, screwing the air hose connector to the barrel, then used surgical tape to strap the barrel to his forearm. The frozen magazine and its contents, now wrapped in sportsman's insulating plastic, would be loaded into the upper tube of the barrel at the last minute.

With the weapon in place Rhinelander kicked off his Nikes and dressed himself in Axworthy's uniform, including the radio. Clothed, he put on the lace-up shoes, then tossed the runners into the Dumpster. Finally he removed the paintball magazine, a compact, battery-powered Bosch ratchet screwdriver, and a two-inch plastic-handled awl from the pack. He put the magazine into the left inside pocket of his uniform jacket and the screwdriver and awl into the right pocket. He adjusted the broad strap of the Sam Browne belt and patted the holster. It was the final touch to the uniform; using the James Smythe identification provided by Cooper's people, he'd legitimately purchased a standard-issue Smith & Wesson .38 police special loaded with Hornady wadcutters. With the knapsack empty he threw it into the Dumpster as well.

Finally he unhooked the bungee cords from the bicycle frame and removed the dummy end of the truck baffle he'd created. It was identical to the one he'd seen in the Secret Service refrigerated truck, complete with recessed screw heads. On the inside of the plywood board he'd screwed and glued a kitchen cabinet handle and four spring clips to hold the baffle end in place after he'd left the vehicle. With the board removed he set it aside and manhandled the bicycle up and into the Dumpster.

The first stage of the operation now completed, Rhinelander took out a package of gum from the side pocket of the uniform jacket, removed a piece, and put it into his mouth. Chewing slowly, he stepped back into the recessed doorway of the delicatessen and pulled down his fly. He

325

urinated against the scarred wooden doorframe, emptying his bladder completely.

For the last twenty-four hours he'd regulated his food and fluids carefully, restricting his intake that morning to a thick high-protein drink of yogurt, raw egg, brewer's yeast, and desiccated liver. It would have to last him well into the night, and the last thing he wanted was a judgment error brought on by nature's call. A small detail perhaps but potentially disastrous.

A brief vivid image snapped into his mind: a Vietcong, black pajamas around his ankles as he squatted in the bush, smoking an early-morning cigarette and loosening his bowels. The wiry black-clad insurgent never even saw Rhinelander or the bright flashing blade that slit his throat.

Rhinelander glanced at his watch: six thirty-five. He eased out of the doorway, removed the peaked cap, and poked his head out around the corner of the Dumpster. Almost time. From where he stood he could see the rear entrance of McCreery's Provisioners. The lane was too narrow for the truck to back up against the loading dock, so it parked sideways.

There would be two Secret Service men and four workers on hand from McCreery's. Two of the McCreery's men would stand in the truck, while the other two loaded. One of the Secret Service agents would stand at the rear of the vehicle to supervise the loading while the second, usually the driver, handled the paper work in the office.

Rhinelander had watched the proceedings on three separate occasions and knew the routine. The truck arrived between six-forty and six forty-five. The two Secret Service men left the truck and went into the rear of the McCreery's building. Between six fifty-five and seven they would reappear, this time with the McCreery's workers. The loading took roughly fifteen minutes, and the truck left the lane between seven-fifteen and seven-twenty. By seven-thirty the truck would be arriving at the West Executive Avenue entrance to the White House for its security check.

Rhinelander heard the heavy rumbling of an engine echoing along the upper laneway and ducked his head back behind the side of the Dumpster. He checked his watch again: six-forty, right on schedule. Listening, he heard the flatulent sigh of brakes as the truck stopped in front of the rear loading bay. A pause, and then the sound of two slammed doors—the Secret Service agents leaving the vehicle. Staring at the sweep hand of his watch, Rhinelander counted the two men down. Lead man pushes the buzzer to the left of the door. Fifteen seconds for the Frisco Bay surveillance camera tilted in the upper right of the doorframe to check the two men. The metal door swings open and—Rhinelander smiled to

326

himself as he heard the faint sound of the door closing behind the two agents.

Without hurrying, the assassin walked out from around the Dumpster and headed up the lane toward the truck, counting silently. He checked quickly. Loading bay door closed, the surveillance camera tilted far too steeply to pick up his approach. Nobody in the alley. A drunk, overlooked, dozing in a doorway could ruin it all now. Thirty seconds.

He reached the rear of the truck and paused again, holding his breath, letting his senses warn him if warnings were needed. Still nothing. Gently he gripped the rear latch on the door and lifted it slightly, just enough to disengage the hook. One minute. He eased the door up with one hand, then boosted himself up and into the refrigerated compartment, tossing the dummy baffle in ahead of him. Once inside, he lowered the door, pushing hard for the last few inches so that the outer latch clicked back into place. Ninety seconds. Cold enough to see his breath if there had been any light.

He eased to the right and swept his palm over the Kemlite wall until he found the toggle for the overhead light. He switched it on, blinking in the sudden glare. He *could* see his breath, and he could also hear the steady hum of the Thermo King unit. Two minutes, ahead of schedule. He picked up the baffle and went to the front of the compartment. Leaning the baffle against the wall, he went to work.

Using the battery-powered ratchet, he removed the side panel of the baffle, being careful to put each screw into the pocket of his jacket. Four minutes now, but even in the cold of the truck compartment, sweat was beading lightly on his brow. Screws out, he took the awl out of his pocket, slipped it into one of the screw holes, and jimmied the side of the baffle out of its position. Having turned the baffle on edge, he slid it back into the now-opened box of the baffle, then peered inside. Ten inches wide, sixty long, and fifty high. Enough room to slide in sideways, half crouched, one hand on the dummy baffle handle, clips or no clips. Too long, and he'd cramp, but it was an unavoidable risk. Six minutes. Quick check of the compartment to make sure there was nothing suspicious. Ratchet placed in the far end of the box. Finally the light. Out. Seven minutes. One minute left to his self-imposed limit. In the darkness he made his way back to the baffle, found the dummy, then eased himself into the box, making sure that he was facing the rear of the truck and that the awl was in his free hand.

Hat off and held between the side of the box and his chest, Rhinelander crabbed sideways, then pulled the baffle into place. The clips

327

made a small noise as they locked into place, but he still kept his hand on the handle. He tried to ignore the mild claustrophobia he felt with the unseen wall of the baffle inches from his face. Eight minutes, and he was in.

Closing his eyes, Rhinelander forced his breathing to slow and his heartbeat to follow suit. Moment by moment he went over the details of the plan, searching for the smallest flaw, finding none. Ten minutes. Five more, and they would begin to load. Thirty-five, and he'd be through the gates. It was going to work.

"Jesus," Mort Kessler whispered, staring at the two men standing in the hallway. "You guys really do look like hell." He stepped aside and let Stone and Travkin enter the recently rented hotel room at the Key Marriott. They'd called Kessler an hour and a half before from a roadside booth just outside the small town of King's Dominion and asked him to get the room as well as some fresh clothes. The room had been easy enough, but the clothes were a different matter. Kessler was shorter than either Travkin or Stone, so his own clothes wouldn't do, and he'd had to resort to a twenty-four-hour K mart just south of the Pentagon. The result was twin sets of jeans, cheap running shoes, and a pair of T-shirts. Travkin chose the "Iron Maiden" shirt, leaving Stone no choice but to put on "Cyndi Lauper."

Kessler ordered a room service breakfast while his disheveled guests washed up and changed. The meal arrived, and the red-haired FBI man drank coffee as the other two men wolfed down the eggs, bacon, hash browns, and toast, telling their story between bites.

"How'd you manage to get a car?" Kessler asked as Stone wiped up the last of his egg yolk with a sliver of toast.

"He stole it," Stone answered, hooking a thumb at Travkin, seated across from him at the round table. "From a fishing camp on the other side of the lake. A Suzuki Samurai. Hot-wired it."

"They teach you that kind of thing at GRU school?" Kessler asked.

"No." Travkin took a sip of coffee, shaking his head. "The Suzuki is much like the Soviet Lada Niva, one of which I own in Moscow. During Russian winters you tend to become intimate with your ignition system. The wiring of a Lada is an education in itself."

"Where is it now?" said Kessler.

"Downstairs in the parking lot," the Russian answered blandly. He sat back and lit a cigarette from the fresh pack Kessler had ordered with breakfast. Stone joined him. There was a brief silence.

328

"You're sure the people who shot Debbie were Spetznaz?" Kessler asked cautiously, his eyes on Stone.

"Positive," Travkin responded. "One of them spoke in Russian."

"It couldn't have been some sort of ruse?"

"It's a pretty good actor who keeps to his part with a hatchet buried in his back," Stone answered wryly. "Why do you ask?"

"You asked me to check her apartment. I got over there around nine last night, and the whole place had been torn apart. I mean, trashed, Stephen. It looked as though they went through the place with sledge-hammers."

"If they were Spetznaz, why were they after your wife?" Travkin asked, frowning.

"Ex-wife," Stone answered, clearing his throat. His jaw tensed as he tried to keep the emotion back. There was no time for grief now. "Uh . . . oh shit, I don't know! She worked for the European Studies Institute at the university; everybody knows it's a CIA front. She's—she was an intelligence analyst."

"It still does not explain it." Travkin shrugged. "They had three targets last night: you, me, and your ex-wife. Logically the primary target should have been me if it was a hit team sent out by Gurenko. Instead, they chose her."

"A mistake," Stone muttered, making a sweeping gesture with his hand. "And it's not important right now." The FBI man turned to Kessler. "Anything on the list I gave you? Or the President's schedule."

"Both," the red-haired agent answered, nodding. "If you were a White House groupie, you'd know that today was Tucker's birthday, complete with fireworks on the lawn. Then he spends three days at Camp David before flying out to that World War Two thing in France."

"Nothing here? No speeches at the Hilton, dinners, tree plantings, that kind of thing?"

"Nope," Kessler answered, shaking his head. "Not a thing."

"Shit!" Stone grunted, butting his cigarette. "It doesn't make sense. Duncan is here, so the hit has to be made here, not Camp David or somewhere in France."

"It's not Duncan anymore," Kessler interjected. "It's Smythe. Traveling on a New York driver's license that turns out to be a phony. I've got an address, too, which doesn't match the name. According to our friends at the telephone company, Mr. Smythe of the phony license is staying at the residence of a Mr. and Mrs. John Gray in the Wyoming Apartments, just off Connecticut Avenue behind the Hilton."

329

"I'll be damned," said Stone, managing a small, tight smile. "How'd you get all that so fast?"

"I ran the names on the list, and Smythe turned out to be the only phony. The powerboat company needed a telephone number to confirm the speedboat rental for yesterday. Our man had to give them a number that worked, and that gave me the address."

"So, what do we do with this information?" said Travkin.

"Normally we'd go to Ruppelt and request about fifty backups from the D.C. office and a SWAT team from Metro," Kessler answered with a snort. "I figure that option's out for the moment. Same as your trying to get help from Comrade General Koslov."

"No," Travkin agreed. "Not a wise move."

"We hit the address at the Wyoming," Stone said firmly, lighting another cigarette. "What we're looking for is hard evidence that someone is trying to off the President. Without that we don't have a leg to stand on, and in the end we *will* have to go to Ruppelt or someone like him."

"Unless he happens to be there when we bust in," said Kessler. "In which case we'd have to defend ourselves."

"With what?" Stone asked.

"This," Kessler answered. He lifted his attaché case from the floor beside the table and opened it. He took out a plastic-bodied Glock 9 mm automatic in a spring-clip holster and handed it across the table to Stone.

"It's my own backup gun," Kessler explained.

Seated on Kessler's right, Dmitri Travkin pursed his lips thoughtfully, then drew a clawed hand down the line of his bearded jaw. "There is no weapon for me?" He asked finally.

Kessler glanced at Stone, who shrugged. "I'm not used to this *glasnost,* hands-across-the-iron-curtain shit." The red-haired man frowned.

"He saved my ass in the woods last night," said Stone quietly. "We're in this thing together, Mort." The FBI man grinned. "Not to mention the fact that he knows how to hot-wire Suzukis."

"Okay," Kessler said finally. "You're the boss. I've got a cut-down Franchi shotgun in the trunk of the car. You can use that."

"*Spasibo.*" Travkin smiled, glancing at the two men with him at the table. "As you Americans say, let's boogie."

"Jesus!" Kessler muttered, shaking his head. "Who'd have thought I'd ever wind up partnered with a jive Russky?"

330

\*     \*     \*

William Osler, thirty-eight and bored, sat in the east side security kiosk of the West Executive Avenue entrance to the White House. Osler, with only five months on the White House detail, had drawn the midnight-to-eight shift on outside duty. This meant that he spent most of his time patrolling the grounds and regularly stepping in dog shit left around by Tucker's three Scotties, Huey, Duey, and Looey. At 7:25 A.M., with thirty-five minutes left in the shift, Osler was having an illicit cigarette in the kiosk, tapping his ash into the partially filled Dr Pepper can kept in the booth for that purpose. Standing in the kiosk entrance was Corporal James Corcoran of the Executive Protection Branch, crisply outfitted in a spanking clean uniform.

In addition to safeguarding the life of the President and anyone else who happened to be in the White House, Corcoran, three years into the service and an ex-marine, was keeping his eyes peeled for Lyall Spencer, Osler's boss, or his own topkick, Sergeant Wayne Dillabaugh of the carrot-colored hair and short temper. Neither man appeared to be in the general vicinity. Directly across from Corcoran on the west side of the avenue was an identical kiosk, manned by Chuck Zimmerman, who'd been in the same class with Corcoran when they joined the EPB. Looking across the road, Corcoran could have been staring into a mirror. Both he and Zimmerman fitted the EPB profile perfectly: tall, fit, and young, every inch the picture postcard cop with the country's most famous residence for a backdrop. The only difference was hair color. Zimm's hair was coal black, and Corcoran's dirty blond.

"What time is it?" Corcoran asked, glancing over his shoulder at Osler. The Secret Service man tipped his butt into the can and tucked it back under the shelflike seat. He stood up, yawned, and glanced at his watch.

"Seven twenty-nine and change," he answered, joining Corcoran in the doorway. "The chow truck should be here anytime now."

"Then we can all go home." Corcoran sighed. Like Osler, the uniformed Executive Protection officer was on the midnight-to-eight shift.

"Just be thankful we won't be on duty for the birthday bash," Osler said. The Secret Service man reached out and plucked the duty clipboard off the inside wall of the kiosk. "Dragon One is on the warpath from what I hear. Everything by the book and no slipups."

"How many on the list?" Corcoran asked, more to make conversation than out of any real interest. The Orioles were playing an afternoon game, and he and Zimm fully intended to be there.

331

"Sixty," Osler answered. "Full checks, metal detector at the door, magnetic stripe coding on the invitations, the works."

"What's the beef?" Corcoran asked. The bells and whistles were usually reserved for state visits.

"I'm not sure." Osler shrugged. "Some kind of rumor about terrorists, I think."

"Terrorists again?" Corcoran snorted. "Shit, we've been waiting for those guys ever since they installed all that crap in the road." He gestured with his chin at the barely visible crease in the asphalt. Drive through an equally invisible infrared beam too quickly, and a saw-toothed steel barrier flipped up out of the ground. Get beyond that, and a string of hydraulic rams came out of the road like gigantic fists, slamming into the underside of the errant vehicle.

Osler stepped out of the kiosk and looked beyond the sliding wrought-iron fence that blocked off the street between the kiosks. He spotted the white unmarked cube van and smiled. Right on the button. He walked onto the road, clipboard in hand, as the truck pulled up in front of the gate. He recognized Ted Loates, the driver, and his partner, Sandy Hansen; both men worked out of the Transport Division. He turned and nodded to Corcoran back in the kiosk. The uniformed man hit the button that opened the gates, and the truck drove through slowly. Corcoran hit the button again, and the gates closed behind the tailgate. Yawning again and thinking about breakfast at the Sixteenth Street Burger King a few blocks away, Osler went up to the driver's side of the cab and did a cursory check of Loates's ID and lapel badge. Today it was bright yellow, which checked out, and the transport man's ID was in order. As he went through the paper work with Loates, Zimmerman strolled out of his kiosk on the far side of the road with the long-handled mirror. The EPB guard dropped into a squat and ran the mirror under the truck, switching on the built-in flashlight. Satisfied that no crazed killer was clinging to the transaxle, he went around to the rear and checked the lead and wire seal the driver was supposed to crimp over the latch when he finished loading. Everything was intact, and Zimmerman came around the truck and gave Osler the nod.

"Clean," he said. Osler looked up at Loates, immutable behind his aviator's glasses.

"Happen to know the day's password phrase?" Osler asked.

"Bully Pulpit," Loates answered, quoting Teddy Roosevelt's description of the White House.

332

"Wooly Bullshit?" Osler frowned, cupping one hand over his ear, then checked the clipboard. "That's not it, I'm afraid."

"Screw you," Loates answered, grinning good-naturedly.

"And the horse you rode in on," Osler shot back. Loates dropped the van into gear, and Osler waved him forward with his clipboard. He watched the truck head down the road, then turn in at the west wing parking lot. He shook his head. Dragging his ass around the dew-damp grounds of the White House all night sucked the big one, but it was still better than driving a truck. He checked his watch again. Seven thirty-five. Twenty minutes of walking around, clock out at the main office in the west wing basement, then on to Burger King.

# CHAPTER 24

Having used the awl to bore a tiny eye-level hole in the baffle, Eric Rhinelander waited until the last pallet had been removed from the truck before he slipped out of his hiding place. Smoothing down his uniform and adjusting his cap, he walked quickly to the rear of the truck and dropped down over the tailgate. From the videotape he knew that the truck usually remained at the White House for forty-five minutes before being returned to the executive garage.

Directly in front of him was the large door leading into the kitchens. Keeping his pace casual, Rhinelander walked by the open doorway and continued on along the service pathway to the mansion entrance located behind the main stairway. He opened the door and stepped into a narrow corridor that led between the stairway and the curator's office on the right. To his left, lit from above by a single bulb, was the set of stairs leading down to the upper-level basement.

Descending, he reached the bottom landing and paused, listening and trying to keep his breathing slow and even. He closed his eyes for a moment, visualizing the layout both above and below. It was almost 8:00 A.M. and there would be some minor confusion as the Secret Service and Executive Protection Branch shifts changed over. At this hour the new shift of Secret Service agents would be concentrating their energies on the west wing executive offices and the President's private quarters on the second floor. With the heavy influx of tourists the EPB men would have their attention focused on the east wing entrance and the six ground-floor rooms included in the public tour.

Visitors to the White House on official business were required to wear plastic identification cards, their color coding based on a series of zones established within the mansion and the two wings, east and west. Visitors wearing cards good for the east wing offices set aside for the First Lady would be stopped by Secret Service or EPB personnel if they attempted to leave their area, but the various EPB and Secret Service people could cross zones at will. A man like Rhinelander, dressed in an EPB uniform, would not be challenged unless he made an obvious mistake like trying to invade the Oval Office or the presidential living quarters. Down in the cavernous basements the assassin could reasonably assume that he was on safe ground.

The first-level basement contained a maze of small offices used by junior assistants, storage areas, the carpenter's shop, the entrance to the rarely used west wing tunnel, and several large storage rooms. A narrow, dimly lit corridor also led to the furniture and service vaults located under the north portico. This was Rhinelander's initial objective. Watching the videotape and observing the flow of traffic into the west wing parking lot, he had noted that most people coming to work at the White House arrived between eight and eight-thirty, so the first-level basement would almost certainly be relatively empty now.

The second-level basement was a different story. It contained the Signal Corps communications center, occupying the old bomb shelter, a cafeteria directly below the ground-floor kitchens, the main laundry, and the entrance to the new east wing bomb shelter. Since the communications center was manned on a twenty-four-hour basis, there was always one shift on hand, but there was little reason for anyone working the second-level basement to come up to the first.

Heart rate and breathing slowed, Rhinelander turned onto the short landing, went down another three stairs, and walked past the men's and women's washrooms. Skirting the service elevator, he turned right down the central corridor running from east to west. As he'd predicted to himself, the passage was empty. Forty-five feet farther on the corridor widened slightly, and the assassin paused. On his left were the double doors leading into the furniture vaults and beyond to the heating and air-conditioning equipment.

The doors were metal-clad and fitted with push bars, while the floor of the corridor was done in a dark speckled linoleum. He scanned the doorway quickly, checking for any signs of an alarm system. There was nothing, and no sign of any visual surveillance either. He wasn't surprised. Considering the number of rooms, offices, and hallways in the building, total surveillance and wiring would be impossible, requiring scores of camera positions and alarm points; at best the Secret Service and the EPB were capable of monitoring key routes and intersections used by the public and the first family. The basement areas were obviously not a priority.

He stepped forward and pushed on the bar of the left-hand door. It opened easily, and he stepped inside and closed the door firmly behind him. The furniture vaults were lit from above by banks of fluorescents. There was a main alleyway between the floor-to-ceiling metal storage racks and half a dozen side aisles running off to left and right. Each rack was filled to overflowing with furniture no longer in use, but still potentially valuable. Stuffed chairs, chests of drawers, sofas, side tables, and lamps all were cataloged and in their proper places.

Rhinelander scanned the racks and walls, once again looking for surveillance cameras. Nothing. Nodding to himself, he walked rapidly down the central aisle to the rivet-studded dark green door at the far end of the cavernous room. Opening the door, he was instantly assaulted with a blurring array of sounds emanating from a dimly lit assembly of compressors, fans, heat exchangers, and refrigeration units, all of them joined by a snaking system of thick conduits and sheet metal ventilation pipes.

The assassin stood quietly, orienting himself. With his back to the door he was facing due north toward Pennsylvania Avenue. The main sewer conduit running up to and then below the metro line was on his right. He turned in that direction, made his way between the banks of shrouded compressors, and finally reached the far wall of the large, underground chamber.

The corner of the room was partially hidden by a loop of ventpipe, but pacing off from the corner, he found his position between a tall, slightly oily transformer unit and the vent. Just to the right of the transformer he could see the gasket opening for the conduit feeding power into the vault from the outside. With the awl from his pocket Rhinelander picked away at the gasket, watching as the old plaster fell away easily.

Part of the Truman renovation, the vault was set on a poured cement floor, with double brick walls sheathed in a two-inch-thick unstressed concrete shell. The bricks, plastered and painted over a score of times since then, were badly spalled, the mortar crumbling. The concrete skin, eaten away by the acidic, swampy soil, was in equally poor shape.

Rhinelander glanced around. He was almost forty feet from the door and well hidden. In the unlikely event that anyone came into the room, he'd have lots of warning. The killer glanced at his watch: eight-twenty. A fraction more than twelve hours left. He crouched down, measured up from the floor with his spread hand as a guide, then settled down to work with the awl.

The three men stood on the roof of the Holiday Inn and looked across Connecticut Avenue to the Wyoming Apartments. Stephen Stone was using Mort Kessler's binoculars, scanning the windows of the large nineteenth-century building behind the Washington Hilton.

"Fifth floor on that side," Kessler instructed. Stone moved the binoculars fractionally. Beside him, Dmitri Travkin waited, a box containing a dozen red roses in his hands. It also contained Mort Kessler's cut-down Franchi shotgun.

"All the blinds are drawn," Stone said, finally fixing on the right apartment.

"And no one is answering the telephone," Kessler added.

"It means nothing." Travkin shrugged. "He could still be there."

"No shit, Sherlock." Kessler grunted. "Which is why Stephen here wants the trick with the flower box. Myself I'd prefer twenty guys with Kevlar vests and some sharpshooters up here."

"The flowers will work," Stone said, lowering the binoculars.

"They better." Kessler snorted. "Because if they don't, Comrade Travkin here is in the shit can."

"You have a wonderful way with words," the Russian answered. "In my country you could have been a poet."

"Yeah, right," the red-haired FBI man said, frowning as he searched the Russian's face for some sign that he was being teased.

"Let's get to it," Stone said quietly.

Ten minutes later the trio had assembled in the fifth-floor foyer of the Wyoming. Travkin, holding the box, stood in front of the door, while Stone and Kessler were out of sight against the far wall of the elevator. Before entering the old-fashioned apartment complex, Kessler had used his penknife to slit the end of the flower box, allowing Travkin to reach in and get his hands around the trigger of the Franchi while he waited. If the assassin answered the door with a drawn weapon, Travkin would take the expedient course of action and blow the man's brains out.

After the third try at knocking on the door it was obvious that no one was going to answer, and Kessler appeared from behind the elevator. He motioned Travkin to stand back while he knelt and used his FBI-issue lockpicks to open the door. Less than a minute later they were inside the large gloomy apartment, and four careful minutes after that they knew their quarry had gone.

While Kessler and Dmitri Travkin began working over the apartment room by room, searching for anything that might be useful, Stephen Stone sat down at the telephone in the den and called the telephone company's security office. Using his FBI authority, he requested a list of all incoming and outgoing trunk calls made to and from the Grays' number at the Wyoming. The supervisor informed Stone that it would take at least half an hour. The FBI man told the woman to call him when it was done.

Stone checked with his companions, neither of whom had turned up anything, then returned to the opulently furnished den. After going through the desk drawers, filing cabinets, and wastepaper basket, he was satisfied that "Duncan" had cleaned up after himself thoroughly, if in fact he'd ever used the apartment at all. Frustrated, he went to the bookcases built into the room and began scanning the titles, wondering what sorts of things the real owner of the apartment found interesting. It wasn't until he reached the shelves closest to the desk that he realized what he was seeing.

"Son of a bitch!" he whispered, going back to the first shelf. He checked the other bookcases quickly, then yelled for Travkin and Kessler. He moved back and forth, eyes flashing over the bindings, pulling out book after book and piling them on the bare desktop. Travkin and Kessler appeared in the doorway and stopped, watching the feverish activity.

"What the hell are you doing?" Kessler asked.

"Check it out!" Stone boomed out. "The books were scattered all over the place, so it took me a little while. He didn't want to take a chance throwing them out, so he salted them around the room."

"Salted what?" Travkin asked.

"The books, man, read the fucking titles!"

The Russian began going through the books, stacking them in piles on the desk. Kessler joined him, reading off the titles as he worked. "*The Living White House, Jacqueline Kennedy's White House Tour, L'Enfant's Washington, Confessions of a Secret Service Agent, Protecting the President, Ring of Power: The White House Staff and Its Expanding Role in Government,* a 1935 *National Geographic* with a story on Washington and the White House, *A Day in the Life of the President, Washington's First Ladies, Upstairs at the White House*—Jesus, there's even one here called

338

*Murder in the Oval Office.*" The red-haired agent stared at Stone. "My
God, Stef, it can't be!"

"Why not?" Travkin queried. "It would be the ultimate act of terrorism. A Libyan perhaps or a Colombian—that would tie in with
Cooper's visit to Barbados, would it not, and the little charade during my
incarceration at the Bowie facility?"

"It's madness!" whispered Stephen Stone. He shook his head.
"Maybe it's just a coincidence, maybe the man who actually owns this
place collects books on the White House."

"I think we can dump that theory," said Kessler, flipping through the
pages of a black hardcover book. "The son of a bitch made notes in the
margin and used one of those fluorescent highlighting pens." He cleared
his throat. "This is one of the passages he underlined from *Ring of
Power: 'On the inner protective perimeter are the agents in civilian clothes;
there are over a hundred on the White House Detail.'* A little later there's
another bit: *'The Presidential protective command post is located directly
under the Oval Office. Throughout the White House Establishment electronic locator boxes tell agents, including the chief of staff, where the principal protectees are at any given moment of the day or night. Red Teams
practice penetration to make vulnerability assessments, fixed base ground
to air missiles are reportedly in the White House area, and shoulder-fired
Redeye missiles are stored for use.'* The bastard has done his homework."

"Incredible," Travkin murmured, turning the pages of another book.
"This is from a volume called *Upstairs at the White House:* '. . . for every
dinner we went to the vaults beneath the North Portico and packed up
the crystal, gold flatware and china.' In the margin he has written the
single word 'basement.'" Travkin fluffed the pages of the paperback.
"There are dozens of entries like that; he has annotated the entire book."

Stone stared at the pile of books on the desk. "Shit, we can't go
through all this now."

"Why bother?" Kessler shrugged. "This is the evidence you wanted."

"This is a bunch of books with notes in the margins and sentences
underlined," Stone answered. "It still doesn't prove anything."

"We're not going to have proof until our man blows away the President," Kessler answered. "We'll have to go with what we've got."

"Stephen is right," Travkin answered slowly. "We have nothing, except now we know that Mr. Duncan, or whatever he is calling himself
now, intends to strike down President Tucker in the White House, perhaps even the Oval Office. I'm sure that we might be able to decipher his

339

method of access if we went through all this material, but I'm afraid we don't have time for that now."

"We're in a big rush all of a sudden?" asked Kessler.

"I'm afraid so, Tovarich Mort." Travkin nodded. "Think for a moment. Stephen assumes a tying up of loose ends by Mr. Cooper, you yourself saw Mallory 'excised,' yes? And now we are here. Mr. Duncan is not. He, too, has cleaned up. That can only say he is ready to make his move in the very near future. Perhaps today."

"Oh, shit!" Kessler groaned. "The birthday party!"

"I beg your pardon?" said Travkin.

"It's the President's birthday today," Stone explained. "They're having a big blowout at the White House tonight."

"He will strike then," Travkin responded firmly. "I'm sure of it."

"We have to give this to someone," Stone said, biting his lip. "We can't go after him without help."

"You said Ruppelt was out, so who do we go to?" Kessler asked.

"General Koslov would laugh in my face." Travkin shrugged. "And then he would hand me over to Gurenko at the KGB and his assistant, the Weasel."

"Nice guys," Kessler muttered.

The phone rang six inches from Stephen Stone's hand, and he jerked nervously. He picked it up on the second ring, then tucked the receiver between his shoulder and ear as he fumbled in the desk for pen and paper. He listened for several minutes, taking down notes as he went, then hung up.

"Who?" Kessler asked.

"Phone company," Stone answered tersely. He looked down at his notes. "Well," he said after a moment, "we don't know how he's getting in or how he's getting out, but I think we know how he's getting away."

"Explain," Travkin asked.

"What do you do when a major crime goes down and the roadblocks go up?" Stone asked. "The train station is being watched, the bus station and the airports, too."

"Rent a balloon," Kessler answered sourly.

"Close," Stone replied. "From the phone record it looks like Mr. Duncan-Smythe has rented a houseboat from a charter place downriver on the Potomac."

The first exchange took place at noon at the foot of the Key Bridge on the Georgetown side. A steel gray Volkswagen van drove down Wisconsin Avenue, turned west onto K Street, and puttered slowly along underneath the booming Whitehurst Freeway until it reached the bridge. The van then pulled off onto the dirt parking area beside the river bank and waited. The vehicle had a small refrigeration unit on the roof and a bumper sticker which read: "Caution—Show Oysters on Board." It had no windows and carried North Carolina plates.

Inside the van, securely packed in a wooden crate, was the chilled corpse of Nezar Hassad, the Lebanese terrorist previously affiliated with the Abu Nidal group. Hassad had been dead for several days, shot through the right ear with a soft-nosed bullet from a Smith & Wesson .38 Special. Since that time he had been kept on ice. Also in the box with Hassad were a six-pound charge of plastic explosive connected to a timer and a tape-activated switch that would detonate the charge when the box was opened.

Prior to his murder Hassad had been dressed in an off-the-rack J. C. Penney suit and penny loafers from Kinney. The wallet in his jacket contained his own identification papers, and his passport showed that his last destination prior to arriving in North America had been France.

Included in his effects was a bogus address book that included Paul Mallory's home telephone number in Alexandria, a D.C. post office box number that had been purchased in Mallory's name, and the international telephone number of a small hotel on the Left Bank in Paris.

The hotel was known to most intelligence organizations as headquarters for the FLI, the Front for the Liberation of Iran, an antiayatollah group financed by the Central Intelligence Agency since 1982. William Casey, director of central intelligence at that time, never had great expectations for the FLI but thought it was useful as a front for other anti-Iran operations. Hudson Cooper had inherited the group through Covert Operations and had kept it on the payroll at the same rate as Casey—a hundred thousand dollars per month. Now the investment was about to pay off.

A second van appeared, approaching from the boathouse on the other side of the bridge. It was dark blue with D.C. plates. The blue van pulled up so that its side door was parallel to the Volkswagen's. Both van drivers then opened their doors, screening the exchange from prying eyes. A short rolling conveyor was placed between the two vehicles, and the crate containing Hassad's body and the explosive booby trap was transferred to the blue van. Exchange completed, one of the men in the Volkswagen dropped out of the open door and spray-glued a large official-looking decal onto the windowless side of the blue van. The decal said: "GRIFFIN

SECURITY SERVICES INC." Griffin Security was the company hired a number of years before to protect and occasionally to patrol the empty confines of the Iranian Embassy, abandoned since the days of the hostage crisis.

With the decal in place the sliding doors of both vans were closed, and the two vehicles went off in different directions. The blue vehicle turned up the service road exit and reached the foot of Wisconsin Avenue a few moments later. Keeping well within the speed limit, the driver piloted the van north to Q Street, then turned east, crossing Rock Creek at the Dumbarton Bridge. The van then went around Sheridan Circle to Massachusetts Avenue and turned in at the gates of the embassy. The driver's companion, dressed in a dark blue Griffin uniform, climbed down from the vehicle and unlocked the heavy chain securing the high wrought-iron gate. The van went down the narrow litter-strewn laneway to an enclosed courtyard at the rear, while the uniformed man relocked the gate.

The two men, both members of the FLI, had clear and simple orders. After parking the van, they were to return to their hotel and wait. If they had not received further instructions by seven-thirty that evening, they were to go back to the van and wait for a rendezvous with their American FLI contact. At nine-thirty they were to open the crate in preparation for handing over its contents. The two men had no idea what the crate contained, nor did they care; as one-time members of the shah's secret police, SAVAK, they were used to following orders without question, and in this case they had been told that their mission was vitally important and would bring them one step closer to reestablishing the house of Pahlavi in Iran. That was enough. After locking the van securely, they slipped out of the abandoned embassy compound and returned to their hotel.

# CHAPTER 25

$E$ric Rhinelander had done his research well, and his timing for the projected assassination could not have been more precise. Any social event at the White House invites logistical chaos that spreads from the State Department's Office of Protocol down to the head of the Secret Service White House detail and eventually to the chief usher. Daily routines are set aside, extra staff is brought in, and security procedures become nightmarish. The presidential birthday party was no exception.

Normally the White House residence staff numbers just under a hundred, not including social aides and the staff of the messroom in the west wing. For Tucker's birthday party the number quadrupled. A sit-down dinner for sixty, followed by a reception for three times that many, required contract staff hiring for the kitchens, thirty social aides from the four-service military pool, twelve extra drivers from the White House garage for chauffeuring guests without vehicles, twenty-five valet parking attendants, also from the military pool, and almost a score of volunteers from the visitors' office who would be required to do anything from combing through the State Department briefing book to make sure that allergy concerns were taken care of to using blow dryers to make sure the rosebuds at each place setting were sufficiently unfolded. On top of all these were the entertainment staff and their entourages as well as a CBS television crew that had been invited to record the proceedings for posterity.

All these people, whether staff, contract, or volunteer, had to be provided with identification and security passes allowing them into a variety of areas within the mansion. Extra Secret Service staff from the district office and beyond, EPB and National Park Service police as well as Metro officers brought in to handle potential traffic snarls all had to be briefed on the evening's activities and procedures. In all, there were 178 new faces present at the White House, not including Eric Rhinelander, the uninvited one hundred and seventy-ninth.

By six that evening the White House was a swarming madhouse of preparty activity, while deep in the vaults beneath the north portico, Rhinelander had completed his preparations and was sleeping lightly, hidden from view by the bulk of one of the air-conditioning compressors. He had removed several bricks from the inner skin of the vault, reaching the bundled electrical cables and planting the timer-detonator that would plunge the White House into darkness for the few moments he needed.

To a civilian, unaccustomed to the violent interludes that were Rhinelander's professional life, sleeping, however lightly, might have seemed an odd thing to do in the assassin's situation, but Rhinelander knew better. He'd seen it in Laos, Cambodia, and Vietnam—a final clearing of the subconscious or perhaps a fleeting confrontation with personal demons before confronting death itself. From his own experience he knew that it was less sleep and more self-hypnosis.

Within some corner of his consciousness Eric Rhinelander knew that madness had stalked him as far back as he could remember, but he knew, too, that he had lived a life in which the potential for insanity was nothing more than an occupational hazard. It had occurred to him from the beginning that his acceptance of Hudson Cooper's assignment was suicidally dangerous, but at the same time he knew that it could also free him forever.

Dozing, always on the edge of wakefulness, Rhinelander went over his plan, point by point, assessing his chances and concluding, as he had a score of times before, that barring the unforeseen, the attempt and the escape that followed would be successful. He knew though, that there was a flip side to that coin: The unforeseen could never be barred completely, and historically, no attempt on the life of a head of state, successful or not, had resulted in the assassin's escape.

Yawning briefly, Rhinelander awoke fully and checked his wristwatch: six forty-five. The first guests would be arriving in the Diplomatic Reception Room. He smiled calmly in the semidarkness. In a little more than two hours from now perhaps the thread of history would be broken.

\* \* \*

Lyall Spencer sat beside the duty agent at the video console in the Secret Service communications office in the basement of the west wing and scanned the monitors carefully. The ventilating fans in the room were blowing hard, keeping back the oppressive heat from outside and also sucking out the steady cloud of cigarette smoke the detail chief was producing. The duty agent's name was Roy Donner, and the smoke was driving him crazy. He'd quit smoking two weeks previously, and even the sight of someone smoking on an old movie made him twitchy.

"How do they handle smoking at these things?" Donner asked, nodding at the monitors and trying to throw Spencer an oblique hint. Donner had been on the White House detail for a year and knew perfectly well that all White House social functions were nonsmoking and had been that way since Jimmy Carter's time.

"I smoke a lot when I'm nervous, Donner," Spencer answered sourly. "And I'm always nervous when the boss throws a party." The detail chief glanced at the screens. Cars all over the parking lots, limousines at the portico, black ties and evening dresses milling around the Diplomatic Reception Room. Thank God he didn't have to listen to the bad Gershwin being pumped out by the four-piece band. "By the way, where is he?"

"Toilet," Donner answered, checking the digital map on the console directly in front of him in the semidarkened room. "Second-floor north in the family quarters. He's been in there for about ten minutes. Lousy protocol. Must be taking a dump with *Time* magazine or something."

"Presidents don't take dumps," Spencer answered. "They defecate if they do anything at all."

"They used to sell the dalai lama's shit, did you know that?" Donner said.

"No, Donner, I did not know that," Spencer said, sighing.

"It's true," the younger Secret Service man assured his boss. "He used to crap down this long pipe on the top floor of his palace, and they had guys down at the bottom who caught it. They dried it out and made good-luck charms. Made a lot of money."

"You wouldn't make a dime recycling Tucker's shit," said Spencer. "Now pay attention to the screens."

The detail chief butted his cigarette and stared over Donner's shoulder. The boss and his family all wore location beepers, but keeping track of the hordes of intruders who had now descended on the White House was impossible. He had cameras for all the rooms on the ground and state floors as well as the kitchens, main hallways, and staircases; but the lighting was half-assed, the cameras kept on fading out, and even with a perfect picture you could barely make out whom you were looking at.

Spencer shook his head. The average American watching the White House on the news probably assumed the Secret Service and the other agencies involved in protecting the President had the most up-to-date equipment. Sometimes that was true, especially when it came to perimeter surveillance, but by and large, just like everyone else, they had to stumble along with aging goods. The same held true for the White House itself. The floors, brand-new in 1950 after the Truman renovation, had already been replaced in some of the rooms, worn through under the feet of thirty-seven million tourists who'd tramped through the place since then.

A telephone built into the main console rang, and Donner picked it up. He listened for a moment and then handed it to Spencer.

"It's for you," said the duty agent, "some guy from the FBI named Stone."

Daniel Waxman paced nervously back and forth in front of the guardrail surrounding the Great Falls lookout, the turbulent waters of the Potomac north of Washington making him feel slightly queasy. Behind him, only yards away, was the peaceful basin of the Chesapeake and Ohio Canal with its locks and large canal house. He would have much rather waited on one of the benches close to the canal, but his instructions had been specific: The meeting was to take place overlooking the thrashing waters as they pounded over the tumbled granite falls.

Waxman, forty-four, was a short, slightly overweight, Columbia-educated career bureaucrat with the State Department. During the early stages of his career and his marriage Waxman had seen himself rising to great heights in the department, sometimes postcoitally confiding in his wife, Brenda, that he could sometimes see himself as an assistant secretary, and when he was feeling particularly pleased with himself, he could actually envision the ultimate phone call from the White House asking him to become the presidential press secretary.

Eighteen years, a vague connection with Oliver North, and simple attrition had seen to those ambitions, and now he was content to keep a low profile, have sex with his wife once or twice a month, and do his job as senior editor of the morning summary. The summary was produced by a division of the department's Bureau of Intelligence and Research and was designed to inform the secretary and his principal deputies of current events and current intelligence relating to U.S. foreign policy. Once upon a time Waxman had made a few melodramatic comments at parties about being in "intelligence," but he didn't bother any more. INR was nothing more than a place to gather Washington gossip, and he was as far as you could get from being a spy.

That was why the call that afternoon had been so confusing. With Brenda visiting her mother in New York, Waxman had decided to spend the morning catching up on the latest Tom Clancy novel and the afternoon down in the basement working out the board for the war game he was designing. Between the book and the basement he decided to make himself a sandwich, and that was when the call came. The man on the other end of the line actually had quite a thick accent, and for a few moments Waxman thought he was being made the butt of a joke by the guys down at the office. Eventually, though, the man, who said his name was Horst Richter, convinced Waxman that he was serious.

Richter told him that he was an East German journalist who had been asked to do a favor for a friend. The friend had some information he thought might be of interest to the State Department. Richter then asked if Waxman would care to pass the information on. When the bureaucrat hesitated, Richter went on to say that the information was vitally important, and by helping Richter out, Waxman could collect some of the glory for himself. Briefly Waxman saw himself with a White House parking sticker on his car again, and in that moment he agreed. After all, what did he have to lose?

Now he wasn't so sure. Here he was, twenty miles out of town with the sun going down, waiting for some East European with a package. Standing there, staring down into the rushing water and feeling mildly ill, he found himself wishing he hadn't been so rash.

Hearing a shuffling sound, his heart suddenly pounding, Waxman spun around. Two men, both wearing jogging suits and sneakers, had joined him on the raised concrete platform. The plump little man swallowed hard. They sure as hell didn't look like Russian spies, but who the hell knew? The shorter of the two men was wearing a bright yellow knapsack across his shoulders.

"Mr. Waxman?" asked the taller man. No German accent. Something else. Shit, they were spies. Waxman felt his bowels turn to water.

"Who are you?"

"You are Daniel Waxman?"

"Yes." Oh, God! If he didn't find a bathroom, there was going to be an accident.

347

"Good." The taller man cleared his throat. "I am sorry to bring you out here on false pretenses, but I can assure that it is most necessary."

"What false pretenses?" asked Waxman, his mouth drying to alum almost instantly. Bizarrely, all he could think about was the fact that his mouth had always dried up like that when he smoked pot back at Columbia. If he didn't shit his pants first, he was going to faint. Christ! Why hadn't he listened to Brenda and gone to work for her old man?

"There is no Horst Richter. There is no friend."

"I don't get it," Waxman answered weakly. The other man had stepped back, blocking the exit from the platform.

"You are here because of who and what you are," the taller man explained. "You work in the Department of State, but you have no real power; you work in intelligence, but you have no control. You are neutral."

"I'll go along with that." Waxman nodded. He'd go along with just about anything at this point. Just so long as he got out of here. The tall man made a small gesture with his hand, and the shorter man stripped off the knapsack and handed it over. The tall man in turn handed the knapsack to Waxman, who looked down at it blankly. The tall man stepped forward and took Waxman by the elbow. He led the frightened man to the rail and pointed to the island splitting the river into two fuming channels. The island was attached to the Virginia side of the river by a footbridge.

"Now then," the tall man said, "on the island you will see a man in a bright blue sailing shell, yes?"

"Yes," Waxman answered, squinting.

"He is using a professional-quality video camera, color, of course. He has just recorded our little transaction."

"I—I don't get it," Waxman stuttered. "Who the hell are you people?"

"My name is Vladimir Gurenko, Mr. Waxman. I am a general in the KGB and resident here in Washington. My companion is Major Valentin Ivashutin."

"Jesus!" Waxman whispered, horrified. He'd read enough John le Carré to know that KGB generals and their assistants didn't prey on middle-grade civil servants for nothing. "What do you want from me?"

"Rest assured, very little," Gurenko said, his voice soothing. "As you were told on the telephone, we would like you to pass some information on to the secretary, Mr. Swanbridge."

"I haven't got access to Swanbridge!" Waxman moaned. "You've got the wrong guy for this job, General."

"You are the perfect man," Gurenko assured him. "As I said, you are neutral."

"But how do I get to Swanbridge?" asked Waxman plaintively.

"By invoking my name," Gurenko answered simply.

"And when do you want this done?" Waxman asked.

"Immediately," Gurenko ordered. "Swanbridge is at a White House reception. You know the chain of command. Get to him." The Russian's voice was horribly blank and emotionless.

Waxman felt as though he were arguing with a machine. "You want me to get to Swanbridge, in the White House, just by using your name?"

"Precisely." Gurenko nodded.

"You're nuts," said Waxman, summoning up a shred of courage from some unplumbed depth. "And what will you do if I tell you that I won't do it?"

"I won't do anything"—Gurenko shrugged—"although the tapes we've just recorded could be rather damning." He shook his head. "No, Mr. Waxman, we won't do anything to you, but your countrymen almost certainly will."

"Just what the hell is that supposed to mean?" Waxman asked.

"The information in that knapsack contains material relating to the possible assassination of Geoffrey James Tucker, President of the United States. Your President, Mr. Waxman, not mine. The information contained in the bag is not conclusive; but it is accurate, and we came upon it accidentally while engaged in other intelligence pursuits."

"I don't believe this is happening," Waxman whispered. His complexion had become ashen, and there were beads of sweat at his hairline.

"It is happening," Gurenko assured him. "Act with speed and with courage, and you will perhaps save the life of your President. Hesitate, and go to your grave knowing that you could have prevented his death." The KGB file on Waxman was slim, but it did note that he seemed to enjoy melodrama. Gurenko's words had been designed to appeal to that weakness.

"Look, I can't guarantee anything . . ." Waxman said uneasily.

Gurenko shrugged philosophically. "You can only do your best," he said. "But you will reach Swanbridge."

"At the White House?"

"If possible. If not, go to his home. You know where he lives, yes?"

349

"Bradley Hills Grove, out by the Burning Tree Golf Club."

"Very good." Gurenko nodded.

"Okay," Waxman blurted. "What if I do get to see him, what if he doesn't believe me?"

"He'll believe you." Gurenko smiled. "And if he shows any hesitation, you can say a few things to him as verification of your sources."

"Like what?" Waxman said.

"Mention Shrenk, Cooper, and Macintyre. Mention the meetings they had in the house on Cherry Hill Lane."

"Shrenk, Cooper, and Macintyre," Waxman repeated. It sounded like a law firm, but the little man knew better. The only Shrenk he knew of was the U.S. attorney general, and he was willing to bet that Cooper was Hudson Cooper of the CIA. Waxman was feeling worse with each passing second, but he was also experiencing a thrill he'd never felt with Brenda or down in the basement with his board game. Sick-making or not, this was the real thing. Screw reading Tom Clancy. He was living it!

"Do you have any questions?" Gurenko asked. From the look in Waxman's eyes the KGB resident knew he'd taken the bait and set the hook. The wide-eyed State Department flunky would go through the fires of hell to give Swanbridge the assassination plot, thus absolving his own people of having any connection to it, and get Gurenko off the hook. He smiled to himself, wishing he could be on hand to see Swanbridge's reaction.

"No questions," Waxman answered, clearing his throat dryly.

Gurenko patted the smaller man on the shoulder. "Excellent," he said quietly. Then he turned Waxman around gently and once again pointed to the man with the camera. "And remember, I will be sending these tapes to your immediate superior within forty-eight hours. They will either prove your patriotism or damn you forever if you decide not to deliver the information to Swanbridge. You understand this?"

"I understand." Waxman nodded. The weight of the knapsack in his hand seemed enormous. He looked across the rushing waters to the small wooded island and the man with the camera. James Bond receded, replaced by Mrs. Waxman's little boy, Daniel. He turned to ask Gurenko a question, but the tall Russian and his blond companion were gone, small figures on the path that led down to the locks and the canal house. He was on his own.

# CHAPTER 26

"**I** must be out of my fucking mind!" Lyall Spencer fumed. Behind him loomed the massive pinnacle of the Washington Monument, three sides now in dusky shadow, only the west facade still colored by the setting sun. The parking lot to the north was almost empty, and the state flags encircling the monument hung limply in the sullen, overheated air. It was 8:20 P.M.

"That's what I thought," said Stephen Stone, leaning against the Secret Service chief's unmarked car, smoking a cigarette. A few feet away Dmitri Travkin was pacing nervously, watching the parking lot and the service roads running up to the huge obelisk. "But I'm convinced there's a conspiracy under way to assassinate Tucker. All the evidence points to it."

"You don't have any goddamn evidence," snapped Spencer. "You've got a lot of bullshit and a Russian defector!"

"He does not believe you, Stephen," said Travkin wearily, pausing in front of Stone. "We might as well give up."

"How can I believe you?" asked Spencer. "You're telling me that I've got a fucking assassin inside the White House right now, and here I am, talking to you guys beside the Washington Monument! Christ, give me proof!"

"We can't give you proof," said Stone. "We told you what's been going on, and the only possible conclusion is that Hudson Cooper, Hollis Macintyre, and God knows who else are planning to assassinate Tucker, probably because he's suffering from something called Creutzfeldt-Jakob

351

disease, a disease that leads to a psychotic behavior. We've run down this man Duncan as far as we can go. He rented a houseboat from a marina downriver at Indian Head, complete with charts all the way up to Great Falls. The guy at the marina says he saw Duncan loading all sorts of scuba equipment on board, as well as a couple of steamer trunks. Then we checked with the Eastern Power Boat Club down by the Anacostia Bridge—close to where he made the exchange with Mallory. Duncan, or Smythe, had the houseboat there all right, but now it's gone."

"So where is it now?" Spencer asked. He glanced at his watch, a worried expression on his face. He was off home base in the middle of a major social event, and if headquarters ever found out, he'd be dead meat.

"The Beach Boys are playing on the Watergate Barge tonight. You know the way it gets out there when there's a big concert. Boats crowd in from all over. I think he's dropped anchor out there, and he's using the concert as camouflage."

"And you think he's inside the White House?"

"All the research books were about the White House. The notes in the margins all relate to the building: history, construction, renovations, floor plans . . . everything."

"Jesus!" muttered the Secret Service man. He stared at Stone and then glanced at Dmitri Travkin. "What the hell am I supposed to do about him?"

"He's with me," Stone answered firmly. "He was the one who figured this thing out in the first place, he saved my ass at Lake Anna, and if we abandon him now, the KGB will burn him."

"I've got to check all this information," Spencer said. "I can't just—"

"There's no fucking time for that!" stormed the FBI agent. "Mort's going to see if he can round up people to cover the barge. We've got to stop Duncan—now!"

At 8:31 P.M. Eric Rhinelander went over the wiring bypass to the main electrical trunk for the last time, then initiated the timer. Standing, he brushed down his uniform, then turned on the Secret Service radio, feeding the earphone wire up through his web belt in exact imitation of a real on-duty EPB officer. He tuned the radio slightly, adjusting the volume, then listened to the backchat from the various Secret Service and EPB personnel. As far as he could tell, everything was going smoothly with the exception of a guest who'd had a little too much to drink and was being discreetly escorted back to her limousine. It took the assassin a few minutes to connect call signs to locations, but eventually he had it figured out. Dinner was almost over, with Diamond and Emerald still at the head table, along with Cobalt, the Vice President, and Flint, the secretary of state, also in attendance. Heliotrope, the White House physician, was in his ground-floor offices attending to a member of the kitchen staff who'd suddenly developed a bleeding nose. Nothing out of the ordinary.

Then Rhinelander stiffened. There was a call from the West Executive Avenue security booth, requesting a double check with Dungeon, the Secret Service communications center, on a scheduled meeting between Diamond and Hudson Cooper, the DDO for Central Intelligence. The duty officer was querying the call list since it seemed like an unlikely time for a meeting. A few seconds later there was confirmation from Dungeon, and Cooper's limousine was allowed entry. The security desk at the west wing main entrance would give Cooper his pass. The assassin took a deep breath and let it out slowly. It was time to begin.

At eight forty-four the digital screens in both the chief usher's office at the north foyer and Dungeon, directly below the Oval Office, showed that the President and Vice President had left the State Dining Room and were now proceeding to the Oval Office. As Dungeon alerted the security staff that Diamond was moving along with Cobalt, two Secret Service agents patrolling the grounds peeled off and headed for their positions outside the Rose Garden windows. Another pair of agents went up the narrow stairway that led from the basement to the corridor beside the Cabinet Room.

The first agent, a woman named Beth Sheldrake, took up a position in the private secretaries' office which stood between the Oval Office and the Cabinet Room. The second agent, John Donnelly, stood beside the main entrance to the Oval Office, giving him a view along the Cabinet Room corridor to the foyer at the colonnade entrance to the west wing. Neither Sheldrake nor Donnelly was in a particular hurry; both knew it would take the better part of five minutes for the Man to reach the west wing and the Oval Office.

As the Secret Service agents took up their places around the Oval Office, Eric Rhinelander left the gloomy security of the vaults below the north portico and headed for the rarely used entrance to the west wing tunnel. He turned right along the main east-west corridor and continued west past the silent carpenter's shop. From above he could hear the faint, muffled sound of music as the band began playing in the Library. The assassin glanced at his watch: eight forty-six. Dinner would be coming to an end, and if things were going according to plan, Tucker and Teresi would now be on their way to the Oval Office.

Rhinelander reached the tunnel entrance and paused. From the empty metal bracket it was clear that there had once been a surveillance camera over the door, but it had been either removed for servicing or simply deemed unnecessary. Ignoring the lucky lack of technology, the assassin pulled open the heavy door and entered the tunnel.

Two minutes previously Lyall Spencer had returned to the White House with his two ill-dressed companions sharing the rear seat. There had been a raised eyebrow or two from the security people at the West Executive gate, but Spencer's badge and ID got them through. The Secret Service chief rolled the car around to the main parking lot across from the west wing main entrance and escorted Stephen Stone and Dmitri Travkin past the marine guard at the doors. He took them to the correspondents' bull pen across from the presidential press secretary's office and sat them down in the empty lounge.

"Now don't you fucking move!" he ordered in a harsh whisper. He shook his head, staring at the two men. "Christ, jeans and T-shirts. Cyndi Lauper yet!"

"What happens now?" Stone asked. He found a package of Larks on the littered desk in front of him and lit up.

"I go down to the basement and start checking through all the contract staff in the building."

"You should be looking for Duncan directly," Travkin insisted. "There is no time to look through files."

"So tell me." He scowled. "Who am I looking for?"

"A little over six feet tall, good-looking, dark-haired, mid to late forties," said Stone. "That's the description we've been able to put together."

"It applies to half the men on my staff, for Christ sake!" Spencer shot back. "Not to mention maybe twenty waiters serving dinner."

"He will not be a waiter," Travkin said slowly.

"Why not?" asked Spencer coldly. "Sirhan Sirhan took out RFK in a hotel kitchen."

"Tucker will not be inspecting the kitchen tonight," the Russian answered. "Look for someone who has access to all parts of the building."

"No such animal except for Secret Service and some of the uniformed types," Spencer answered, shaking his head.

354

"Uniforms?" Travkin asked.

"Executive Protection Branch," Stone explained.

"How many on duty?" Travkin asked quickly.

"Tonight?" Spencer said, arching his eyebrows. "For something like this they've probably pulled out most of their staff. Make it a hundred and fifty. Most of them on the outer perimeter."

"How many outside?"

"A hundred."

"Fifty inside?"

"Something like that. It's hard to say during an event like this."

"He will be one of those fifty," Travkin said. "They are the ones to check."

"Your Russian sounds pretty sure of himself," Spencer said, turning to Stephen Stone.

"My Russian, as you call him, is pretty goddamned smart, Spencer, and I think he knows what he's talking about."

"What if he's wrong?" Spencer retorted.

"What if he's right?" Stone answered.

"All right, but just stay where you are," said Spencer. He turned and left them, heading for the Cabinet Room stairs and the Secret Service office in the basement.

Eric Rhinelander reached the west wing exit from the tunnel at eight forty-nine. He straightened his uniform jacket, adjusted his cap, and opened the door. He stepped through into the basement offices and walked briskly forward. To his right was a darkened short corridor that led down to the photo office and the presidential barbershop. Beyond that was the Secret Service communications center.

The killer followed the passageway directly in front of him, mentally counting down, his mind's eye giving him the route forward. He turned right, then left, then right again, walking past the closed doors of half a dozen vacant offices. He finally reached the curving stairway that led up to the press room on the main floor. He checked his watch again, noted that he was slightly ahead of schedule, and climbed the stairs, his right hand gently brushing the highly polished leather holster on his hip. Five minutes left. Ignoring the cool skin of sweat building up under the wet suit, he continued to climb the stairs, keeping up his silent count.

At the top of the stairs Rhinelander turned right, following the hallway past the open expanse of the correspondents' bull pen, empty now except for two men in jeans and T-shirts, taking a cigarette break at one of the desks in the center of the semidarkened room. Cleaning staff? A factor to consider on his way out. He ignored them for the moment and continued on, heading back toward the colonnade.

According to the floor plans he'd examined, the next hurdle was the corridor leading to the Oval Office. From under the peak of his cap he could see the double surveillance cameras discreetly mounted in the ceiling, one pointing down the corridor, the other facing him. He walked under the camera mount, catching a brief glimpse of the Secret Service man at his post outside the Oval Office door. Ten steps beyond he reached the colonnade entrance to the Cabinet Room and stopped.

He opened the door a few inches, poking his head around it as though following a patrol routine. The room was empty, the draperies pulled across the line of tall windows that looked out onto the Rose Garden. Without pausing, he slid into the room, closing, then latching the door from the inside.

The room was dark, but he'd studied enough photographs so that he was able to orient himself. Fireplace to his left, long oval conference table running down the center, twenty leather armchairs arranged around the table. Door at the far end of the room leading directly into the private secretaries' office.

Working swiftly in the darkness, Rhinelander stripped off the Executive Protection Branch uniform, grateful for the cool breeze from the air-conditioning unit. With the uniform off he gently pulled the tape from around his arm and assembled the air gun, checking the $CO_2$ feed line connection carefully. He laid the weapon gently on the smoothly burnished surface of the table, then squatted and dug the tubular magazine out of the EPB uniform jacket. He pulled off the layers of insulating plastic and felt the tube. Still cold.

He tipped the magazine up, caught one of the paintball capsules in his palm, then tested it with his thumb and forefinger; the contents were still frozen, the water barely liquid around the inside edges. Good enough. He loaded the magazine into the upper barrel of the weapon and then, barefooted, made his way down to the other end of the room. Finally he checked the luminous dial on his watch. One minute. Concentrating on keeping his breathing steady, the assassin waited patiently for the clock to run down. It was 8:53 P.M.

Beth Sheldrake, one of the five woman Secret Service agents on the White House detail, shifted in her chair and leafed through a battered copy of *U.S. News & World Report* she'd found on the coffee table in the private secretaries' office. The thirty-nine-year-old brunette yawned, covering her open mouth with her palm, wondering how long the boss and Teresi were going to be in the Oval Office. She knew they were having a meeting with Hudson Cooper, a CIA heavy, but that was all.

It seemed like a strange time for a meeting, and she frowned, wondering if she wasn't witnessing the opening moves of a latter-day Cuban missile crisis. She'd been a kid back then, but those few days had scared the shit out of her anyway; for two weeks she and her classmates had done A-bomb drills, skulking under their desks while the sirens wailed and their teacher walked around with a transistor radio plugged into her ear.

To hell with that kind of thinking, she told herself. It was hard enough spending forty or fifty hours a week at the White House without worrying about what its occupants were doing, and she was suddenly glad that the private secretaries' office was soundproof; she couldn't have eavesdropped if she'd wanted to.

At exactly 8:54 P.M. Eric Rhinelander pulled open the door leading from the Cabinet Room into the private secretaries' office. His eyes swept across the relatively small room and found the figure of Beth Sheldrake. She was seated—a fatal error on her part—and seeing him, she tried to drag her weapon from the spring-loaded shoulder holster dangling beneath her two-button blazer.

During regular practice sessions at the Secret Service training center in Beltsville, Maryland, the strongly motivated woman consistently beat out most of her colleagues, her draw, aim, and fire times always under two seconds. In real life, with a magazine in her hands, seated on a padded couch and completely unprepared, she took almost three and a half seconds to close her hands over the butt of the standard-issue S&W .357 slung under her arm. It took Rhinelander less than two seconds to pick his target and fire his weapon and a further one fiftieth of a second for the flash frozen projectile to impact.

From a range of only twelve and a half feet the effect of the mercury-and-ice "bullet" was devastating. The Secret Service agent's jaw had dropped in surprise as Rhinelander entered the room, and the ball struck her open mouth, easily penetrated the soft palate of her tilted head, and smashed up into the medulla, shattering and sending shards of frozen metal into her brain. She died instantly, respiratory and motor functions wiped out in an instant. She slumped down onto the couch, brain matter and blood draining down into her mouth and throat. There had been no sound except for the paper bag pop of the $CO_2$.

Barely pausing, Rhinelander took three silent steps to his left, then gently twisted the dead bolt knob on the door leading from the office into the corridor. Ignoring Beth Sheldrake's body, he skirted the desk beside the hall door and stepped across to the door leading into the Oval Office. He took a deep breath, fixing the floor plan of the famous room in his mind.

Fireplace on his right, grandfather clock on his left. Directly ahead there were two couches, divided by a coffee table and a padded spindleback captain's chair facing the coffee table and the fireplace. From the photographs he'd examined he assumed that the captain's chair was reserved for the President. Fifteen feet behind the chair was the President's large oak desk, and beyond that, the triple set of floor-to-ceiling windows facing due south. To the left of the desk, beyond the flagstaff, were the French doors leading out to the Rose Garden and, on the right, the door leading to the President's private office and the full four-piece bathroom.

The President would probably be seated in the captain's chair with Teresi on the couch to his right. Cooper would be seated with his back to Rhinelander. Range for the President would be twenty-three feet, and for Teresi twenty-five. The assassin checked his watch: 8:55:30. It all would be over within the next ninety seconds. Rhinelander flipped the rate of fire lever above the trigger from single shot to automatic and reached out for the brass doorknob.

"Where the hell is Spencer?" Stephen Stone asked angrily.

"Sweat," Dmitri Travkin murmured, dropping his cigarette into a half-empty styrofoam coffee cup on the desk between him and Stephen Stone. The Russian stood up suddenly, turning to stare out toward the hallway behind him.

"What?" the FBI agent frowned.

"Sweat," Travkin repeated. "A few minutes ago I saw a uniformed man walk down the hallway . . . there." The Russian pointed.

"So?"

"He was sweating," Travkin said, anxiety in his tone. "I noticed it. Sweat on his sideburns and jawline. There was a dark stain on the collar of his jacket, at the neck. Sweat."

"What are you getting at?" Stone asked.

"The building is air-conditioned," the Russian explained. "I can feel it."

"So why would he be sweating?" said Stone, completing the thought.
"Sick?" Travkin frowned.
Stone shook his head. "Not on a night like this. You don't want the guards sneezing on the guests."
"He was the right size and coloring," Travkin mused. "I only saw him for an instant but—"
"It's worth checking out." Stone shrugged. "It beats sitting here doing nothing." The FBI man reached out and picked up the telephone on the desk, punching up the main switchboard.

"Anything?" asked Lyall Spencer, staring over Roy Donner's shoulder, examining the computer screen.
"Nothing out of the ordinary." The duty officer shrugged. "Everyone assigned to duty tonight signed in properly. The only way to check for sure is to do a radio count, make sure they're all where they should be."
"How long will that take?" Spencer asked.
"Better part of an hour," Donner answered.
"Shit!" Spencer swore. "That's no damn good!" He looked up at the big IBM clock set above the surveillance monitors. There was a faint click as the minute hand jerked forward. It was eight fifty-six.

Rhinelander burst into the Oval Office and gave himself a two-beat count to get his bearings. Dark green draperies were drawn over all the windows and the French doors, and the room was brightly lit by hidden rows of fluorescents around the ceiling wainscot, giving the office a glowing, almost theatrical look.
The three men were in almost exactly the positions he had envisioned, except that Teresi was a little farther along the couch from Tucker's chair than he'd expected. Both the President and Vice President were dressed in evening clothes. Cooper, with his back to Rhinelander, was less than ten feet away.
For a brief frozen splinter of time everything remained as it was: Tucker slouched in the captain's chair, palm supporting his chin as he looked across at Cooper, a small smile masking obvious strain. Teresi, youthful, his clothes more stylish than the President's, his collar stud open and his bow tie askew as he leaned forward, tapping cigar ash into the cut glass receptacle in the center of the table. Cooper's voice, ragged and worried.
Then everyone began to move. As the door crashed open, Cooper turned, giving Rhinelander a brief look at his pale, lean face. Tucker

359

gripped the arms of the captain's chair, eyes widening as he began to push himself upright, and Teresi, the most telling, rolling down across the couch, trying to duck beneath the coffee table as the searching muzzle of the assassin's weapon swept around the room.

Rhinelander fired three bursts, one directly at the President, one at the diving figure of Teresi, and the last toward the figure of John Donnelly, the Secret Service agent posted at the formal hallway entrance to the office, who had rushed into the room at the sounds of Tucker's frightened yell and the ripping, stuttering explosions of released $CO_2$ from the paintball gun. In all Rhinelander fired nineteen of the twenty rounds in the magazine, with at least a dozen hits. Then, right on schedule, the lights went out all over the White House as Rhinelander's "mine" detonated deep underneath the north portico.

"Jesus Christ!" Spencer roared as every monitor screen went dark. Scores of alarm lights began to flash on the board in front of Donner, the duty officer. Although both the Signal Corps radio communications center in the second-level basement of the mansion and the Secret Service communications room were serviced by secure, dedicated electrical and fiber-optic lines, the mansion and wings were serviced from a transformer vault on East Executive Avenue that, although regularly inspected, was not immune to sabotage at its electrical duct access point in the north portico vaults. With no light in any of the rooms, all the Secret Service surveillance equipment was made useless with the exception of the panic buttons located throughout the entire building. The panic buttons were in turn connected to a system of bells and horns that alerted the Secret Service and everyone else within hearing that the President was in trouble.

"We've got a PB alert in the Oval Office!" Donner boomed. Spencer could hear the faint sound of bells. He knew that the guests, most of them halfway between the State Dining Room and the Library, would be panicking, but he couldn't have cared less.

"Go, Hurricane! Now, goddamn it!" Spencer yelled. Blindly Donner hit the transmit button on the console in front of him and then spoke firmly and clearly into the microphone headset that curved in front of his mouth.

"This is Dungeon. We have a Hurricane Warning in the west wing. No response. All agents converge immediately."

Hurricane Warning was a scenario that Spencer had developed and practiced with every shift of men on the White House detail. It was a three-stage intrusion alarm, based on the concept of a lunatic member of a tour somehow managing to gain access to the west wing and perhaps even the Oval Office. The initial response called for every Secret Service agent on building perimeter control to converge on the Oval Office, while outer perimeter agents and EPB officers would seal every exit. During drills Spencer had worked it down to an art, with his inner perimeter agents reaching the west wing within two and a half minutes and full outer perimeter security in place in two minutes and fifteen seconds.

Those were drills, however, and did not take into account the possibility of total darkness within the building or the complication of what amounted to a state dinner, with guests and staff suddenly plunged into blackness. In fact, it took Spencer's agents almost four minutes to ring the west wing offices, and even then, only a third of the agents actually made it. Outer perimeter security was somewhat better and was fully in place within three minutes. In both cases however, it was definitely a case of closing the stable door after the horse had bolted.

"What the hell!" Stephen Stone rose out of his chair in the press room as the lights went out and the booming tremor of the vault explosion shuddered through the building.

"Bomb?" asked Travkin, peering into the gloom at his companion.

"No," said Stone, shaking his head in the darkness. "I think it's going down. I think it's Duncan!" Frantically the FBI man looked down at the dark outline of the desk, searching for a weapon. The best he could do was a memo spike complete with half a dozen unanswered messages. Scooping it up, Stone pushed around the desk and joined the Russian, who was already heading for the open archway leading out to the hall.

"He went to the right," said Travkin.

"That leads to the colonnade and the Cabinet Room, I think," Stone answered, feeling his way along, one hand against the wall. The FBI man reared back suddenly, spotting the darkened figure of a man less than twenty feet ahead, running hard.

Stone didn't hesitate. He dropped into a half crouch and tried to catch the running man in a waist grip tackle. Beside him Travkin acted more directly, lunging forward, arms outstretched. Stone made contact, then felt a terrible pain in the side of his head, followed by a blinding flash and a deafening roar. He could feel consciousness fading, but in a final moment of lucidity he drove his left arm up, the memo spike against his palm. He had the brief satisfaction of feeling the spike connect with flesh and bone, and then he passed out, assuming, logically enough, that he'd been shot in the head and was now in the process of dying.

At eleven forty-five that evening, almost three hours after the Oval Office attack, Hudson Cooper was returned to the Watergate apartment hotel with a full escort of Washington Metropolitan Police and four Secret Service agents. Immediately after the attack he had been taken from the White House to George Washington University Hospital for examination. Leaving the grounds of the presidential mansion, he had seen Marine One lift ponderously off the south lawn, presumably taking Tucker and Teresi to Walter Reed.

The CIA deputy director had allowed a short debriefing while he was examined, but then, pleading exhaustion, he had asked to be taken home. At his apartment he locked the front door, leaving two of his four-man Secret Service contingent in the hall outside. The other two agents were patrolling the main floor, and half a dozen metro police had been attached to the Watergate until further notice or until the assassin was found.

Numb with fatigue, the stooped, thin-faced man poured himself a drink and eased himself down in front of the television in his living room. He lit a cigarette from the box on the coffee table, nervously rubbing the cool metal of his late wife's lighter in his hand as the TV sprang to life. Using the remote control, he flipped through the channels, all of which were still broadcasting news of the terrible event. He finally settled on WDVM, the local CBS station.

Ironically it was only then that he learned exactly what had transpired over the last hours. The attack had taken place so rapidly he never had time to think, and after he was whisked away from the White House, his escort, the doctor examining him, and Spencer, the Secret Service man who debriefed him, had divulged no information at all.

It appeared that Tucker at least had been killed during the attack, struck twice in the head, once in the throat, and once in the chest. There were confused reports regarding the Vice President, but at that point he was known to be at least in critical condition, if not already dead. Cooper's presence in the Oval Office at the time of the assassination was not being reported yet, but the aging intelligence officer knew that it would only be a matter of time.

There was virtually no news at all about the killer. The Secret Service wasn't talking, but the marine guard on duty at the main entrance to the west wing reported that an ambulance had removed at least two people

362

from the west wing. According to the guard, one of the men was an FBI agent, and the story being circulated was that he had injured and possibly managed to kill the President's assailant. There were no confirmed reports of this, however.

Searching for more news, Cooper flipped to NBC's Channel 4 and found a sidebar story being reported: An audiotape, purportedly recorded by a man named Nezar Hassad or Assad had been dropped off at radio station WNTR. On the tape Assad took full responsibility for the assassination in the name of his organization, the All Islam Liberation Front.

The tape went on to say that rather than endure the possibility of capture and trial, he preferred to die a glorious death at his own hand. Shortly after the tape was received, there had been a large explosion at the vacant Iranian Embassy compound on Massachusetts Avenue, which was now under investigation by the FBI and Metropolitan Police. Initial reports stated than at least one person and perhaps more had been killed by the blast.

The NBC channel was also now confirming reports that an FBI agent named Stone had managed to injure President Tucker's assassin. From what the on-site reporter understood, the assassin, wounded, had made his escape through the sewer and service tunnels running beneath the White House and had left a blood trail indicating that he had been seriously wounded by Stone. The FBI man and his unidentified companion had been taken to Doctor's Hospital on Eye Street. As yet there was no word on their condition or any information about the man with Stone at the time of the assassination.

Taking a swallow of his drink, Hudson Cooper, now drained of all emotion except a deep, unspeakable depression, watched as the all-news network broadcast a brief taped segment showing a haggard Joseph Swanbridge at the podium of the newly designed Press Conference Room in the east wing. The secretary of state, flanked on either side by at least a dozen Secret Service agents, was describing the Succession Act and explaining his position.

With letters of intent long on file by both the president of the Senate and the speaker of the House, and in light of the Twenty-fifth Amendment sections relating to presidential and vice presidential inability to govern, he, Joseph Swanbridge, as next in line, was assuming the role of Acting President until such time as Vincent Teresi, in writing, declared himself fit to take the office vacated by President Tucker on his death.

Sighing, Cooper dropped back against the padded cushion of his chair and used the remote control to turn the television off. He sat quietly for a few moments, sipping occasionally from his drink, the cigarette forgotten in the ashtray in front of him on the coffee table.

He closed his eyes, and instantly he found himself reliving the horrifying events in the Oval Office. He remembered turning in his seat on the couch, knowing what was about to happen, and seeing the face of the man he'd hired to assassinate Tucker and Teresi. Somehow he would have felt better if it had been the face of a madman or fanatic, but the face he saw was only cold and methodical, handsome perhaps, except for those flat, empty, expressionless eyes.

And then he'd seen the long black barrel of the gun, heard the coughing, ripping sound, watched Tucker lift half out of his favorite chair, only to be slammed back into it and tipped backward onto the huge carpet inlaid with the presidential seal, dead certainly before he struck the ground.

The telephone trilled on the end table at his right hand. He lifted the receiver and listened, staring blankly out across the room to the drawn curtains over the living-room window. The one-sided conversation continued for the better part of five minutes, and then Cooper hung up the telephone softly. He paused for a moment after he hung up to watch the slight tremor in his hand.

He stood up then and made his way through the apartment to the bedroom. He brought down an ordinary shoebox from the shelf in his cupboard and removed a deeply blued Springfield Armory 1911-A1 .45-caliber automatic pistol. He slipped a full magazine into the butt of the weapon, pulled back the slide, and pushed one of the fat-nosed shells into the breech. Taking the gun, he went to the kitchen, where he poured himself a glass of cold water. Then he returned with gun and water to the living room. He stood in front of the fireplace, staring at the painting over the mantel, then turned away. He didn't want to make any mistakes and knew that liquid would increase the concussion effect tenfold, so he took a long drink of water, which he held in his mouth while he inserted the gun barrel between his lips. Eyes wide open, he squeezed the trigger without flinching, and blew his brains out all over the painting of his wife on the wall.

# CHAPTER 27

Seventeen days after the assassination of Geoffrey James Tucker and four days after the release of Vincent Teresi from Walter Reed Hospital, Stephen Stone drove down the winding, treelined drive leading to Stone-acres, Hollis Macintyre's estate on the Potomac, south of Washington. The sun was lowering, casting long, cool shadows over the rolling lawns of the estate, and Stone was tired after a day which had begun with a farewell breakfast at Dulles Airport, an hour before Dmitri Travkin stepped onto the Aeroflot jet waiting to take him back to Moscow.

After two weeks of testimony behind closed doors for the newly formed Morgentaler Assassination Committee Travkin was returning home in his new role as media darling, sporting fresh shoulder boards on his GRU uniform marking his promotion to colonel. Stone was sorry to see his friend leave, and over breakfast he'd made one last and only partly serious attempt at getting him to defect.

Travkin appreciated the gesture but declined; if he defected, the best he could expect was a book contract and some brief notoriety before he faded into obscurity. Back home, considering his hero's role in helping track down Tucker's assassin, it seemed that the sky was the limit. As a representative of a new era in East-West relations he couldn't beat tackling a President's killer, even if he had wound up being kneed in the groin and left stunned on the floor as the assassin escaped.

Stone brought the car to a halt in front of the imposing columned entranceway and climbed out into the cool early-evening air, a slim briefcase in one hand. He touched the small bandage covering the all-but-healed wound at his temple and took a deep breath, enjoying the scent of new-mown hay and the flowers, massed against the stone walls of the house. He went up the short flight of steps leading to the door and rang the bell. A few seconds later an elderly black man, his hair grizzled, answered the door. Stone nodded. According to the dossier he had built up on Macintyre, this would be Benjamin, his butler-valet.

Benjamin led him into the foyer, then guided Stone around to the large high-ceilinged library. Macintyre had left the draperies open, allowing Stone a fine view of the sloping grounds leading down to clumps of shadowed trees at river's edge. Beyond the trees the Potomac flowed down to the sea, and beyond, Stone could just make out the eastern shore.

Benjamin left him at the doorway, and Stone made his way across the pegged oak floors to the big coffee table in the center of the room. Macintyre was waiting for him, bulk arranged on a love seat, one small hand holding a tiny crystal liqueur glass, half filled with some gleaming amber liquid.

"Agent Stone," Macintyre said, his voice as rich as the liqueur in his glass. He inclined his huge, leonine head briefly. Stone watched the man's eyes: wary and analytical. He was on his guard.

"Mr. Stone will do," Stone answered. "As of ten days ago I was seconded from the bureau as special investigator for the Morgentaler Committee."

"I was aware of that," Macintyre answered, nodding again. "What I am not aware of is your reason for requesting this interview. As you know, President Tucker and I were only barely acquainted."

"Yes, I know that," Stone replied. He snapped open the briefcase in his lap and withdrew a sheaf of paper. "As of this moment our interview is strictly off the record."

"Really?" said Macintyre, raising an expressive eyebrow. "I'm not sure I want any interview I have with your committee to be off the record."

"I'm conducting the meeting at the express wish of Senator Morgentaler himself. In his own words he'd like you to have as many options available to you as possible. I'm not sure I agree."

"Agree with what?" Macintyre asked politely.

"He's willing to let you off the hook, just to keep things on an even keel," Stone answered. "Personally I think you should be tried for treason and then executed."

366

"Good Lord!" said Macintyre, amused. "You seem to be a man of strong convictions. What do you base this fervent animosity upon?"

"Facts," Stone answered. "According to the information I've been able to put together so far, on my own and with the help of Dmitri Travkin of Soviet Military Intelligence, you were part of a conspiracy to assassinate the President and the Vice President of the United States. You and several others, including Hudson Cooper, deputy director of operations for the Central Intelligence Agency, as well as Mr. Shrenk, the attorney general of the United States, became aware that President Tucker was suffering from an advanced form of a dementia known as Creutzfeldt-Jakob disease.

"On the basis of your knowledge of the disease, or rather Hudson Cooper's knowledge through his connection with Dr. Barron at Walter Reed, you and the others of your group decided that the best course of action would be assassination. You included the Vice President in your scenario, knowing that his policies were far from being in accord with your own."

"Poppycock!" Macintyre laughed, taking a sip of his drink. "Babble. You have no proof of any of this."

"I'm afraid we have a great deal of proof, Mr. Macintyre, some of it provided by Gennadi Koslov of the GRU and even more from Vladimir Gurenko of the KGB. They have been most forthcoming, Mr. Macintyre, and it appears that your meetings at Cherry Hill Lane were better attended than you knew."

"You intend to swear information at a Senate committee meeting from known Soviet agents?" scoffed Macintyre. "Good luck, my friend."

"We have more than that. We have Hudson Cooper."

"Cooper is dead."

"He sure is," said Stone. "He was very emphatic about cashing in his chips. He had good reason."

"Indeed?" Macintyre asked.

"Yup." Stone nodded. "He was the one who hired Duncan. We still don't have a real name for the man."

"Or the man himself. Much like Lee Oswald," Macintyre added.

"They found a blood trail in the sewers all the way down to the main junction," said Stone. "My people also had the houseboat covered. Duncan never appeared. The odds are he drowned in the main sewer or got trapped in one of the muck catchments."

"Perhaps." Macintyre shrugged. "But the truth of it is, you have no

367

killer, you have no conspirator who hired the killer, good Lord, you don't even have his name."

"No," Stone answered, "not his name, but I do have a list of other names. Names even the committee doesn't know about. In fact, the only one who's seen these names is Josh Morgentaler."

"What names are these?" Macintyre responded coldly.

Stone smiled to himself. Cold or not he was getting to the slug son of a bitch.

"These are names my ex-wife sent me," Stone answered, trying to keep his voice steady. "She sent them to me before she was murdered by a KGB Spetznaz group. I didn't find them until I got out of the hospital."

"Ah," Macintyre said theatrically. "Now I'm beginning to see your drift. You wish to give information from the KGB to the Morgentaler Committee, but you also say they murdered your ex-wife."

"That's right. They were worried because they thought she was going to blow a huge net of agents who'd been in place for years, some of them for decades."

"What does this have to do with Tucker's killing? From what you say it would appear that your ex-wife was working for the Russians."

"That's right." Stone nodded. "She was part of the group of illegals and deep-cover agents the KGB was trying to protect when they killed her. I've met with General Gurenko, and he showed me her file. It doesn't do my ego much good, but presumably being married to me seemed like a good idea from an espionage point of view."

"I still don't see what this has to do with Tucker's death," said Macintyre, "and what it has to do with me." The fat man's tone was exasperated.

"She also worked for Hudson Cooper as a courier and sometimes as an intelligence analyst. She was a CIA mole."

"And you got this information from Gurenko at the KGB?" Macintyre asked coolly.

"You bet," Stone answered. "These guys have got strict orders from the top: Any help we need, we get. They're willing to cooperate completely, just so long as we don't implicate them in an assassination plot."

"And this list of names," said Macintyre. "They know you have it?"

"They don't even know it exists," Stone answered, grinning at the grossly overweight man across from him. "Debbie was being run by one of their top people at Moscow Center, a man named Kuryokhin, an old-style spymaster. According to the material Debbie sent me, she was his personal asset within the CIA."

"I still don't know what this has to do with me," Macintyre said wearily. He glanced pointedly at his wristwatch, a thin gold Patek Philippe. "It's getting late, Mr. Stone, and I'm an old man. I need my sleep."

"I won't take much more of your time," Stone said. "And my reasons for showing you the list are personal. I know I'll never be able to tie you absolutely into this conspiracy, any more than Cooper, Shrenk, or any of the others. Morgentaler knows it, too. But we want you to know you're being watched. We want you to know that *we* know—that's all."

"All right, you've come down here to see what rattles when my bones are shaken. Consider it done," Macintyre said. "And frankly, I don't really think I'm interested in your list. I think you should be on your way."

"You want to see the list," Stone answered. The room was almost dark now, the light in the room a blue glow. Macintyre made no move to turn on any lights. Stone pushed the photocopied list across the coffee table at the fat man. "It's the name underlined on the third page."

Macintyre leaned forward heavily and picked up the list. He turned to the third page, turning it toward the windows and holding it close to his face.

JOSEPH SAXON SWANBRIDGE/enlisted—Yale University/24/3/1940/key as code MARYBELLE

"You can't be serious!" said Macintyre, turning to look back at Stone.

"Keep reading." Stone zipped up his briefcase and stood up, his jaw tight with anger. "It's all there, Macintyre. Rich boy at Yale, father a doctor, mother a radical poet. It's 1939, 1940, and the world's going to hell. Europe's in flames and the U.S. isn't far behind. Time for a new order. Your pal Swanbridge went for it all, and they kept him away from any obvious demonstrations or groups. They had him pegged as someone who'd go a long, long way. And he did."

"It's insane!" Macintyre whispered.

Stone leaned forward and plucked the list out of the man's hand. He opened the briefcase far enough to slide in the list and then stared down at the slack-jawed man on the love seat.

"You thought you knew it all, didn't you, Macintyre? You and your invisible friends, your government by secret committee." Stone's voice was dry and hard. He bent closer, his face no more than a foot away from Macintyre's. "Well, you screwed up badly, Hollis. If your killer had finished the job, your man Swanbridge would have made it. Bad enough he became Secretary of State, Hollis, but you actually made him President of the United States, even if it was for only a few days." Stone straightened and shook his head.

"Think about that," Stone said softly in the gloomy half-light of the book-lined room. "You almost put a KGB sleeper in the Oval Office." The counterintelligence agent smiled grimly. "And you know what, Hollis? Everyone who's anyone, every power broker who counts is going to find out about what you almost did. Cooper was smart enough to kill himself because he knew what would happen to him when it all came to the surface. The senator wanted to give you the chance, and so did Teresi, but I'm willing to bet you don't have the guts to do the same thing."

Stone tucked the briefcase under his arm and walked away, heels tapping on the shiny wood floors. He paused in the doorway and turned back to the fat man, slumped silently in the love seat, his huge head silhouetted in the last light coming through the French doors behind him.

"Prove me wrong," Stone said, staring at the huge old man. "By all means, prove me wrong."

Macintyre waited until Stone had gone and then stood up slowly. He opened the doors and stepped out onto the small patio, edged with a waist-high stone wall. The fat man crossed to the wall and put his palms down flat on the cold granite as he stared out over the river.

Stone was right, he had no stomach for suicide, but God only knew, the prospect of his name and reputation's being fouled was equally horrific. Without power he was nothing, and if he was nothing, he would die. Sighing, he turned away from the darkening view of the water, and at that exact moment the bullet from the Marlin .444 hunting rifle struck him full in the chest, slicing through the fatty tissue below his collarbone and blowing through his heart like a copper jacket fist. It was a perfect shot.

Two hundred fifty yards away, hidden in the trees beside the rushing river, Eric Rhinelander watched through the Tasco scope as his quarry fell. He lowered the rifle and nodded. As best he could, he'd completed the assignment and closed the last door. All that remained now was the future.

# THE WHITE HOUSE
## SER. / ENGIN. 1988

1861 STORM SEWER

WEST
WING

PASSAGE TO
EXECUTIVE OFFICE
BUILDING

WEST WING

OVAL
OFFICE

PASSAGE TO
WEST WING AND
OVAL OFFICE
(B-2)

1861 STORM SEWER
PASSES BELOW PASSAGE
TO WEST WING (B-2)